P9-DDD-215

"If you really knew what went on in my head...

Annabelle lowered her attention to Blake's lips, remembering all too well how they felt against hers. It made her wonder how he'd be in the bedroom—a dangerous thought, because she wasn't sure how much longer she could keep holding back.

"If you don't stop that, Annabelle, I'm going to give you what you're asking for," Blake warned in that gruff, low voice of his. A bedroom voice. Made for whispering and teasing and tickling the sensitive skin below her ear.

A shiver ran through her body, and it wasn't from the cool breeze.

"Do you miss it?" she asked, trying to regain control of the conversation.

"What, kissing you?" he asked.

"I meant football," she corrected as heat burned her cheeks. But, yeah, the kissing too.

"Are you sure?" he pressed, touching a finger to the warmth of her face.

"If I say no, what will you do?"

His face inched closer to hers. "Whatever you want, Annabelle..."

PREVIOUS BOOKS BY ERIN KERN

Along Came Trouble
Here Comes Trouble
Looking for Trouble

PPB
KER

WINNER TAKES ALL

Champion Valley #1

ERIN KERN

HOMEWOOD PUBLIC LIBRARY

SEP -- 2016

FOREVER

NEW YORK BOSTON

This book is a work of fiction. Names, characters, places, and incidents are the product of the author's imagination or are used fictitiously. Any resemblance to actual events, locales, or persons, living or dead, is coincidental.

Copyright © 2016 by Erin Kern
Excerpt from *Back in the Game* copyright © 2016 by Erin Kern

Cover photography by Claudio Marinesco
Cover background images from Shutterstock
Cover design by Elizabeth Turner
Cover copyright © 2016 by Hachette Book Group, Inc.

Hachette Book Group supports the right to free expression and the value of copyright. The purpose of copyright is to encourage writers and artists to produce the creative works that enrich our culture.

The scanning, uploading, and distribution of this book without permission is a theft of the author's intellectual property. If you would like permission to use material from the book (other than for review purposes), please contact permissions@hbgusa.com. Thank you for your support of the author's rights.

Forever
Hachette Book Group
1290 Avenue of the Americas
New York, NY 10104
forever-romance.com
twitter.com/foreverromance

First Edition: August 2016

Forever is an imprint of Grand Central Publishing.
The Forever name and logo are trademarks of Hachette Book Group, Inc.

The publisher is not responsible for websites (or their content) that are not owned by the publisher.

The Hachette Speakers Bureau provides a wide range of authors for speaking events. To find out more, go to www.hachettespeakersbureau.com or call (866) 376-6591.

ISBNs: 978-1-4555-3598-9 (mass market), 978-1-4555-3597-2 (ebook)

Printed in the United States of America

OPM

10 9 8 7 6 5 4 3 2 1

ATTENTION CORPORATIONS AND ORGANIZATIONS:

Most Hachette Book Group books are available at quantity discounts with bulk purchase for educational, business, or sales promotional use. For information, please call or write:

Special Markets Department, Hachette Book Group
1290 Avenue of the Americas, New York, NY 10104
Telephone: 1-800-222-6747 Fax: 1-800-477-5925

ACKNOWLEDGMENTS

I would like to extend a huge thanks to my husband, whose unwavering and endless support always keeps me going even when I want to stop.

Also, and equally important, the team at Grand Central who collaborated with me to cultivate this series. Without their enthusiasm and nonstop belief in me, I wouldn't have had the chance to delve into the exciting, and oftentimes confusing, world of high school football. Leah, thank you for your patience and helping to fill in gaps in my football knowledge. Lauren, you are missed greatly, but I will always cherish the time we had to work together.

And for my amazing agent, Kristyn Keene, who's been there with me from the beginning and opened a door for me when everyone else had slammed it shut.

WINNER TAKES ALL

ONE

Half these kids don't know a blitz from a fumble."

Blake Carpenter had to admit this assistant coach wasn't wrong. Most of these kids couldn't pass for shit. The kicker couldn't find the goalposts if they had flashing lights on them. And these boys couldn't take the Colorado heat without bitching like a bunch of little girls. Damn, Blake hated it when his best friend was right.

How had his life come to this?

A year ago he'd been playing pro football, something he'd dreamed of since he was a little kid. Making more money than he knew what to do with and enjoying every advantage and privilege a multimillion-dollar contract could throw his way.

Yeah, life had been good.

Great, actually.

Until it had all come crashing down after multiple knee surgeries and an early retirement due to a positive drug test. Testing positive once had been bad enough. But after his coach had warned him that his second test would most likely be positive, Blake had taken matters into his own hands and retired. He'd warned his trainers to not give him that "medication" they kept injecting because of his torn ACL. He should have known better.

It had cost him everything he'd worked for. His contract. His career.

His passion.

And no football organization in their right mind would hire someone who had a history of using performance enhancing drugs, not even for a front office job. So he'd left football and returned to Colorado, where he'd grown up, fully intending to live out the rest of his life in peace. That had lasted about a year before he'd been bored out of his mind, since there was only so much solitude and hiking a person could do before that got old real fast.

It was only after watching the high school football team die a slow death of humiliation and defeat, ending their eighteenth losing season, that Blake ended his pity party.

Now here he was, a week into his new job of coaching a high school football team that hadn't seen a winning season since the Clinton administration.

Needless to say, it had been a pride-swallowing moment.

He had no one to blame but himself for his fall from being a football god to a thirty-four-year-old high school coach who'd received more wary looks from parents than a stripper at confession.

Apparently some moms and dads didn't want the likes of him coaching the children they felt could be the next Aaron Rodgers or Peyton Manning.

Whatever.

Blake didn't have the heart to tell them the only way

these kids could be Aaron Rodgers was if they stole the guy's identity.

In other words, not gonna happen.

In other words, he had his work cut out for him.

And you've only got one season to make it happen, pal.

That was another little tidbit that chapped Blake's ass. If he couldn't pull off a winning season, then he'd be shown the door faster than he could call his next play.

The school district's athletic director had made that point very clear when he'd hired Blake. Bring the team to the play-offs this season or find another job.

Sure.

Piece of cake.

"What the hell is number twenty-four doing?" Cameron muttered. Cam's blue eyes were hidden by a pair of dark sunglasses, despite the overcast day. But Blake could feel his best friend's gaze, analyzing and scrutinizing each move the kid on the field made.

Cameron Shaw was a play-calling genius who could turn a ballerina into the next Heisman winner. He and Blake had played ball in high school together, then in college, and Cam had been coaching high school ever since. Blake had agreed to do the job only if he could have Cam by his side.

"Strickland!" Cameron bellowed to number twenty-four, whom he'd had a close eye on since practice started. Cam crooked his finger for the kid to approach.

Brian Strickland, a junior with the heart of a lion but the talent of a ten-year-old, whipped his helmet off and ran toward them.

"Yeah, Coach?" Brian asked with a noticeable tremor to his voice.

"You decide to take a nap out there, or what?" Cameron barked.

Brian's gaze flickered to Blake's, then back to Cameron at the same time that his Adam's apple bobbed up and down like a buoy in a storm.

"No, sir," the kid answered as he licked his lips and cleared his throat because his voice had cracked. Actually cracked.

"You got some hot rally girl on your mind?" Cam asked.

A pink flush filled the kid's cheeks. Oh yeah. There was definitely a rally girl.

Brian shook his head, then swiped the back of his hand across his sweaty brow. "No, sir. I mean, she's not really my rally girl but—"

"Yeah, okay," Cameron cut him off. "I'm just trying to figure out why you're not running the play I gave you."

Brian shook his head, as though not sure how to answer the question. Probably because he didn't know. Probably the kid thought he had been running the play, only the play in his head wasn't the play Cam had given them.

Blake kept silent while Cameron did his thing with the player.

"Remember, ninety percent of the game is in here," Cameron said as he tapped the kid on the forehead with his knuckle. Then he slapped Brian on the shoulder. "Now get your ass back out there."

Instead of responding, Brian replaced his lid and sprinted back on the field. Blake hooked his hands on his hips, blew his whistle and clapped his hands three times. The kids, recognizing the signal to lend their undivided attention to their coach, snapped their heads toward Blake. Some of them removed their helmets; others tried to get their labored breathing under control.

"You expect to win games with that half-assed display

you just showed me?" Blake called out to his players. The kids alternated between panting and shifting their feet on the grass. "If you expect people to spend their hard-earned money on tickets to watch you play, you've got to do a hell of a lot better than that. Otherwise all they're going to get is a bunch of sorry-ass pansies who couldn't outplay a peewee league."

The team stared back at Blake with wide eyes, reminding him he was dealing with a bunch of kids who didn't have the hardy exterior of professionals. Were they not used to a coach who told them like it was? Blake rolled his shoulders, attempting to loosen his muscles and the tension that came with the enormous responsibility of whipping these kids into shape.

"I didn't hear a 'yes, Coach'!" Cameron called out.

The kids responded with a "yes, Coach" that sounded like a bunch of defeated rejects, bringing Blake back to the reality of their situation. Seeing their faces, looking into the eyes of kids who'd never tasted victory, who'd never known the exhilaration of having the town at their backs, stands filled with screaming fans, was like someone letting the air out of Blake's balloon. Having experienced that firsthand, Blake knew how walking around on cloud nine could fuel a player's motivation to exceed to the next level. To elevate the game even higher so the fans knew they could depend on them to bring them another win.

These poor kids didn't have the first clue what that was like, and they deserved to feel it, even for just a brief moment. Blake swore to himself they would have that for more than just a moment.

"Again!" Cameron demanded. "Make them hear you in Pagosa Springs! Remind those guys that we're still here!"

This time their collective "yes, Coach" was loud enough to be heard on top of Chimney Rock.

Blake blew his whistle again. "Y'all will keep running that play until you can execute it in your sleep!"

The grunts and smacking of helmets that followed brought a fresh wave of nostalgia over Blake. There wasn't quite anything like the sounds and smells of the game. The feeling was something only someone with a passion and drive for football could understand. For years it was all Blake had known. All he had cared about and he had never wanted or imagined doing anything else with his life.

He only had himself to blame for effing it all up. Knowing how things ended, would he have done anything differently?

Hell yes, he regretted the use of illegal drugs to enhance his body. And, sure, he could've outed the trainers. But ultimately, he was the one responsible for his own body. Ultimately, he'd allowed them to do whatever it took to win.

Blake turned his attention back to the kids on the field as Matt West, his cousin's son, executed some serious blocking, paving the way for Scott Porter to move forward and receive the ball.

"Now that's the kind of passion I like to see."

Blake gritted his back teeth when Drew Spalding sauntered up next to him. The school district's athletic director managed to radiate cockiness and charm all at the same time.

"Something I can help you with, Drew?" Blake asked as he kept his focus on his players, hoping Drew would take Blake's not-so-subtle hint and go the eff away.

"Just thought I'd stop by for a few minutes and watch the first practice of the season," the guy answered.

Invaded was more like it, because they both knew Drew was there to see the coaching staff more than the kids. Drew and Cameron had a rivalry that went back to high school, and things had only gotten worse from there.

Drew pointed toward the end of the field. "Why is Cody doing push-ups over there? Seems to me he ought to be running the play with his team."

The muscle in Blake's jaw clenched even tighter. "He mouthed off to Cameron." Damn, was this guy going to question everything he did?

"You shouldn't overwork your quarterback," Drew scolded. "He could pull a muscle."

He shot the athletic director an impatient look. "Then he shouldn't be talking back to his coaches. The kid needs to understand that he's not in Texas anymore."

Cody Richardson was one of the few kids on the team with real talent. The problem was he had a chip on his shoulder the size of Rhode Island and an entitled attitude to go along with it. In Blake's world, respect had to be earned. Apparently Cody had gotten used to it being handed to him.

Blake whistled and motioned for Cody to rejoin his team. He tugged on the bright red practice jersey and jogged toward the huddle.

"Maybe Cameron was being too hard on the kid," Drew commented.

"Cameron was doing his job," Blake shot back. He jerked his head toward the benches behind them. "Why don't you take a step back and let me coach my team, Drew."

Drew looked as though he wanted to argue. Knowing the guy, he probably did. Blake didn't give a shit. Drew might be Blake's superior, but on the football field, Blake always had the final word. The kids needed to know that just as much as Drew did.

"This isn't high school anymore, Blake, so you don't

need to keep one-upping me," Drew commented in a hard voice.

Blake turned to face the athletic director. "I'm not trying to one-up you, Drew. I'm trying to do the job you hired me to do."

The guy held his hands up in surrender, but the slight tilt of his mouth contradicted the benign gesture. "I just wanted to see how the team looks." He lowered his hands and took a few steps backward. "It might be too early to tell, Carpenter, but one season may not be enough time for you to get the job done."

One season was more than enough time, but Blake kept the argument to himself as Drew walked away. Let the cocky asshole think he had the upper hand. Blake would prove himself on the field; then Drew would have to keep that trap of his shut. The play ended and Cameron signaled for the kids to run it again. They got halfway through when a shadow appeared beside him. A long, slender, and curvy shadow, followed by the scent of…something flowery and feminine. Blake didn't know the distinction between the smell of a rose and a carnation, but whatever it was was damn good. Like attention-getting, hair-standing-on-the-back-of-his-neck good.

And the soft voice that followed was the perfect match to the knock-you-on-your-ass scent messing with his concentration. "Coach Carpenter?" the woman asked.

Blake kept his attention on his players. "If you have a problem with the way I talk to your kid, then I suggest you don't come to the practices," he told the woman.

"Uh…," she started, clearly taken aback by his abrupt statement. "No, I'm not related to any of the players, Mr. Carpenter."

The play finished and Blake blew his whistle. "Water

break, gentlemen," he called to his players. He waited a moment before turning to the woman who'd interrupted his practice. When he did, the hazel eyes that blinked back at him just about knocked him on his ass. And yeah, she was way too young to be the mother of a high schooler.

So what the hell was she doing here?

Besides clouding his thinking with whatever the hell she sprayed on herself.

"What can I do for you, Miss..." He waited, arching a brow above his sunglasses.

She blinked at him, then stuck her hand out. "Turner," she answered. "Annabelle Turner."

Her full lips curved into a small but oddly seductive smile, which was like a punch to Blake's gut.

What the hell?

He took her hand, noting how much smaller and softer it was than his. Her petite fingers curved around his palm, but instead of shaking her hand, he just held on to it. As though he were some jackass who had never gone through a hand-shaking ritual before.

"Again, what can I do for you?" he wanted to know.

She withdrew her hand from his and rubbed it up and down the top of her thigh, which was covered in some kind of black spandex. As though she'd just come from the gym. Probably had considering how lean she was.

"I wanted to come and introduce myself before we started working together," she answered.

His brow twitched in confusion. "Working together?" he repeated.

"With the players," she clarified with a wave of her hand toward the field.

"I'm not following you, Ms. Turner."

"I'm the physical therapist," she explained. Her teeth

stabbed into her full lower lip when he didn't respond to her announcement. "Drew Spalding hired me to work with the kids," she went on. "Do you know Drew? He's the athletic director—"

"I know who Drew is," he interrupted. Out of the corner of his eye, he saw Cameron walk onto the field to speak to the players.

Annabelle smiled, creating a shallow dimple in her right cheek. "Sorry, but you were looking at me like you didn't know what I was talking about."

He turned to face her, noting how her long thick hair kept teasing her jawline when the wind blew. The strands were dark on top, the color of a rich Tennessee whiskey, which slowly faded to a brighter blond on the ends, curling slightly into a perfect outward flip.

"That's because I don't, Ms. Turner," he explained.

Her brow crinkled at his abrupt tone. Excuse him for being an asshole, but he had a team to coach and this woman, with her provocative scent and legs for days, was pulling his thoughts off of play calling and onto lazy afternoon sex.

"Drew hired me last season to work with the players," she explained, which still wasn't much of an explanation. "Since the team doesn't have an official doctor, he thought I could help them."

"Help them with what?" Yeah, he knew what physical therapists could do for football players. As a professional, he'd been treated by some of the top PTs in the country. What he didn't know was why she was here, with a high school football team. He'd never heard of a high school football program hiring their own therapists and doctors, unless it was a wealthy 5A school, which Blanco Valley wasn't.

"Stretching," she answered. "Conditioning. Treating old injuries that might hinder their abilities."

Blake hadn't been made aware of a physical therapist working with the team. That sort of practice was unorthodox and unnecessary in Blake's mind. Professional football teams had all sorts of trainers and doctors to make sure the players were kept in the best shape possible.

But this was high school, for crying out loud. What the hell did they need a physical therapist for?

"Talent is what these kids need, Ms. Turner. Not stretching exercises."

Her mouth opened to say something, then shut again. "Drew thinks I can—"

He crossed his arms over his chest. "Last I checked, Drew Spalding wasn't this team's head coach. I am. I don't know you from Adam, so I'm not about to let you walk in here and step on my toes." He turned from her and walked onto the field, determined to get his mind back on his players and off this woman.

But the tenacious little thing had other plans because she grabbed his forearm, digging her sharp fingernails into his flesh, giving him an impression of delicate, soft skin, which was odd given the firm grasp she had on his arm.

"Are you dismissing me, Mr. Carpenter?" she demanded.

He spared the hand on his arm a quick glance, noting how trim and neat her fingernails were. Unpainted. Practical. Then quirked a brow at her. "Beautiful and insightful. Quite a combination."

She stared at him for a moment, drilling her greenish-brown eyes into his and touching a place deep inside that hadn't been touched in a long time. The one that had to do with arousal and reacting to a beautiful woman. Then the angelic look on her face was replaced with a firm set of her full mouth, a look she no doubt mastered.

"You can't just shrug me off, Mr. Carpenter. Even though

you didn't hire me, I can be helpful to your players." She took a step toward him. "You haven't even seen what I can do yet."

He allowed his gaze to drift over her lithe body, touching on her flat stomach, then skimming down her toned legs. As a football player, Blake had mastered the art of intimidation, often being able to get inside his opponent's head with a simple searing look.

But he had to give this five-foot-nothing sprite some credit. She held her ground almost as well as some of the fiercest players he'd gone up against.

"I don't need to see what you can do, Ms. Turner." He ended the conversation by turning his back on her and walking the rest of the way to the center of the football field. Whether or not she actually left, he had no idea. But he could have sworn he heard the words *impossible asshole*.

Yeah, he was that.

TWO

Blake Carpenter was a surly son of a bitch who needed the giant stick up his rear end to be surgically extracted.

By a team of world-renowned doctors.

Annabelle had known some obstinate people in her life. Hell, she could be pretty darn stubborn when she wanted to be. But this guy practically gave new definition to the word.

She didn't back down from anyone, though, and she wasn't about to let some gorgeous ex-football player think he could bully her. If he didn't want to talk to her on the field, fine. She'd ambush him in his office. She'd only been working with the team for one season, but they'd quickly become like her little brothers. They were good kids who loved football and deserved every chance at success. Would Blake Carpenter finally be the one who helped them achieve that?

Of course Annabelle knew who he was. The guy had been one of the top quarterbacks in the game and was also a native to Blanco Valley. What she hadn't known was what a grumpy shithead he was.

All those Gatorade and Under Armour commercials he'd starred in not only showed a guy with muscles cut from marble, but also someone who was halfway likeable.

And if posing in nothing but those spandex boxer brief things—because she had no idea what the technical term for those babies was, other than penile enhancer—hadn't been enough to turn her head, his charity work had sealed the deal. She'd seen a special on *Dateline* talking about the large amount of money he'd donated to the children's wing of a Green Bay hospital. After that, she figured anyone who spent his off days with terminally ill kids, starting an afternoon program for them so they could get outside for a few hours and learn football, was someone more than just a pretty face and deliciously hot bod.

Who would have known that Blake Carpenter, one of the most feared quarterbacks in the NFL, would have no problem getting eye level with a four-year-old so he could show the kid how to cradle a football? At the end of the segment, Blake had leaned down and kissed the boy on top of his head, which had been covered with bandages from a recent surgery to remove a brain tumor.

Unfortunately, all that had eventually been overshadowed by his steroid scandal, which had taken the media and country by storm. Instead of being remembered as an amazing athlete and as a hero to terminally ill children, he'd been hailed as a liar and a cheater. Annabelle had tried not to fall in line with the rest of the country by slinging mud at the guy. How could he be that innocent after testing positive for performance-enhancing drugs and then abruptly retiring?

So which one was the real Blake? The man who got choked up over a kid with brain cancer? Or the man who was willing to shoot God knew what into his body in the name of winning.

She glanced at her watch and noted how much time she had before her first appointment at her studio. Her physical therapy practice was located in the heart of town and offered services for those recovering from an injury or some kind of surgical procedure. She loved what she did, but more than that, she loved being able to help people get their lives, and health, back on track.

She'd be damned if she'd allow their head coach to push her away from helping these kids.

And then they were there. The team filed down the hallway, the sounds of their conversations and cleats clunking on the cement floor invading the once peaceful locker room.

She stood back while the kids made their way to their lockers to change out of their gear. Cameron followed, along with two other coaches. Blake was the last one off the field, and she took the opportunity to catch his attention.

His Bobcats baseball cap was pulled low over his eyes, which were still shielded by a pair of dark sunglasses. The hard line of his mouth, set on a clean-shaven square jaw, and his straight nose were the only things visible on his face.

Annabelle strode up next to him, determined not to let the don't-speak-to-me vibe radiating from his imposing six-foot-whatever frame deter her.

"Still here, Ms. Turner?" he said without slowing his long-legged stride, which threatened to leave her in the dust.

"Five minutes is all I'm asking," she pushed. When Blake kept walking and didn't respond, she pressed on. "I just want to offer my thoughts on some of the players."

"Do you have coaching experience, Ms. Turner?" he asked as they rounded a corner that led to his office.

Did he have to walk so damn fast? She practically had to trot to keep up with the guy.

"Do you have to call me that?" she asked instead of answering his question, which was ridiculous anyway. "I would prefer you use my first name."

He came to a sudden stop and she almost plowed into him.

"I'll use your first name when the alternative stops making you blush," he answered in a low voice. Then he turned around and kept walking, leaving her gaping at shoulders so wide she was surprised he could find T-shirts that fit him.

Had he really just said that to her?

And did she really blush whenever he addressed her so formally?

You know you do.

Something about the way he said *Mizzzz* Turner, so gentlemanly. And yet, the guy was anything but a gentleman, which made the way he said her name sound more sinful than it should have been.

The heat flaming her cheeks was unmistakable. She knew perfectly well what it was. What she hadn't counted on was Blake being able to notice it so easily. Hopefully it had more to do with his ability to be detail oriented and less with her being so damn readable.

Hopefully.

Yeah, that was it.

She blinked and realized he'd ditched her. Yet again. She took off after him, into his office, but Blake was already there, removing his sunglasses and settling in the chair behind his desk.

She pushed through the door without bothering to knock or waiting for an invitation. He wouldn't give her one anyway.

"I'm beginning to think you don't understand English, Ms. Turner," he said as she closed the door behind her.

"I—" she started, then snapped her mouth shut, knowing

chastising him for using her last name again wouldn't do any good.

His office was big but cluttered with shelves, photos, books, and a television. Her gaze roamed for a moment before settling on the big man leaning back in his office chair as though he didn't have a care in the world. His hat still covered his hair, which, she knew from TV and magazines, was dirty blond. The kind that had probably been white when he'd been a kid but had darkened naturally over time. The fact that his hair wasn't visible beneath the hat, except for the back of his neck, meant he kept it trimmed neatly. She bet he had the type of hair that a woman could run her fingers through.

Odd that she would think such a thing. As though she wanted to test it out for herself.

But she didn't.

Blake folded his hands across his flat stomach and stared at her out of eyes so blue, it was like looking at a cloudless summer sky.

The same, and now familiar, heat slid low in her belly and spread all over, to every limb, until she felt like coming out of her skin. The uncomfortable sensation was as foreign as it was exciting but also left her feeling unnerved and confused. The out-of-sorts feeling had been the same with her ex-husband. Nathan had used his good looks, though Annabelle doubted Blake had the same vanity, to make women discombobulated, which she'd fallen for. Only this time, she tamped the feeling down, refusing to spiral down the same tunnel of lust she'd fallen down before.

To mask the jittery nerves, Annabelle lifted her chin and jabbed her hands onto her hips. "I'm not leaving until I have my say."

One corner of his mouth kicked up. "Clearly."

She opened her mouth, then shut it, expecting more headbutting. His quick agreement, or maybe *surrendering* was a better word, left her momentarily speechless. "I've been working with these kids for a year, Mr. Carpenter," she told him. She tilted her head to one side and studied him as he leaned farther back in his chair. "Or would you rather I call you Blake?"

One of his thick shoulders moved in a half shrug. "You can call me whatever you'd like. I don't really care."

How about I call you asshole? "Fine. The point I'm try-ing to make is that I don't want to intrude on your coaching. But these kids need proper training—thorough stretches be-fore and after practice."

"I'm giving them proper training, Ms. Turner." Blake stared at her for a moment; then his office door opened. Pat Walters, a senior, and one of the kids Annabelle had worked with last season, poked his sweaty head in. "Coach, do you have a minute?"

"In a sec," Blake answered.

Pat shut the door, and Annabelle was left alone with Mr. I-Don't-Need-Anybody's-Help.

"Him, for example." She jerked her thumb over her shoulder, indicating where Pat had just been. "Pat has a his-tory of pulling his groin muscle. It's going to continue to give him a problem unless it receives proper treatment. I started working with him at the end of last season and he's made a lot of improvement." She held up an index finger when Blake opened his mouth to argue. "In fact, I was help-ing him so much that his dad started bringing him to my studio on Saturday mornings."

"Is that right?" Blake asked.

"Yes," she reiterated. "And last season, your forward, Connor Phillips, asked me if I could help him with some stretches too."

"If these kids want to take physical therapy on their own time, that's their business," Blake stated.

Annabelle pulled in a deep breath, utilizing the relaxation techniques she'd learned in yoga years ago. The guy sitting across the wide desk from her was rapidly threatening the calm atmosphere she'd worked so hard to create for herself. Ever since her divorce, Annabelle had sworn she'd never allow a man to create a ripple in the life she'd established. Her ex-husband had obliterated the reality she'd lived in and had shattered her confidence. After she'd put the pieces of her life back together, she'd been careful not to allow another man to make her feel less than she really was.

She studied Blake for a moment, allowing her gaze to touch on the scar bisecting his left eyebrow. "Why are you so against me being here?"

He swiveled the chair back and forth. "If you want to work with the players on your own time, that's your business. But once these kids are on the field, they're my business. They need to be focusing on plays and honing their skills. The stretching I have them doing is more than enough."

"I'm not saying it's not. But I can work one on one with them and focus on their individual needs." The guy either had a major superiority complex, or he didn't trust anyone else being on the scene with him, especially someone who wasn't affiliated with football. Given what he'd been through with his team and retirement shrouded with questions, Annabelle wouldn't be surprised if he was once bitten, twice shy. The more she thought about it, the more trust issues would make sense. He'd been through a nightmare, had probably been abandoned by people close to him, and now he was hesitant to let anyone else get too close. How could she get him to see that he could trust her?

His brow twitched. "You're a tenacious little thing, aren't you?"

"When it's something I'm passionate about, yeah. Look"—she leaned forward in the chair—"give me a month to prove it to you. I'll stay out of your way and not give my opinion on any of the players unless you ask for it." She threw that last part in just to make him feel better. But they both knew darn good and well that he'd never ask her opinion on anything. "I would like to have weekly meetings also, if you have the time."

Blake shook his head. "I don't—"

"Here's my number," Annabelle interrupted, knowing if she gave him the chance, he'd shoot her request down. Inhaling a deep breath, Annabelle channeled the confidence she'd worked hard to regain after her divorce.

Don't show your insecurities.

She passed her cell number across the desk, which, of course, he didn't accept.

What a surprise.

"Call me," she told him, and stood from the chair without waiting for a response. That stare of his was unsettling and made her skin feel itchy and uncomfortable. She smoothed her hands down her shirt because if she didn't occupy them, she might do something stupid. Like fiddle with her hair. Or check her pulse. And, damn it, she would not be the same second-guessing woman she'd been after her divorce. She'd worked too hard to reclaim her independence and confidence and she would not allow another man to shake that. Again.

Annabelle lifted her chin. "The next practice, I promise you won't even know I'm there," she stated as she rounded her chair and opened the office door.

"Don't make promises you can't keep, Ms. Turner."

She glanced at him over her shoulder, just in time to catch the devious tilt of his mouth.

THREE

Six hours later, after back-to-back appointments, Annabelle left her studio, still fuming over Blake Carpenter. The man was the most obstinate thing she'd ever encountered. And that was saying something, considering Ruth Turner, Annabelle's mother, could argue the color of the sky. Growing up with a woman like Ruth had given Anabelle the tools she'd needed to go head-to-head with even the most stubborn people.

One conversation with Blake had turned her into the same insecure, second-guessing woman she's been after her divorce. The entire time she'd been in his office, she'd felt out of sorts. Like a child who'd been stripped of her security blanket.

Not since meeting her ex-husband had Annabelle had this sort of crazy-physical attraction to a man. She shook her head at her own stupidity as she locked the front door to her studio and walked to her car.

Bottom line, Blake Carpenter, former professional football

player and all-around jerk-face, was just about the hottest thing she'd ever laid eyes on.

Unbelievable.

She started the car and pulled away from the curb, then flipped a U-turn at the intersection. Her normal routine was to close up her studio, then head to her mother's house to make dinner and catch up with household chores.

This evening she decided to make a detour to the administration building of the Blanco Valley school district to have a little chat with Drew Spalding. She wasn't sure how much good it would do, but at the very least she could make her issues with Blake known to the man who'd hired her. Chances were there wasn't a whole lot Drew could do about it, but she had to try anyway.

Her phone vibrated from the depths of her purse, and Annabelle took advantage of the red light to dig the thing out. She had a feeling she knew who the text was from and tapped the screen to pull up the message.

I'm out of toilet paper. And milk.

Annabelle couldn't help the grin that broke across her face. Leave it to her mother to get right to the point.

A second later another text came through.

And Charlie needs more doggie treats. Be sure to get the vegan kind.

Annabelle's smiled faded when she read the last line. Charlie was her mother's Boston terrier, who had the attitude of a diva and a bark that was like an ice pick to her eardrums. Annabelle had never liked her mother's dog, mostly because she got the distinct feeling he turned his nose up at her whenever she came to the house. Never mind the fact that she was now the one feeding him and brushing his damn teeth.

And what did it matter what kind of treats the dog ate?

But she was happy to do it. Her mother had enough on her plate that she didn't need to worry about what the dog had on his. Ruth had had two hip surgeries in the past year. After the first time, Annabelle had taken as much time off as she could to take care of her mother for a week, then had returned to Denver. Shortly after that, her mother's health had taken a turn for the worse, and Annabelle had made the difficult decision to leave Denver. She'd sold her physical therapy practice and her condo and moved to Blanco Valley. Ruth had protested, saying it was unnecessary for Annabelle to rearrange her entire life just for little ol' her. But they both knew it had been for the best. Ruth wasn't getting any younger, and she had no one else to depend on with her other daughter, Naomi, so far away. It had been a good thing, too, because a week ago, Ruth had needed a second surgery on the same hip. Her mother's mobility was becoming more limited in her old age, so Annabelle thanked the Lord she'd made the decision to be closer. She made a note to stop at the market after leaving Drew's office. On the plus side, perhaps feeding some weird vegan treats to King Charlie would take her mind off Blake. And his world-class rear end.

Doubtful.

She shoved her own negative thought away and pulled into the parking lot of the school district's administration building. The interior of the building was quiet and blessedly cool. The front desk was empty, but all the lights were still on. Annabelle rounded the first corner and strolled down a short hallway to the open door of Drew's office. She rapped on the door frame to announce her presence and smiled when Drew lifted his head.

"Annabelle," he said with an openmouthed grin that should have sent her heart fluttering. Drew was a good-looking guy who could probably have any woman he wanted. As far as she knew, he had remained single after his divorce and didn't date very often. Probably because he was married to his job.

Why couldn't she be attracted to him instead of Blake Carpenter? Or notice how great his ass looked in a pair of shorts? Drew was a great catch and he didn't make her teeth grind together whenever he opened his mouth.

"Hi, Drew," she said. "Sorry for showing up unannounced. I'm not interrupting you, am I?"

He shook his head. "Not at all." He gestured toward one of the desk chairs. "Have a seat."

She dropped her purse to the floor and lowered to the chair. It was one of those ergonomic things with no armrests and no padding. Uncomfortable as hell, is what it was.

"What brings you by?" he asked after tossing his pen on the desk and leaning back in his own ergonomic chair.

"I went to practice today to check out the team," she answered.

Drew gave her a slow nod. "And you met Blake," he concluded.

Obviously she wasn't the only one Blake had conversational issues with.

"Yes," she confirmed. "He's..." Her words trailed off as she sorted through her mind, trying to find the correct word to describe such a complex man.

"An ass?" Drew helped with a lifted brow.

Exactly. "That's not the word I was going to use," she hedged, instead of agreeing with him. "But he does seem a little...socially challenged."

Drew chuckled. "That's one way of putting it. But the guy was one of the top players in the NFL. He knows his stuff, which is why I hired him. You're not going to have issues working with him, are you?"

She licked her lips and puffed out a breath. "I'm going to

do the best I can for those kids, because they deserve that. But Blake did try to fire me today." Actually, blatant dismissal had been more like it

Drew's brow furrowed. "That's not surprising. I went to high school with him, so I know how obstinate the guy can be. Just don't let him push you out the door. If you stay out of his way, you shouldn't have a problem with him." Drew tilted his head to one side. "Do you need me to set him straight for you?"

Annabelle lifted a brow. "I can fight my own battles, thank you. I'm not about to let Blake Carpenter bully me into leaving the team."

Drew nodded. "Good. Because I still believe those kids need all the help they can get. You just do your thing, let Blake do his and you shouldn't have to butt heads with him."

Yeah, easy for him to say. Drew didn't have to worry about his pulse fluttering whenever he was near Blake. Doing her job side by side with him was one thing. Doing it while trying to suppress the butterflies in her stomach or mask the heat blooming across her cheeks whenever he said *Mizzz* Turner was a different story.

The market didn't have vegan dog treats, so Annabelle went to the pet store. They didn't have any either, so she grabbed some that had all white meat chicken and brown rice. She could have gone to the dog groomer's, because they had things like vegan dog treats and all natural shampoo. But she was tired and wanted to go home.

So Charlie would just have to deal and so would Ruth.

She pulled up to her mother's house, making a note to call the landscapers and bitch at them for not cutting the grass this week. Her mother had enough to deal with without having to worry about her yard getting done.

Annabelle got out of the car, retrieved the groceries from the backseat, then walked up to the front door. She let herself in without knocking, knowing Ruth wouldn't hear it anyway. Her mother actually had excellent hearing but tended to be selective, which sometimes made for some interesting conversations.

The short entry hall opened up to the living room where her mother was kicked back in the recliner, her wooden cane leaning against the side. Charlie, the little pain in the ass, jumped off her mother's lap, ran up to Annabelle, and yapped and jumped as though he'd never seen her before.

Heathen.

She kicked her leg out to pry the little shit's sharp nails off her yoga pants. "Get off me," she ordered the dog. "I thought you were going to get him a bark collar," she said to her mother.

Charlie kept up his barking and followed Annabelle to the kitchen. "Those things are inhumane," her mother called. "They electrocute the dogs."

Good grief. Annabelle lifted her eyes to the ceiling as she set the plastic bags on the counter. "No, they don't," she called back. "They make a high-pitched sound when the dog barks. It trains them to be quiet." She strolled back into the living room where Charlie had climbed back onto his throne. Annabelle jutted a finger at him. "He needs one, Mom. The dog's a menace."

Her mother ran an arthritic hand over Charlie's tiny head. "He does what he's supposed to do. He alerts me when someone's at the door."

The tiny black-and-white dog with short fur and black eyes stared back at Annabelle with one eye dropping closed and the other kept firmly on her, as though to say, *You don't fool me.* Annabelle didn't want to fool him; she just wanted him to stop shrieking like a banshee whenever she walked in the door. "It's more than an alert. It's an instant migraine." She stared at her mother. "It makes people want to kick him." Charlie's ears perked up as though sensing he was in immediate danger of Annabelle's size 8s.

Yeah, sleep with one eye open, dog.

"Did you get his treats?" Ruth asked without acknowledging Annabelle's statements. Probably because she knew they were true.

She went back into the kitchen, snagged the bag of cookies, then ripped them open. Charlie's ears perked up when he saw the food, and Annabelle barely resisted the urge to snarl at the animal. He simply blinked at her because she either wasn't good enough at conveying her contempt for the dog or Charlie wasn't easily intimidated. Knowing the animal, it was the latter.

Ruth's eyes narrowed when she saw the bag. She held up a hand before Annabelle could reach in and grab a treat. "Wait a minute. Those don't look like the ones I normally buy."

If Annabelle ever owned a dog, it'd be eating Alpo. Not that she didn't like dogs. Really, Annabelle had a fondness for dogs, at least ones that didn't have superiority complexes. But wasn't dog food, dog food?

"They were out of the other stuff," she told her mom.

"Let me see it," Ruth said with an arm extended.

She handed the bag over, knowing exactly what her mother was going to say before she even said it.

"See," Ruth stated with her index finger tapping the bag. "This has chicken in it." She offered the bag back to Annabelle. "I'm not giving animal bits to Charlie. It's bad for them. I saw it on Animal Planet."

Oh Lord. If there was one thing her mother was obsessed with, besides Charlie the douche, it was Animal Planet.

She held her hands up in surrender. "Okay, whatever. I'll go get the other stuff, but it'll have to be tomorrow."

"Charlie thanks you," her mother called to Annabelle's retreating backside.

She didn't do it for Charlie, but who was she to argue?

Her mother turned the volume up on the TV, which was tuned to some show about marine life that lived in the Great Barrier Reef. Annabelle put away the lactose-free milk, then took the package of toilet paper and stored it in the hall closet. After taking care of that, she pulled a casserole from the freezer and preheated the oven.

The first time her mother had surgery, Annabelle had learned the hard way that it was easier to prepare a week's worth of dinners, then store them in the freezer. Coming over here every single night and making dinners from scratch, as her mother liked them, was simply too much work. So she'd prepare them at home, usually on a Sunday, and bring them over Sunday night.

Tonight's dinner was a chicken broccoli casserole, topped with corn flakes. One of her mother's favorites.

Annabelle set the dish on the counter. She'd just turned around to go back into the living room when her mother came shuffling in, leaning heavily on her cane.

"You shouldn't be moving around, Mom," Annabelle told her. "We've talked about this before, remember? You need to heal properly before you can start that aerobics class." As a physical therapist, Annabelle knew the importance of making a healthy recovery after a major surgery such as her mother had. Keeping the muscles mobile and limber post-surgery was imperative to healing properly. Ruth seemed to think she could rely on her cane, which made Annabelle's fingers itch to throw the damn thing in the closet. Because they both knew the cane was more for security than anything else.

"I'm not an invalid, Annabelle. I can get up and get myself something to drink." She opened the fridge and took out a bottle of water. "Besides, my doctor told me I need to try moving around if I feel like it."

Even if her doctor hadn't told her that, Ruth would still try to do everything for herself. The woman rarely asked for help and seldom accepted it when offered. The only reason she allowed Annabelle to do as much as she was doing was because she knew Annabelle wouldn't take no for an answer.

"I need to regain my strength if I'm going to do cardio in the park with Patty and her friends." Ruth waved her hand in the air. "I'd rather do that than some dumb class at the community center."

Annabelle blinked at her mother and swallowed back a groan. "Mom, not the Beehive Mafia. Those women are nothing but a bunch of gossips."

Patty Silvano was her mother's neighbor. She and Virginia McAllister, Beverly Rowley, and Lois Jenkins were all born during World War II. They'd convened into a group of four because they were Blanco Valley's longest living citizens, not to mention two of them were descendants of the town's founders. They'd earned the nickname the Beehive Mafia because they styled their slate-gray hair as a throwback to the sixties and loved to chirp in people's ears about the goings-on in town. They also met at the city park twice a week for cardio in the park.

Lord help them if Ruth Turner joined that horde of busybodies.

"Honey," Ruth commented. "They hate being called that."

Annabelle was pretty sure they thrived on the notoriety of it, but whatever.

"How did the first practice go today?" Ruth asked, changing the subject. Yet again.

Annabelle reached for the cookie jar and snagged an oatmeal raisin she'd made a few days ago. "As expected," she hedged. No need to go into her already developing issues with their coach. The one who made her feel like she needed to fluff her hair.

"I heard that Blake Carpenter is something to look at," Ruth commented.

Annabelle merely shrugged. "I guess so." Understatement of the year.

Ruth only lifted a brow.

"Why are you looking at me like that?" she asked her mother.

"Patty told me a woman would have to be dead not to notice that guy."

Annabelle finished off the cookie and reached for another. She'd have to do an extra thirty minutes of yoga to burn them off. "And?" *And let's please end this conversation now.*

"And is he as hunky as Patty says?" Ruth grinned, creating deep lines in the paper-thin skin of her cheeks. "Does he have a rippling chest and a cement-hard butt?"

Annabelle nearly choked on a raisin. "Mother, it really creeps me out when you talk about men that way."

"Honey, I might be old but I'm not dead. And I want grandkids." She gulped some more water. "It's obvious I'm not getting any out of your sister," she muttered.

Annabelle left that particular subject alone and stared at her mother. "What do grandkids have to do with Blake Carpenter?" But, yeah, she knew. Thinking of kids made her think of how they were made. And no way did she want to think about sex and Blake Carpenter at the same time.

Ruth waved a hand toward her daughter. "You're single. He's single. And from what I hear pretty darn easy on the eyes."

Annabelle lowered her brows. "How do you know he's single?"

Ruth lifted one shoulder. "Patty told me. She's friends with the mother of Blake's best friend."

"The guy's been in town how long, and you're already gossiping about him?"

"It's not gossip, Annabelle. It's just"—she waved her hand in a circle—"neighborly conversation."

Yeah, right.

Annabelle replaced the lid to the cookie jar and crossed her arms over her chest. "Well, I work with the guy, so getting involved with him would be inappropriate. Besides, I have no desire to get married again."

"Honey, not all men are selfish pricks like Nathan," Ruth said in a soft voice.

Not only had he been cheating, but also the woman he'd cheated with had no idea he'd even been married. It was a small comfort to know she hadn't been the only one to succumb to Nathan's charm and deceit.

Ruth had been supportive, to the point where she'd been all Annabelle had to lean on. Deep down, though, she knew her mother had been disappointed her oldest daughter hadn't been headed for that typical white-picket-fence life. The one Annabelle and Naomi had growing up.

"That's true, Mom," she responded. "But not all men are princes like Dad was."

Ruth's mouth turned up in a small smile. "Your dad was one of a kind, wasn't he?"

The oven dinged, and Annabelle turned to slide the casserole in. The task was a welcome distraction, for she knew the tears would come if they talked about her father any further. Annabelle had adored the man and his death had left a gaping hole in their family.

Behind her, Ruth sighed. "Honey, I just can't bear the thought of you being alone. It's not natural."

Annabelle set the timer on the oven and straightened. "I'm not really alone, Mom. I have you. I have Stella," she said of her best friend. "And I have my work." She placed a hand on the counter. "I stay plenty busy."

"That's not what I mean," Ruth said.

Annabelle smiled at the woman who'd always been the rock of their family. "I know," she agreed. "But I'm happy."

Ruth opened her mouth to counter Annabelle's statement but was interrupted by a knock on the front door, followed by Charlie's furious barking.

The two women left the kitchen, trailing behind Charlie as he leapt off the recliner and scampered toward the front door. The dog jumped up and down, yapping like a maniac as the door opened and Patty Silvano poked her head through.

"Hello." The older woman, with her traditional up-do, waggled her fingers and managed to shove her way past Ruth's guard dog.

"Come on in, Patty." Ruth waved a hand, then motioned for Charlie to settle down. "Charlie, that's enough."

Patty, cradling two jars of some kind of food in one hand, knelt before the dog and scratched Charlie between the ears. "Oh, aren't you a good boy," she crooned to him.

Charlie, instead of going on a wild rampage like he always did with Annabelle, rolled over onto his back and stuck all four legs in the air.

Ruth slid Annabelle a sly look. "See, you just have to know how to work the dog."

Annabelle barely resisted the urge to bare her teeth, because Charlie had never been that calm for her. Maybe it was fear of the towering beehive that had Charlie admitting submission.

Yeah, that had to be it. And not having anything to do with Charlie simply not liking his owner's daughter.

Patty straightened and smoothed a hand down her blue polyester pants. She pasted a wide smile on her pale face, which deepened the grooves in her forehead and cheeks. "I wanted to bring over some of my peaches." Patty held up the two jars, which had sliced peaches floating in syrup.

Ruth accepted the gift from her neighbor. "Aren't you sweet, Patty? Thank you." She gestured next to her, toward Annabelle. "You remember my daughter Annabelle, don't you?"

Patty's grin deepened. "Of course I do, and you're even more beautiful than the last time I saw you."

Annabelle was about to thank the woman for her kind compliment, when she continued. "No wonder the new coach was all flustered this morning." Patty actually winked, and Annabelle had the feeling she was trying to be coy, or something equally horrifying. All Annabelle could feel was the heat flaming into her cheeks as the two women stared at her, as though she was supposed to respond with something. But what?

Thank you?

Yes, you figured out my evil plan?

Or how about, mind your own business?

Annabelle shook her head, but Patty shoved past her as she linked arms with Ruth. "Lois's daughter was at practice this morning because, you know, her oldest son is a junior on the team." Patty tossed Annabelle a half grin over her shoulder, as though sharing some inside secret about that piece of information. "And Lois's daughter told her that Mr. Carpenter didn't seem too happy to have Annabelle there today."

Ruth jammed her hands onto her bony hips. "Now why would that man have an issue with my daughter?"

Patty leaned toward Ruth and whispered, "Because clearly he's threatened by a beautiful woman."

Oh good Lord.

Ruth slowly nodded as though the truth had just been revealed to her. "Oh, he's one of those," she whispered back. "A man who can't handle when a woman is in a position of authority." She stepped toward Annabelle and wrapped her thin fingers around Annabelle's shoulders. "Honey, you don't back down from him, you hear me?"

Annabelle smiled, because if she didn't, she might scream at the ridiculous conversation Patty had started. Reason number one she didn't want her mother doing cardio in the park with the Beehive Mafia. Also, she didn't want to come over one day and see Ruth's hair styled in a five-foot twist on her head.

"Mom," Annabelle started as she peeled her mother's fingers off her shoulders. "I think Lois's daughter is mistaken. I'm sure Blake isn't threatened by me."

"Honey, a man as good-looking and dominant as he is would never take kindly to a female, especially one who looks like you, invading his territory," Patty commented. "Virginia confirmed it, you know," she said to Ruth.

"Virginia was at practice too?" Annabelle asked.

Patty waved a hand in the air. "No, honey. She saw Mr. Carpenter the other day when he was at his cousin Brandon's house. Said he's a hot piece of ass." Patty held her arthritic hands up, jingling the beaded bracelets on her wrist. "Her words, not mine."

Annabelle almost gagged. "You know what? I just remembered I have a root canal I'm late for."

Patty forged on. "We were hoping to catch a glimpse of him this morning when we were doing our cardio, but Brandon was jogging by himself." Patty nudged Annabelle in the ribs. "You know that's why we started cardio in the park, right? It's the best way to catch all those young studs without their shirts on. Lois managed to snap a picture of Brandon and added him to our Tumblr page. It's under the Queen Bees."

Gag me. Though Annabelle wouldn't mind seeing Blake without a shirt on...

Okay, no. That would be bad. She didn't need any more reasons to be fantasizing about the man.

Patty glanced at her jeweled watch. "I have to get home and catch me some *Judge Judy*." The old woman shot Annabelle and Ruth a smile. "I love how she doesn't take crap from anyone. Kind of reminds me of me."

With a chuckle that some people would construe as mildly devious, she was out the door, Charlie running after her as though he wanted just one more belly rub. The terrier lowered to his hind legs and tilted his head to one side at the closed door.

Okay, the dog could be cute sometimes. When he wasn't being so damn annoying.

Annabelle turned toward her mother, who was still clutching the jars of peaches in her arms. "Mom, please don't do cardio in the park with them."

Ruth turned toward the kitchen. "Oh, honey, they're harmless."

"More like ridiculous," Annabelle corrected.

Ruth shot her daughter a glance over her shoulder. "Honey, I thought you would be happy that I found something to do with myself. You were just telling me the other day that I needed to get in some exercise after I'm healed."

"Yes, but not with the Beehive Mafia." She jutted her index finger toward her mother. "If you come home with a hairstyle like that and polyester pants, I'm disowning you."

Ruth clasped Annabelle's face in her soft hands and placed a kiss on both her cheeks. "I love that you worry about me."

Annabelle couldn't help the smile that crept up her mouth. At times she felt like the worst nag, always telling her mom she needed to do this or more of that. Over the years, she'd become convinced that her mother was ignoring her, that Annabelle was wasting her breath on a woman who wanted to do her own thing.

"I just want you to be happy, Mom," Annabelle admitted.

Ruth's smile slipped. "You're starting to sound like your sister."

When Naomi had first left the states at the age of twenty-one to finish her college studies in Central America, Ruth had been supportive and even excited for her youngest daughter. But the excitement had faded when Naomi announced her plans to stay abroad.

One more year had turned into six, during which time Annabelle's sister had flitted from one Latin country to the next. Her most recent endeavor was Cusco, Peru, where she'd obtained financing to open a hostel.

It left Annabelle no choice but to be the primary caregiver for their mother.

Annabelle knew Naomi didn't intend to be selfish. She just went where she wanted without giving much thought to anything else.

Not that Annabelle was bitter or anything.

Really, she wasn't.

"I'd like to bring you to my studio one day next week and work on some exercises," she said, needing to change the subject from her sister. When Ruth only stared, Annabelle pushed. "The doctor said you need to be working with a physical therapist. It's important that you work on your hip."

"I know that, Annabelle."

Great. Now her mother was upset, which turned into irritable. And irritable Ruth was about as pleasant as a wild cat.

"Why don't you go sit back down and I'll bring you some dinner when this is done cooking," she suggested.

Ruth swiped the back of her hand across her eyes. "Charlie needs his dinner first."

The glittering moisture that had been wiped away from Ruth's eyes gave Annabelle a moment's pause. Her mother had never been a crier, or showed any kind of emotion for that matter. That sort of thing was awkward for a woman who had an easier time telling her kids how to use proper table manners than she did saying "I love you."

Nevertheless, Annabelle approached her mom just as she opened the refrigerator door to where the dog's chicken and rice was stored in a container. She placed her hands on her mother's bony shoulders and turned her around. "I'll get Charlie's dinner. You go sit down."

Ruth nodded but looked everywhere but at Annabelle.

"Mom," she said in a gentle voice. "Naomi doesn't stay away because she doesn't care about you. She doesn't realize." Annabelle looked into her mother's rheumy green eyes. "She's always been like that. It's not because she doesn't love us."

Ruth nodded again, then said, "I know. I just wished she knew how much I miss her."

"She knows," Annabelle assured her. "She misses you just as much." She gave her mother's shoulders a soft squeeze. "Now please go sit down and let me take care of this."

"So bossy," Ruth commented with a crooked tilt of her mouth.

Annabelle straightened. "I had to get it from someone."

FOUR

Blake paused as he stepped into the locker room, twenty minutes before he was supposed to meet with Matt West for extra practice. It wasn't the dark interior that gave him pause, nor was it Cameron kicked back in Blake's office, watching game film. It was the muted conversation coming from the weight room. The deep rumbling of one of his players, mixed with soft laughter. A woman's laughter.

And not just any woman. A woman who'd barged into his life and threw his hormones into all kinds of chaos. A woman he didn't want or need hanging around and telling him how to deal with his players and run his team. But here she was anyway, when no one else was supposed to be around, sending his automatic suspicious meter haywire.

Blake set his bag down, sending Cameron a quick glance before heading toward the weight room. The voices grew louder as he neared the door. The kid, who sounded like Matt, said something to Annabelle, prompting a giggle from her.

A carefree bubble of laughter like that of someone who had no ulterior motive. No agenda lurking in the shadows, waiting to pull a fast one on him. Even if Annabelle Turner didn't really strike him as manipulative or sneaky, Blake had yet to make the final decision for himself.

He stood in the doorway of the weight room and watched as Annabelle performed some kind of neck exercise on Matt. The kid was lying on his back on a bench, with Annabelle standing at his head, cradling the kid's neck in her hands. She spoke to him in a low, comforting voice, telling him to relax.

"I'm going to give your head a gentle tug," she told Matt. "Just take a deep breath for me, and then slowly let it out."

Matt's eyes dropped closed and Annabelle performed the stretch, with her petite hands gripping Matt's jaw and chin.

"How's that?" she asked the kid.

"It's good," Matt muttered.

Annabelle adjusted her stance. "Okay, I'm going to pull a little harder this time."

Matt cleared his throat. "Just don't dislocate my head from my shoulders," he joked. "I don't think Coach would be too happy about that."

The corners of Annabelle's mouth curled up and Blake was hit with the new and odd sensation of lust. New because…well…he hadn't had it this bad for a woman in a long time. And odd because he'd never had such a powerful reaction to a woman quite like Annabelle Turner. Opinionated. Headstrong. Stubborn.

Kind of like him. Totally opposite from the type of woman who usually floated his boat.

Blake didn't know how to handle it, nor did he like it.

"You should give your coach some more credit," she told Matt. "He may push you hard, but it's with the best intentions."

Blake hung back, not sure how to take her words but damn sure they'd shifted something inside his chest.

"My dad says a lot of the stuff people said about him isn't true," Matt commented. "He says Blake's not that kind of guy."

Annabelle shifted her hold on Matt's head. "I suppose your dad would know, being his cousin and all, wouldn't he? Also, the media has a way of exaggerating the truth."

Blake was just about to turn and leave, not wanting to eavesdrop on their conversation any more than he was, when Annabelle said, "Coach cares about you, you know. He hasn't exactly had a warm welcome from some of the parents, so he has a lot to prove."

His skin prickled along the back of his neck as Annabelle finished the stretch and motioned for Matt to sit up.

"What about you?" the kid asked. "What do you think?"

Blake could practically feel Annabelle's deep sigh. "I think he'll be a good coach for the team."

Matt laughed and swung his legs to the side of the bench and stood. "Is that all you think, Ms. Turner?"

Annabelle hooked her hand over her slim hip and tilted her head at the boy. "I think Mr. Carpenter is mis-understood by a lot of people." Her ponytail slipped over her shoulder when she shrugged. "I think he's had a rough couple of years and maybe just wants to put his life back together. After all, doesn't everyone deserve a second chance?"

Blake turned from the doorway, not waiting to hear Matt's reply. Because the ringing in his ears would have drowned it out anyway.

How could one woman confuse him so much, yet under-stand him more than anyone else?

He didn't want her understanding him, but at the same time her words had been something he'd yearned to hear for a long time. Whether he wanted to admit it or not, heck yeah he wanted a second chance. Perhaps that was why he'd taken this job in the first place. To prove to the world, and himself, that he wasn't down and out. That he wasn't the dirtbag, lying cheater people thought he was. The fact that Annabelle Turner, a woman who'd narrowed her eyes at him as much as she'd mentally undressed him, saw right through his I-don't-give-a-shit attitude shocked the hell out him.

Because he either wasn't as closed off as he thought he was.

Or Ms. Turner was more in tune to him than he wanted.

"You getting tired, old man?" Brandon prodded as they pounded the pavement of the greenbelt that cut through the city park. Brandon's dog, Duke, kept pace with them on his red leash, tongue lolling out of his mouth as he slung doggy slobber everywhere. Blake had a fierce competitive streak, one of the reasons he'd been such a successful quarterback. Unfortunately a bum knee put a serious cramp in his need to outrun his cousin. Blake knew he shouldn't be pushing himself so hard, but giving less than 100 percent wasn't his style.

Thirty-four wasn't old, but, shit, some days he felt like his body was falling apart. The OxyContin he'd popped that morning, prescribed by his doctor, numbed the pain enough for him to run. But he still felt out of sorts. Out of shape. Off his game.

And the burning need to toss back another pill coursed through his veins like an attack of fire ants.

"I'm fine. Just wouldn't want you to trip and ruin your

pretty face." Blake quickened his pace and resisted the urge to rub his knee. "Heads up. Beehive Mafia at two o'clock."

Brandon muttered a curse.

"I'm sure they'll have the pics up before you're done with your shower." Blake couldn't help smirking. As much as he teased his cousin, though, he knew more than anyone that Brandon would give a stranger the shirt off his back and his last dollar if they needed it.

Blake often teased his cousin that he was one of the last heroic bachelors left in Blanco Valley. All one had to do was look at how he'd single-handedly raised a rowdy little boy into an ambitious teenager. Matt was Brandon's world, which for some reason had women practically tripping over themselves to get a piece of the guy. Few women had succeeded to penetrate that tough armor Brandon placed around himself and his son, though.

"Matt looked good on the field yesterday," Blake told his cousin after they'd jogged in silence for a few minutes. He tossed Brandon a quick look, but the expression in his eyes was hidden by a pair of dark sunglasses. And the sun wasn't even out. "Better than the first practice."

"Then you know more than I do," Brandon answered. "The kid won't talk to me."

"He's a teenager, Brandon," Blake reminded him. "How open were you at that age?"

Brandon only grunted. Yeah, like father like son.

They rounded a corner and jogged over a wooden bridge, the dog's nails clicking over the wood that arched above a shallow creek. "Come to a practice and you'll see. He still has a long way to go, but he shows promise."

"I've been busy with work. Those early morning practices are hard. It'll be easier once school starts and you switch to afternoons."

A bead of sweat ran down Blake's temple. "He just needs to work on keeping his focus," he told Brandon. "He lets his mind wander and that's when he runs into trouble. Plus I've noticed tightness in his neck."

Matt loved the game of football. In fact his passion for the sport rivaled Blake's. But the kid was far from a natural talent. He was tall and bulky, which worked in his favor, but his forty-yard dash was one of the slowest on the team.

That morning he'd pulled Matt aside and talked to him about hanging back after practices so Blake could work with him on some techniques.

"He said working with Annabelle has helped," Brandon said, cutting into Blake's thoughts.

The mention of that name almost sent Blake tripping over a boulder on the edge of the path. The same monster, the one created when his career imploded, came scratching to the surface, whispering in the back of his mind that this woman was a stranger. That he didn't really know her. That this was *his* team, and he didn't want strangers encroaching on what was his and his responsibility. He'd learned the hard way not to turn a blind eye to what was most important to him. He didn't know Annabelle Turner enough—other than that she was tenacious as hell—to allow her around his kids.

Yeah, despite his efforts to scare her off with his best ornery attitude, she kept showing up. Every. Single. Morning. There she'd be in her yoga pants, practically spray painted on those long slim legs, long and thick ponytail dusting the slight indentation of her backbone. Swinging back and forth whenever she moved. Irritating him. Distracting him.

Turning him on.

Okay, yeah, she turned him on. He'd be a liar if he tried

to deny it, even if it was only to himself. She was as hot as a Colorado summer and as cool and collected as a boardroom executive.

Just that morning she'd texted him, way too early in the day for a human being to be awake and functioning. His phone had buzzed as he'd dozed in bed and when he'd finally gotten around to checking it, there had been three messages.

I'm assuming the reason you haven't contacted me about the meetings I mentioned is because you either lost my number or you've been kidnapped.

He'd only grunted to himself as he swung his legs out of the bed and read the second message.

If it's the former, here's my number again, after which she repeated the same phone number she'd already given him.

Blake stood from the bed as he thought about the cell number she'd scrawled on a napkin, which was still sitting on the kitchen counter.

If it's the latter, she went on, *then the kidnappers have my sympathies.*

One side of Blake's mouth had twitched. Shit, he hadn't been about to smile, had he? The woman, who rubbed him all kinds of the wrong way, had been able to pull some emotion from him.

Blake had sent her a quick reply as he'd readied for his jog with Brandon.

How did you get this number?

Her reply had been immediate, probably because she'd had a pencil hovered over her calendar for the moment he'd give her part of his schedule.

A little birdy.

Cameron.

Blake had made a mental note to add *ass kicking of assistant coach* to his list of things to do.

A little while later, as Blake had walked out the front door to meet his cousin, his phone had buzzed again.

So next week then? Sounds good. I'm free Thursday.

Did the woman just have conversations with herself? He'd never even agreed to meet with her, and she'd gone ahead and set the damn thing up.

"So, is the lack of comment because you don't agree?" Brandon asked, pulling Blake out of his morning memories. "Or does the smokin' hot physical therapist already have you tongue-tied?" Brandon's brows shot up his forehead. "Don't tell me you don't notice what she looks like."

Blake shook his head. "Didn't say that." And that was all he was going to say about one Annabelle Turner.

Brandon burst out laughing. As in tossing his head back and guffawing like he did when they were kids. "Oh, I see how it is," he said after calming down.

Blake glanced at his cousin, noting the smile still turning up the corners of his mouth. "See what?"

"How she's already under your skin," Brandon answered.

Blake slid his cousin a narrow-eyed glance. Truth.

"Again with the no comment," Brandon mused. "That stony silence might work on others, but you forget I've known you since we were in diapers."

Blake didn't need reminding. "I don't even know her," he corrected his cousin.

"Don't have to know someone to lust after them," Brandon pointed out.

Blake kept his pace up, even though his knee was on fire now. Damn his injury and damn his need for more pain pills. "Who said anything about lust?"

"Your denial is enough, my friend."

Blake shook his head. "She's not under my skin."

"Matt said some of the kids on the team are calling her Tantalizing Ms. Turner."

Blake stopped running and jabbed his hands on his hips. Brandon did the same and used the hem of his T-shirt to dry his sweat-drenched brow. A woman walked in the opposite direction, with her cell phone glued to her ear, and allowed her gaze to drop down to the strip of flesh exposed beneath the lifted shirt. His cousin shot the woman a grin, and Blake swore the woman's cheeks reddened just as she passed them.

Yeah, his cousin was a chick magnet. Always had been.

Blake waved a hand in the air. "Whatever. Say what you want, but I'm not getting involved with her."

"Who said anything about involvement?" Brandon gave Blake's shoulder a shove. "I just want you to admit she gets your panties in a twist."

"You mean the same way Trisha did for you?" Blake asked, mentioning Matt's mother.

Brandon let out a humorless laugh. "You always did play dirty, didn't you?"

Blake moved one of his shoulders. "Just returning the favor."

"I guess I had that one coming," Brandon admitted.

They walked in silence for a moment, allowing their breathing to slow down and soaking in the mid-Saturday-morning sun.

"Yeah, okay, she's hot," Blake finally said.

Brandon just grinned. "There it is."

Blake jabbed his index finger toward his cousin. "But I'm not getting involved with her."

"You keep mentioning that, but I never said anything about getting mixed up with her," Brandon pointed out. "So is it me or you you're trying to convince?"

Blake stared back at his cousin for a moment, then turned away. Damn the man for knowing exactly what Blake was thinking, then having the balls to call him out. Brandon West always got some kind of sick satisfaction out of watching Blake squirm. The thing was, it had never mattered before. His cousin's ribbing, even if it was playful, because everything about Brandon was playful, never made Blake want to sock one to him.

Which meant Brandon was right.

Annabelle was under his skin.

The three of them, men and dog, stopped at a water fountain where Brandon pulled a foldable mesh water bowl from his shorts pockets, filled it with water, and placed it on the ground for Duke. The dog, tongue hanging about a foot out of his mouth, bent his big old block head down and lapped the water up, sloshing the stuff all over the concrete.

"I can't imagine what your kitchen floors look like," Blake commented as Duke continued to drink.

Brandon grunted. "He can't help it if his tongue is the size of a surfboard." He bent down and scratched the dog's ears. "Ever think of getting one?"

Blake shook his head and swiped his forehead with the back of his hand. "If I could ever keep a plant alive for more than a week, maybe."

"Maybe one day I'll just surprise you with one," Brandon commented with a sly grin. "I'll stick a red bow behind its ears and leave him on your doorstep."

Blake lifted a brow. "Do that and I'll send your baby pictures to the Beehive Mafia."

Brandon straightened. "You're cold, man."

Speaking of the Beehive Mafia, the four women, who'd been rotating the cardio stations the entire time Brandon and Blake had been jogging while simultaneously snapping pictures of them with their camera phones, because they were *damn* fast with those things, came strolling up to them. Their polyester shorts hit each of them at the knee, with loose T-shirts, pristine white tennis shoes, and their signature beehives making them stick out like they had neon signs on their heads.

Blake wondered if they coordinated their outfits.

Brandon lifted the hem of his shirt and used it to wipe more moisture from his brow. Patty Silvano, the most camera happy one of the bunch, whipped her phone out and snapped a picture so damn fast that Blake barely registered the flash.

She tucked the phone back in her shorts and sent Brandon a coy grin. "The people of Blanco Valley thank you, Mr. West."

Brandon let his shirt drop and he jabbed a finger at Patty. "You don't have my permission to use that. I own all the rights to pictures of me."

Patty waved a hand in the air, dismissing Brandon's concern. "Oh, it's just for my personal page. No one will see it but me."

That was pure bullshit, and they all knew it. The four of them may be in their seventies, but they could shoot the shit like a bunch of sailors.

"In fact"—Patty took her cell out again—"let me get one more shot of you. Just lift your shirt a little higher this time."

Virginia McAllister, Brandon's neighbor and vocal activist for the demise of Duke, yanked the phone out of Patty's hands. "Give the kid a break, Patty. Or at least wait until he's jogging without a shirt on."

The other women chuckled, joined by Blake because Brandon looked like he was about to shit his pants.

"Why don't you get a shot of this guy," Brandon

said, jerking his thumb in Blake's direction. "He's got more packs in his stomach than I do." He whipped a hand out and grabbed the bottom of Blake's shirt. "Blake, lift your shirt up."

Blake tried to yank himself out of the way, because, for God's sake, he didn't need this bunch stalking him with their phones and ridiculous hair.

But Brandon was fast, and Patty was even faster, and *how* did she do that? She snapped the picture and slid the phone away before Blake had a chance to cover his torso up.

"What the hell?" he demanded of his cousin.

Brandon sniggered and Lois Jenkins clapped her hands together like a little kid who'd been given a new bike. "Oh, we finally got one!"

Beverly Rowley, who seemed to be the least concerned with violating Blake's and Brandon's rights, crossed her arms over her chest. "Can we cool it with the pictures and get on with our workout, please?" she demanded. "The two of you are worse than Lois's grandkids."

Virginia spoke up. "Who do you think she gets it from? That little girl of hers was the one who showed her how to use the camera phone in the first place."

Patty's chin tilted up. "Neither one of you appreciate real art. I'm doing the city of Blanco Valley a favor."

"If any of those pictures end up on your Beehive page, I'm going to let Duke loose in your yard." Brandon pinned Patty with a hard look. "And Duke loves hydrangeas."

Patty stepped forward and got right in his face. "If I see this animal in my plants, I'm going to sic Lois's grand-daughter on you. And if you think I'm fast with a camera? That little girl will have pictures of you doing things you won't even remember doing."

Blake slid his cousin a look because, shit, Patty Silvano,

five-foot-nothing that she was, could be damn scary when she put her mind to it.

"Do you hear me, son?" she said to Brandon.

Blake leaned closer to Brandon. "She called you son," he commented, smirking.

Patty slid her death stare toward Blake, effectively shutting him up real fast.

"Yes, ma'am," Brandon said.

Patty grinned, softening her features and bringing back the sweet woman who had the spryness of a forty-year-old. "Good man." Then she patted him on the bicep. "Oh my." Her brief touch turned into a lingering caress as she ran her fingers over the grooves of Brandon's muscles.

"Oh for heaven's sake, Patty." Beverly stepped forward, hooked her arm through Patty's, and practically dragged her friend away. "By the way, Mr. Carpenter," Beverly addressed Blake. "There might be some people in this town who oppose you coaching our boys, but not us."

Lois nodded. "That's right, son. We know you'll bring pride back to the Champion Valley."

At the mention of the nickname, given to Blanco Valley during its glory days of football, Blake's gaze automatically touched on Haystack Mountain. Looming over the valley, like a cruel reminder of the weight Blake had on his shoulders, were the words *Champion Valley*, arranged out of giant white boulders. The words were visible for miles around, letting everyone know of the powerhouse that once resided here and the pride the town carried with the high school's multiple state championships. Blake had been a part of that, as had Brandon and Cameron. In fact, the three of them used to take weekend trips hiking up the mountain, then sit by the sign and gaze back down at the town, like the immortal football stars they were.

At the end of their senior year, the school had held a ceremony, a sort of inaugural for the painting of their jersey numbers on the Champion's rock. The rock sat in the middle of town, next to a wooden sign that said, *Welcome to Blanco Valley, home of the undefeated Bobcats*.

Of course, the sign had been erected twenty years ago when they'd been undefeated. Unfortunately, no one had changed it, either because people had stopped caring or they held out hope they'd be undefeated again.

"They tried taking the sign down," Beverly commented.

Blake cleared his throat past the lump that had formed. "What sign?"

"Well, that one, of course." The older woman waved her hand toward Haystack Mountain. "The mayor wanted it removed, but the city council voted against it."

Lois stepped toward Blake, and he got a whiff of the Aqua Net holding her hair together. "There are people in this town who still believe in you. We wanted the sign to stay up because we believe you can make us great again."

Virginia piped up. "What Lois is trying to say is that we don't have a lot of years left. We need you to make it snappy."

Blake wanted to chuckle at Virginia's attempt at humor, but he couldn't manage to even force one. Because, as much as he didn't want them to, the old woman's words meant something to him. Over the past few years, he'd grown complacent with the doubt, the rumors, and the pity, so hearing someone affirm him, showing the kind of faith he'd been longing for, made him feel…uncomfortable.

As though he didn't deserve it. Because wasn't that what people had been saying about him? That a cheater and a liar didn't deserve people's sympathy?

Eventually he'd told himself he didn't need it. That the

public's support didn't mean anything to him. That he could do it on his own. It wasn't until he heard the words that he realized the powerful effect they had.

And hadn't Annabelle said something similar the other morning in the weight room? When she'd been talking to Matt?

Yes, now that Blake thought about it, she had. Something about giving him the benefit of the doubt. Perhaps that's why he'd slipped from the doorway without alerting them to his presence. Knowing the woman, Annabelle would have seen the vulnerability all over his face.

Blake nodded. "I'm going to do my best, ma'am," he told her. "The team's showing a lot of promise."

Beverly grinned, crinkling the corners of her eyes. "That's what we like to hear. Prove that mayor wrong. Show him why that sign needs to stay up."

Yeah, no sweat. What they didn't realize was that Blake had been given a broken team with kids who were hungry for it but parents who didn't want him around.

"We have a problem," Cameron said a few days later when the team had shuffled into the locker room after another practice.

Blake leaned back in his chair and didn't remove his attention from notes he'd made. "What now?"

Cameron sat, adjusting the bill of his Bobcats baseball cap, which was already pulled low over his dark blue eyes. His too-shaggy chocolate brown hair was badly in need of a cut and curled over his ears. "Keith Montague and Randy O'Connell have been pulled from the team."

"Why?" Blake asked, though he was pretty sure he could guess the reason, judging by the look of sympathy in his friend's eyes. It was the same look given to him by everyone else close to him after the scandal. His parents, when he'd visited them in Arizona. Brandon. Hell, even Matt looked at Blake like that. But sympathy was the last thing he wanted from them. What he needed was their support. Their confidence that he could do the job he was hired to do.

"Randy's dad says his grades last year weren't the best and they want him to focus on academics. Randy didn't love the game anyway, so why make him continue playing?" Cameron rasped his hands along his scruffy jaw. "That's according to the kid's old man anyway."

Blake nodded. "And what did Keith's dad have to say?"

Cameron leveled Blake with a no-bullshit stare. "That he doesn't want his son playing for you."

"Well, shit," Blake muttered. It shouldn't matter. What a couple of know-it-all jerk-offs thought about him shouldn't get under his skin. But it did. Blake wasn't that guy. He wasn't a liar. And he wasn't a cheater.

Even though 90 percent of what had been reported about him was complete bullshit, people didn't care. All they saw was the latest football star fall from grace and land flat on his face. Few people had stood by him and had been willing to give him another chance. Oddly enough, Drew Spalding, for however much of a jerk the guy could be, had been willing to overlook the dark cloud following Blake around like a curse. Even though the two men didn't see eye to eye, Blake was grateful to him.

"We'll have to pull in our backups," Blake commented, pushing aside his other thoughts.

Cameron shook his head. "They're not good enough, Blake."

"Hell, Cam, what choice do we have? Two-thirds of the team couldn't hold on to the ball if I put superglue on their fingers."

One side of Cameron's mouth turned up in a sardonic smile. "Bet you're wondering what you were thinking when you accepted this job."

Blake snorted. "No doubt. You have an awful lot of faith in me," Blake pointed out.

Cameron lifted both shoulders in a lazy shrug. "I wouldn't have left my other coaching job for anyone else but you."

Blake had known that and had known what Cameron had given up to coach with him. Cam was a true friend through and through, and Blake would be damned if Cameron's loyalty would be in vain. He'd turn this team around if it was the last thing he'd do. Blake would be damned if he'd allow all of his doubters to have the last word.

This was one promise he wouldn't step away from.

He'd also be damned if he'd allow a couple of narrow-minded fathers keep him from coaching this team to victory.

"So," Cameron stated as he leaned forward and snagged a handful of M&M's out of a bowl on Blake's desk. He leaned back in his chair, dropped a couple in his mouth, and crunched them between his teeth. "I couldn't help but notice Ms. Turner still coming around practices. Apparently you didn't growl at her hard enough after the first practice." Cameron ended his statement with a final crunch of chocolate and a grin.

"Or I did and she's too stubborn for her own good," Blake argued.

Cameron took some more M&M's. "Or that," he agreed. "But I've never known someone not to cower when you level them with that death stare of yours." Cam jerked a thumb over his shoulder. "Those kids practically piss their pants when you get that look on your face."

"Your point?" Blake demanded. Except he knew his friend's point and it pissed him off.

Cameron's grin grew, creating a crease in his stubble-covered cheek. "My point, my friend, is that she's the first person in I don't know how long not to tuck tail and run the other direction when you exert your dominance."

"You're making me sound like a porn star, Cam."

Cam waved a hand in the air. "You know what I mean." He wagged an index finger in Blake's direction. "I see the way you pretend she's not around."

"Obviously I'm not pretending well enough," Blake muttered.

"So you do have a thing for her," Cameron guessed.

Blake shook his head. "Shit, not you too."

Cam chuckled. "Brandon does it to piss you off. I do it because I'm concerned for your well-being."

Blake coughed and said "bullshit" at the same time, which enticed a full-fledged laugh from his assistant coach.

"Both of you do it to annoy the shit out of me," Blake accused.

"Because you need it," Cameron said matter-of-factly.

One of Blake's brows arched. "I need you to annoy the shit out of me?"

"How else would we get you to do anything other than eat/breathe/sleep football half the time and live like a recluse the other half?"

"Maybe I like living like a recluse." Except he didn't. He'd just sort of tumbled into that solitary life after he'd left the NFL. Now it was just him, his bum knee, and his pain pills. But Brandon and Cameron didn't know that. Oh, they knew he had knee trouble. Anyone with eyesight could see his slight limp. What they didn't know was that he still needed his OxyContin like he needed his next breath. The bottle he'd tossed in the desk

drawer that morning was still there. Blake opened the drawer
and glanced down as the bottle rolled forward and bumped the
front panel. There were still pills in the bottle. He heard them
rattling around. Probably plenty for him to toss one back now
and maybe take another one before bed.

But not with Cam sitting there... also, shouldn't he stop
taking the stuff?

His fingers gripped the edge of the drawer as a layer of
sweat coated his hand. Cam tossed back some more M&M's
as Blake slammed the drawer shut, the sound of the bottle
rolling around inside like a whisper in his head.

That he'd never tell anyone. He didn't want or need anyone's pity, especially his two closest friends. Bad enough
they were already pushing him to... whatever it was they
thought he should be doing with Annabelle Turner.

He knew what *he* wanted to do with her, but he'd be
damned if he'd tell anybody else that.

"No one likes living like a recluse," Cameron argued.
"Not even you."

Blake leaned back in his own chair. "Please tell me more,
Mr. Master of Relationships. And while you're at it, remind
me how the last one ended for you."

The playful gleam in Cameron's eye dimmed a bit. "I
told you I had no idea she was married." Cam's mouth tilted
and he picked up a pen and chucked it across the desk,
where it hit Blake in the shoulder. "Douche."

The pen landed on the floor, so Blake snagged another
one out of the holder and sent it sailing, hitting the bill of
Cameron's hat. "Prick."

Cameron gave the pen on the floor a glance, then clucked
his tongue. "Temper."

"Says the guy who threw the pen first," Blake reminded him.

Cam slouched lower in his chair. "Touché. And you've still got a pretty good arm."

"Gee thanks."

"For an old guy," his friend said with an evil grin. "Who obviously needs to get laid."

"Keep on, Cam."

But yeah, that was true. Blake did need to get laid. He needed a warm, soft woman to spend a few hours in bed with so he could exercise the tension and stress from his body.

Or he could just go for a bike ride or something.

Or get laid.

With Annabelle.

Except it'd probably be so good he'd want to come back for more and that would definitely be a bad idea. He had more demons and baggage than he knew what to do with and a casual hook-up was all he was capable of giving right now.

Besides, he'd like to think he was more professional than to have a one-night stand with a woman he worked side by side with.

Yeah, that was it.

Cameron's phone vibrated. He withdrew it from his pocket, touched his finger to the screen a few times, then slid the thing away. "I've got to go meet with special teams," his friend announced.

"Three o'clock, game film," Blake told him.

Cam nodded and headed for the office door. "You got it." He opened the door, stepped out, and poked his head back in. "Miss Thang's swaying her hips this way. Throw the lock on the door and I'll stand guard for you."

The image of swaying hips and what Blake would like to do to them, especially with a big sturdy desk, had that muscle between his thighs twitching for the umpteenth time in as many days. To wipe the cocky grin off his friend's face, Blake bypassed the cup of pens and went for the paperweight. The thing went flying and only missed Cameron's smug look by an inch when it hit the door frame and crashed to the floor.

Yeah, he still had a good arm.

FIVE

Annabelle was about to let herself into Blake's office when something hard flew up against the wall and hit it with a thud. Cameron shot her a grin and managed to close the door seconds before the object probably would have hit him in the head. She was just about to ask him what the heck that was when he poked his head back in the door, said something to Blake, then shut the door again.

Something else crashed against the door, making Annabelle jump because the thing sounded heavy and probably expensive.

"What the heck are you two doing?" she asked the assistant coach.

Cameron folded his arms across his wide chest. "It's an old ritual Blake and I have. Instead of saying good-bye, we throw stuff at each other. Makes us feel all macho and shit."

She narrowed her eyes at him, noting the faint smile that tugged at the corners of his full mouth. Then she shook her head and pushed down on the door handle. "Men are weird," she muttered.

When she stepped into the office, Blake was just...there. As he always was. There. A commanding presence who couldn't be ignored even if she tried.

And she'd tried.

The guy was too...well, everything to be put out of her mind.

I see the way you pretend she's not around.

Yeah, she'd heard what Cameron had said. Okay, she'd heard the entire conversation. Should she have felt guilty for eavesdropping?

Probably. Anybody would. A tiny frisson of guilt had threaded through her system as she'd stood outside his office door and listened to him and Cameron talk about the team. Her guilt was because she hadn't exactly been invited. She'd been relentlessly texting him about meetings and he'd managed to talk around her purpose. Either ignoring her altogether or answering her questions with non-answers.

Acknowledging her without giving her what she wanted.

So she'd decided to just show up, because how else was she supposed to get through to him? Wait for him to cave?

Not bloody likely.

She'd heard Cameron mention the only reason he'd accepted the position was because it was Blake. Meaning he wouldn't have come to the Bobcats for anyone else. Meaning they had a special bond. Meaning Blake wasn't the ogre he wanted her to think he was.

She cleared her throat and pushed the door closed. "Do you have a minute?"

He eyed her from beneath the bill of his baseball cap, which was pulled down low enough to cast his eyes in shadow. "If I say no, will you go away?"

I see the way you pretend she's not around.

Cam's words floated around in her mind, like a temptation, a dare to see how far she could push Blake. But at the same time, other parts of the conversation warred with her desire to break his tough exterior. She'd heard the stress in his voice when he and Cameron had discussed options for the team. Before now, Annabelle had never considered the pressure he was under. How conflicted he must feel with the school district, hiring him, pushing him to win and then the opposition from the parents who didn't understand Blake.

A strange feeling, close to sympathy for a man who'd been through hell, warmed her chest. Annabelle pushed it away, because sympathy would turn to compassion. Not that she didn't have compassion for the man, because she did. Probably a lot more than half the town. But compassion would melt the stern resolve she'd developed after her divorce. That resolve was the only thing keeping her from melting for Blake Carpenter completely.

She graced him with her sweetest smile, the one that used to wrap her daddy around her little finger. "No," she answered.

"Then I guess it doesn't matter, does it?" he asked.

"No," she said again.

"Then why'd you ask?"

She stepped away from the door and took a chair that was still warm, obviously from Cameron. "To be polite."

One side of his mouth turned up and the butterflies in her belly did that dancing thing again. "How magnanimous of you."

"What can I say? My mother raised me right," she told him, even though that wasn't the reason. She did it to irritate him. To entice some kind of reaction from him. A laugh. Anything to crack the ironclad exterior he'd erected around himself. She supposed the almost-smile was a start. A small stepping-stone to revealing who Blake Carpenter really was.

But still not enough for her.

"You might as well tell me why you're here, then," he told her. He slouched low in his chair and rested his hands across his flat stomach. Yeah, she'd noticed that about him too. How in shape the guy was. How his Bobcats football T-shirts molded over the bulk of his shoulders and wide chest, then loosened over his narrow waist.

Was it wrong of her to want to lift the hem of the shirt? Just a little peek to see if the flesh beneath was as smooth and hard as she'd imagined.

Bad Annabelle.

She cleared her throat and shifted in her seat.

"Um...," she started. "So I know we're only about a month away from our first game..."

His brow twitched. "And?"

Yes, Annabelle. And what?

"Well, I think the kids are looking pretty good. They respond well to you," she added.

Blake slowly nodded. "I'm glad you approve, Ms. Turner. Is that all?"

"No," she answered quickly, fearing he'd toss her out if she didn't get to the point. Problem was her tongue had a habit of ceasing to work around him. As did her brain, especially when he used her name like that. It rolled off his tongue like a drip of sweet honey. "Having said that," she went on, pushing thoughts of dripping honey from her mind, "there are a few kids I'm concerned about."

"Who specifically are you talking about?"

Blake continued to sit rigid in his chair, not moving a muscle, except the one in his jaw that kept clenching. The speech she had in her head about moving forward with the kids, and her determination to lend a hand, paused. In its place was a need to make sure Blake understood that she would never do anything shady.

"Blake," she started, turning the words over in her head, trying to find a way to convey her message. "I hope you know I would never put these kids in jeopardy. My only concern is making sure they heal properly. Even if that takes an entire season."

Something flashed in his eyes, but it was gone too quick for Annabelle to label it. Not only that but the shadow cast by his cap made his expression difficult to read. Whatever it was had softened his expression enough for Annabelle to know she'd cracked him. That he understood she wasn't here to work against him.

"I understand that," he told her. "I know you would never do anything to hurt my players."

"Because I'm not like the trainers you knew," she went on. "I don't put my own desire for winning above my patients. I care about those kids."

That muscle in his jaw kicked in again, contradicting the softening of his blue eyes. She'd gotten so used to seeing them hard with determination and resistance that she almost missed it. But once she realized she'd gotten through to him, Annabelle wondered how she'd ever see him the other way again.

"I appreciate that," he finally said, as though he'd been searching for the words. Had she really managed to stump him?

"Just for the record," he told her, "I never pegged you for that type."

Annabelle nodded. "But you've made your distrust of me pretty clear."

"Only because I take this job personally. Those are my

players out there," he said with a nod toward the locker room. "And I've learned the hard way not to give too much control to anyone else."

"I understand that," she assured him. "I'm not trying to take over. I'm trying to help."

He waited a moment, staring back at her out of those clear blue eyes and sending a shiver down the center of her back.

He nodded. "Go on."

"Scott Porter has a tight hamstring that he keeps pulling."

Blake swiveled back and forth in his chair. "I'm aware of that."

"I'm doing what I can for him, and I think the stretching is helping," she assured him.

Blake was silent a moment, as though sensing she had more to say, which she did but she knew he wasn't going to like it. "But?" he asked.

Annabelle held her breath for a moment, then slowly expelled it. "I think it would help Scott if he didn't participate in the practices. At least in any kind of full contact." She waited for him to snarl at her or tell her she'd lost her mind. He didn't. Instead he did something she'd yet to witness from him.

He laughed.

The heat that sat low in her belly spread throughout her body and settled in all her girly parts. Parts that hadn't been used in way too long. So long she'd almost forgotten how to use them. But more than that she'd forgotten how alive they made her feel. How aware of herself she became. Itchy. Uncomfortable.

And so unbearably hot.

The man had a deviously sexy laugh. So much sexier than she'd imagined. Not that she'd been thinking about what his laugh would sound like.

"That's not happening, Ms. Turner," he finally said after he'd stopped chuckling.

"Players are just as at risk of injury during practices as they are during games. I just think until his hamstring loosens some more, he needs to take it easy. If it suffers one more good pull, he'll be unable to play the rest of the season." When he didn't respond, Annabelle continued. "Surely you have a backup you can use for a little while."

"Of course we do," he answered. "But he's not nearly good enough. Scott's one of the few good players we have and we need him on the field."

Annabelle blinked at him. "All the more reason for him to focus on his leg. So he's ready to play when the season starts."

Blake leaned forward in his chair and folded his burly forearms across the desk. They were covered in a soft dusting of dark hair. Funny how *soft* would be used to describe arms that looked like corded steel. "Ms. Turner," he said. "I can take it easy on him during practices, until the leg heals, but I can't bench him altogether."

"Well, I guess that's a start," she muttered, grateful he was at least willing to heed her caution.

He blinked and his mouth twitched. She almost swore he was about to smile, but that wasn't possible. Because Blake Carpenter didn't smile.

"I don't like people interfering with my work, Ms. Turner," he told her.

Gee, really?

"And I don't like people telling me what to do," he added.

Again. Shock.

"You're used to having your way, aren't you?" he asked with a tilt of his head.

Always. "Sometimes," she lied.

"Well, so am I," he stated.

"No kidding? I never would have guessed that."

This time he did smile. A slow curling of his lips that matched the curling of her toes in her cross trainers. "So who do you think will win, Ms. Turner?"

"You might if you ever stop calling me that."

He grin grew. "Why would I want to do that?"

Because it turns me on. "Because it's too formal. Just call me Annabelle."

"That's not why you don't like it," he countered in a low voice.

They stared at each other like two caged fighters waiting for the other to wave the white flag. Only Annabelle didn't give up, and she wasn't about to start now. If Blake Carpenter thought she'd admit defeat, he had another thing coming.

She lifted a shoulder in what she hoped came off as nonchalant. "Call me whatever you want, Mr. Carpenter. It doesn't really matter."

"Oh, but it does," he argued, then leaned even closer. So close that she could smell his shampoo mixed with his early morning sweat. "Because you don't like being defied. You need that control, don't you?"

She lifted one brow. "You're going to talk to me about control?" she countered, rather than give one hint he was right. Because she did need a certain amount of control. Because if she didn't, things tended to spin out of control. Like a cheating spouse. Like a mother with failing health and no one to share the burden, worry, and stress.

"You're right, I do like to be in control," he admitted. "The difference between you and me is I have no problem admitting it."

She leaned back in the chair and crossed her arms over

her chest. Mostly to keep him from noticing her heart thumping against her ribs. Because he'd already noticed way too much about her.

"At least I'm not afraid to admit when I need help."

He sat still for a moment, she swore, not even breathing. "You think I need help coaching this team?"

"No, that I think you can do. Probably better than anyone else could. I'm just wondering how much longer you're willing to go with that bad knee of yours."

A muscle in his square jaw ticked. Direct hit.

"You should know enough about old injuries to know they never fully go away," he muttered.

"True." She nodded. "But I think we both know it's more than just an old injury. It's still a problem for you. In fact, I'm willing to even bet you still take medication for it."

"What's your point, Ms. Turner?" he asked.

She chewed her lower lip. "My point is that I can help you with it. I see you favoring and rubbing it when you think no one else is watching."

"In other words, you can't take your eyes off me," he countered.

She lifted her gaze to the ceiling and prayed for patience. "Joke all you want, but I'm serious." She tilted her head to one side and studied him. It was barely lunchtime and his strong jaw already showed a five-o'clock shadow. The kind that could rub a woman's skin raw.

"It's just an old injury that aches sometimes. I have it under control."

"Really?" she asked. When he nodded, she continued. "You know when most people come to me, it's only because their doctor has ordered physical therapy. Most of them don't think they really need it. But they're always glad they came." She snagged a tablet of Post-it notes from his desk and a pen from the holder. Then she jotted down the address of her studio. "If you change your mind, here's where I am." She set the information down, knowing he wouldn't take it if she offered. "I can see the pain on your face, Blake. Pills don't always cure everything."

Without another word, she left his office, hoping somehow she'd gotten through to him.

As Annabelle left the school, she forced her mind away from Blake.

It was ten-fifteen and she had a ten-thirty appointment with her friend Stella.

She parked her car along the curb in front of her studio, gathered her bag from the backseat, and went inside the building. She'd just flipped on the lights when Stella breezed through the doors like the breath of fresh air she was.

And Annabelle could use a breath of fresh air right then.

"Sorry I'm late," Stella said on a breathy voice.

Annabelle glanced at the clock on the wall and lifted a brow. "It's ten twenty-nine, Stella." If the woman were abducted by aliens, she'd still find a way to be on time.

"Obviously your idea of late and my idea of late aren't the same thing," Stella replied, then toasted her with the paper cup of coffee she held in one hand. "Love this new thing you're doing with your hair, by the way. Evidently the new football coach is having a positive influence."

Only Stella could get away with such a comment. A year ago, when Annabelle had come back from Denver, she'd signed up for ballet aerobics. The teacher of the class, a tall, willowy classic beauty named Stella Davenport, had bitched at Annabelle to "stop slouching" in that commanding way ballet teachers were so famous for, and they'd been close friends ever since. Probably the closest friend Annabelle had ever had.

Annabelle fingered the loose curls that she'd actually taken the time to blow-dry. "I had a few extra minutes this morning," she answered. "And it has nothing to do with a football coach."

Lies.

Stella snorted, then set her purse down on the floor. "Please. The only time a woman takes care in her appearance is if there's a guy. One of our principal dancers in Chicago used to take her hair out of its bun after every single rehearsal. We all thought it was the strangest thing until we saw the hottie medical resident pick her up for dinner one night."

"That doesn't mean—"

"And then," Stella went on, "the mother of one of my students, who always had a god-awful Denver Broncos baseball cap covering her beautiful red hair, started picking her daughter up with her hair all styled and curled. I thought maybe she found her self-worth after losing it for Lord only knows how long, when I remembered the single dad of a different student."

Annabelle lifted a brow at her friend.

"You see?" She took a sip of coffee. "Throw some man candy into the picture and a woman starts doing things she doesn't normally do." She pointed an index finger at Annabelle. "Like wearing jewelry."

"I'm just worried about the holes in my ears closing," Annabelle argued as she absently fingered the earring dangling from her lobes. So what if she'd dug them out of her jewelry box after going nearly a year without wearing them?

Stella giggled. "I know perfectly well what Blake

Carpenter looks like. The man's practically another species. Tell Auntie Stella all about it."

Annabelle shrugged and led Stella to the mats on the floor to start her exercises. "There's nothing to tell." At least nothing she wanted to share with anyone. Not even Stella. Because Stella wouldn't rest until Annabelle had acted on her feelings and urges. The woman pretty much wore everything on her sleeve and encouraged everyone around her to do the same.

Annabelle had lost her ability and desire to live like that after her divorce. Stella knew this and understood where Annabelle was coming from and she knew her friend meant well.

"Okay, answer me this," Stella said as she downed the last of her coffee and tossed the cup in the trash. "Is he as hot in person?"

"You already know he is," Annabelle answered.

Stella waved a hand in the air. "And the reason you don't want to jump his bones is…?"

Annabelle laughed. "Just because a guy is hot doesn't mean I'm going to jump his bones." But, yeah, she wanted to.

"Then there's something wrong with you," Stella stated.

Annabelle crossed her arms over her chest. "Okay, so how come you don't want to jump his bones?" Even though it was meant as a rhetorical question, the thought of her tall, beautiful friend throwing herself at Blake Carpenter did something funny to Annabelle's insides. Her stomach tightened unexpectedly.

"I never said that," Stella countered. "He just seems like more of your type. Besides, I'm not looking for a guy right now."

Ah, yes, her beautiful friend dated about as often as a

groundhog came out during winter. She thought she'd remembered Stella going out on one date a few months ago, but she'd said the date hadn't ended well.

Annabelle gestured for Stella to take her place on the floor.

Before she'd left Chicago, Stella had been a principal dancer for the Chicago Ballet. She'd been one of the best who'd had a starring role in just about every show she'd performed in. Then a fall during a pas de deux had torn Stella's MCL and ACL. Surgery had repaired the damage, but the time off during her recovery had knocked Stella down a few notches. Not to mention her mobility hadn't been the same. A year after her injury, she'd retired from professional ballet and moved to Blanco Valley after her grandmother had suffered from her second heart attack.

Like Annabelle, Stella was her grandmother's only caregiver. Another thing the two women had in common.

Annabelle had never met a more kindred soul.

Even though she swore she was happy, Annabelle sensed Stella missed ballet like an amputee missed their arm. Annabelle had a feeling her friend had another plan B in place after her retirement that didn't include living in a Colorado mountain town.

"How's the knee today?" Annabelle asked. Last week, Stella had cut their session short, complaining about pain in her knee.

"Better," Stella commented. She yanked her hooded sweatshirt over her head and lowered to the floor. "Last week was a bad one for me. I had to use my ice machine for a few days."

"You should still be using your ice machine." She gestured toward Stella's leg. "You're supposed to be wearing your brace too. You're still prone to swelling."

Stella only rolled her eyes and moved her leg into position for her reps. She pretended otherwise, but Annabelle knew Stella suffered from a lot of pain. An ACL tear was a major injury that could take a lot of time to recover from. Most people suffered from pangs and stiffness for the rest of their lives. Stella put on a face of steel and made the world think her knee was fine. As though a forced early retirement had been in her plans all along and no big deal.

That had to be about as true as Annabelle planning on a cheating husband and painful divorce.

"Start with ten reps," Annabelle told her friend. "Then I have some new exercises for you." She hung back, watching Stella instead of touching her. Stella had a weird thing about direct contact with other people.

Stella huffed out a breath as she pushed through her first set. "I'm going to remember the hell you put me through during your next aerobics class."

Annabelle smiled as a bead of sweat rolled down Stella's temple and slid back into her dark hair. "I push you because I love you. You push because you're a sadistic bitch."

Stella answered Annabelle's grin with one of her own, followed by a wince. "You have to be a little sadistic to be a ballet dancer. And most of us are bitches because we have huge egos. Those who aren't don't make it very far." She slid her friend a sly look. "You shouldn't be friends with me, Annabelle. I'm not as nice as you think I am."

Annabelle smacked Stella on her shoulder. "You want people to think you're a hard-ass, but you're all mush on the inside."

"Lies." Stella gasped as she straightened her leg to finish the rep.

"Forget it," Annabelle argued. "I know you too well."

Stella slid her friend a look. "Or do you?"

"Okay, let's stretch," she instructed her friend.

Stella lowered her leg, moving slower than normal. Annabelle moved into position to assist Stella with the stretches, taking care not to make any sudden movements that would strain the knee. Or make too much contact. Stella's muscles stiffened when Annabelle touched her.

"Okay, how about this?" Stella asked after they'd been stretching for a few seconds. "I'll admit I have a gooey soft center when you decide to go for it with Mr. Football."

Annabelle lifted a brow. "That's not much of a deal. What is with you and this guy anyway?"

Stella shifted positions into a new stretch. "Because you, my friend, need to get laid."

"Why Blake Carpenter?"

"Why not Blake Carpenter?" Stella countered.

Yeah, Annabelle. Why not?

"He's hot, for one thing," Stella continued. "He's big and muscular. And hot."

Annabelle grinned. "You said that already." Probably because Blake was so damn hot that it needed to be mentioned twice.

"Well, he is. Some other woman is going to jump the guy's sexy bones if you don't do it already."

"They can have him as far as I'm concerned," Annabelle replied. Then she slanted her friend a look. "What makes you think the size of a man's muscles or his looks is all that matters to me? Maybe I'm after a more intellectual type who likes to read horoscopes and clean in his spare time."

A laugh popped out of Stella. "Honey, every red-blooded woman wants a man who smolders like that guy does." Stella's mouth curled in a slow grin. "A man who can whisper in a woman's ear and make her breath hitch." Stella lifted her head off the mat. "And horoscopes? Really?"

Annabelle lifted a shoulder. "Just saying."

Stella let her head fall back on the mat. "For all you know, maybe he does read horoscopes. Maybe underneath that sculpted torso is a guy who can scrub calcium stains off a faucet like a boss."

Yeah, right. Blake was 100 percent prime alpha male who only knew how to beat his chest and make a woman's heart flutter.

Problem was, Annabelle couldn't think of one thing wrong with that.

The bell above her door dinged, and Virginia McAllister shuffled in, her orthopedic shoes scuffing across the carpeted entryway.

"Hi, Mrs. McAllister," Annabelle called to the woman. "I'll be with you as soon as I've finished with Stella."

Virginia's head, which was capped by her signature beehive, was bowed over her cell phone. "Oh, don't rush on my account. I'll just use the time to update my Tumblr page." She shot the two women a grin, accentuating the grooves etched in her cheeks. "This morning we caught our coach jogging without a shirt on. Him and his cousin," she added with a single nod of her head. "They tried to be sneaky by jogging on the other side of the park." Virginia chuckled, which sounded wicked coming from a seventy-something-year-old woman. "Those boys think they can outsmart the Queen Bees. I'll show them who's smart."

Stella bit back a laugh as she moved into another stretch.

"Mrs. McAllister, do they know you're taking pictures of them?" Annabelle asked. When what she really wanted to ask was, *What does Blake look like without his shirt on?* But she wouldn't. Not because she didn't want to know but because her mind was already conjuring up enough images that she didn't need to see the pictures.

Yeah, he'd look good. Athletic shorts clinging to those narrow hips. Maybe a trail of sweat running down the center groove of his carved abs. Back muscles bunching and tensing, glistening under the morning sun from the sweat covering his smooth skin.

"Want to see?" Virginia asked as though she'd read Annabelle's thoughts.

"We'd love to see," Stella piped up before Annabelle had a chance to say No Effing Way.

Annabelle smacked her friend in the shoulder.

Stella slapped her back and gingerly rolled to her feet.

"Traitor," Annabelle mouthed to her friend. Stella tossed a grin over her shoulder and strolled toward Virginia. She took the phone from the older woman and thumbed the screen. Annabelle reached her friend's side in time to see a photo of Blake and Brandon, shirtless of course, because life was just that unfair, jogging through the Blanco Valley City Park.

"Do you have one of just Blake?" Stella asked.

Virginia looked at Stella like she had a screw loose. "Of course not. Why would I take a picture of one when there were two of them? They are both equally nice to look at."

Stella scrunched her nose and watched the tumbling pictures. Annabelle watched, too, because, well, what else was she going to do? And she was curious.

One picture was of Blake and Brandon jogging side by side, no shirt on either of them. Dark sunglasses, low-slung athletic shorts.

It was pretty much like she pictured. Every woman's fantasy wrapped up in one big, sweaty, chiseled package.

The pictures continued to scroll, and one of just Brandon popped up. He and his dog Duke and a red do-rag tied over Brandon's head, covering most of his rich brown hair.

Stella made a sound and shook her head.

"Girl, what's wrong with you?" Virginia demanded. "You have a problem with a man that looks like that? Because I could find a hundred other girls who would appreciate that fine piece of work." Virginia pointed at herself. "Me being one of them."

Stella looked up from the phone, and she and Annabelle stared at the woman, who had bright red lipstick on her thinning lips. Virginia yanked the phone out of Stella's hand. "Just because I'm old enough to be your grandmother doesn't mean I'm blind. I can still appreciate a young man who can get a woman's pulse fluttering." She waved the phone in the air. "How much do you want a bet the first game of the season is packed?"

Of course Annabelle hoped the whole town turned out to watch the Bobcats play. But not because they'd been stalking the Queen Bees' Tumblr page and now knew what Blake Carpenter looked like without a shirt on. Chances were half the town had already seen the photos. The Beehive Mafia had a staggering following on their Tumblr. Mostly because they posted pictures of Blanco Valley's hot young bachelors. For some reason they'd targeted Brandon West, who seemed to be featured on the page more than anyone else.

Not that Annabelle cared. She rarely ever looked at the page.

But you will now.

No. No she wouldn't. Because she didn't need another reason to salivate over Blake Carpenter. His confidence and dark brooding were enough without adding his naked, sweaty torso to the mix.

Virginia pocketed the phone. "Are you ladies going to the pancake breakfast on Saturday?"

Stella nodded. "Of course. Best pancakes of the year."

The pancake breakfast was a fund-raiser the football team organized. The players made breakfast and half the town showed up to offer their support and funds for the football program. It was typically held at the school gym before the first game.

Only when Stella elbowed Annabelle did she realize she'd been standing there without giving an answer.

"I wouldn't miss it," she answered.

SIX

Blake tossed his keys around in his hand and strolled onto the football field, his shoes sinking into the soft, freshly cut grass, and the early morning sun edging above the craggy mountain peaks. The air was crisp with a cool breeze blowing across the back of his neck and reminded him that winter wasn't far away. He zipped his jacket up higher, wishing he'd put on a longsleeved shirt underneath instead of short sleeves because—

"What the hell?" he muttered when his attention was snagged by his players—*his* players—on the field in the middle of warm-ups... with Annabelle.

His eyes narrowed behind his sunglasses when the meddlesome—and *damn* she was hot in spandex—woman jabbed her hands on her hips and nodded as the players moved from one stretch to the next. She meandered across the grass, weaving around the players, nodding at some and making corrections with others.

"She's a sight, isn't she?" Cameron said after he'd strolled up alongside Blake. Casual as you please, as though Annabelle Turner, a woman who'd caused Blake to take more cold showers than a nymphomaniac, wasn't completely stepping on Blake's toes.

"What the hell is she doing?" Blake inquired.

You mean other than turning you on?

Cameron made a pair of quotes in the air. "She's 'helping.'"

Blake turned to his friend and assistant coach. "Was that before or after you told her to get lost?"

Cam smirked. "Are we talking about the same Annabelle?"

Blake shook his head. "Never mind." Then he walked away from Cameron and approached the woman he fully intended to tell to back the eff off.

What the hell did she think she was doing, warming up with *his* team without him? How did she just think she could stroll in here and take over? As though she had every right? As though he wasn't doing a good enough job with his own players?

He knew she thought she was helping, but shit.

Even worse than her encroachment was his reaction to her. Damn, from the moment he'd laid eyes on her with the team, his heart had lurched up into his throat, a previously unfamiliar feeling that was growing more familiar each time he saw her. Then she'd laughed and tilted her head and the erratic beating of his heart had bloomed into warmth across his chest.

Damn it, but he could not develop feelings for this woman. Hell yeah, she turned him on. But that's where it needed to end. She rubbed him the wrong way. She annoyed the shit out of him. She was too opinionated and stubborn for the likes of him.

So why did he get all kinds of warm fuzzies in his belly when he saw her?

That's the irritation talking.

Yeah, that was it.

Irritation.

Annabelle took another turn and walked in between the players, eyeing each one and making more corrections. When she was within hearing distance, he called, "Were you going to take over coaching too?"

Her head jerked around, her high sleek ponytail swinging around her shoulders and brushing her breasts.

Then she smiled. Honest to God grinned, like she was happy to see him. "Oh good, you're here," she responded, instead of uttering something more appropriate like, "Please forgive me for taking over your team." But she didn't. She said something even more horrifying. "I just wanted to try out some new stretches and get them warmed up for you."

Blake dropped his bag on the grass. "So should I take a seat in the stands and hand over my whistle?"

Her grin grew. "Don't be so dramatic, Blake. I just wanted to make sure they were properly stretched before practice."

One of his brows arched. "And I don't?"

"I didn't say that. I—" She stopped midsentence and studied him, tilting her head in a way that made him feel like he was under a microscope. "Blake, do you think I'm trying to take over your job?"

What the hell was he supposed to think?

"Gee, I don't know, Annabelle. I arrive to start practice with my team, and here you are. Without my knowledge or my permission."

"I didn't realize I needed your permission to stretch with them." She gestured toward the boys behind them. "I've been doing it for weeks."

"Not in this capacity," he pointed out.

She was silent for a moment. "How is this any different?" *Yeah, Blake. How?*

"It just is." *Good answer, asshole. Maybe next you can drag your knuckles on the ground.*

She stared back at him, her lush lips set in a firm line. "Oh, I get it," she said slowly. "So all that talk in your office before about trust and you assuring me that you know I'm not that kind of person..." She turned and walked back through the kids. "And saying you trust me and coming to an agreement about the players..." She turned back around and pinned him with a hard stare. "That was all bullshit?"

Had they come to an agreement? "Uh..."

She held up a finger to stop him. "Setting aside the fact that you want what's best for these players, which you've stated several times. Am I wrong?"

Why wasn't his brain working? "Annabelle—"

"Am I wrong, Blake?" She jabbed her hands on her hips and tapped her foot on the soft grass.

"Well, no, but—"

"Then what is your problem?" she demanded while jabbing a finger into the center of his chest. "Seriously, Blake. Why don't you want me here?" Her pointy little finger stabbed into his chest one last time for emphasis.

He wrapped his hand around hers so she couldn't poke him again. "Ow."

"Oh, don't give me that," she said. "I've poked boulders softer than you."

He couldn't help the grin that crept up his mouth. "Thanks. I think."

She crossed her arms over her chest. "So what gives? Why are you so eager to get rid of me?"

"It's not that..." His words trailed off because, damn.

Was he trying to get rid of her? Yeah, he supposed he was. But not for the reason she thought.

She circled her hand in the air. "Okay, so..."

He grabbed her elbow and maneuvered her away from the kids. "Maybe next time you could just give me a heads-up."

"Why, so you can tell me to butt out?" she asked.

She's got your number.

"Not...exactly," he replied.

She shook her head. "I was right. You are full of shit."

Huh?

"The only reason you don't want me here," she told him, "is because your massive ego won't make room for any-body else. Well, get over yourself because I'm not going anywhere." And then she was gone, spinning around on her heel and sashaying across the grass with that 'tude, holding her head up high.

And damn if he wasn't half proud of her.

"Don't look now," Cameron whispered to Blake. "But the Dollys have targeted you and set their course for destruction."

Blake bit back a groan as he dumped syrup all over his pancakes. His mother would scold him for sending himself into sugar shock, and his father would tell him to add a side of bacon.

Whatever.

Out of the corner of his eye, he spotted Dawn Putnam and Rhonda Powell, aka "the Dollys," aptly named for their minuscule waists, which some people claimed had been surgically altered, and their teased blond hair. As though the style were still popular thirty years later. To be honest, Blake had always thought they looked like something that had stepped out of *Steel Magnolias*. They'd both attended

Blanco Valley High School, cheered, were voted homecoming queens—a tie two years in a row because, apparently, the student body couldn't decide which one of the girls they liked more.

Now they both had daughters who cheered and would most likely follow in their mother's footsteps as part of the homecoming monarchy. Both their husbands were wealthy developers who'd been responsible for building up half the town. And they served on the PTA. Basically any other way they could use to make school/football/cheerleading/student body stuff their business.

Personally, Blake had never had a problem with them. He'd graduated three years before them and considered them busybodies who thought nothing existed outside of high school. As long as they stayed out of his way and didn't stick their nose in his coaching business, like everyone else had this morning, he was fine with them.

Blake had just cut into his pancakes while cradling his paper plate with one hand when the two women approached them.

Dawn extended her hand first. "Mr. Carpenter, we wanted to stop by and introduce ourselves. I'm Dawn and this is Rhonda."

Blake stuck a forkful of pancake in his mouth before shaking the women's hands.

Dawn turned and gazed around the school gym. "Isn't this a great turn-out?" she said.

When Blake and the team had arrived at 7:00 a.m. that morning, there had been a line wrapped around the gym. The people had cheered and waved at the team, like they were a bunch of celebrities. No one had expected this kind of attendance, mostly because in recent years, the town hadn't shown much interest in the team.

Now the gym was packed with students, teachers, and citizens, eating pancakes, mingling, and discussing the upcoming season. The Beehive Mafia was there, as well as Brandon, who'd been headed their way when he spotted the Dollys and made an abrupt U-turn in the opposite direction.

Sneaky bastard.

He'd also spotted Annabelle because, well, why wouldn't he spot her? His Annabelle radar was always turned on.

Cam elbowed him when Blake hadn't answered Dawn's question.

"Yeah." He nodded, not really sure what else to say. "Looks like we're going to bring in a lot of money for the football program."

"You know, Rhonda and I rallied most of these people to come this morning," she told them, and the two women bobbed their heads in unison. Blake briefly wondered if they coordinated their lives to match, down to the way they styled their hair. "We're good at getting people involved. Last week we went to the Cat and put a special announcement on their blackboard," Rhonda chimed in.

The Cat, as known by the locals, was the Bobcats' diner and a popular hangout of students and players. They usually gave free breakfast to the players on game days and stayed open extra late on Friday nights.

"We told people to come on out here and meet their new coach," Dawn continued. "Then Rhonda went into Screamin' Beans and put a big colorful poster in the window." Dawn spread her hands in front of her. "'Come and have breakfast with the Bobcats.' That's what it said." Dawn glanced at her friend. "She even painted little orange and black paw prints on the storefront window."

Blake nodded because, really, he wasn't sure what else

to do. He just wanted to eat his breakfast. "Well, we're grateful for your effort. I'm sure it's brought the team a lot of money."

Rhonda stepped even closer and, shit, were they trying to invade his personal space? He could practically drip his syrup on the woman's cleavage. "Well, if there's anything else you need from us, we're real good at gathering a crowd. We could gather up boosters for you because, word has it, the team could use some more."

He paused with a bite of pancake halfway to his mouth and glanced back and forth between the two women, who were practically nose to nose with him. Cameron coughed into his juice, and Brandon, from across the room, gave him a crooked grin and mock salute. And Annabelle...

Shit, why was he thinking about her again? They hadn't bumped into each other yet this morning, even though they'd committed plenty of mental undressing from across the room.

When was the last time he'd mentally undressed a woman before?

"You should talk to Cameron, here. He handles the... rallying of people," Blake blurted, using Dawn's words.

Cam jerked him a look, then coughed and said "asshole" into his fist. Neither woman seemed to notice.

Rhonda, who was always looking for a man to keep her company while her husband all but ignored her, pulled a pen out of her pocket.

Who in the hell kept a pen in their pocket? Especially with pants tight enough that they probably ripped when she sat down?

"Well, then," Rhonda said with a devouring grin. She took it upon herself to take a hold of Cameron's hand and jotted her number on his palm. "Here's my number in case you want to get together and bang it out."

Blake choked on his pancakes and Cameron sent him a death-upon-you look that had Blake chuckling after forcing his food down.

Rhonda finished with Cam's hand and he had to pull it from her grasp because the woman wasn't about to let go. He glanced at the number, which had little hearts drawn around it. Blake was surprised she didn't write *Mrs. Rhonda Shaw* with a little bubble around it.

Dawn hooked her arm through her friend's. "Rhonda, come on. There's donuts."

The two women strolled off, swaying their slim hips like the seasoned professionals they were. "Don't forget to call me," Rhonda said over her shoulder with a little finger wave.

Cam downed the last of his juice and pinned Blake with a stare. "Do you want to get your ass beat now or later?"

Blake bit back a chuckle, knowing it would get him an uppercut to the jaw. "You've got to admit, the woman's good."

Cameron's dark blue eyes narrowed. "She's a viper."

"Maybe it's because she knows your history with married women," Brandon said as he approached them. "She figures she's fair game."

"You're both douchebags."

"I'm just glad someone else is being stalked for a change." Brandon slanted Cam a look. "Do you know what it's like to go jogging and have seventy-four-year-old women chase you down with their camera phones? Man can't even run in peace."

"That's why I go shooting in the woods. No one to bother you out there. You should give it a try sometime."

"You go to the woods because you can't shoot for shit and you don't want anyone to see you," Brandon told his friend. "And trust me, they'd find me," Brandon told them.

"By the way," he told Blake. "Mac Armstrong's been looking for you. Said something about giving you a discount on a club membership and getting your own golf polo with matching sweater."

Blake would have laughed, except that was all too close to how Mac Armstrong was.

He glanced around the gym, past the kids making pancakes like a bunch of line cooks, past the tables of people eating the food and talking about who-knows-what. Past Annabelle talking it up with Stella Davenport. Stella said something and Annabelle tossed her head back and laughed, exposing her long, creamy neck, the delicate muscles gently curving into her narrow jaw.

Blake's gut tightened as her hazel eyes lit up with laughter, the sound dancing over his skin like the caress of soft fingers.

"Yo." Brandon elbowed him in the ribs. "Mac's over there."

"Nowhere near Annabelle," Cameron added, obviously looking for payback for Rhonda Powell. He pointed toward the stage. "On the other side of the room."

Blake ground his back teeth together. "I have eyes, dickwad."

"Which were busy undressing *her*," Brandon added like the asshole he was. "Seriously, you're not even discreet about it."

Blake turned away from Annabelle and managed to catch Mac Armstrong's attention.

Mac waved when he saw Blake, then excused himself from the group of men he'd been talking to.

Cam heaved a sigh, then tossed his paper cup in a trash can. "Really. That guy?"

Mac Armstrong was a wealthy golf club and resort

owner who'd graduated from Blanco Valley high the same year as Blake, Cameron, and Brandon. He'd even played for the team and had his jersey number on the rock, near Blake's own number. Blake had heard through the town grapevine that Mac had been a booster for the team years ago but for whatever reason had pulled his support from the team. The lack of his funds had hurt the program, and that had only prompted other boosters to follow his lead.

As much as Mac could suck the oxygen from a room, because he was such a dominant personality, Blake had actually been meaning to reach out to the guy.

"The team could use his resources, Cam," Blake reminded his friend. "The program's got no money."

Cam sighed again. "The guy's obnoxious. He's like the Energizer Bunny on crack."

Brandon chortled. "We could call the Dollys back over here. Talk to them about getting their husbands to donate some money."

"Hell, you've already got Rhonda's number," Blake added.

Cam shot his friend a dark look. "Seriously. Gonna murder you."

Mac reached the three men, clapped Cameron on the back, and shook Blake's and Brandon's hands. At six foot five, Mac towered over the men in both size and personality. His thick head of sandy blond hair was combed back from his wide forehead, giving him what some people called a "wise-guy" appearance. His face was always clean shaven because, some people suspected, his beard already had a healthy dose of gray in it and Mac wasn't about to stand for that.

"Blake, how're you doing?" Mac asked, pumping Blake's hand so hard it practically gave him whiplash. "Listen, I've been watching team practices and I feel real good about this season."

Blake nodded. "Thanks. The boys are working really hard."

"I'm telling you, this town deserves some wins after the drought we've had. The champion's rock is collecting dust, you know what I'm saying?" Mac punctuated his rhetorical question with a laugh. Then he jabbed Blake in the chest with his beefy finger. "Your number was the last one to be painted on there. Did you know that?"

Blake glanced at Cam and Brandon. Cam shrugged and Brandon scowled. "No, I didn't know that," Blake told Mac.

Mac snorted again. "Well, we need change that, don't you think?"

Blake blinked at the man and realized Mac was waiting for an answer. "Of course I do. That's why we're doing everything we can to bring in a winning season." *And the point of this conversation is?*

Mac slung a heavy arm around Blake's shoulders like the guy was about to share a dirty secret. "You see all these people here?" Mac turned the two of them around so Blake could see the whole gym. The boys flipping pancakes and cracking each other up. Flirting with the cheerleaders and rally girls. Parents mingling with one another and talking about each of their kids' college plans. Bobcats pride posters posted all over the walls. Black and orange paw prints leaving trails from one side of the gym floor to the other.

Looking around, Blake realized, that yeah, the town did deserve a win. They were relying on him to bring it to them, even if some of the parents didn't want their kids playing for him. Blake had forced those people from his mind, because he didn't need to be focusing on the people who didn't want him around. The players—those kids slinging batter at each other and making pancakes in the shape of paw prints— were the ones who need his attention. They were the ones he'd sworn his dedication to and he wasn't about to witness another bout of disappointment from a kid he'd made a promise to.

"Yeah, I see them," he told Mac.

"These are the real fans," Mac stated. "They expect great things from you because this town needs it. We've lost our excitement, Blake."

Blake pulled out of Mac's hold and crossed his arms over his chest. "I realize that, Mac, but I'm not sure what your point is."

"Well, I want to help you all out," Mac went on as he retrieved his wallet from his back pocket and pulled out a business card. "I don't have time to get into everything, because my beautiful wife over there has been giving me the stink eye for the last thirty minutes." He glanced up at the three men. "Call me so we can talk further." The man gave a quick wave to his wife, who shot him an impatient look with a tap to her wristwatch. "I'm comin', baby doll," he called to her.

Then he turned and ambled away, leaving Brandon shaking his head. "See?" he said to Blake. "You didn't even have to charm him. He came straight to you."

"Just be careful," Cameron said. "What he didn't tell you was that the last coach didn't like to be told what to do. That's the real reason Mac pulled his funding from the program. The guy wants what he wants when he wants it."

Before Blake could form a reply, Drew Spalding was in his ear. "If you're smart, you'll do what the man says. Imagine that money for new helmets or new practice equipment."

Blake crossed his arms over his chest. Out of the corner

of his eye, he saw Brandon edging away, as though sensing something brewing and not wanting to get involved. But Cameron, being the no-backing-down kind of guy he was, stayed put. "I'll always do what's best for the team, Drew. If Mac decides he wants to become a booster, we'll spend the money where it's needed most."

Drew nodded. "With my approval, of course."

"He doesn't need your approval, Spalding."

Drew turned his hard gaze to Cam, sending rays of contempt in the man's direction. "Oh, but he does."

Cameron took a step closer. "You and I both know he doesn't."

"Cam, shut up," Blake warned his friend.

Of course neither one of them listened. Drew's mouth curled up. "You think I'm going to listen to a man who has no respect for other people's marriages?"

"That's enough, Drew," Blake told him.

"What's really on your mind, Drew?" Cam asked, goading the man in a way that only Cameron Shaw could do. Cam was good at stirring shit up, as he'd been famous for in high school. Quick to grin at the ladies and quick to throw a right hook at anyone who looked at him the wrong way. He'd mellowed in his older age, but underneath that cool exterior was the same hot-headed teenager who'd been sent to the principal's office for telling his history teacher to shove his classroom rules up his ass.

Blake settled a hand on Drew's shoulder, hoping to remind the man they were in a crowded gym with players and parents. "What's on my mind is that I'm looking at a man who can't get a woman of his own so he steals other people's wives."

Cam's square jaw hardened, settling his mouth into a firm line that Blake recognized as simmering trouble.

Brandon pressed a hand on Cam's chest. "Take a minute to remember where you are," Brandon said to his friend in a low voice.

Drew's chin shot up. "You'd best listen to him, Shaw."

Brandon shot Drew a dark look. "I suggest you quit while you're ahead, Drew. Trust me when I say you don't want to go a round with Cameron. He'd enjoy pounding that smug smile off your face. So why don't you take a step back before I turn him loose?"

Drew jabbed a finger in Cam's direction. "Your days are numbered."

Then he was gone, taking his contempt for Cameron with him.

"If I never see another pancake again, it'll be too soon," Stella stated as she and Annabelle exited the gym, sliding their sunglasses on to shield their eyes from the bright midday sun. "I think I ate about five pounds of syrup."

"You and me both," Annabelle agreed.

The pancake breakfast last year hadn't drawn nearly the amount of people this one had. She knew that had as much to do with Blake as anything else. People wanted an up-close-and-personal view of the new, famous coach. Whether they were in favor of him being here was another story. But the important thing was, the large crowd had to have drawn in some significant funds for the team.

The players had been at ease behind the grills, pouring batter and serving half the town. They'd joked around, been themselves, and had relaxed, which was a far cry from how she'd seen them on the field. Getting their butts kicked, sweat running down their faces and hair matted to their heads. They'd been...

Lighthearted.

Annabelle's spirts had lifted for them, as she'd watched the team she'd fallen in love with. Seeing the support from the town had been exactly what those kids had needed.

And then her lightheartedness had turned to something else when she'd spotted Blake. Of course, she'd seen him the second she'd entered the building. Because how could she not? The throngs of people, kids laughing and conversations hadn't stopped them from finding each other.

Stella had nudged her in the ribs. "Will you just go over there already?"

First he'd been trapped by the Dollys, which, Annabelle knew, anyone was susceptible to. They were like younger versions of the Beehive Mafia. Without the cell phone cameras and the obsession with Brandon West. Although Rhonda Powell seemed to have her meat hooks in Cameron Shaw's side. After that he'd been in deep conversation with Mac Armstrong, which had followed by him mingling with the players' parents. She hadn't wanted to interrupt, because it had been Blake's time to shine, and her body had already been humming without getting that close to him.

So she'd left it alone, despite Stella's many attempts to get them closer with her lame attempts like, "Hey, let's take a closer look at that poster over there." Or, "I think that table on the other side of the room might be more comfortable than this one."

Annabelle had rolled her eyes at the last one. Or all of them because her friend was anything but subtle. Then Brandon had inserted himself next to Blake and Cameron and Stella had changed her mind real fast. Annabelle had no clue what that had been about, but she hadn't pushed the issue.

Now they were full of pancakes and sausage.

The two of them were headed toward Annabelle's car

when she spotted Matt leaning into the passenger seat of his dad's truck. Annabelle made a detour because she'd been meaning to talk to the kid.

"Hey, Matt," Annabelle called out to the kid. Matt backed out of the truck and graced her with a wide grin when he saw her.

"Hey, Ms. Turner," he returned just as his dad strolled up to the truck, holding a box of stuff that he slid into the bed.

Stella tapped Annabelle on the shoulder. "Give me the keys. I'll go wait in the car."

"Just a sec," she told her friend.

Brandon turned and strolled back into the building, whistling and twirling his keys around as he ambled with that easy grace of his. Stella exhaled and leaned against the vehicle.

Annabelle slid her friend a look, then returned her attention to Matt. "I just wanted to see how your neck was feeling."

"Oh." Matt ran a palm over the back of his neck. "It's a lot better, thanks for asking. And thanks for spending that extra time with me."

She offered the boy a warm smile. "That's what I'm there for. Next time we meet, I can show you some stretches you can do at home. You might have to get your dad to help you with some of them."

Matt kept his hand on his neck. "Is it possible I'll injure it again?"

"Well," Annabelle said, not really sure how to answer the question. Further injury really depended on the person and the amount of stress they were putting their body through. "It depends. If you keep your muscles loose and stretched, then you shouldn't have to worry about it."

Brandon came back out of the building, his beefy arms

clutching another box. His shirtsleeves had been pushed higher up his shoulders, revealing the definition and cut of muscles. His denim-covered long legs carried him across the parking lot until he reached the truck. He slid the box in the bed, then tossed the car key toward Matt.

"Start it up," he told his son.

Matt caught the keys with the ease of someone trained to catch a football.

Stella pushed away from the truck. "Can we go now?"

"What's your hurry?" she asked her friend.

"I have a twelve o'clock class. Not good form for the teacher to be late."

Annabelle crossed her arms over her chest. "How are you going to get home if I'm driving you there?"

Stella jerked when Brandon slammed the tailgate closed. She glanced back at the guy, whose eyes were covered by dark sunglasses.

He shot the two women a quick grin.

"I was going to walk," Stella answered after taking her attention off Brandon.

Annabelle's eyes flew up her forehead. "With that?" she asked, gesturing toward the ace bandage wrapped around her friend's knee.

"Why does everybody always look at me like I have six heads when I tell them I'm going to walk somewhere?"

"Because you're—"

"Problem?" Brandon asked when he sidled up to them. Annabelle hadn't even heard him approach.

Stella glanced back at him. "We're fine, thanks."

Brandon hooked an arm on the edge of the truck bed. "Do you need a ride somewhere?"

One side of Stella's mouth twitched. "I don't live that far from my studio."

"Because you're limping," Brandon stated as though he hadn't heard her.

"I— What?"

He pointed toward her bandaged leg. "You've been limping all morning."

Stella shook her head, sending her long dark hair sliding over one shoulder. "I haven't been limping."

"Yeah, you have," he reiterated.

Stella opened her mouth as though to argue again, only to shut it. "No," she finally stated.

One of Brandon's brows arched above his sunglasses.

"Dad, I have to be at work in ten minutes," Matt said as he climbed into the passenger seat of the rumbling truck.

Brandon glanced at his son, then back at Stella. "Last chance. I'll be around so I can swing by and pick you up."

Annabelle stood back and watched the exchange, wondering why Stella was so adamantly against Brandon helping her. She was pretty sure the two didn't have anything against each other. In fact, as far as Annabelle knew, the two of them hardly knew each other.

"I'm fine," Stella said again.

Brandon snorted and shook his head. "Guy can't catch a break," he muttered before rounding the back of the truck and hopping in the front seat.

The two women stood back as he pulled away.

"Stella, that was rude," Annabelle told her friend. "He was just trying to help you."

Stella hooked her arm through Annabelle's. "I told you I would rather walk. I don't need him giving me a ride anywhere."

Annabelle was just about to ask Stella what the hell her problem was when she spotted Blake sauntering, because that's the only way the guy walked, out of the gym.

Cameron was by his side, the two men equally tall and wide and imposing with their dominating personalities and hard gazes. Cam slugged Blake in the shoulder, which Blake returned with a grin.

Something shifted inside her as she watched the two men. There was a closeness between them that only true friends could understand. Even though she didn't know much about their relationship, she'd guess they were more like brothers. Much like Blake's relationship with Brandon.

Cameron offered Blake a mock salute, then meandered to his own car.

Annabelle paused as she watched Blake and opened her car door when he spotted her. Hard to tell for sure with his eyes covered, but she just knew. The instant his gaze connected with hers, she'd felt it. Down to the pit of her stomach where all those butterflies lived. The hard set of his mouth, framed by stubble just starting to grow in, probably because it had been hours since he'd shaved, sent those butterflies all over her midsection.

"Annabelle," Stella called as she stood by the passenger door. "Are we going to go?"

Blake continued to advance, his long legs eating up the concrete with wide, sure steps.

"Yeah," she told her friend. "Just give me one minute."

Stella glanced back at Blake and grinned. "I'm guessing you'll be more than one minute," she dared. "At least give me the keys so I can turn the radio on."

She tossed her friend the keys, then closed the distance between her and Blake.

"Hi," he said when they reached each other.

"Hi," she returned. "I meant to say hello in there, but you were pretty tied up."

Blake glanced back at the gym. "Yeah," he agreed. "I don't think I had two seconds to myself."

"That's good. It means you raised a lot of money," she pointed out. "Listen," she went on. "I wanted to see when you'd be free to meet with me again."

Blake tossed out a laugh and shook his head. "You never give up, do you?" he questioned as he walked around her.

Annabelle rushed after him. "I would think you'd understand the importance of not giving up, Mr. Carpenter."

He paused and turned toward her. "I thought we'd moved past the Mr. Carpenter stuff."

She narrowed her eyes at him. "I guess it depends on how much you're annoying me."

"In that case," he continued walking again, "we may never move past it."

Damn it, hadn't they come to an understanding? She'd thought, at the very least, they'd reached a mutual respect where they could work together. So why was he blowing her off?

"Blake, please," she pleaded with a hand on his arm. Which was a big flippin' mistake.

Because. Oh. My. Hard. Muscles.

Blake faced her, dropped his gaze down to her hand on his arm, and lifted a brow.

"Yes, Annabelle?" he queried, throwing the first-name thing back at her.

"I . . ." Her words trailed off because she was momentarily thrown by the use of her name. "I thought we had come to an understanding." Why was she still touching him?

"We did," he agreed. "I understand you can come, on your own time, to work with the players. Before or after practice."

"Yes, but I would still like to meet with you to discuss the kids." The heat from his skin had her dropping her hand.

"I'm pretty busy."

"You had time for me last week."

His mouth twitched. "That's because you just showed up. I don't remember scheduling anything with you."

"Then I'll just keep showing up," she said with arms crossed over her chest. "And texting you. Until your phone blows up. Or maybe I'll just sic the Dollys on you."

"Now that's just cruel."

She shrugged, trying to downplay the pounding of her heart. "Take your pick."

Blake stared at her for a moment, saying nothing, that firm mouth of his turning her insides into cottage cheese. What would it be like to have those lips pressed to hers? Would they soften? Annabelle bet they would.

She also bet she'd spontaneously combust if she kept thinking things like that.

Blake blew out a breath and yanked his sunglasses off. "Look, I've told you before, I don't want just anyone interfering with this team."

No matter how many times she saw them, Annabelle could never fully prepare herself for his blue eyes. They were deep, like the deepest part of the ocean, where the sun couldn't penetrate. And intense. Perhaps that was the biggest difference between him and Nathan. Nathan had been gorgeous but carefree. Lovable, fun, and always up for a good time.

Blake was intense to the point where it made Annabelle squirm. As though he took himself too seriously. He'd love hard; she knew that much. Probably to the point of distraction. But he'd also be single-minded and focused. Nathan hadn't understood that because he'd been too busy spreading his love to other women.

No, Blake wouldn't be like that. He'd give a woman

everything he had and make her feel like she was the only woman in the world. Annabelle shivered at the thought.

She shoved the thought aside and focused on the discussion at hand.

"I understand your hesitation," she assured him. "In fact, I would be suspicious if you weren't so suspicious. But I'm protective of these kids too. They've become like family to me and I just want to do my part to help them."

Blake blew out a breath and gazed over her shoulder for a moment. He withdrew his keys from his pocket and twirled them around in his hand.

"Check back with me on Monday," he told her. "But," he added, "this doesn't mean I completely trust you. That you need to earn."

She nodded. "Of course. Also...I'm sorry for taking over your practice the other day. I was out of line."

Blake shifted his stance and studied her. "I wouldn't have expected anything less from you, Annabelle."

Was he still mad? "You have every right to still be upset with me, but I did what I thought was right for the team."

"I'm not upset with you," he clarified. "When you believe in something that much, like those players, you go after it. I respect that."

Huh? She'd expected the riot act. A good lecturing. A don't-overstep-your-bounds-again spiel. But respect?

"I..."

He chuckled. "Are you surprised?"

To say the least. She offered him a smile. "Thank you," she said instead of questioning him further.

He started to turn, then stopped himself. She froze as he lifted his hand, bracing herself for his touch. His thumb and index finger grasped her earlobe, rubbing it between the two digits. The contact sent a zing down her spine.

What was he doing?

He looked at the one ear, then the other, holding on to her lobe the entire time. Skimming his thumb back and forth. She wondered if he realized he was caressing her like that.

"You're missing an earring," he finally said.

Her hand automatically flew to her ear, which then collided with his hand. He dropped his so fast that she barely had time to register the contact before it was over. But it left her hand burning as she fingered her empty ear.

"Oh," she breathed. "I didn't even realize it fell out."

He replaced his sunglasses. "Why don't we go back inside and I'll help you look for it."

Annabelle shook her head. "No, it's okay. They were an old pair and I have to get Stella to her studio."

He bent so he was eye level with her. "You sure?"

She nodded, because her throat was suddenly tight.

He'd offered to find her earring for her.

Why was that a big deal? It shouldn't be.

Only, Nathan had never offered to do anything like that. He'd just smile and tell her to go buy herself a nicer pair. Because that had been easier than putting in the actual effort. And she'd have done it because she'd been too inexperienced to know any better.

With Blake it was different. She'd been burned enough to know when to jump back when the fire got too hot.

And Blake Carpenter was definitely too hot.

SEVEN

After several more hours, and twenty-five more text messages from her mom, asking for things like pineapple chunks and cheese cubes, Annabelle locked up her studio to run some errands of her own. She picked up her mother's groceries, as well as some for herself, then headed to the hardware store to purchase a few more things for home repairs.

The pipes underneath the sink in the hall bath had been leaking and she needed some plumber's tape to fix it. Then the garage door started squeaking and she'd been fresh out of WD-40. So she was browsing the aisles of the place, trying to think of anything else she might need for the home, when she came across a fireproof safe that was on sale for 40 percent off.

As she stared at the thing, her mother's voice chimed in, reminding Annabelle the importance of always being prepared.

Anything could happen, Annabelle, her mother would say.

What would you do if your house burned down and all your important documents were gone?

Her mother could have given doomsday preppers who stockpiled food in case of a zombie apocalypse a run for their money. Who really needed to have battery-operated radios and heat-resistant blankets lying around?

When my uncle Barney's house burned down, he lost everything. Even his driver's license and Social Security card were lost. Do you know the hoopla he had to go through to get all that stuff replaced?

Yeah, she knew. Because her mother had told her twenty times.

Annabelle stared at the safe for a good ten minutes before relenting. She flagged down a store employee because, *damn,* the thing was heavy.

She told herself it was more of an impulse buy and nothing to do with quieting her mother's nagging voice. Which was stupid. Because who just impulsively tossed a forty-five-pound fire-proof safe in one's cart as though it were a Milky Way bar?

Daughters who care way too much about pleasing their mothers.

After paying for the stuff, and gritting her teeth against the highway robbery of paying for a hundred-dollar safe, Annabelle left the hardware store and pushed the cart through the parking lot. When she came to her car, which thankfully had one of those automatic opening back doors, she stuck her foot under the sensor to open the door and then turned back to the cart. While the door slowly lifted open, she hefted the safe in her hands, struggling to hold on to one side, and waited. As soon as the door opened wide enough, she planned on sliding the thing right in so she wouldn't have to hold it longer than necessary.

And kudos to her for being all smart and prepared and stuff.

Except she'd completely forgotten about the plastic grocery bags covering all the space in the tiny back end of her SUV.

She took a tiny step toward her car, gritting her teeth against the quivering muscles of her arms. "Shit," she breathed. Not one ounce of spare space to set the thing down.

How could she have forgotten she'd crammed all these groceries in?

With no place to set the safe down, Annabelle turned back toward her cart before she dropped the damn thing. Only the cart was rolling away.

And there it went, backward down the slight incline of the parking lot. One, two, now three parking spaces away.

"Uh, wait...," she huffed as the cart continued its journey until it nudged the bumper of a jacked up truck and stopped. "Double shit."

Okay, so she could either put the safe on the ground and break her spine in half or smash her groceries.

Nothing but great choices.

"Someone please kill me," she muttered to herself.

Just as she was about to drop the damn thing, a set of big, strong, and thickly muscled arms took the safe from her trembling hands. Just lifted the box right from her as though it weighed no more than a sack of chips. Annabelle jolted forward from the sudden loss of weight and gasped as Blake Carpenter stood before her.

One brow slowly arched above the rim of his sunglasses.

"Much as I'd love to stand here and hold this thing...," he told her.

She blinked at him, momentarily distracted by his out-of-nowhere presence and then his rumbling voice. "Oh," she blurted out. "Right, sorry." She spun around and began haphazardly rearranging the groceries so Blake would have a place to set the safe down. She attempted to move aside but bumped into him, which only solidified the impression that he really was as steely and sculpted as he looked.

"Just set it right there," she instructed with a lick of her lips because all the moisture in her mouth had dried up.

He set the thing down, with way less effort than what she would have done. And she would have resented the hell out of him for the ease in which he did everything, but the way his athletic pants glided over his smoothly rounded butt cheeks took all the resentment right out of her.

Damn, the man was a sight.

She cleared her throat. "Thanks," she told him with a grin.

"That wasn't planned out very well, was it?"

"I grabbed it at the last minute and forgot the back end of my car was full," she told him. Saying it out loud made it sound just as dumb as it was.

He slid his hands into his pants pockets. "You bought a fireproof safe on impulse?"

See? He's thinks it sounds just as implausible as you do.

"Yeah, well, it was on sale, so…," she answered with a lift of her shoulders.

One side of his mouth kicked up. "And you like to be prepared for everything, don't you?"

"You say that like it's a bad thing," she answered.

He leaned closer to her and lowered his voice. "Like I said before. Control freak." A chuckle rumbled deep in his chest when she opened her mouth. "There's nothing wrong with needing to be in control, Annabelle."

The name tumbled so effortlessly from his lips, just like everything else about him, that it was mildly disconcerting. The intimacy of using her first name created a whole new set of feelings.

He'd muttered it in a way a lover would whisper in one's ear.

And she liked it way more than she should have.

"So I like things a certain way," she agreed with a casual lift of her shoulder. "So what?"

"So nothing." He slid his sunglasses off his face and tapped them against his thigh. "I just don't think you realize how sexy it is."

Say what?

Annabelle didn't know many men who'd think control issues were sexy. It was true she liked things a certain way. And she liked knowing she had a modicum of control over her circumstances. That way she would never be blindsided ever again like she'd been by her ex-husband.

But sexy?

"Uh…" Her voice trailed off because she was speechless. For, like, the first time ever.

A gust of wind picked up, whipping her hair across her face. Blake lifted a hand, the one not endlessly tapping those sunglasses against his thigh, and tugged the strand of hair off her face. Just barely glanced his index finger over her cheek, sliding the piece down and tucking it behind her ear. Slowly. Almost too damn slow so that the tip of his finger left a tingling trail across her cheek and then blazed back up into her hairline.

Where had that come from?

Men had touched her before. A lot more purposefully and thoroughly than that. So why did this touch seem so much more intimate? Why did it make her breath feel short and her pulse flutter?

"You're wound so tight, you're practically vibrating," he told her.

Did he have to mention vibrating while she was so damn turned on?

"Says the guy who doesn't know the meaning of easy-going," she argued.

His brow twitched. "That's because you've only seen me on the field. In the right setting I can be the easiest going guy you'll ever meet."

She doubted that but had to push him anyway. "I find that hard to believe. Today was the first time I've ever seen you crack a smile."

"I smile plenty," he said. "But my players would hardly take me seriously if went around grinning and cracking jokes all the time."

She crossed her arms over her chest. "No, but they might find you more human."

"You think so, huh?"

"Yeah."

Then he took another step closer. As if he weren't already invading her personal space. In fact, he was so close that he'd managed to dominate her personal space. Forget invade. The man conquered.

Before she could figure out what to do next, her cell vibrated from her back pocket. She retrieved it, touched the screen, and groaned at her mother's text, which read:

Marshmallow cream.

"Good grief," Annabelle said to herself, and put the phone away. Her mother would have to get her cream another day. Annabelle had already gone to the store and was tired. Not to mention the physical drain of her banter with Blake.

"Problem?" he wanted to know.

Annabelle shook her head. "It's just my mother. She's been texting me her grocery list all day and I've already done my shopping for her."

Blake's brows lowered over his eyes. "It takes your mother all day to send a text message?"

His assumption coaxed a smile from her. "No, she's been texting one item at time. Starting from this morning," she added.

"You do your mother's shopping for her?"

Annabelle leaned against the back end of her SUV and sighed. "Yeah, she's had two hip surgeries in the past year. She's also epileptic and had a seizure while she was driving."

Blake visibly winced. "Not good."

"Nope. She had her license taken away, so she's pretty dependent on me. I take her out when I can, but…mostly I just run her errands for her and make her dinners."

Blake nodded as though he understood her situation. "So you do it all, then?"

She stared back at him, trying to read the meaning behind his words. But his deep blue eyes gave away nothing. The man was damn good at that. She lifted a shoulder in a casual shrug, even though, to Annabelle, the situation was far from casual. "I'm her daughter. It's my job to take care of her."

Blake tilted his head to one side, passing his sunglasses back and forth from hand to hand. "That's not why you do it."

A heavy breath escaped from her. "You're right, it's not. But I'm all she's got, so if I wasn't around to do it, she'd be on her own."

"You don't have any brothers and sisters?"

Now that was a subject she didn't want to explore. "I have a younger sister, but she doesn't live in the area."

"What about your father?"

"He died several years ago. So it's just me and Mom now."

Blake was silent a moment as though processing the information and possibly even understanding her situation. Then he slowly nodded. "Loyal as well as controlling. No wonder you refused to leave when I tried to let you go."

Annabelle pursed her lips. "First of all, you didn't have the authority to fire me. Second of all, I'm only controlling where it matters. Besides, I think you like having me around and just won't admit it."

"Why is that?"

"For one thing, you know I can help," she told him.

Blake finally stopped passing his sunglasses back and forth and slid them over his eyes. "And the other?"

Annabelle was silent a moment, suddenly realizing how much she enjoyed coaxing a smile from him. Stony-faced, the man was something else. When he smiled? He could downright melt concrete.

"Because I'm under your skin," she told him.

One of his brows arched above his sunglasses. "Sure of yourself, aren't you?"

She shrugged. "I know how to read people."

He took another step toward her, until she could count the stubble shadowing his square jaw. The coarse hair along his chin was a shade darker than the dirty-blond locks on his head. "*I* know how to read people, Ms. Turner."

She couldn't see his eyes, but she felt the heat of his gaze over her face, then lower to the fluttering pulse and the base of her neck. Then he did something that made her want to jump out of her own skin.

He touched her. And not to brush away a stray piece of hair. It was a stroke of the back of his hand over the erratic thumping of her pulse. His knuckles rasped across her sensitive skin, sending an electrical current through her system and igniting a fire that had been extinguished a long time ago.

"Case in point," he murmured as the rough pad of his thumb continued to stroke the soft flesh of her neck.

Annabelle licked her lips, which had grown dry with each circular motion of this thumb. If her body reacted to such a basic gesture, how would it react if he were to kiss her?

More important than that, why was she thinking about him kissing her?

Maybe because his mouth was so close. A whisper away from her own that she could feel each gentle breath that left his mouth.

Man.

That's what he smelled like.

All man and heat and desire.

If it were even possible, his mouth moved a centimeter closer. "Now who's under whose skin?" A heartbeat later, he took a step back. Then he turned that fine backside to her and sauntered away, each long leg taking him farther across the parking lot.

Yet he lingered. His heat, his scent, and his devastating aftermath curled around her like fingers digging into her flesh.

Oh boy, she was in some big trouble.

Blake had always considered himself to be an intelligent person. After all, he'd gone to Texas A&M on a full football scholarship and had been an honor student. Then he'd been drafted into the NFL at the age of twenty-three and had been one of the best QBs, and he hadn't squandered all his millions away like a lot of athletes did.

So the fact that he'd just acted like a complete ass in the middle of the hardware store parking lot was beyond him. Anyone with brains would have accepted Annabelle's thanks and moved on. But he'd stuck around and goaded her. Because that's what he did best when he was around her.

As though he'd never had an interaction with a woman before.

He gripped the steering wheel tighter and left the parking lot.

As he'd pulled into the hardware store, he'd seen her exiting with her cart. As usual, his attention was drawn to her and the way her hips moved in that sensual sway of theirs. She'd left her hair down, which was a change from the usual long ponytail, and it fell in thick layers past her shoulders. The response his body had was instantaneous and also troublesome. Because he didn't want to want her. She was meddlesome and too opinionated for his taste.

But as he'd exited his car, he'd seen her struggling with that ridiculous safe and something made him stop. Call him old-fashioned, but he hadn't been able to turn a blind eye to a woman in need. Even if that woman made him want to drop to his knees and howl like a wild animal. So he'd intervened.

And had a bitch of a time trying to hide the tenting action in his pants.

The woman was something else.

One minute allowing her authoritative nature to call the shots, and the next giving him a glimpse of her vulnerabilities.

He shook his head at his own stupidity. If he were a smart man, which he was, he'd stay away from her.

The trouble was he couldn't. Not only was she there every morning before practice, but she was also in his head.

Now who's under whose skin?

That had been a load of shit, if he'd ever heard it.

She was under his skin, no doubt about it. He'd only said that to deflect the fact that she'd been right. And he'd wanted to see her squirm as she made him squirm.

Why should he be the only one juggling feelings he didn't know how to handle?

From the cup holder of his truck, his cell vibrated. Blake picked it up and touched the screen.

Damn, but he hated texting. It was nothing but a lazy and drawn out way to have a conversation.

I just drove past the hardware store and saw you making out with Ms. Turner. What's that about?

Brandon.

Blake ignored the text and tossed his phone down.

A second later it vibrated again. With a heavy sigh, he picked it up.

No response? Is that because your tongue is still lodged down her throat?

"You son of a bitch," Blake muttered to himself while one-handedly dialing Brandon's number.

His friend picked up on the first ring. "Nice of you to come up for air long enough to answer."

Blake ignored the jab and made a left on Canyon Drive. "If you have something to say to me just call. You know I hate texting."

Brandon snorted. "Because you're a dinosaur."

Blake hung up on his friend and set the phone down again. Thankfully, Brandon left him alone.

"Asshole," Blake growled, more about himself than Brandon. Brandon was just being Brandon.

He turned into his neighborhood and gripped the steering while tighter.

When had he turned into such a grumpy prick?

When you effed up your life.

His knee throbbed like a son of a bitch. It had been hours since he'd taken his pain pills. Leaning across the console, Blake dug around in his glove compartment and wrapped his hand around the prescription bottle. Only three pills left.

Shit.

He managed to get the top off and tossed back a pill, swallowing it in one gulp.

Soon the pain would edge away and he could think coherently again.

Maybe that's why he'd pushed Annabelle the way he had. Because the throbbing in his leg had muddled his brain.

Yeah, that was it.

Definitely.

Except when he made a right turn, he spotted her again.

Always there. Always haunting him.

How had he not known she lived in this neighborhood? Not the same street, but still close enough to be too much of a temptation.

Who are you kidding?

She didn't need to live in the same neighborhood to tempt him. Simply existing was enough.

Her house was a modest bungalow-style one story, similar to his. A large tree dominated the front yard with colorful flowers lining the front porch and a kerosene-style lamp mounted by the front door.

Quaint and charming. The house suited her. And maybe a couple of kids running around with a golden retriever.

The picture his imagination created only reminded him of why he needed to stay away from her. She was a forever kind of girl. Three kids. A couple of dogs. A husband who sat at a desk all day and didn't have a broken body that was dependent on pills.

But he stopped along the curb anyway and watched her.

Because he was creepy like that.

Then she attempted to lift the safe from her car. And failed.

She took a step back from the car, inhaled a deep breath, then tried lifting again. This time she managed a step back but quickly set the box back down.

He ought to help her. She couldn't get that thing inside her house by herself. At least not without breaking something.

But if he got out of his truck, there'd be no turning back, and their interaction would go beyond a senseless yet scorching touch.

So he rolled down his window and his mouth detached from his brain.

"Need another hand?" he called.

She spun around, hair flying all around her shoulders, making him wonder what it would feel like to tunnel his hands through the thick strands.

"I think I can get it this time," she called back.

He rested his elbow on the open window. "How many more times are you going to try before you drop it on your foot?"

Her teeth stabbed into her lower lip.

She needed to not do that.

Because his willpower was only so strong.

With a sigh, after she'd only stared at him without answering, Blake climbed out of his truck and slammed the door shut.

"You really don't need to trouble yourself again," she told him.

"I'd rather trouble myself with this than trouble myself with taking you to the emergency room after you've broken a toe."

Her mouth kicked up. "Gee, thanks."

He returned her grin. "No sweat."

"That wasn't a real thanks, you know," she told him.

"Really? It sounded so genuine," he argued.

She stepped back while he hefted the safe from the back of her SUV. "You're just loving this, aren't you?"

"What, you needing me?" he countered, because she made him say weird things.

She sent him a mocking smile and led the way to her front door. "I meant your gloating."

He ignored the statement and allowed his gaze to wander down her trim backside. The sleek indentation of her backbone. The subtle flare of her hips and the way her always-present yoga pants outlined the heart shape of her delectable rear end.

She glanced at him over her shoulder and lifted a brow when she caught him staring.

Just returning the favor, sweetheart.

He'd seen her checking him out more than once.

She opened the front door and stepped back for him to enter. He brushed past, a little too closely, so his arm just glanced off her breasts. The contact was instant and brief but enough to reaffirm his thoughts that she really was as soft and full as she seemed. Probably a nice handful. Just like he preferred.

"Just set it down here," she told him, gesturing toward a small office shut off from the rest of the house by a set of double French doors.

The place smelled good. Fresh and clean and like wild-flowers. Sort of like her. Bright light spilled in through wood-framed windows and the hardwood floors gleamed in the stream of sunlight as though she'd just cleaned them.

She probably spent her spare time cleaning. Annabelle struck Blake as the sort of person who grabbed a toilet wand when she was stressed. Or maybe even bored. He followed her down a short hallway, taking in the family photos strategically placed on the wall, creating a small photo gallery of family and nature scenes.

Blake stopped in front of one and took in the much younger picture of Annabelle, shorter hair nudging her narrow jawline but still beautiful and full of life.

"Is this your mom?" he asked, pointing to the older woman next to her in the picture.

Annabelle stopped and came back to where he stood. "Yeah." A smile tipped her mouth. "That was the summer we took a road trip through the Midwest."

"Sounds exciting," he commented.

"Not many people would be into that sort of thing. But my mother could make anything exciting."

He slanted her a look. "You look like her."

Annabelle tilted her head to one side and studied the old photograph. "Yeah, I guess I do. My sister takes more after my father."

Blake pointed to another picture of Annabelle with a woman younger than her. Both women had the same dark hair, but Annabelle was shorter with fuller lips and a pointier chin. "Is this her?" he asked.

"Yeah, that's Naomi."

The tone in her voice was different, and Blake wasn't sure she even realized it. He turned and looked at the woman who had him tied up in knots. "You said she doesn't live in the area."

Annabelle shook her head, turned, and continued walking down the hallway. "Right now she's in Peru."

Blake followed her. "What do you mean right now?"

Annabelle pushed through a door that led to the kitchen. He followed her in and watched as she pulled a coffeepot out from a bottom cabinet and set it on the counter. "Naomi doesn't stay in one place for more than a year or so. She's been in Peru for a few months and just opened a hostel. Before that she was in Panama. I'm sure it won't be long before she picks up and goes somewhere else."

The undercurrent of resentment wasn't hard to pick up. Blake leaned against the opposite counter and folded his arms over his chest. When she mentioned taking care of her mother, Blake had assumed Annabelle was doing what most other children of aging parents did. But after her comments about her sister, he realized it was more than that. It was more than an obligation.

She no doubt loved her mom and took pride in helping out, but there was also a necessity she'd assumed because there was no one else to do it. Hadn't she told him in the parking lot she was all her mother had?

In that moment, as Annabelle filled the coffee carafe with water, Blake saw her as more than the bossy woman who was interfering with this work. She was a woman with burdens, who'd willingly made room in her life to take care of an ailing parent. When a lot of children would have hired a day nurse or put them in a retirement community, Annabelle had assumed the responsibly.

Control freak.

She didn't trust anyone else to do the job. Her mother meant too much to her for that.

"Why are you looking at me like that?" she wanted to know after she'd turned the coffeemaker on.

The machine gurgled to life, filling the kitchen with the scent of brewing coffee, something that made Blake's mouth water. "I was just thinking you're not really the person you put out there for people to see."

She leaned against the counter and mimicked his stance. "How do you figure that?"

"How long has it been since you've seen your sister?" he asked instead of answering her question.

"Two years maybe," she answered automatically.

He nodded. "International travel is no doubt expensive."

She rolled one shoulder. "I wouldn't know."

"You've never gone to visit her?"

"I don't have that kind of time."

He waited a moment before answering. "Because you're so busy doing things for other people?"

"You must think I'm super-woman or something. I just have my job and my mother. That's all I do."

The coffee gurgled a few more times, then stopped brewing. Instead of reaching for a mug or two, because he could really use a cup, she remained in her spot, staring at him.

He stared right back because he wasn't about to let her off the hook so easily. Finally realizing there was so much more than the woman who tried to tell him how to coach his players, Blake dug for more. "No, it's not. You volunteer your time to work with a bunch of high school football players—"

"Even though you tried to fire me," she interrupted.

Blake didn't slow down. "You offered to help me with my knee. You shop for your mother and make her food. I'll bet you even clean for her too."

"My mother's sixty-three and has bad hips. She can hardly get down on her hands and knees and scrub a bathtub."

"So hire a maid service," he offered.

Annabelle snorted and opened an upper cabinet, pulling down two mugs. "Do you take cream or sugar?"

"Black," he told her.

She slanted him a look over her shoulder. "Somehow that doesn't surprise me." She filled both mugs, handing over his while reaching for a canister of sugar. "Maid services cost money," she finally responded to his suggestion.

He took the mug, allowing a slow grin when she sucked in a breath at the contact of their fingers. The skin on her hands was just as velvety as it was on her face. "Or you just don't trust them to do the job right," he said.

"Or that," she agreed while hefting spoon after spoon of sugar into her coffee.

He narrowed his eyes at her. "You're going to give yourself a heart attack." The coffee was good. Bold and strong and just how he liked it.

"I haven't had one yet," she answered with a grin.

He matched her smile with one of her own. "*Yet* being the key word there."

She finished with her coffee, then blew on the surface. "Worried about me?"

He just shrugged because, damn, he sort of did worry about her. Worried she was giving more of herself to others than she had time for. Human beings could only stretch themselves so far before they broke. "I'm just wondering who'll clean your mother's bathtub if you slip into a sugar coma."

One of her thinly sculpted brows arched. "You're a funny guy."

"Glad you noticed." He lifted his cup and took a shallow sip. "So how did you and your sister end up so different?"

"I don't really like to talk about Naomi," she immediately said. When he only stared at her, she heaved a sigh of defeat. "To tell you the truth, I don't know. We were raised by the same parents in the same home. But we're totally different people. Don't ask me how that happened because I don't know. Naomi's always lived for herself. She does what she wants and goes where she pleases."

"In the meantime, you go where you're needed," he concluded for her.

Annabelle waited a moment before answering. "I guess you could say that." She stared off into the distance and shook her head. "Don't get me wrong, I love my sister. I mean, we're only two years apart in age and we were like best friends growing up. But..." She shook her head again, as though she couldn't quite figure it out for herself. "We just grew into two completely different people. I'm not sure what happened, and that bothers me."

Blake lifted the cup but paused before taking a sip. "What does?"

"The fact that I don't have anything in common with my own sister." She blew out a long breath. "She cares about seeing the world and diversity and expanding her knowledge of other cultures. There isn't anything wrong with that. It's just..."

He waited for her to finish and when she didn't, he did it for her. "You resent her."

The moment the words left his mouth, her shoulders sagged. "It's such a horrible thing to say, but it's true." Her hazel eyes searched his. "What kind of a person resents her own sister?"

"The human kind," he reassured her.

"Don't make me out to be a hero, because I'm not," she warned him.

Blake took a slow sip of his coffee, allowing the drink to burn down his throat. "What you're doing sounds pretty heroic to me."

"What, cooking my mother dinners and scrubbing her toilets?"

"Offering your time without being asked and not expecting anything in return."

"How do you know I'm not expecting anything back?" she asked before sipping her coffee.

"Because you're not that type of person." He paused a moment. "Are you?"

She watched him over the rim of her Minnie Mouse mug. "You seem to have me all figured out, don't you?"

Blake shook his head. "There you go answering questions with questions again. Do you ever give a straight answer?"

"When I want," she answered with a nonchalant shrug.

Blake set the mug on the counter, more focused on the woman so intent on keeping herself a mystery. Shouldn't that be the way he wanted it? The more he got to know her, the more he liked her. And that needed to stop.

The thing was, he couldn't bring himself to stop.

He took a step toward her. Slow, deliberate steps that took him across the small kitchen. "You don't want to, is that it?" he queried. "Because you don't want me figuring you out."

Her lips parted slightly. "You seem to be doing a pretty good job so far."

"Am I?" he asked with a quirk of his mouth. He stopped in front of her, close enough to see the flecks of brown in her hazel eyes, and realized they weren't as green as he originally thought. Funny how one day they seemed as green as fresh-cut summer grass and the next they were more gold.

"Blake," she whispered.

He was pretty sure he grunted, something that made him sound like a caveman instead of an intelligent person capable of speech. Because he was too busy roaming his gaze over her delicate features and realizing what a classic beauty she really was. Milky skin, petite nose, and long dark lashes. How hadn't he realized just how beautiful she really was?

From the moment he'd met her, he'd known she was intriguing. Intelligent, sassy, and independent. Until that moment, he hadn't allowed himself to see just how captivating she really was.

How could you have missed it, asshole?

Then his brain took a leave of absence when he lifted his hand and tested the softness of her lips against his thumb. The second contact was made, his fantasy came to life and he realized just how correct he'd been. He skimmed his thumb back and forth across her lower lip, barely resisting the urge to lower his head. Which was hard when she parted her lips as though in invitation to do whatever he wanted.

And he wanted.

Oh, how he wanted.

But if he indulged himself now, he wouldn't stop. Once their lips made contact, the strange attraction and pull between them would explode and the animal inside, the one desperate to own her, would come out and take over.

Despite his thoughts, he liked to think he was more of a gentleman than that.

Only, the woman was crafty and sneaky. Because one minute he was simply touching her—just an innocent caress—and the next she'd lifted her head just enough to bring her lips in contact with his.

The movement was quick and minimal but unexpected enough to throw him off guard. Blake didn't like being thrown off guard. Made him feel out of control and he liked having the upper hand in everything he did.

But Annabelle had swooped in and stolen the advantage without warning. The second their lips met, his good intentions evaporated. His restraint fled and he pressed even closer to her, sliding his hand from her mouth to tunnel through the silky coolness of her hair.

And, yeah, he liked it when she wore it down. Gave him ample opportunity to give the strands a gentle yet firm tug, applying just enough pressure to tilt her head back. His tongue slipped past her lips in time to swallow her surprised gasp.

Who has the upper hand now?

He could get used to having the upper hand over Annabelle Turner. She struck him as the type of person who didn't give it up so easily. Kudos to him for snatching it from her with such little effort.

Her hands, those nimble little works of magic, crept over the dips and curves of his chest. He applied more pressure to her scalp with his hand, just as her finger traced the sculpted edge of his pecs. Then her tongue was tangling with his with as much, if not more, enthusiasm than his own.

Something vibrated. Blake could have sworn it was him, considering how hot and turned on he was. All she needed to do was move those curious fingers to the hem of his shirt and lift. The rest of their clothes would follow soon after.

The vibrating started again and Blake realized it was a cell phone. It couldn't have been his because he'd left his in the truck. Just as the kiss was heating up, Annabelle tore her mouth away, taking a step back so fast that she stumbled against the counter. She probably would have fallen down if the thing hadn't been there to hold her up.

She licked her lips and gripped the edge of the counter. "I'm sorry," she whispered.

Blake stared at her and didn't speak, mostly because his heart was thumping too wildly. But also because her apology threw him for a loop.

"You're sorry," he repeated.

"Yeah, I…" She wiped the back of her hand across her mouth. "I shouldn't have done that."

"Why not, Annabelle?" he wanted to know, because, damn, the last thing he wanted to hear from her was sorry. What did she have to be sorry about? "Because you allowed yourself to lose control? Or because you don't know how to handle whatever this thing is between us?"

She shook her head and opened her mouth. Then closed it again. Then opened it. "There's no 'thing.' It was just a kiss."

Blake laughed even though the situation was far from funny. "Kisses like that don't just happen, sweetheart. Not unless both people want it badly enough."

She opened her mouth to argue, but he cut her off. "Don't tell me you didn't want it. Or that it wouldn't have gone further if your phone hadn't interrupted us."

"No," she said, as though trying to convince herself. "I wouldn't have let it go any farther."

He arched a brow at her. "Really? You're telling me that if I had slipped my hand under your shirt, you would have stopped me?"

She pushed from the counter and edged away from him. "Stop it," she warned him.

"Stop what?" He turned and followed her movements around the kitchen. "Stop being honest? Come on, Annabelle. We both know you would have let me do whatever I wanted."

She spun around and faced him. "Okay, maybe I would have. But that's why it had to stop. Also, the team can't be aware of whatever this is. We're supposed to be setting an example for those kids, and how can we do that if we're making out?"

Blake narrowed his eyes, then opened his mouth.

"Come on, Blake," she went on. "What do you think those kids would say if they found out? Don't you think it would change the way they look at both of us?"

"I think they know my personal life is my own business," he told her.

She jabbed a hand in his chest. "Yes, but you value what they think of you. You loathe the thought of letting down another kid. Don't you?"

Blake immediately shook his head and turned from her. "You don't know what you're talking about."

"Oh, I think I do," she urged. "Because that," she emphasized with a gesture between the two of them, "can't happen again."

"Because I make you feel things you're not comfortable with. And you can't stand that," he added.

She stared at him with color staining her high cheekbones. "Okay, so what if I like to keep my emotions in check? What's wrong with that?"

"Nothing's wrong with it as long as you don't allow it to run your entire life."

Her brows pulled low over her eyes, which had gone even greener than he'd seen them. "Isn't that the point of having control? So I can run my life?"

Blake stepped toward her, but she backed up until she nudged the fridge. "But you're not running your life. It's running you."

"You don't know anything about me," she whispered.

He didn't stop his pursuit of her. Just kept stalking her until he could see the fluttering pulse near her collarbone. "I know you have yourself so closed off that no one can see anything but what you want them to see. I know you like to have everything just the way you want it. Anyone can see you've been doing it for so long that you probably don't even know the woman you are underneath anymore."

Her nostrils flared and the color brightening her cheeks deepened. "You think you know everything," she told him.

He lifted his hand and cupped her cheek. The usually cool skin was warm. Heated from her passion and temper. "I know more than you think I do," he whispered.

Then he dropped his hand and left her standing there.

What he didn't say, or allow her to see, was that he was just as shaken as she was.

The depth of passion behind their kiss had been enough to scorch the clothes right off their bodies. Oddly enough, that wasn't what rattled him.

The mystery he usually saw behind her green eyes had melted away. For one brief moment, he saw the woman underneath her cool exterior. She'd been hurt deeply and had probably spent a lot of time and energy burying it. The scars on her soul had reached out to him with trembling fingers and latched on.

And he feared they wouldn't ever let go.

EIGHT

The burning was back.

Actually, if Blake were to be honest, the burning never went away.

But it was especially bad this morning because he'd skipped his Oxy the night before. As he'd climbed into bed, he'd eyed the bottle sitting on the nightstand. Just waiting for him to pick it up and toss back a few. Instead, he'd gone to bed and hadn't slept for shit because his knee had been killing him.

Now, as the first gray light of daybreak slatted through the wooden blinds, Blake eyed the bottle again. He swung his legs over the edge of the bed and scratched his bare chest.

Pills can't fix everything.

Hadn't Annabelle said that to him the first day they met? Anyone who said that had never suffered from a dependency before. Because, when the medication coursed through his system, it sure as hell felt like they could fix anything. The pain. The headaches. The burning sensation that coursed through his veins and itchy skin.

Simply tossing back one of those little pills could make all that go away.

At the same time, Blake had enough experience with drugs surging through his system to know he wasn't doing himself any favors.

So shouldn't he wean himself off them or something?

Was it healthy to quit cold turkey?

He stood from the bed, knowing he had about thirty minutes to get to the field. A shower would help with his jitters. But only temporarily. It was always temporary.

His back teeth ground together as he grabbed the little orange bottle.

You take them because you're weak.

One of the things he'd sworn to himself after his retirement was no more weakness. He'd been weak all through his surgeries, through his recovery and his dependency on his trainers and doctors.

And another thing, Blake thought as he replaced the bottle on the nightstand, how could he preach to people about being a role model for his players when his own life was still upside down? What kind of role model doped himself up on painkillers?

Didn't his players deserve the best from him?

Blake shook his head as he strolled into the bathroom and stripped his boxers.

Yeah, those kids deserved, and needed, someone who had all their wits about him. So he left the pills on the nightstand and readied for practice, telling himself the shaking and burning would go away.

Not sure if he believed his own lies.

"We're going to get our asses handed to us," Blake muttered an hour and a half later as the offensive line tried, and failed, for the third time, to execute the play Cameron had called.

The assistant coach blew his whistle "For God's sake, Richardson!"

Brandon, who'd swung by on the way to a jobsite, clapped Blake on the shoulder. "Ever the optimist. That's what I love most about you," he said, and just barely dodged an elbow to the ribs. The guy popped the piece of gum in his mouth and clapped when his son Matt intercepted the ball and ran it for twenty yards.

Blake ignored his cousin and blew his game whistle. The kids stopped play and turned their attention toward their coach. "Water break, then huddle," he called to them.

While they did as they were told, Brandon said, "I don't hang up on people."

Blake jammed his hands on his hips and pushed the brim of his baseball cap up his forehead. "Your point?"

"I'm trying to remove the bug that crawled up your ass and died," Brandon told him.

"Don't bother," Blake responded, then left his cousin standing there. He strode down the sidelines, past the practicing cheerleading squad, to address the group of kids who essentially held his future in their hands. They were good kids who loved the game and always gave 100 percent. Blake wished that alone was enough to win games, but it wasn't. He needed rushing power, accurate kicking, and effective defense. As it stood, the defensive line couldn't keep a kitten from slipping past and getting to the QB.

Cameron and the other coaches had pulled a few kids aside to review the play and talk about fine-tuning. Their first game was little more than a week away, which meant the pressure was mounting. When he'd arrived at the field earlier, there had been a couple of news vans and reporters from papers wanting to interview the new coach. He'd indulged, as was expected of him, and gave the customary speech about optimism and all that. Whether or not they believed his practiced speech was anybody's guess.

Blake hated the press, as much as it could draw attention to the team and their efforts. He wasn't here to please reporters and help the six o'clock news fill air time. His focus was the team and getting them game ready.

He blew his whistle again and the kids replaced their lids and gathered around for tackling drills. They formed a circle, big enough for Blake to stand in the middle and two players to tackle each other.

The kids started the drill, beginning with chants. Most of it was just noise and nonsense, at least to anyone else watching. But to the kids, the rhythmic grunting and hollering, synchronized with bouncing on the balls of their feet, was just as important as the drill itself. Blake couldn't explain it, but the thumping of the kids matched the thumping of their hearts and got their blood pounding.

He tooted his whistle again. "Thirty-six and seventeen," he called. The two players came forward, bouncing from foot to foot, readying themselves for the crunching of pads and brute force that would send one of them to the ground. When Blake blew his whistle again, the kids went at each other, slamming themselves against each other, each one using all his strength to knock the other down.

Number seventeen, Connor Phillips, went sprawling on his backside and the other players hooted and hollered. Blake stayed in his spot and stared at the boy. "On your feet, son," he told the kid. When he didn't get up right away, Blake hunched down and got in the Connor's face. "Our first game is one week away and these guys are going to come after you with all they've got. Are you really going to lie there like a pussy?" The kid immediately stood and took his place back in the circle.

They went through the drill, each kid getting their turn to tackle another. Blake blew his whistle and motioned for the team to huddle. The kids came closer, removed their lids, and pressed them together in a gathering above their heads.

After one more good grunt, the kids dispersed and retook their places on the field, waiting for another play call. Cameron came forward, blew his own whistle, and called the play.

The offensive line readied, and when the center hiked the ball to QB Cody Richardson, the play unfolded. What should have been a beauty of a throw turned into a debacle that was not only intercepted but also left Cody completely unprotected. Blake's optimism turned to annoyance.

"For God's sake, Richardson," Cameron bellowed, repeating his earlier frustration with the quarterback, who seemed to be off his game today.

Blake blew his whistle and walked farther onto the field. "Cody," he called to the kid. Cody whipped his lid off his head and jogged toward Blake. "You've gotta get that pass off faster than that, son."

Cody nodded vigorously, beads of sweat trickling down his face. "Sorry, Coach."

Blake shook his head. "I don't want to hear sorry. I want you to hit them on the break, you hear me?" When Cody nodded, Blake went on. "When they run deep, you throw deep. Understand?"

"Yes, Coach!" Cody replaced his lid and trotted back to his position.

Cameron blew his whistle "Again!"

The players resumed their positions, with the offense lining up and the center snapping ball to Cody. The QB cradled the ball and sent the thing flying. The only reason the receiver managed to catch the ball was because of a last-minute ten-yard sprint. But the ball landed in his hands and he was tackled shortly afterward. Technically the play was completed, but not very well.

Blake knew the kids knew this, but they celebrated anyway, hooting and clapping each other on the back.

Cameron stepped forward and blew his whistle. "I don't see what you're celebrating about!" he told the players, which got their attention. "Because y'all looked like a bunch of Girls Scouts out there! You're not watching your wide receiver, and your QB is down on the ground." Cameron looked at each player. "Learn your offense," he told them. "I want you to know your offense so well that your children will know your offense."

Blake stood next to Cameron and addressed the kids. "We're playing our first game against the number two team in the district. They're a team that knows how to win, and they'll be out for blood, you feel me?" When the kids shouted their "yes, Coach," Blake went on. "No one wants to spend their hard-earned money to watch a team who can't complete a play. Now, your moms and dads and girlfriends are going to be watching." He glanced at each of his players. "Do any of you remember the last time this team brought home a win?" When the kids shook their heads, Blake answered them. "That's because it was before any of you were born. Do you see that sign up there?" He pointed toward the Champion's Valley sign on Haystack Mountain. "Did you know the mayor wanted it removed? Well, we're not going to let him because we're going to show them a championship team. Now get your heads out of your asses and quit acting like a bunch of babies!"

"Yes, Coach!" The players moved into huddle once again

and repeated the ritual of removing their lids and chanting. Blake left the kids to it and approached the other coaches. Out of the corner of his eye, Blake saw Brandon, who'd moved to the other side of the chain-link fence separating the stands from the field, lift a hand in farewell. Blake waved good-bye to his cousin.

An odd sense of satisfaction at the team's improvement, mixed with frustration at Cody's performance, made him irritable. If the QB was off, the whole team was off, and at this point, they were out of time. With the first game less than a week away, they needed to be more in sync than this.

The team filed into the locker room, each of the players going to their spots and taking a seat on the benches. Cameron took a moment to say a few words to the team, reviewing the plays they made with rudimentary drawings on a chalkboard. Blake stood to the side, eyeing the players and noticing the deadpan look on Cody's face, thinking something was off with the kid.

Blake shifted his weight off his bad knee, admitting he should have taken his Oxy after all. As good and noble as his own pep talk had been, pep talks didn't ease pain. Since he knew himself, he'd grabbed the bottle at the last minute and tossed them in his car.

A movement out of the corner of his eye caught his attention. There in the doorway leading to the weight room was Annabelle, waiting for a free moment with the players. She didn't see him and he used the opportunity to watch her. A week had passed since the incident in her kitchen. Also known as the kiss that had haunted his dreams every night since then. Yeah, he'd seen her since then, in passing before and after practices, but they'd barely spoken.

The strange thing was, he missed her. He missed her in his business. Barging into his office and offering her opinion on the players. Her recent lack of interference should have pleased him. After all, wasn't that what he wanted? For her to slink into the background so she wouldn't distract him?

Only he didn't want that.

Today her hair was pulled back in its usual high ponytail, accentuating her sharp cheekbones. Funny, but he found he liked it better loose. The strands were thick and soft, which he knew firsthand since he'd had his fingers tangled in them. The appearance of her hair sort of reminded him of how she really was. Not the sharp Annabelle she'd first been with him but the Annabelle who'd fused her lips to his the other day. The Annabelle who constantly talked about how much she loved the kids and wanted to protect them. That was the real Annabelle, Blake realized.

As though sensing his thoughts, she turned her head and glanced at him. Her eyes, which were particularly green to-day, contradicted the serious set of her full mouth. Her long lashes swept down with a slow blink and then she smiled at him. Not the full smile he was used to seeing from her when she worked with the kids. Just a slight tilt. Hesitant, perhaps even testing.

Yeah, she was testing him.

Testing to see if he'd blow her off. If he was still pissed about the kiss.

Hell yeah he was pissed. But at himself for not having more self-control. And then for acting like an ass.

He offered a tight nod. Because if the other coaches caught him grinning at the smokin' hot physical therapist, he'd never hear the end of it.

Cameron finished his speech to the players, and everyone dispersed. Annabelle diverted her attention to Scott Porter, the kid with the hamstring problems. Her half-smile quickly blossomed into a full one when she laid a hand on Scott's shoulder. She said something to the kid, which prompted a smile from him.

Damn it, Blake wanted her to smile like that at him. The fact that he was jealous of a freakin' high school student was an official new low for him. Wasn't it enough that they'd kissed, and now he wanted more from her?

Annabelle and Scott disappeared into the weight room and Blake pushed away from the wall. He headed toward his office but made a detour to Cody's locker, where the kid was removing his game pads.

"Cody," he said to the QB. "A word in my office."

Cody set his pads down and followed Blake across the locker room. Blake opened the door and gestured for the kid to enter first. Cody took a chair, and Blake sat in his own, leaning back and pushing the brim of his hat up his forehead.

"Do you have any idea why I called you in here?" Blake asked as he folded his hands across his stomach.

Cody shook his head. "No, Coach."

Blake watched the kid for a moment, noting his utter stillness, which was an unusual change to the cocky attitude they'd all grown used to. Something about Cody reminded Blake of himself. Living and breathing football. Only caring about being on the field but at the same time not wanting to listen to anyone. Blake had been just as cocky, just as cocksure of himself. Thinking nothing could bring him down. Except a torn ACL.

"Is there something on your mind you'd like to talk about?"

Cody shook his head again. "Everything's fine."

Bullshit. Just like Blake always told Annabelle his knee was fine. Blake read the lies all over Cody's face. Had Blake been that easy for Annabelle to read?

Blake decided to take a different tactic. "Okay, then. Let's talk about your field performance." He grabbed his clipboard and glanced over the notes he'd made during practice. "Your pass completion rate has improved, but your timing's been off."

Cody shifted in his seat. "I'm sorry, Coach. I didn't sleep good last night and—"

"It's not just today, Cody. You've been off all week. Your handoffs are sloppy and you're not following through with the play. If this had been a real game, the other team's defensive tackle would have annihilated you." He leveled Cody with a hard look. "So, I'll ask you again. Is there anything you'd like to tell me?"

On some level, Blake understood Cody's unwillingness to open up. Hadn't Blake been that hesitant to let anyone in after his banishment? All the phone calls from his parents in Arizona checking in on him? How many times had he uttered the words *I'm fine*?

Blake leaned forward in his chair. "Listen," he told the kid. "Our first game is next week. Do you understand what I mean?"

Cody nodded.

"You're the quarterback. The captain," Blake told him. "You've been on a winning team before, and most of these kids don't know what that feels like. Not only have you played in an arena three times the size as ours, but you're also older than most of them. Now, you may not realize this, but most of those kids look up to you."

Again the kid nodded and Blake continued. "I'm sure I don't have to tell you that the attitude of the quarterback sets the tone for the entire team. When your attitude sucks, it rubs off on them. When you have no faith, it sucks what little faith they have. You understand what I'm saying, son?"

"Yes, Coach," the kid replied automatically.

Blake studied him for a moment. "You don't really want to be here, do you?"

Cody lifted one shoulder. "I just want to play football, Coach."

"But not for the Bobcats," Blake guessed.

"I didn't say that," Cody argued.

Blake shook his head. "You didn't have to. Your attitude on the field says it all. You may have been a team player in Texas, but you haven't been much of a team player here."

Cody didn't say anything, effectively affirming Blake's assumption of the kid.

A heavy sigh flowed out of Blake's lungs. Time for a different attempt. "I understand playing for a small-time 3A team isn't the same as the Texas state champions. But those other players out there?" Blake asked with a nod of his head toward the locker room. "They don't understand that. Every time you step onto the field with that piss-poor attitude of yours, you're letting them down. Now, how are you going to look each one of them in the eye, knowing you're not giving them the same 110 percent they're giving you?"

The sullen kid slid deeper in his chair and averted his gaze to the ground. "I'm sorry, Coach."

"You keep apologizing to me, Cody, but I don't want to hear you're sorry." Blake rested his arms on his desk. "You really want to prove to me and the other coaches how sorry you are? Bring it on the field and leave it there."

Cody nodded. "Yes, sir."

Blake jerked his head toward the door. "You're dismissed."

Cody jumped out of the chair like his ass was on fire and jerked open the office door.

With another heavy sigh, Blake dug the heel of his hands into his eye sockets, wishing he could rip them out of his head.

A kid who had no desire for the game was more of a lost cause than the one who couldn't catch a ball.

The biggest problem was that Cody had more talent in his pinky finger than half the other kids on the team. If he stopped caring, it would affect his play and then they'd be screwed.

His cell buzzed from the desk and Blake picked it up, thumbing the screen. The message was a text from Brandon with a photo attached. He pulled up the picture and stared at the screen.

"What the hell?" he muttered as he gazed at a photo of a dog lying on the front seat of Brandon's truck. The animal, with shaggy golden fur and perky ears, had his head tilted to one side, as though posing for the picture.

Found this dog, Brandon's text said. *Interested?*

Blake shook his head and answered.

Not just no, but HELL no.

Brandon's response was immediate.

You're going to make me look in this dog's eyes and tell him no? Heartless bastard.

Blake typed his response.

I'm not making you do anything. But if you leave that dog at my house, I'll tell everyone you wet the bed until you were eight.

Brandon didn't respond right away.

Why can't you take him? Blake asked.

The phone vibrated. *I already have a dog. And I thought you hated texting.*

Blake chuckled and shook his head. *I do so I'm ending this conversation. DO NOT leave that dog at my house.*

Brandon didn't respond.

"I can't believe you wouldn't paint your face with me," Stella complained as she and Annabelle made their way through the entrance of the football field.

"I was going to," Annabelle replied as she took her ticket from the woman inside the booth. "But then I remembered I'm not a high school student."

Stella took her own ticket and the two of them weaved their way through people. "You also remembered that you're no fun?"

Annabelle slanted her friend a look and took in the orange paw print on her left cheek. "I'm fun," she argued. "I'm here with you, aren't I?"

The two of them moved past a group of girls wearing the jerseys of their favorite players. "Yeah, because that coach has one fine ass," Stella teased.

"I...I...that's not why..." Annabelle could feel her face flush, and she forced herself to take a deep breath. "I'm here for the kids," she finally said.

The stadium was already crowded with students, parents, and half the town. Since the Bobcats weren't a very good team, most of the attendance had to do with their new ex-pro coach. Many were rooting for him to succeed and bring the team back to its former glory. But Annabelle knew full well that there were as many people hoping to watch the scandal-plagued coach have to admit to more failure.

"Fine. You be here for the kids. I'll be checking out that fine backside," Stella replied. "I doubt I'll be the only one."

For some reason the thought of other women looking at Blake, even remotely close to the way she looked at him, had Annabelle's stomach flipping over. Which was stupid. Preposterous.

Stella burst out laughing as they maneuvered through more people and headed toward the concessions stand. "I can see you don't like that idea," her friend commented. "When are you going to admit you want to jump the guy's bones? Do the nasty? A little horizontal mambo?"

Annabelle stopped at the end of one of the long concession lines. "What decade are you from?" she asked her friend.

"Obviously a different one than you," Stella answered, and crossed her arms over her chest and turned to face Annabelle.

"All right, when was the last time you went out with a guy? Look, I know you get tired of me bringing this up. But I worry about you. I see you spending all your free time cooking and cleaning for your mother and you never get out."

The two women took a few steps closer to the open counter of the food stand.

Annabelle lifted one shoulder. "Maybe I like cooking and cleaning for my mother."

Stella snorted. "Honey, nobody likes that. Okay." She grabbed Annabelle's shoulders and turned her. "I'll leave this alone if you promise me you'll go out with the next man who asks you."

Annabelle narrowed her eyes at her friend. "What if I don't like him, though? What if he has BO and scratches his balls?"

Stella shook her head. "Doesn't matter. You have to go out with him anyway."

Annabelle blinked at her friend. "Why?"

"Because," she started, then was interrupted when someone bumped her friend from behind. Stella turned around, probably to tell the guy to back off, and both she and Annabelle blinked up at the very tall and very broadshouldered Brandon West.

Brandon towered over both of them, even Stella who was tall for a woman. He blinked his dreamy brown eyes at the two women.

"You're not going to throw up on me, are you?" he asked Stella.

Annabelle looked at her friend, then back at Brandon, who stared down Stella with an unreadable expression.

Stella offered Brandon a sweet smile. "That depends on how nice your shoes are."

The slight tilt of Brandon's mouth might have been considered a smile. Obviously Stella didn't because she didn't smile back. She lowered her gaze to the huge hot dog wrapped in a piece of aluminum, cradled in Brandon's equally large hands.

"That's quite a sausage you have there," Stella commented.

Brandon lowered his gaze to the hot dog, then one of his thick, dark brows arched. "You know what they say. The bigger the sausage"—he lifted the hot dog to his mouth and took an enormous bite—"the bigger the appetite."

Stella tilted her head to one side. "I was going to say the bigger the mouth."

Brandon's one-sided grin grew, and then he chuckled and Annabelle could have sworn a layer of goose bumps rose on her friend's bare arm.

Brandon peeled more aluminum away from the hot dog. "You are something else, Stella Davenport." And then he walked away. Actually, sauntered was more like it. Because men like Brandon West, who had more testosterone in his baby toe than most men had in their entire body, didn't simply walk. They maneuvered.

Stella blew out a breath, which came out as more of a shudder.

"What," Annabelle said with a poke to Stella's shoulder, "was that?"

Stella turned and faced the front of the line again. They

were only three people away from the counter now. "What do you mean?"

"What do I mean?" Annabelle parroted. "I mean the eye raping you just committed in front of me. And why did he ask if you were going to throw up on him?"

"I don't know," Stella answered. "Maybe he was just making conversation."

Yeah, because every conversation started with questions about upchucking.

"Stella." She nudged her friend's shoulder.

A heavy sigh left her friend's shoulder's sagging. "Do you remember that one date I went on a few months ago? The one I said ended badly?"

Annabelle nodded. "Yeah." She waited for her friend to continue. When Stella didn't elaborate, the lightbulb clicked on. "Wait a minute. The date that ended badly was with that guy?"

At Stella's jerky nod, Annabelle laughed. "You threw up on Brandon West?"

Stella glanced around at the other people. "Why don't you say it a little louder? I didn't mean to throw up on him. I got some kind of weird food poisoning from the restaurant we went to and threw up right as he leaned in to kiss me."

The two women approached the counter and Annabelle withdrew the twenty bucks from her pocket. "You never went out again?"

"Would you want to go out with the woman who threw up right you tried to kiss her?"

"Yes, you have a point," Annabelle agreed. "Maybe you should take your own advice and jump the guy's bones already."

"If and when I jump a guy's bones again, they will not belong to Brandon West."

Funny, that was the same thing Annabelle kept saying about Blake Carpenter.

They finally approached the snack shack, after having to shove their way through people who were still waiting for their food. Stella shouldered a man out of her way and signaled one of the women.

Unfortunately, the woman was Dawn Putnam, aka homecoming-queen-PTA-mom-extraordinaire. Annabelle swallowed a groan as Dawn plastered a grin on her face, accentuating the orange lipstick—orange, for God's sake— covering her surgically overfilled lips.

Not that Annabelle didn't like the Dollys. Really, they were fine women. Just a bit . . . well, exhausting.

"Well, hello there, Annabelle," Dawn greeted. She'd spray painted her hair orange and black and had teased it into two high pigtails, thus making her resemble a teenager. A look, Annabelle was sure, Dawn had been going for. Rhonda was busy helping other people, which was a relief because Annabelle wasn't sure she could handle both of the Dollys at once.

"What can I get you girls?" Dawn asked.

"Two corn dogs and two Cokes," Stella told the woman.

Dawn switched her attention to Annabelle. "So, do you think our boys can bring it home tonight? How was Coach Carpenter feeling about the opener?"

Annabelle blinked at the woman and was bumped from behind. "How would I know how the coach was feeling before the game?" She'd almost called him Blake, but thought better of it, knowing how Dawn and Rhonda practically made gossip a sport.

Dawn tilted her head and blinked her long black lashes. "Well, haven't you been spending a whole bunch of time with the team and the coach?"

Stella leaned close. "She's fishing," she whispered in Annabelle's ear. "In case you haven't noticed," she said to Dawn, "there's a huge line of hungry fans behind us. Perhaps you could just get us our food now."

"I only see the team and Coach Carpenter during practices," Annabelle informed Dawn, before Dawn could respond to Stella's request. "When I come to work with the kids."

Dawn lifted her shoulders, which were clad in a throwback Bobcats T-shirt. "Well, I only know what I hear." She turned for a moment, then came back with two corn dogs wrapped in aluminum foil. She graced them with a wide smile, showing her white teeth, which had probably also been altered, and handed over the food. "You know how this town likes to talk." When Stella accepted the food, Dawn leaned over the counter, smashing her generous breasts over the edge. "Not that I believed any of it."

"Our drinks?" Stella demanded.

Annabelle held a hand up to silence her friend. "I'm sorry, but believe what?"

Dawn meandered toward the soda machine and began filling a paper cup with Coke. "Just that you and Coach discuss things other than the kids."

The one cup reached its limit, and Dawn stuck another cup to be filled.

"I'm sure I don't know what you mean, Dawn," Annabelle commented.

The second cup was filled and Dawn placed two plastic lids over the cups. "Oh, I don't either," she agreed with an airy laugh. "Like you said, this town loves to talk. A lot of it isn't even true. I told you, I don't believe most of it anyway." She worked the cash register and gave them the total.

Stella had cash thrown down before Dawn could even

finish. "Keep the change," Stella ordered; then she scooped up her drink and nudged Annabelle away from the counter. "That woman is ridiculous."

Annabelle took a sip of the soda, wishing she'd ordered water when the bubbles mixed with the churning of her stomach.

"Don't listen to a word she says, Annabelle," Stella warned when Annabelle hadn't said anything. "She and the other one stick their noses in everybody's business because they can't grow out of high school and their husbands ignore them."

"But what if she's right?" Annabelle mused as they wove around the throngs of people toward the bleachers.

"She's not," Stella confirmed. "Okay," she amended. "Let's say, for argument's sake, she is. So what? Since when have you cared what people have thought?"

Yes, that was true. But what if there was a thread of truth to Dawn's prodding, because that's what it had been. That's what she and Rhonda were best at. Finding out people's dirty little secrets and "accidentally" telling half the town. She cared about the team too much to allow whatever was going on with her and Blake to overshadow their success.

And they would be successful. They had to be because they, and Blake, had everything riding on this season.

NINE

The Bobcats managed to squeeze out a last-minute win, even though they'd been shut out in the first half. The defense had managed to pull their shit together and did their jobs effectively enough to push back the offense. Cody had executed two beautiful fake passes and the Bobcats had scored two touchdowns in the fourth quarter.

Considering where the team had been during the first week of practice, Blake was pleased. Cautiously optimistic. Not that he was going to have play-off T-shirts made just yet. But if they could keep playing the way they played tonight, they stood a chance. Provided their players could stay healthy. Scott Porter had to be taken out in the third quarter due to tightness in his hamstring.

When Scott had walked off the field, Annabelle's warning had flashed through Blake's mind. Blake had meant what he'd said about not being able to bench Scott. At the same time, Blake knew Scott was one injury away from being taken out for the season. The kid's health weighed as heavily on his mind as the team's performance. As the coach, not only was Blake responsible for the team's record, but also for the kids' safety and well-being. They needed Scott, but Blake didn't want to push him past what his body was capable of.

The parking lot was almost empty as he left the field house. It was late, and his body felt drained from the crash after the adrenaline rush from their win. And his knee was throbbing. Thank goodness he had some Oxy in his car.

Blake strolled toward his truck, keys dangling from one hand and his gym bag in the other. As he approached, he noticed a figure leaning against the driver's side door.

A petite, luscious figure in a pair of tight jeans and a Blanco Valley High hooded sweatshirt.

Just the sight of Annabelle turned his beat-up body on high alert. Over the past week, Blake hadn't been able to get that kiss out of his mind. Not only the feel of her lips pressed to his, but also how perfectly her body fit with his. Each one of her curves had molded seamlessly against his harder and bigger one, as though they were two pieces of the same puzzle.

And look at him with all the lame metaphors.

Blake approached the truck, twirling his keys around in his hand. Because if he didn't keep them busy, he'd yank her away from the door and kiss her again.

"Hi," she greeted when he stopped in front of her.

He tossed his bag in the bed of the truck. "Hey," he replied. "You're here awfully late."

"I wanted to hang around and congratulate some of the kids. You guys played a good game tonight," she told him.

"Thanks." Why did her praise have to mean so much to him? The parents and the school district was what mattered. Not some hazel-eyed opinionated goddess.

Annabelle scraped the toe of her tennis shoe along the ground. For some reason Blake found the movement endearing.

He was turning into such a pussy.

"I spoke to Scott's parents and he's going to be coming to my studio three days a week now."

Blake nodded. "That's good." Man, he was an idiot. One kiss with this woman and now he didn't know what to say to her.

"Blake," she said on a sigh. She pushed away from the truck and tucked a strand of hair behind her ear. "I'm sorry," she told him. "About before."

"For what? The kiss or the apology?"

She blinked at him and inhaled a deep breath. "For the way I acted afterward," she clarified. "To be completely honest, I'm not sorry for kissing you. I thought that maybe..." Her words trailed off. "I thought I had taken you off guard and acted inappropriately. I didn't want you to think I was being too forward. The sorry just kind of popped out before I could think."

Blake pocketed his keys. "You did take me off guard. But that didn't mean I didn't like it as much as you did. I think we both know I did." She'd been pressed up against him hard enough to feel the evidence between his thighs.

As though sensing his thoughts, Annabelle's gaze dropped down, lingering long enough to elicit a reaction. "I think it's safe to say we both liked it. A lot," she added. "Probably too much, actually."

"How much is too much?" Because that was part of his confusion.

One of her shoulders moved. "To be honest, I'm not sure. I'm still trying to figure that one out."

"Maybe we should try it again, just to see," he suggested.

Her attention lowered to his lips. "I don't think that's a good idea, Blake."

"Why?" He took a step toward her, but she didn't back up. "Are you afraid you'll realize how good we could be together?"

"Actually, yes." She placed a hand on his chest when he leaned closer. "I have trust issues, Blake."

"Really?" he asked with an arched brow. "I couldn't tell. So what happened? Some dickhead didn't realize what a good thing he had with you?"

A slow smile graced her beautiful features, as though warmed by his roundabout compliment. "Something like that, yeah."

Any man who trampled over the heart of Annabelle Turner didn't deserve two seconds of her time.

She lifted a hand again, and for a moment, he thought she was going to push him farther away. Instead, her palm rested on his chest, her fingers lightly tracing the edges and grooves. "So now are you going to tell me that you're no better? That I need to stay away from you?"

Her question prompted a smile from him. "I wasn't going to say so, but yeah. I'm no good for you. You should stay away." His head dipped so the tips of their noses touched. "You're standing next to my truck, Annabelle."

"Maybe that was my plan all along."

Blake gave a small shake of his head. "You're a conundrum, Ms. Turner. You think this is a bad idea, and yet here you are. Telling me you have trust issues and rubbing yourself all over me like a cat in heat."

"I can't figure it out either. I know I should stay away from you, but..."

He nudged his face closer to hers, so their mouths were a breath away from each other. "But what?"

Her throat moved up and down as she swallowed. "I just think—"

"Why don't you stop thinking for once?" he demanded and wrapped an arm around her trim waist, bringing her flush up against him. Just as she opened her mouth to respond to that, he closed the remaining distance between them, fusing their lips together. In that instant, something inside him exploded. The animal she'd been teasing since he met her lashed out, and their kiss went from subtle to hard.

He yanked her closer and sucked her startled gasp into his mouth, along with her sweet tongue. Her body, so soft and touchable, in all the right places, was plastered to his. Pressing and touching and turning him on so damn much he felt like they were about to go up in flames.

And when she tunneled her hand into his hair, the rest of his logical thinking went out the window. The kind of rational thought that told him they were a bad idea. That she obviously did have trust issues, just as she told him, and he had demons of his own. A relationship between them couldn't go anywhere. At least beyond the physical and he wasn't sure that would be enough for her. Just as he wasn't sure he could give her more than that. He was still on the path of putting his life back together. There wasn't enough room in it yet for anything else. Especially the kind of time and effort a relationship with Annabelle Turner would need.

Her tongue slid along his, infusing more heat into his body and momentarily making him forget about the pain in his knee. About his uncertain future and whether or not he could really bring the Bobcats a winning season. Blake was a winner, always had been, and the thought of losing anything made his blood run cold.

But being with Annabelle made all that go away. With her, there was no winning and losing. Only Blake Carpenter, a man with flaws and scars and a beating heart beneath his chest.

When he'd returned to Blanco Valley, he'd just been through the worst time in his life. A time he should have left behind him, but he hadn't. It had followed him home, trailing after him wherever he went, reminding him he wasn't invincible. That he wasn't the football god he thought he was. Annabelle had a way of dissolving that. With one touch of her hands, with one sly look beneath those dark lashes, she chased away his failures and restored a small semblance of the man he used to be.

He liked it. And he liked her for it. Way too much.

Just as the kiss was getting good and heated, she pulled away from him. Slowly inching back, but leaving her hands on him. Blake didn't know if she realized how close she'd pressed herself to him. Not that he cared.

"Yeah, I can see what you mean about that being a bad idea," he muttered.

She smiled and ran her tongue along her lower lip, which was moist and swollen. "So, maybe it's a good idea. But still kind of bad."

Blake removed his hand from her lower back and skimmed the pad of his thumb over her jawbone. "Now you're not making sense." But he totally knew what she meant.

"Because you muddle my brain. You make me say stupid things."

His mouth turned up in a grin. "I'll take that as a compliment," he told her.

She removed her hands from his hair and stepped back. "I can't do a relationship right now."

Blake didn't believe that for a second. "Who says I'm looking for a relationship?" he asked, instead of saying what he'd been thinking.

"No one," she answered with a shake of her head. "I just felt like I needed to make that clear."

"I think we both know you're not built for casual flings," Blake said.

She nodded, but something dark flashed across her eyes. "There you go again, thinking you know me so well."

He rolled one shoulder. "I don't hear you denying it."

She didn't say anything for a moment. "Okay, so why don't you do relationships? What is so wrong with them?" she countered, as though she couldn't think of a response to his accusation. Probably because she couldn't.

"There's nothing wrong with them. They're just not for me," he told her.

"Why is that? Because some gold digger ditched you when the going got rough?"

Exactly. But she didn't need to know that. If things remained casual, there was no chance of his balls being extracted from his body.

"Excuse me for pointing out the obvious," she went on, "but you should take your own words to heart. You know, the ones where you say we should just go for it?"

One side of his mouth kicked up because damn if she didn't have him on that one. "I don't remember saying anything like that."

"Maybe not those exact words, but it's what you meant," she told him.

Shit. Hadn't he told himself she was smart and too meddlesome for her own good? The woman kept getting inside his head and taking the words right out of his mouth. Yeah, he did want to go for it with her.

The problem was, he didn't know what *it* was.

They had two different definitions of relationship. He

wanted casual. She told him that's what she wanted, too, but he wasn't so sure about that.

He stepped back from her and winced when he placed too much pressure on his bad knee. Her gaze dropped down as though sensing his pain.

"I told you I could help you with your pain," she reminded him.

He reached around her and opened the truck door. "I told you I've got it under control."

"With pills?"

As she said the words, he reached across the front seat to the glove compartment. Feeling her eyes on him, scrutinizing every move he made, he withdrew the Oxy, pried open the lid, and tossed back a pill.

"They just help with the pain," he told her after turning to face her again. Maybe if he said the words enough he'd start to believe them. That he didn't have a problem that needed attention.

She lowered her gaze to the bottle still clutched in his hand. Ironically symbolic of how he couldn't let them go. Man, he was such a mess. First he poked and prodded a woman who not only messed with his head, but also had his number down so well that she practically wrote the damn thing.

Without warning, she snatched the bottle out of his hand. Surprisingly, he didn't try to take it back. Had it been anyone else, Brandon or Cameron, he'd have tackled them to the ground to save face. With Annabelle he had no inhibitions. Because she'd see through them anyway.

"OxyContin?" she asked with a lifted brow. "You shouldn't still need this stuff, Blake."

Yeah, no shit.

"How do you know that?" he countered.

"Because I don't live under a rock. I watch the news often enough to know when you had your surgery and should have been off Oxy a year ago." She held the bottle up. "Why are you still taking these?"

He yanked the bottle out of her hands. "I'd think that'd be obvious. Especially to a woman who claims to know everything about me." Yeah, his words were harsher than they needed to be. And yeah, the flash of hurt in her eyes was like a jab to the ribs. But he didn't need her figuring him out. Because then she'd see him for the fraud he was.

"I never claimed to know everything about you, Blake, but that stuff is meant as a temporary pain reliever immediately following a major surgery. You have a problem if you're still taking it."

He turned from her, not wanting her to see how right she was. She placed a hand on his upper back. The soothing gesture relaxed him, yet at the same time put him on edge. "I can help you, Blake. You really need to talk to someone if you're addicted to pain pills."

Her words shouldn't have meant anything to him. They should have infuriated him. Simply for the fact that she'd seen it so easily when he'd worked so hard to pretend he wasn't a complete mess. Another reason he needed to stay away from her.

Annabelle Turner had her finger on his pulse, reading and seeing him for the person he really was. In reality, it should have pleased him. To have a woman see past the dollar signs and the icon the American public had made him to be. But in truth, it scared the shit out of him. There was no pretending with her. He was exposed, raw and vulnerable and weak.

He didn't like it. No one had ever done that before and he didn't know the first thing to do about it.

"I told you before, I don't have a problem," he growled at her. He got in the truck and Annabelle stepped back as he reached for the door. "If you're looking for a quick roll in the sack, you know where to find me. Otherwise, keep your nose out of my business."

Then he slammed the door and started the truck, tearing out of the parking lot and leaving her standing there alone. He should have felt vindicated for putting her in her place.

Yeah, he should have felt good, especially after that world-shattering kiss. Instead, all he could think about was the hurt darkening those beautiful eyes of hers. As he drove home, he cursed himself for the asshole he was, thinking she'd only been trying to help. Because that's what Annabelle did. She helped people whether they wanted to admit they needed the help.

Maybe it wouldn't be the worst thing in the world to pay her studio a visit. After all, it would give him an opportunity to feel her hands on him.

Normally Annabelle could function on about five hours of sleep. Any less than that, and she went about her day growling like a zombie.

From the moment she rolled out of bed, she knew today would be one of those days. Even though she'd had a full night's sleep, it had been rough and interrupted. Tossing and turning, alternating between erotic dreams about Blake and replaying his accusatory words in her head.

Her mother had always told her she'd been too outspoken for her own good. Always thinking she knew what was best for others. Case in point, her mother's care.

Last night, standing next to Blake's truck and turning a perfectly lovely moment into a nightmare had been a perfect example of that. She'd seen the man struggling to keep his cool and she'd taken it upon herself to butt in. As usual.

How had she expected him to react? Confess his addiction with eager acceptance? Most addicts reacted to that sort of confrontation with anger, and Blake was no different. No matter how much she wanted him to be.

Why she always thought she could save people from themselves was beyond her. All those years she'd tried talking sense into her sister for living like a nomad should have been enough. But she kept on doing it. Because she never learned her lesson.

Now the only man she had growing feelings for, since her husband, probably hated her.

She opened up her studio an hour before her first appointment. The coffee cup she clutched in one hand trembled as she pushed through the glass doors. Today was definitely a two or three cup kind of day.

The place was cold, so she turned up the heater and flipped on all the lights. Annabelle left her sunglasses on, mostly because she wasn't in the mood to deal with bright light or her own reflection in the wall of mirrors. Because then she'd see what an idiot she really was.

Whatever Blake was going through shouldn't matter to her. Obviously he was a wounded soul and she identified with that. Maybe that was why he called to her so much. She saw someone trying to overcome a struggle, on his own, and she'd been in that situation before. She'd picked up the pieces of her heart, without burdening anyone else, and moved on.

The bell above the door dinged and Annabelle turned. She froze in the act of sliding her bag down her shoulders.

There, big and tall and so wounded her heart broke for him, was Blake.

He, too, had sunglasses on, and his mouth, surrounded by dark stubble, as though he hadn't bothered to shave that morning, was set in a hard line. His hands were casually resting in his pants pockets, but the rest of his body language was anything but casual. Normally his unruly blond hair was covered in a baseball cap. In fact, Annabelle couldn't remember ever seeing him without something covering that thick hair of his. Today, he'd left it off. But his hair was still unruly, still a bit too long and pushed back from his forehead from too much finger combing.

In a word, the man was devastating.

Devastatingly handsome and devastating on her heart. Because she longed for him, longed to feel his arms around her and longed to chase away his pain and regrets.

"I'm not open yet," she said by way of greeting.

He didn't move a muscle. "I heard you work with people recovering from an injury." His voice was deep and gravelly, as though he'd rolled out of bed a few minutes ago. Given the state of his hair, he probably had

"I only help people who are nice to me."

His mouth twitched, which could have been mistaken for an almost smile. Annabelle knew better than to expect spontaneous smiles from Blake Carpenter. He slowly removed his sunglasses and hooked them in the front pocket of his black athletic pants. By now she ought to have been prepared for the impact of those crystalline blue eyes, one of his best assets, in her opinion, but she couldn't quite steel herself for them. Flanked by dark lashes and hooded by thick brows, they were a force to be reckoned with, and they knocked the breath out of her every time.

"Yeah, about that," he started, taking a few steps toward her. "I shouldn't have spoken to you that way last night. I'm sorry."

Annabelle nodded and caught a whiff of his shampoo, something musky and spicy and so very male she wanted to weep. "It's all right. We're all susceptible to douchebag moments."

"Are you calling me a douche, Annabelle?" His eyes narrowed, but his lips quirked up.

Oh man, the way he said her name. "I said you had a douchebag moment."

He nodded. "Fair enough." He looked around, taking in the studio. "So, this is a nice place."

"Thanks," she replied. "It just so happens my first appointment canceled, so I have some time for you."

This time he did smile, and the butterflies in her stomach kicked into high gear. "Lucky me. I guess I should have called first."

"No, that's all right." She led him to the weight machine that she usually used with Stella. "I guess I can make an exception for you."

"You shouldn't after the way I talked to you last night," he told her.

His Green Bay Packers T-shirt stretched over his wide shoulders and gave definition to his chest. Over his narrow waist, the shirt was loose, but when he moved to take a seat at the machine, she got the occasional impression of corrugated abs.

"I told you, it's all right. We all act like douches sometimes. Even me."

Blake leaned back against the padded bench and folded his arms over his stomach. "You were just doing what you thought was right. Nothing douchey about that."

"I should have minded my own business," she told him.

"That's not who you are," he reassured her. "And you're right. I do have a problem."

She studied him, noticing the hard set of his jaw and lines of stress and pain bracketing his mouth. Had she been so enamored by his good looks that she'd never noticed the battle lurking behind his gorgeous eyes? How long had he been going through this? Had he been dealing with it alone?

"How often do you take them?" she asked.

He hesitated before answering, then said, "Every day."

"How are you even getting them so long after your surgery?"

"I have a doctor who doesn't ask a lot of questions. I tell him I'm in pain, and he writes the prescription."

"That's not very responsible of him," she countered. "All he's doing is enabling you."

"I'm aware of that."

"Have you thought about talking to someone about it?" she asked, again without thinking. She'd crossed a line with him last night and didn't want to do so again. "I mean like counseling or something."

A humorless laugh popped out of him. "Wouldn't that make a great headline: 'Disgraced football player seeks therapy for pain pill addiction.'"

"Is that how you see yourself?" she asked. "As disgraced?"

"That's how everyone else sees me."

Her brows lowered. "How do you know that?"

"How else would they see me?"

The defeat in his voice tugged at her heart. All his cocky attitude was a façade to conceal the turmoil inside. How many other people had misjudged him the way she had?

"You don't strike me as the type of man who cares what other people think," she told him.

"Not usually," he replied. "But there are some people worth impressing."

Something about the way he said the words made her squirm. As though her skin had grown too tight for her body, stretching thin and wanting to snap. Even her ex-husband, who could have charmed the panty hose off a librarian, hadn't made her feel so...aware of herself. Aware of her heart beating erratically in her chest and the fine layer of sweat gathering in between her breasts.

Lord, but the man was potent.

His attention dropped down to her hand, still resting on his injured knee, reminding her she'd left it there, as though she had every right in the world to touch him.

"You know, you can talk to me about it," she said out of the blue. "Your retirement," she clarified when he didn't respond.

But he still didn't respond, unless one would call a ticking jaw a response. She supposed, knowing Blake, that was a response. Considering he was a man of few words, he wouldn't exactly come out and say, "I don't want to talk about it."

"If you...you know..." She shrugged, suddenly not knowing what to say. Because, why would he want to share something so dark with her? It's not like they had that kind of relationship. "Wanted to get it off your chest or anything."

His chest puffed out when he inhaled a deep breath. "Not right now," was all he said.

She got it. It's not as though talking about her divorce was an easy thing for her. So what had she been thinking asking him?

That she wanted to know him better. What made him tick. What had shaped him into the man that he was now.

"Can I see it?" she blurted out.

One of his dark brows lifted, giving her a sardonic look.

Her eyes dropped closed. "I meant your knee."

And then the half-smile playing around his mouth turned into a full-force grin. "Are you sure?"

Actually, she wasn't. At least until he called her out on it. The man had a bad habit of doing that.

"Go for it," he told her. He lifted his leg, giving her room to pull his pant leg up, past a defined calf sprinkled with dark hair and over his knee.

The joint was riddled with scars. A single incision line cut down the center of his knee, along with another, longer one down the side. On the top of his knee were three dots, formed into a triangle.

Annabelle touched the tip of her index finger to them. "What're these from?"

"Laser scars," he answered in a low voice. "And this," he went on, running his thumb down the frontal scar, "is where they had to rebuild my ACL using my patella tendon."

Annabelle looked up at him, realizing how close their hands were to touching, which shouldn't have sent her heart all aflutter. Especially after kissing, twice. But it did. With both their hands resting on his knee, his thumb just centimeters away from her palm, all she had to do was shift her fingers. Just a little and she could place her hand on his.

Instead, she focused on the other scar. The thing was long and gnarly, going from the top of his thigh and wrapping around to the bottom of his knee. "What about this one?"

"That's from both the ACL and MCL."

"You tore both of them?" She hadn't remembered hearing that bit. "Sounds pretty painful."

He shook his head, as though he couldn't believe it himself. "You can say that again."

"What kind of therapy did you do after your surgery?"

Blake leaned his head back on the bench, looking exhausted and tired of his own life. "After the first one, I had access to the best trainers in the NFL, so my therapy was pretty extensive."

"You had more than one surgery?"

"About a year after the first one, I had to have another to clean the joint up and drain fluid. But that was after I retired and my recovery was in my own hands, so I never really did anything about it."

Because he hadn't cared. The words didn't need to be said for Annabelle to understand them. Most people saw a man surrounded by scandal. Performance-enhancing drugs. Career-ending injury. Rumors of an affair with the team owner's wife. Annabelle dismissed that last one, already knowing Blake well enough to realize he had more integrity than to mess around with a married woman.

But the rest would have been enough to send anyone spiraling into depression and whatever other hell he'd been through. Beyond that, Blake was a broken man who'd been forced to give up a game he'd no doubt lived and breathed for. Not only that, but he was also in Blanco Valley coaching high school football, probably because he hadn't had any other career options.

Once again, she saw past the brash exterior, past the melt-you-into-a-puddle eyes to the human man underneath.

"So you never went to physical therapy after your second surgery?"

He gazed back at her beneath lowered lids. "The second surgery wasn't as invasive, so I didn't feel the need to," he told her. "And before you launch into a lecture, I realize now I should have."

She narrowed her eyes at him. "You think I lecture people?"

"I think you thrive on it," he answered with a smirk. "You should have been a teacher. Or a lawyer."

Annabelle answered his smile with one of her own. "That's what my mother used to tell me."

"So how'd you end up doing this?"

She removed her hand from his knee and rubbed her damp palm down her pants. "I like to help people."

"That's obvious," he agreed. "But there are a hundred different careers for that. Why physical therapy?"

Annabelle shook her head, not sure how to answer because no one had ever asked her that before. "I'm not sure. I guess because I don't like to see people in pain. I like to think I'm doing my part in helping them put themselves back together."

"Such a humanitarian," he muttered.

She snorted. "Hardly." She smacked his thigh. "Now quit stalling, and let's get to work." His pant leg was still pushed past his knee, revealing a long, strong leg. An athlete's leg, finely tuned and sculpted from years of training. A man's leg shouldn't turn her on, but Lord help her, Blake's did.

Worse than the tingling sensation in the pit of her stomach was imagining those legs on top of hers, pinning her to a soft mattress. Doing the horizontal mambo, as Stella liked to put it. Annabelle bet it would be good with Blake. He looked like a man who knew how to make use of his own body and who knew his way around a woman's. There was no greater turn-on, or emotional threat, than a man who could lick and touch his way from one end of a woman's body to the other.

Annabelle grabbed the hem of Blake's pant leg and started pulling it down, covering up all that male perfection. Despite the knee that looked like it had been put together in Frankenstein's lab. Just as she edged the material past his scars, Blake's hand covered hers, forcing her gaze up to his.

"Thank you," he muttered.

His face was expressionless, but his eyes gave him away. They were deep and bottomless, reaching out to her and grabbing on to her heart.

"For what?" she asked with a whisper.

"For not judging." His hand lingered on hers and his thumb traced a torturous pattern over her knuckles, dipping in and out of the grooves. "Thank you for taking the time to actually ask."

"Because I care."

"You shouldn't," he warned.

She tilted her head to one side. "You're so hell-bent on making me think you're nothing but a jerk."

His thumb continued its journey. "You've seen firsthand how true that really is."

"That's not who you are, though. I think you've gotten so used to people thinking the worst of you that you expect it from everyone."

"Maybe I want people to think the worst of me," he countered.

Her brows flew up her forehead. "Why would you want anyone to think that?"

He paused before answering, watching their joined hands resting on his knee. His scarred and broken knee. Just like the man. "Because they won't be as disappointed when I let them down."

And there went the last of her heart. The last piece intact, just barely holding on, slipped away, leaving her exposed and vulnerable to Blake Carpenter.

"Sounds like the people in your life have unattainable standards," she reassured him, because, damn it, someone had to. Someone had to make him understand he didn't have to be superman all the time. That it was okay to be human and make mistakes and stumble when the burden became too much.

Blake's brow twitched, signaling a crack in the tough exterior he'd erected. Before she realized what he was doing, he dropped her hand, skimmed the back of his knuckles up her arm, curved over her shoulder, oh so slowly, and then wrapped around her neck. Sucking the breath right out of her lungs.

The man really did have magical hands.

With one gentle tug, he brought her closer so that she was leaning over him. To brace herself, she placed her hands on his chest, gathering the soft cotton of his T-shirt in her hands. Underneath, the curved muscles of his pecs were firm, dipping to a hard line and giving way to equally firm obliques.

He just lay there beneath her, relaxed as she'd ever seen. When she knew perfectly well he was anything but relaxed. The man probably never allowed himself to let go.

"You're dangerous, Annabelle," he whispered against her mouth.

"Me?" she said on a short laugh. "I told you I have trust issues, but you're making me rethink all of that."

"You must be easier than I thought," Blake responded with a ghost of a smile.

Her hand inched higher up his chest. "You think you're so charming, don't you?" she countered instead of indulging the almost kiss they were playing with.

"But it's working on you," he pointed out. "You want me."

Heck yeah, she did. But she couldn't act on it. She still wasn't convinced it would be anything more than a casual hook-up for him, and she wanted more than that. She wasn't sure she'd ever be able to walk away from him, especially with her heart intact.

"Lust is easy to overcome," she said. "It's the other stuff that gets in the way."

His thumb applied pressure to the sensitive spot just below her ear, and her eyes almost rolled out of her head. "You know all too well about that, don't you?"

"Unfortunately, yes."

"That's a shame," he murmured against her lips. "Because I bet we could set the sheets on fire."

The sheets? Probably an entire building.

His lips only got close enough to tease before he set her away from him. The barely-there contact left her burning and frustrated and…incomplete. Like a really good round of lovemaking ending just seconds before a climax could ripple through her system.

"Too bad you don't do casual," he told her, calm and cool as ever, as though she hadn't been seconds away from climbing all over his body.

TEN

Blake stood by his back door, clutching his coffee and eyeing the shaggy golden dog, the same one from Brandon's photo, in his backyard. Shredded screen door, torn up garden hose, and so many holes dug, his yard looked like Swiss cheese. The dog, with its long furry tail swishing back and forth fast enough to create a gale force wind, was panting, tongue hanging out, and then jumped all over the damn shredded screen door when he'd seen Blake enter the kitchen.

"Son of a bitch did it," he muttered to himself as he stared at the animal.

Blake set the coffee on the kitchen counter and took out his phone, snapped pictures of the door and the garden hose. Then he sent it to Brandon with the message, *Watch your back*.

The dog seemed to grin, as though sensing he was the subject of the messages.

"What're you so happy about?" he asked the dog through

the screen door. Which would need to be replaced. The dog barked, a high-pitched *yip* that echoed throughout the yard. The same dog that he'd told Brandon to absolutely not, under any circumstances, leave at his house. The thing had dirt on his nose and mud smeared halfway up his legs.

"You're proud of yourself, aren't you?"

The dog barked again and spun in a circle.

Blake's front door opened, then shut. He turned and spotted Cameron ambling down the front hall with long strides.

"Holy hell," his friend stated. "Are you running combat drills back here?"

Blake stepped aside so Cam could see the gift Brandon had left him.

Cam eyed the shredded screen door, then lowered his gaze to the dog, who was still standing and panting like a maniac. Then Cameron tossed his head back and laughed.

"Something funny?" Blake wanted to know.

"Ah, the dog," Cameron said after his laughter died down. "Brandon tried to pawn him off on me, but I told him no."

"*I* told him no," Blake shot back. "How the hell did you dodge this bullet?"

Cameron fixed his gaze on the mutt. "I told Brandon if he dumped this dog on me, I'd let everyone know he has a pair of Mighty Mouse underwear." He grinned at Blake, then tapped his index finger against his temple. "Dirty tactics, my friend. Can't be afraid to use them."

Blake shook his head. "Shit. What the hell do I know about owning a dog?"

Cameron slid the screen door open. "They just need some attention and exercise." The second Cam was on the deck, the dog was all over him. Jumping and smearing mud down Cam's jeans. Cam shoved a knee in the dog's chest. "Down," he ordered the animal. The dog sat and swished his tail back and forth on the muddy deck. Cameron got down on one knee and stroked behind the dog's ears. "What're you going to name him?"

"Nothing," Blake answered immediately. "I'm not keeping him."

Cam glanced at Blake over his shoulder. Both the dog's eyes dropped closed as Cam continued to massage his ears. "Yeah, you're keeping him."

Blake narrowed his eyes at his friend. "I beg your pardon?"

"You're really going to look this dog in the eyes and get rid of him? Even you're not that heartless."

"How do you know that?"

Cameron stood and held a hand out in front of the dog's face, but that didn't stop the animal from standing as well. Surprisingly, the animal didn't jump. Just looked up at Cam like he was a hero. "Because you know what it's like to be given up on." Cam snapped his fingers and pointed to the deck. "Sit," he ordered, and the dog lowered his hind legs. "Just show him who's the alpha and he'll do anything you say."

"Seriously," Blake told his friend. "You need to take this dog. I don't have time to take care of an animal."

Cameron snorted. "And I do?"

"Yeah, but you know more about dogs than me." He nodded toward the animal, who was still sitting and waiting for his next command. "See how he listens to you?"

"Only because I used a commanding voice," Cam told him. "He listens well, so you can train this dog to do pretty much anything."

Maybe Blake could train him to shit all over Brandon's backyard.

Cam accompanied him to the store to get dog food, chew toys, and a collar. Even if he didn't plan on keeping the dog, which he definitely wasn't, he still needed to get some basics. Might as well give the animal a name or he'd be tempted to call the dog "Son of a Bitch."

His mother had called as he'd been trying to wrestle the damn animal into his collar. The dog had kept trying to bite Blake's hand and had given him a good scrape when he'd finally fastened the damn thing around his thick neck. He'd managed to catch his mom on the third ring, and she mentioned some story she'd heard about Roger Staubach.

And so the dog was called Staubach. Because Blake had been frustrated and annoyed and couldn't make the effort to call the dog anything else.

Blake had learned a long time ago not to count his chickens before they hatched. So when the Bobcats won their second game against the Alamosa Maroons, Blake took the win in stride. They were off to a good start, but still a long way to making the play-offs.

But when Cameron strolled into his office two hours before their third game, Blake was grateful for his tempered optimism.

"Corey Brighton has been put on academic probation," Cameron announced. "He can't play tonight."

Blake tossed his pen down on his desk and shoved his baseball cap up his forehead. "Shit," he said to himself.

"The kid's in the weight room with Annabelle, but he doesn't know yet. I just found out a minute ago. We'll have to call in the backup."

Blake shook his head. "Jason's not good enough." Not that Corey was one of their more stellar players, but the second-string kid was worse. Blake leaned forward in his chair, feeling a headache starting in the back of his neck and slowly easing upward. "What if we switched some of the other players around?" he asked Cam. "Moved Riley

Houghton from special teams to Corey's spot and then pulled Gavin Winstead to cover Riley?"

Cameron rubbed a hand along his rough jaw, then slowly nodded. "Could work."

"You go find Riley and Gavin," Blake told his assistant coach. "I'll talk to Corey."

The two men stood, and Cameron gazed at Blake from across the desk. "So I heard the tantalizing Ms. Turner is working her magic on you," Cameron commented. Damn his friend and his stupid grin.

For a second Blake wanted to ask which magic Cameron was talking about. The medical kind or the kind that happened in the bedroom. Even though they technically hadn't made it that far yet, he was pretty sure they would.

Given the chemistry that exploded between them every time they were together, Blake knew in between some sheets was where they were headed.

"She's just helping me with my knee," Blake corrected his friend.

Cameron narrowed his eyes. "The woman's a walking centerfold, and that's all you're doing with her?" The guy shook his head and chuckled. "I think you've had one too many hits on the head, my friend."

Yeah, wasn't that the truth. And it wasn't like their lack of a physical relationship wasn't for lack of trying on Blake's part. He'd made it clear to Annabelle, on more than one occasion, that he was willing to do anything she was up for. Well, everything except a commitment. The fact that she still held herself back contradicted her assurance that she could do casual.

Funny how she had no problem lip-locking with him, but anything beyond that was too much for her. One way or the other, he'd get the woman to change her mind. He had enough experience with women to know he could drive her out of her mind without even touching her. Before the football season ended, he'd have her begging for it.

Hell, she was already begging for it; she just didn't want to admit it.

"Maybe I'm just taking my time," Blake countered.

Cameron's laugh grew. "When have you ever taken your time?"

Truth.

"Is it because she's not into you? Has the great Blake Carpenter finally met a woman who doesn't chase after him like a groupie?"

That, too, but he wasn't about to let his friend know he was right.

This time Cameron tossed his head back and laughed, the snarky son of a bitch. "I love it," he said, chuckling. "Annabelle won't rip her clothes off for you, and you can't stand that."

Blake came around his desk and barely resisted the urge to land a right hook across his friend's scruffy jaw. "Why don't you do the world a favor and go screw yourself?"

Cam's laughter faded to a wide grin, and he rubbed a hand over the middle of his chest, easing the ache from his laughter. "As much as I love myself, I'd rather have a woman for that."

Yeah, wouldn't they all?

Blake left his friend and made for the weight room to talk to Corey. After years playing football, Blake knew how it felt to be told you couldn't play. For someone who woke up every morning, looking forward to that moment when their cleats would sink into the soft turf of the field, it could be devastating. Having to stand on the sidelines, watching your teammates go for the win and not being able to do your part.

The loss was sort of like having an arm severed.

Nobody knew what that felt like more than Blake. The only difference for him was having it taken away for the rest of his life. One or two games he could handle. Anything more than that was like taking away his reason for living.

He found Corey with Annabelle.

She'd traded in her usual yoga pants for blue jeans. Worn, faded blue jeans with holes in the knee and a tear in the upper thigh. The worn thread exposed just enough for him to get a glimpse of pale skin. Creamy. Maybe a shade lighter than her legs because that part of her body didn't see the sun as much.

The thought had the muscle between his legs twitching.

He approached the two and ran his gaze over her thick brown hair, which was free from its high ponytail. The locks were shiny, reflecting the overhead fluorescent lighting of the room. The strands framed her face and accentuated her high cheekbones, and his hands itched to dive into the thickness.

When she averted her attention from Corey, she saw him, holding his gaze while she worked with the kid through some stretches.

"Hi."

Her soft voice got under his skin and crawled along his nerve endings like fire ants.

"Hey," he said in return.

Something flashed across her eyes, which were exceptionally green today. Blake got the feeling it had something to do with the almost-kiss he'd teased her with at her studio. Other than being a sadistic bastard, Blake had no clue why he'd done that. Because he wanted to show her what she was missing out on by holding herself back.

The sucky thing was, he was missing out too.

"Coach?" Corey asked. "Is everything all right?"

Blake shifted his attention to Annabelle. "Could you give us a minute?"

She nodded her understanding, even though he knew she'd hurtle a hundred questions at him later. "Sure."

Blake hooked his hands on his hips as she left. "Six-week progress reports came out today," he told the kid, not wasting time with beating around the bush.

A deep red colored Corey's cheeks, as though he knew what was coming. Most players did. "Your GPA's slipped," Blake said. "You've been put on academic probation."

Corey swung his legs over the bench and stood. "Coach, you've gotta let me play tonight. We're two and oh," he said as though Blake had forgotten. "You can't bench me now."

Damn if Blake didn't understand the desperation in Corey's voice.

"I have to. District rules," Blake said. "You don't maintain that GPA, you don't get to play."

Corey ran both his hands over his buzzed hair, no doubt trying to find a way around the rule. They both knew there wasn't one.

Blake laid a hand on the kid's shoulder, trying to find some way to reassure him. He knew there wasn't one, but he had to try. "Just focus on getting your grades up and we'll bring home the win. As soon as you get your GPA back up, I'll reinstate you."

Corey nodded and his shoulders slumped. "This sucks, Coach," he muttered.

"I know."

"I mean, there has to be something you can do, right? Can't you, like, overrule them?"

"Sorry, son. This is out of my hands."

Corey stood still for a moment, then lashed out and kicked the weight machine. Blake understood the kid's anger. When Blake had retired early from the NFL, he'd gone home and trashed his weight room, breaking mirrors, along with his treadmill, and tossed a fifty-pound weight through one of the windows. Then he'd taken his Porsche, torn out of the driveway, and ended up at a bar, where he'd picked up some woman whose name he couldn't even remember. The next morning she'd been gone from his bed by the time he'd woken up. Just as well because he'd been too drunk to remember the encounter anyway.

"I understand your anger, son," Blake told the kid. "But taking it out on school equipment won't do you any good." He placed a hand on the kid's tense shoulder. The muscles were practically vibrating. "Finish your stretches with Ms. Turner before the team meeting."

Corey nodded but didn't say anything.

Blake left him standing in the weight room feeling like he'd kicked a puppy. Every coach understood feeling responsible for their players, and Blake was no different. The team had become an extension of himself, and before he'd known it, winning had become more than proving to everyone that he could do it. That he wasn't down for the count.

These were good kids who loved the game and craved the taste of victory. Each time Blake looked in their eyes, he felt their pull over him, their pleading to do for them what other coaches couldn't. The district had discounted the Bobcats. Their losing streak was so long, they'd become a running joke.

If you want to keep your winning record, just play the Bobcats.

Blake would be damned if that tradition would continue. Not on his watch. He'd always been a winner and nothing had changed.

He found Annabelle outside in the hall, talking to a couple of rally girls who'd brought gifts and food for their players.

"Everything okay?" she asked when she stopped in front of him.

No, it wasn't okay. He should be focusing on tonight's game and all he could think about was Annabelle wearing his shirts.

"I had to bench Corey for his grades," he told her.

"Yikes," she replied. She looked over his shoulder, as though searching for the kid. "Poor Corey."

"Yeah, that's rough," he said.

She shifted her attention back to him, those bright green eyes of hers seeing way too much. "You feel for him, don't you?"

He gazed down at her, wondering how she did it. "I know what it's like to have the rug yanked out from under you."

"That's why you're good for them," she told him. "Because it's more than just a game to you."

He hadn't thought about it that way, but he supposed she was right.

"How's the knee?" she asked.

"Sore," he answered, giving his knee a few testing movements.

"That usually happens after your first session because we work on muscles you haven't been using. It'll get better."

Damn, why did she have to care so much? How did she know he'd be back for more? Was it a mere assumption or could she see through him as well as he could see through her?

If that was the case, he was screwed.

"So..." She dragged the word out, and then wiggled her brows. "I'm just waiting for you to say it."

He leaned against the wall, using the movement to crowd her. Behind him, his team was preparing for the game and he should be with them. But at that moment, the only place he wanted to be was as close to Annabelle Turner as possible.

"Say what?" he wanted to know. "How much you want to get in my pants?"

Her green eyes narrowed. "I should smack you for that."

One side of his mouth kicked up. "But you won't."

"Don't be so sure of yourself," she warned. "I was talking about you telling me how right I was."

His brow arched. "About?"

She leaned closer to him and whispered, "About me being able to help you."

He nodded. "Oh, that. Here I thought you wanted to talk about my hot body."

That had her chuckling, which danced over his skin as smoothly and delicately as her fingers. "Always so cocky. I don't know why I give you the time of day."

"Because you can't help yourself," he told her.

She bobbed her head from side to side. "Could be. I also meant what I said about wanting to help you. I don't want you to hurt anymore."

"I hurt all the time, Annabelle." And not just from his knee.

She leaned closer and cupped his cheek with her delicate, cool palm. Her skin was so much softer than his, smoothing over the rough stubble on his jaw. "Poor wounded football star."

"I'm not a star anymore," he corrected.

"You are to them," she argued, nodding her head toward the players. "Just remember that and you can't fail."

When he opened his mouth to argue, to tell her how wrong she was, she lowered her hand over his chest, right above his beating heart. Which thudded wildly like the thing was on crack cocaine. Hell, to him she was crack cocaine.

"I don't mean with winning games. I mean in here." She accentuated her words with a firm tap of her palm, matching the thumping of his heart. "You don't see how those kids look at you. You give them hope. In there"—she nodded toward the locker room—"you're not the washed up football player you think you are. They see a man who believes in them and has put more effort into this team than anyone else has. To them, they've already won."

Blake shook his head, not knowing how to process her words, thinking he didn't deserve them. For so long he'd listened to what the country said about him. Cheater. Liar. Fraud. Sticks and stones and all that.

"Annabelle," he said to her, his voice coming out gravelly. He lowered his forehead to hers, suddenly needing her strength and confidence.

She cupped both his cheeks in her palms. "You don't give yourself enough credit." Then she pressed her cool lips to his, lingered for a moment, but not nearly long enough.

Then she was gone. Sauntering down the hallway toward the field and leaving him wondering how she'd managed to make him feel alive and vulnerable and human. Something he hadn't felt in a long time.

He wasn't sure if he should pursue it—pursue her—or run in the other direction.

Annabelle opened her studio the next morning, steaming cup of coffee in her hand.

"Want to grab some coffee?" a deep voice said from behind her.

Startled, Annabelle spun around, barely managing to keep her drink from sloshing over the rim. There stood Blake, tall and imposing and so damn hot he was practically on fire. Which would match the fire burning in her loins at the moment.

"Never mind," he told her with a smirk. "I can see you already have some."

She wagged a finger at him. "You're not getting out of this." Then she gestured toward the exercise equipment. "Sit."

His lips twitched. "Yes, Mom."

She set her coffee down at the reception desk and admired his super-fine ass in this worn blue jeans. And, *damn*, the man filled out a pair of 501s like nobody's business. "Don't give me that tone," she chastised. "It was your idea to come here this morning."

He took a step closer, towering over her and filling her personal space with his heat and images of tangled limbs. "Just so I could do this." Then his arm wound around her waist and yanked her closer.

She jerked forward, unprepared for the feel of his hardness and the way his thighs cradled hers. "Blake," she murmured while bracing her hands against his chest, more to feel him than to gain her balance.

"Yeah," he whispered against her lips.

"What're you doing?"

His nose nuzzled hers. "If you haven't figured it out, then I'm doing it wrong."

Without thinking, because rational thought always abandoned her when he was around, her arms went around his neck. "Is this why you really wanted to come this morning?"

"I always knew you were perceptive," he said against her ear.

Her eyes dropped closed, because what else was she supposed to do when his fingers were creeping underneath the hem of her shirt? Or flicking his tongue over her earlobe?

"You don't need to schedule an appointment with me for this," she pointed out. "You could just..."

He drew back and looked at her. "Just... what? Just show

up at your house for a quickie? Or maybe grab you during practice and shove you in a utility closet? Because that would sound like something casual, which you say you don't do."

She blinked at him because he was right. Wasn't he? No, he was correct. She didn't want a casual fling, no matter how tempting it was with him. She'd lose her heart and he'd walk away, leaving her to pick up the pieces of another relationship.

On the other hand, this felt so damn right. Having him yank her into his arms like she belonged there. As though he couldn't stand to go another minute without touching her.

"You're right, I don't." She unwrapped herself from him reluctantly and stepped back. "So you can't be doing stuff like that anymore."

He crossed his arms over his chest. "Are you going to sit there and tell me you didn't like it?"

"That's exactly what I'm saying." Biggest lie ever.

He took a seat at the machine, bending his leg and readying himself for his exercises. "You ready?" he asked her with a glance at his watch. "I've got stuff to do today."

Speechless, because he always had that effect on her, Annabelle stood in the middle of the room and eyed his relaxed pose. Arms draped casually at his sides. Head leaned back. One side of his mouth curled in a smirk that made her panties want to spontaneously combust.

She ignored the flutters in her belly and approached the machine.

Yeah, the man was good. Too good. And yeah, a fling with him would be out of this world. But she had to control herself. For the sake of her heart, which had taken too many beatings in the past.

She cleared her throat as she reached his side and got a

whiff of the good stuff he always had on. She had no idea what he washed with or sprayed on his person but, damnation, it was good stuff. Probably called *orgasm in a bottle*.

She narrowed her eyes at him. "You're surprisingly upbeat considering the team's loss last night."

"I'd forgotten about that, so thanks for bringing it up."

She doubted that. "Are you okay?"

He shifted his good leg. "I had a good cry when I got home last night and ate a gallon of ice cream. Watched some *Steel Magnolias*, so I'm good to go this morning."

She lifted her eyes to the ceiling. "All right, you've made your point."

"Just wanted to make sure you realized you've mistaken me for a woman."

As if anyone could mistake Blake Carpenter for a woman. "You have way too much testosterone for that."

His gaze dipped down her front, leaving a fiery trail across her breasts, spearing through her midsection and spreading to her toes. "Here I was afraid you hadn't noticed."

They both knew that wasn't true.

"Let's get started," she instructed, and pushed him through three reps of ten leg extensions on the machine, giving him time to loosen his knee and warm it up. Amazingly, she avoided touching him, when her therapist instincts were to place a comforting and encouraging palm to his leg. But she knew, deep down, the touch would stem from more than comfort. It would be selfish because she'd only be doing it to feel him. To remind herself of how hard and powerful he really was.

Thirty minutes later they'd finished, with Blake slanting her a look as he climbed off the machine. "You're brutal," he told her.

The knowledge that she'd made the great and mighty Blake Carpenter break a sweat had her grinning. "That's why I'm so good." She offered him a bottle of water from the mini-fridge, which he accepted.

His gaze narrowed over the top of the bottle. "Is that what people tell you? If they were honest, they'd call you sadistic."

She leaned closer to him because, *damn,* he smelled good. "I just think you don't like being worked over by a girl."

His attention raked down her body as he took a slow chug of the water. "Girl, huh?"

"What else would you call me?"

He lowered the bottle and stared at her out of half-lowered lids. "You really want to know?"

Okay, bad question.

"Want to grab some lunch?" he asked, throwing her for a loop.

"I'd love to," she told him. "But my next appointment is in twenty minutes." The one morning she'd actually love to have a cancellation.

"Bummer," he stated with a glance at his watch. "I'm heading out of town until tomorrow. Thought I'd catch a minute with you before I left."

Look at him being all relationshipy and stuff. It was almost enough to play hooky with him.

Almost.

"Where are you headed?" she asked him. *Must* she sound like the needy girlfriend? Seriously annoying.

"Wouldn't you like to know?" He grinned.

Cocky bastard. And then he was out the door, leaving her to stare after him and wondering what the hell had just happened.

ELEVEN

The bottle of OxyContin he'd refilled on Friday sat on the kitchen counter, daring him to leave them alone. The one pill he'd popped yesterday before leaving on his overnight fishing trip with Brandon and Matt hadn't been enough. But he'd left the pills behind, in an attempt to do away with the temptation to take more. When he'd returned this morning, they'd still been sitting there. He'd only been home for a few hours, after catching diddly-squat on the lake, and he'd already picked the bottle up half a dozen times, only to set it back down. As Blake placed two cans of soda into a lunch sack, he tossed the bottle another look.

Just take me, they said. *You don't have to deal with the pain. I can make it go away.*

Sweat dampened his palms at the thought of skipping a day.

He turned to the fridge, forcing the desperate need from

his mind, and grabbed a paper sack full of fried chicken and a plastic container filled with sliced watermelon.

The clicking of nails on the tile floor sounded behind him, along with the rapid panting of a dog that had endless energy and was probably drooling all over the floor. Blake kicked the fridge door closed and eyed his uninvited guest.

"If you think I'm leaving you in this house all by yourself, you've got another think coming," he told the dog. Staubach tilted his head to one side, then lowered his rear end to the floor.

Probably waiting for a treat.

"All right, fine," he muttered, then dug around in the pantry for the bag of treats he'd picked up. When he'd gone to the pet store, he'd only planned on buying essentials. Food, bowls, and a collar. But then he'd strolled past the toy section and thought, what the hell. Dogs needed toys, didn't they? And they liked treats and bones. So he'd ended up grabbing a bag of rawhides, biscuits, and half a dozen plush toys. Two hundred dollars later, here he was tossing a dog treat to an animal he hadn't planned for or wanted.

"I ought to dump you back at my bastard cousin's house," Blake told Staubach as the dog inhaled his treat, then wagged his tail, as though waiting for more. "That's all you're getting."

The dog stood and nudged Blake's thigh, wagging his tail so hard, his entire body wagged back and forth along with it.

Okay, yeah. The dog was kind of cute. And fun to play with. Last night they'd played tug-of-war with one of those rope things. Blake had admitted defeat when Staubach had started grunting and thrashing his head back and forth. After letting go of the rope, for fear Blake would have his shoulder dislocated, Staubach had settled on the carpet and gnawed on the rope for half an hour.

Blake walked around the dog and finished packing his lunch. He ought to be watching game film and studying how they'd managed to eff up their last game. Instead he was packing an impromptu lunch for a woman he should be staying away from. Not only should he stay away from her, but she also wasn't even aware of his plans. Going by the seat of his pants had never been this thing. Blake was a planner and thought carefully before each move he made. So when he'd decided to detour from his original plan and starting throwing together food, he'd surprised himself.

Look at him, being all spontaneous.

Funny because spontaneity had never been his thing.

He took all the food and drinks from the counter and stored them together in a bigger bag. Grabbing his keys from the counter, Blake turned to leave. But not before laying eyes on the Oxy one last time.

You need me, they taunted.

It had been about twenty-four hours since he'd taken his last pill. As he'd driven home from the fishing trip that morning, all Blake could think about was snagging the pills and dumping all the contents down this throat. But when he'd gotten home, his self-preservation had won out. He'd stared at the bottle for several seconds before abandoning them and heading for the shower. Except his hands had shaken through the entire thing. They'd trembled as he'd washed his hair and trembled as he'd stood there, head tilted up toward the spray of water. After he'd hastily rubbed a towel over his body, his skin was heated. And he knew it had nothing to do with the temperature of the water.

The lunch bag was clutched tight in one hand, truck keys in the other as Blake stared at the bottle. His back teeth ground together as the pull they had over him intensified.

For however much he told himself he needed the solace

they gave him, even if temporary, Blake would be damned if he'd become another statistic of pain pill addicts. So he turned his back on them, curses flying through his mind, and let Staubach through the newly replaced back door before striding out of the house.

The early afternoon was clear and breezy, perfect lake weather.

Vallecito Lake was a mountain oasis nestled among snowy peaks and flanked by aspens. The resort had just about everything to offer, from fine dining to campgrounds. Blake had spent his fair share there as a kid with his parents and Brandon.

He started the truck and cruised through the neighborhood, toward Annabelle's house. He couldn't help the smile as he exited his truck and walked to her front door.

He gave the solid wood front door a brisk knock and grinned at the sound of her footsteps. Even the way she walked was precise and measured. Controlled, just like everything else she did. Except when she was around him.

But when he got an eyeful of her, the smile slipped. Denim cutoffs, ripped at the knee, left her beautifully toned calves bare, along with gold toenails, slipped into a pair of flip-flops. A snug tank top revealed pale shoulders with a light dusting of freckles and gave the perfect impression of high, full breasts.

"Blake." She blinked at him. Her gaze dipped down his body, in response to his own admiration of her. "What're you doing here?"

He leaned against the doorjamb, only to inch his way closer to her. "I was on my way to the lake and wondered if you'd like to join me." Props to him for making it sound like her invitation had been a last-minute thing. As though he hadn't woken up that morning, in a freezing cold tent, conjuring a way to spend more time with her. At least time that didn't involve a locker room full of sweaty high school kids or a football field.

"Right now?" she asked.

"Yeah." He jerked a thumb over his shoulder. "I've got some food in my truck and wanted to get out for a few hours."

She brushed a chunk of hair over her shoulder, which was pulled back from her face with a scarf thing tied into a knot at the top of her head. "I thought you were away for the weekend."

"I came back this morning," he answered.

Annabelle glanced over her shoulder, then back at him. "I was actually getting some food put together to take over to my mom. I'd love to go, if you wouldn't mind running me over there first."

"Of course," he told her, trying to squash down the satisfaction at her acceptance. He pushed away from the door frame. "I'd like to meet your mother anyway."

Annabelle rolled her eyes away from him. "Don't get ahead of yourself. My mother's not the typical nice little old lady you'd think. And," she continued as her attention skittered over him, "she's not as enamored with charm as—"

"As you are?" he finished for her, knowing instinctively that's what she was about to say.

"Actually, I was going to say, as you'd think she'd be." She tilted her head. "But you can go with that other one if you'd like."

Yeah, he'd like. He also knew she was full of it.

She turned from the door, knowing he'd follow her in. "Let me just get a few things together first."

"Need a hand?" he automatically offered.

She led him into the kitchen, where she had three

casserole dishes on the counter. "No, I got it." She offered him a smile while removing pots from the stove and setting them in the sink. "I'll just be a minute." Then she disappeared through the door and left him standing there.

While he waited, he poured some dish soap on the sponge and went to work on the first pot. She must have been cooking the entire morning, given how many dishes she'd dirtied, not to mention the state of the stove top and counters. Is this what she did with her free time? Cooked food for her mother and whatever other chores were required? When did the woman take time for herself?

A vacation? A boyfriend?

That last thought sent a surge of irritation through his system, and he sloshed water over the edge of the sink. Blake cursed himself for being so...

Well, just being an ass.

So what if she were to have a boyfriend? Or even have a man take her out, indulge her in an expensive meal or buy her something nice?

Seems as though she deserved that kind of attention, given how much of herself she gave to everyone else.

And you want to be that man.

Except he didn't do relationships.

And Annabelle was better than a quick and meaningless screw.

When he'd first met Annabelle, that's all he'd wanted from her. As he got to know her better, that had changed. And the change had been so subtle that he hadn't realized his priorities had shifted until now. Until he'd seen her standing at the front door, in the middle of making food for her ailing mother, Blake hadn't realized he no longer wanted to get in the woman's pants.

At least not in the way he used to. He'd be lying if he

said he was no longer interested in some more intimacy with the woman. And that was just it. He wanted real intimacy. Something that went beyond a quick orgasm and an even quicker good-bye.

Blake finished his second pot and placed it in the drying rack. He reached for a frying pan and went to work on it.

"What're you doing?"

Her soft voice pulled Blake out of his startling thoughts. He glanced at her over his shoulder as he placed the pan he'd been vigorously scrubbing on the drying rack.

"Just thought I'd put myself to use," he told her. He swiped the dishrag off the counter and dried his hands.

"You didn't need to do that."

"I know I didn't," he replied, and set the towel down. "Just like you know you don't need to take care of your mother. But you do it anyway."

She opened her mouth to argue, then shut it. "I'm not as helpless as my mother is," she pointed out.

He leaned against the counter and braced his hands behind him. "I don't think she's that helpless, Annabelle. I think you just like being needed." He came toward her and wrapped his hands around her upper arms. "You don't do things for people just because they can't do for themselves. Sometimes it's just nice to do something for someone."

"That's awfully deep for washing some dishes," she whispered.

"Funny how you bring that out in me," he told her, then released her. Turning toward the counter, he stacked the foil-covered casserole dishes on top of each other. "Ready?" he asked.

She blinked at him, as though she had more she wanted to say to him. Lord knew, the woman always had an argument ready. As though she kept them on index cards, categorized by situation so she was always ready.

Wouldn't surprise him.

"Yeah," she answered. "But don't think doing my dishes is going to butter me up." She pointed a finger at him. "I'm still not having a fling with you."

He grinned at her backside, loving how her cheeks reddened whenever he riled her up. And loving how her ass moved in those cutoffs.

"Be careful, Ms. Turner," he warned her as he followed her to the front door. "I think we might already be there."

When they arrived at Annabelle's mother's house, Blake expected an unkempt yard. Not because Mrs. Turner didn't care. Because she was older and couldn't even make her own food, much less plant flowers and mow grass. But the grass was green, neatly trimmed, and bordered the house with flowers. Apparently Annabelle took care of the yard work too.

As he parked the truck, she glanced at him. "Before you say anything, no, I don't cut my mother's grass," she told him, as though reading his thoughts. "She has a gardening service that comes once a week."

"I didn't say anything."

One of her sculpted brows arched. "You didn't have to. I knew what you were thinking."

Had they arrived at that point already? Where they could read each other's looks and tone of voice? The reality of it sent a surge of uncertainty through his veins.

They exited the truck and Blake carried the casserole dishes, following Annabelle to the front door. As they made their way up the walk, Annabelle eyed a nondescript dark sedan parked in the driveway. Not only parked, but parked badly. The vehicle was crooked and just shy of kissing the closed garage door.

"Thought your mom didn't drive?" Blake wondered.

Annabelle stared at the car. "She doesn't. And that's not my mom's car."

Blake slid the woman a look. "Maybe she has a secret boyfriend."

She elbowed him in the ribs and he thought he heard her mutter, "Yeah right."

So Mrs. Turner didn't date either. Must be a family trait.

Annabelle opened the front door without bothering to knock and held it open for him. The gesture rubbed every chivalrous bone in his body wrong, but since his hands were full of three casserole dishes, he let it slide.

"Not used to that, are you?" she whispered to him as he brushed past her.

Shit, there she went again. Knowing what he was thinking with nothing more than a simple look.

"Just don't make it a habit," he told her, and followed her down the hallway.

"Mom?" she called out. "I came to drop by some food."

A high-pitched yapping and the scurrying of nails on the hardwood floor greeted them halfway down the hallway. A black and white dog that looked like a mix of a giant Chihuahua and a bulldog stopped in front of Annabelle and barked its little head off. Annabelle ignored the thing and kept walking.

When the animal realized it wasn't going to get its desired attention from her, it moved on to Blake, exhibiting the same obnoxious yipping and jumping up and down on its short little legs.

"Just ignore the heathen," Annabelle told him.

Blake eyed the dog, who kept up his constant *yap yap yap*. "What the hell kind of dog is this?"

Annabelle glanced at him, and tossed a death-ray stare at the little animal. "He's a Boston terrier, but he thinks he's a pit bull and has the attitude of a princess." She stopped and lifted her foot, literally sliding the dog across the floor, who barked the entire time. "Just shove him aside." Annabelle lowered her foot, and the dog ran back toward her, jumping on her leg. "Annoying little shit," she muttered.

A television was on in the distance, as well as talking. Two females, conversing back and forth, riddled with laughter. Annabelle paused in front of him, so abruptly that he almost plowed into her.

"Unless you want spaghetti all over your back, give a guy some warning," he told her.

But she didn't hear him. The tense set of her shoulders told him she'd gone somewhere else, a place she wasn't comfortable with, and for a second, Blake thought she was going to turn around and bail on the whole thing.

He underestimated her, because she squared her shoulders and pushed forward. Just like she did everything else.

The woman had a backbone of steel; he'd give her that.

He walked behind her, until she came to an abrupt stop just inside the kitchen. The space was small and about two decades old, but that wasn't what caught Blake's attention. And it wasn't even the elderly woman, leaning heavily on a wooden cane, with the same dark hair as Annabelle, sprinkled with gray and severe-looking glasses perched on the edge of her nose.

It was the younger version of Annabelle, the woman she'd identified as her sister in the wall of photos, standing at the counter in a floor-length cotton dress and long wavy hair hanging halfway down her back.

"Naomi," Annabelle said with an unmistakable note of surprise in her voice.

The younger woman dropped the wooden spoon she'd been using to mix something in a bowl and flew across the kitchen. "Tansie!" she exclaimed, and threw her arms around Annabelle's shoulders, embracing her in a fierce hug.

Of course Annabelle returned the gesture, but the motions weren't as loose or uninhibited as her sister's. The stiffness in Annabelle's shoulders had returned and she dropped her arms before Naomi was ready to let go.

Blake set the casseroles on the counter.

"What're you doing here?" Annabelle asked her sister.

"I flew in this morning," Naomi answered, then glanced back at her mother. "I wanted to surprise you two."

A broad smile graced Mrs. Turner's features as she gazed at her youngest daughter.

"It certainly is a surprise," Annabelle said. "How long have you been over here?"

Naomi moved a shoulder in a loose gesture. "I don't know. A few hours I guess. I just started making a batch of cookies. Want to help?"

"Why didn't either one of you call me?"

Mrs. Turner averted her gaze, but Naomi chimed in. "I wanted to visit with Mom first, and then I got the hankering for some pecan chocolate chip cookies."

"Mom can't eat pecans. They mess up her digestive system."

"Oh." Naomi glanced at the bowl and then at her mom. "I guess I'll have to eat them all, then." And then Annabelle's younger sister turned her inquisitive gaze on Blake, running her green eyes all over his body. "Are you my sister's boyfriend?"

Blake glanced from Naomi, who was still eyeing him like he was a piece of prime steak, to Annabelle, who'd yet to take her attention off her younger sister. "Uh..."

"What's the matter, boy?" Mrs. Turner chimed in. "My daughter not good enough for you?"

"Mother," Annabelle groaned.

"Well, I'd kind of like to know too," Naomi added. "I'd also like to know why my sister isn't boning a man who looks like sex on a stick."

"Naomi, please," her mother chided.

"How do you know she's not?" Blake countered.

"Because if she was, she wouldn't be standing there looking like she has a stick up her ass."

"Can we please refrain from the third degree about Annabelle's life for five minutes? Thanks." Annabelle walked to her mother and offered her a kiss on the cheek. "Did you take your pills?" she asked her mom, who nodded.

"Geez, Tansie, take a chill pill already," Naomi muttered.

Annabelle ignored her sister. "We brought you some dinners," she told her mother, then she took the top casserole and placed it in the fridge. Blake picked up the other two, handed them to her, and brushed his index finger over her hand. The woman was about to shatter, and the comforting gesture was the least he could do.

She offered him a smile. And not the same tight smile she showed her sister. This one was genuine, if not a little small, and it was all he could do to keep from pulling her into the tight circle of his arms.

"I've already got dinner for tonight covered," Naomi said.

Annabelle turned from Blake and stared into the fridge before closing the door. "Who bought this milk?"

Naomi glanced over her shoulder from the cookie mix she was working on. "I did. I saw Mom didn't have any, so I ran out and got some."

Annabelle shut the fridge door. "But Mom can't drink regular milk. You have to buy the lactose-free stuff."

"Since when?" Naomi asked; then she looked at her mother. "Why can't you have milk?"

"Because it makes me sick," her mother answered.

"Mom stopped eating dairy two years ago, Naomi," Annabelle told her sister.

Naomi blinked and held the wooden spoon suspended over the bowl. "You seriously can't have any dairy at all?" she asked her mom.

"Not unless I take those lactose pills, which I can't all the time because they're expensive."

"What're you making her for dinner?" Annabelle asked.

Naomi dropped the spoon in the bowl and turned to face her sister. "What's with the attitude?"

"I just want to make sure you're not making anything that's going to make her sick. She can't eat like she used to and you don't know what she likes."

"I think I know what my own mother likes to eat," Naomi shot back.

Annabelle opened the fridge door and pointed to the gallon of vitamin D milk. "Obviously not."

"What's your problem?" Naomi demanded.

"Both of you hush!" Mrs. Turner shouted with all the force her elderly vocal cords would allow. Both girls snapped their mouths shut, immediately responding to their mother's authority. "Annabelle, it's just a beef stew. Now both of you say you're sorry," she told the girls. "You're sisters, for crying out loud."

"Sorry," Annabelle muttered.

Naomi crossed her arms over her chest and stared at the kitchen floor. "I'm sorry too."

"You ought to be ashamed of yourselves, acting like a couple of children. And in front of Mr. Carpenter too. Yes, I know who he is," Mrs. Turner told Annabelle when she lifted a surprised glance at her mother. "I don't care whether or not you're boning him." She tossed a pointed look at her younger daughter.

"Nobody's boning anybody," Annabelle said firmly.

"Maybe you should," Naomi butted in. "If you're going to do it with someone, it might as well be him."

"How do you know he's not already involved with someone else?" Annabelle asked.

"Are you?" Naomi asked him.

Blake didn't want to be dragged into their weird conversation that kept alternating between boning him and food allergies. "No, ma'am, I'm not."

"Okay." Annabelle grabbed his hand, which trembled slightly under her touch. "We're leaving now."

"I just got here and now you're leaving?" Naomi wanted to know. "We've had all of ten minutes together."

"Seeing as though they weren't very pleasant ten minutes, I'd like to go now." She stopped in the act of pulling him through the front door. "And I already had plans," she stated. "If I had known ahead of time that you'd be here, I could have cleared my afternoon."

He laid his hand on her lower back for reassurance and ushered her out of the kitchen. And away from the gaping faces of her mother and younger sister.

TWELVE

"Why does your sister call you Tansie?" Blake asked after they'd arrived at the lake and spread a blanket on the beach. They'd munched on the food he'd packed in comfortable silence for a few minutes. The fried chicken was good. Greasy and crunchy, just the way Annabelle liked it.

The breeze kept playing with her hair, blowing it across her cheek. The refreshing air felt good, cooling her heated skin, but not quite blowing away the shame for how she'd treated her sister. "When Naomi was little, she couldn't say my name right. She used to say Tansabelle, which eventually got shortened to Tansie." Annabelle cradled a can of soda in her palms and let out a deep sigh. "I'm sorry you had to see all that back there."

Blake glanced at her profile. "What're you talking about?"

"The way I acted with my sister. I was cranky and out of line with her." She stared at the top of the can, trying to force the image of the confusion and hurt in Naomi's eyes. "I mean, I haven't seen her in two years and all I could think about was how wrong she was doing everything. I gave her a hard time about milk, for Pete's sake." Annabelle shook her head, wondering what the heck was wrong with her. "The thing is, if she'd been around more, she'd know my mom is allergic to dairy."

Blake lifted a hand and brushed a strand of hair off her face. The backs of his fingers were warm and rough and sent a chill back into her hairline. All she wanted to do was lean into his palm and not talk about her sister. Not talk about what a jerk she'd been or wonder why she'd acted that way in the first place.

"You're being too hard on yourself," he told her. "We all drop in maturity level around our siblings."

She gazed back at him. "Aren't you an only child?"

"Yeah, but my cousin Brandon came to live with us when he was little, so he's as good as my brother. When he and I get around each other, everything becomes a competition."

"What happened to his parents?"

Blake bit into a chicken strip. "They were killed in a car accident while he was staying the night at my house. Our mothers were sisters, so when his parents died, my mom and dad became his legal guardians."

"That must have been awful for him. How old was he?"

"Six. Brandon doesn't have much memory of his parents," Blake told her.

Annabelle watched him, thinking how handsome he was with the sun glancing off his strong features and highlighting his straight nose. "You two seem like you're really close."

He looked at her. "The guy's my best friend."

"I thought Cameron was your best friend."

He nodded. "We're all a package deal."

She gazed out over the lake, loving the way the sunset glanced over the ripples of the water's surface. "I shouldn't have treated Naomi that way," she whispered, hating herself for allowing her resentment for her sister to claw its way out. Not only that, but also her need for perfection had turned her into a domineering know-it-all who snapped at her own sister over pecans and milk.

"I'm sure your sister knows you love her," he tried to reassure her.

Annabelle shook her head. "See, I've never been good at the 'I love you' thing. We never really said it in our house growing up. Except for my mom, who always tells us she loves us."

"Are you trying to tell me there's something you're actually not good at?" he asked her with a smirk.

There are a lot of things I'm not good at. She forced the thought from her mind and glanced at him, caught his infectious grin with one of her own. "I think you have a skewed image of me, Blake Carpenter."

He pinched her chin. "I like the way you say both of my names. Makes me sound like I'm in trouble."

"You say that as though you like being in trouble," she commented.

He leaned closer and raised a brow. "Only if you're going to discipline me."

Her mouth widened into a smile. Damn if this man didn't have a way of coaxing grins out of her. And he didn't have to even try. "You have a sick mind."

He heaved out a sigh. "If you really knew what went on in my head, you'd probably run the other direction."

She watched him watching the water, wondering if that were true. There was no telling what sort of things he kept hidden from the rest of the world. The thing was, Annabelle wasn't sure she'd turn the other way. On the contrary, she wanted to help him. To ease the lines of stress and worry bracketing that beautiful mouth of his.

As the thought crossed her mind, she lowered her attention to his lips, remembering all too well how they felt against hers. How the man threw all his energy into kissing, making her wonder how he'd be in the bedroom. It was a dangerous thought, because she wasn't sure how much longer she could keep holding back.

"If you don't stop that, Annabelle, I'm going to give you what you're asking for," Blake warned in that gruff, low voice of his. A bedroom voice. Made for whispering and teasing and tickling the sensitive skin below her ear.

A shiver ran through her body, and it wasn't from the cool breeze.

"Do you miss it?" she asked, trying to regain control of the conversation.

"What, kissing you?" he asked.

"I meant football," she corrected as heat burned her cheeks. But, yeah, the kissing too.

"Are you sure?" he pressed, touching a finger to the warmth of her face.

"If I say no, what will you do?"

His face inched closer to hers. "Whatever you want, Annabelle. Remember, you're the one who's keeping this platonic."

His spicy, and so very male, scent washed over her. "*Platonic* isn't the word I'd use."

"You're right, it's not. I was just trying to find a respectful way of putting it. And, yeah," he went on, "I do miss football."

Annabelle set the can of soda on the blanket next to her

and drew her knees up, wrapping her arms around them. "If you hadn't been injured, would you still be playing?" When he didn't answer, she pressed. "I know you didn't want to talk about it before, but you can tell me. I mean, if it's something you want to get off your chest. I can just sit here and listen."

Blake stared over the water for a moment, as though debating whether to share with her before answering. "It's not something I like to talk about."

Boy, did she understand that feeling. Her divorce was something she kept under lock and key. Luckily, Blake hadn't pressed for details about it. However, Annabelle suspected that had more to do with him biding his time rather than a lack of interest.

"I don't know whether I'd still be playing," he surprised her by answering. "If I had to guess, I'd say probably not. Not with the issues with my knee." He placed his attention on her. "You know, you're the only one who does that."

"Does what?"

"You don't tiptoe around me. Most people act like my retirement is a disease they can't mention. I can tell they want to, but they hold back and it becomes like an elephant in the room."

Annabelle could understand that way of thinking. It was a natural assumption to think his past would be too hard to talk about, so they left well enough alone. Probably thinking they were doing Blake a favor. The thing was, Annabelle wasn't that kind of person.

"That's silly," she told him.

Blake shrugged as though it didn't matter to him, when she knew better. "It is what it is."

"You have no idea the kind of shady shit NFL docs will put in a player's system to get them well. Sometimes it's at the urging of the coaches; sometimes it's the player's decision."

"So what was it in your case?"

Blake leaned back on his hands. "The first time I messed up my knee, I told the doc to do whatever he needed to get me back on the field." He looked at her. "The first time I tested positive, I knew it was from whatever they'd been injecting me with, so I told them not to give it to me again."

"But they did," she guessed.

"I kept reinjuring my knee and the doctor kept insisting the drugs were FDA approved and he gave them to all the players. I did it at the coaches' urging and trusted them."

"So what happened the second time?" she asked.

Blake took a deep breath. He'd never really told this to anyone before because he'd been ashamed. Even though retirement, he knew, had been the right thing to do. Still, he'd felt at fault. Responsible, because weren't people responsible for their own actions?

"My coach informed me the test would likely come back as positive."

"That's when you knew, didn't you?"

He tossed her a look. "That they'd screwed me over again? Yeah, you could say that."

"So how could they allow the doctors to keep injecting you with that stuff if they knew it was illegal?"

He shrugged his shoulders, which only accentuated their bulk beneath the T-shirt he had on. "They needed me on the field. It was a chance they were willing to take."

"And what about you?" she asked. "Wouldn't have you been suspicious?"

He paused before answering. "Of course I was. But I trusted them enough not to do it again, but they did."

"That's why you retired?"

"Yeah," he answered without hesitation. "There was no way I could keep playing after a second test came back positive. I knew no other team would touch me. Retirement was the only option."

She blinked at him. "So you would rather have been forced into an early retirement from a game you lived and breathed rather than tell on your coaches and teammates?"

"You don't sell out teammates, Annabelle. And I wasn't forced. My retirement was my choice."

"But that's not the only reason, is it?" When he only stared back at her, she continued. "You didn't want to put your teammates, who I'm guessing were probably also your friends, through the same hell you'd been through. So you sacrificed your own future."

He sat very still, casually leaning back on those well-defined sleekly carved arms as though he didn't have a care in the world. Just a lazy afternoon at the beach, enjoying the late Colorado sun. But Annabelle knew better, because his eyes gave him away. They always did. He may have been able to joke and play his way around his hurt, but his eyes betrayed him.

"Don't make it sound like a Shakespearian tragedy, Annabelle. I'm no hero."

"Oh, that's right. Because you're nothing more than a disgraced ex-football player whose only gig was coaching high school football," she told him. "Is that right?"

"You don't miss anything, do you?"

She shook her head and turned away from him, wanting to strangle him for refusing to see what a good guy he was and for not being able to let go of his demons.

The accusations had to hurt. Living day in and day out, knowing he'd been put in an unfair position, paying the ultimate price, and listening to unthinkable things said about him. The thought that that's what he'd reduced himself to, that he believed all the trash talk, made Annabelle's heart hurt. When anyone could see he was more than rumors and scandal and gossip.

"You really believe what they say, don't you?" she asked him.

The question must have thrown him by surprise, because his brow lowered.

"You think you're damaged goods and that's why you keep people away."

"You think I keep people away?" he asked with a slight tilt of his head.

"How many relationships have you been in since you retired?"

"Depends on your idea of a relationship. Which we've already established is different than mine."

Okay, he had her on that one. So he might have had some casual flings, or whatever his dating life had looked like. Frankly, Annabelle didn't want to think about it and she wanted to smack herself upside the head for even asking in the first place.

"Because you only do casual, right?"

One side of his mouth quirked in that sexy way of his. The man could reduce her to a puddle with a simple tilt of his mouth. "Exactly. Casual is more fun anyway."

"Except that's not why you refuse to commit yourself," she pushed. Now that she knew his bark was much worse than his bite, Annabelle thrived in pushing him. Besides that, she had the feeling not many people in his life had pressed for more beyond what he showed them. People in his life had accepted him at face value, and that was probably the way he wanted it.

Not Annabelle.

"I'll just bet you have a different theory," he said, as though he were enjoying the conversation. As though he were humoring her. Well, she refused to give him the satisfaction.

And heck yeah she had a different theory. And heck yeah she was going to tell him. Someone needed to kick him out of his rut of self-contempt.

"You hold yourself back because you don't think you have anything to offer. You don't think you're worthy enough for anyone to get attached to you." She ought to tell him it was too late for that. She was already attached to him.

"Yet you can't seem to stay away from me," he pointed out, as though her theory was flawed.

"Because I don't see you that way."

"How do you see me, Annabelle?" he asked softly.

She got to her knees and, without thinking about what she was doing, swung one leg over his stretched out ones and straddled his thighs. They were rock hard beneath her. He didn't move a muscle, besides the clenching of his jaw. Maybe some desire flashing through his blue eyes. Oh yeah, she could have him. All she had to do was give him the signal and he'd take her to bed.

A part of her, a huge part that was getting harder to keep in check, wanted that more than she wanted her next breath. But that would be too easy. She wanted, and needed, to prove to him that he was capable of doing more.

He continued leaning back on his hands, watching her beneath heavy lids, his chest rising and falling with each steady breath he took. The slow movement contradicted her own uneven breaths.

Maybe crawling on top of him had been a bad idea.

"You really want to know what I see when I look at you?"

"You're going to tell me regardless," he countered.

Yeah, she would. But she wanted to give him the chance to back away. The fact that he didn't told her he cared more than he'd admitted thus far.

"I see a man who's put up with me, and even humored me at times, even though he didn't want to. I see someone who's put more effort into those kids than any other coach has, including spending his after-hours time with the ones who need it. I see someone who took in a stray dog, takes care of it and has probably already fallen in love with the thing." She leaned closer to him, bracing her hands on the sand next to his hips. "I see a man who put the future of his teammates above his own. Giving up the game you love rather than taking some stupid cop-out deal that would have dragged everyone else down with you." Annabelle paused, giving him a chance to deny it, to tell her how wrong she was and prove he really was the villainous person everyone said.

But he didn't. He just watched her with those cool eyes of his, giving away nothing. Except for the hard set of his mouth and the clenching muscles in his jaw. Yeah, she'd hit a nerve. She'd scratched him raw and would continue to do so until he stopped being such a pig-headed moron.

"Are you really going to keep telling me you're not a hero? Because I don't believe that for a second."

Slowly he pushed forward, placing his hands on her hips. His grip was easy but firm, holding her tight enough so that she couldn't move. Not that she would anyway, because it felt too good. He felt too good beneath her. His thighs cradled her hips perfectly, and she had to squash the instinctive feeling to wiggle her bottom.

"You know what I think, Ms. Turner?" he asked in a rough whisper.

His lips were inches away from hers so their breath mingled together. So close that her mouth tingled, just dying for him to kiss her again.

"I already know what you think, Blake," she whispered back. Her hands had found their way to his shoulders and her fingers dug into the steely flesh of his back. The muscles were bunched and tense and well defined.

"I think you're too meddlesome for your own good." With one good tug, the fingers on her hips tightened and he yanked her closer. "I think you need to mind your own business."

She was sure the bite in his words was meant to frighten her away.

"Maybe I don't want to mind my own business," she argued against his mouth.

He removed one of his hands from her hips and slid it around her neck to cradle the back of her head. They fit nicely together there too. His palm was just big enough to curve over the back of her skull, with this thumb pressed on the pressure point just beneath her ear.

"Blake." His name slipped out in response to the caress his thumb was giving the sensitive skin behind her ear. A tingle zipped down her spin and stole the breath from her lungs. Her eyes dropped closed before she could really help it. The response was as automatic as the uneven beating of her heart.

Then his lips made contact with hers. Just a simple and brief touch, but enough for fireworks to explode inside her midsection.

When he pulled back slightly, she said, "You're doing this just to shut me up," she accused.

"Since when does anything shut you up, Annabelle?"

Yeah, he had a point with that one.

Sneaky bastard.

He had her right where he wanted her. In his arms, trembling and aching and burning up so much she didn't know which way was up. When he finally gave her what she was craving, by sealing his lips over hers, Annabelle was too far gone.

Too far gone to care they were in a public place. Too far gone to care that they'd slid right into that casual/fling or whatever they had. She ought to be offended and feel manipulated by him. But the thing was, he hadn't done very much to manipulate her. Just a few kisses was all it took to discard her relationship-only rule.

It's more than kisses, Annabelle.

As Blake swirled his tongue around hers, Annabelle knew she was right. The spell he had over her had been cast with more than kisses and touches. It was the man. The flesh and blood wounded warrior who'd opened himself up was what had her inching closer and closer each time they were together. Without realizing what had happened, he'd captured her heart. Stolen it right out from under her nose and held it in those capable, strong hands of his.

Annabelle scooted closer to him, so their torsos were pressed together, her breasts against his hard chest. The contrast between their bodies, his so much harder and bigger than hers, sent a chill of awareness through her.

Blake deepened the kiss, angling his head in just the right way so he could suck her gasp into his mouth and swallow it as his own.

Lord have mercy, the man knew how to kiss. Annabelle had never been so thoroughly devoured and claimed. She knew, as the two of them sat in the middle of a public beach, practically climbing all over each other, that's what he was doing. He was claiming her, regardless of whether or not this—whatever they had—

went beyond what she allowed it to. Blake was too much of a gentleman to force anything on her.

The hand on the back of her head tightened, holding her closer to him, and she threaded her fingers through his hair, loving that he'd left his usual baseball cap off. His hair was soft and just long enough to give a gentle tug.

Their tongues danced around each other one more time before Blake pulled back. They were both breathing heavily, their nostrils flared, lips moist and heartbeats matching in rapid rhythm.

"Still think I'm a hero?" he asked.

He was trying to shock her away, but it wouldn't work. She brushed her thumb along his lower lip. "I don't care how much you try to push me away, Blake. I'm too stubborn for that."

He laughed, which sounded more weary than full of humor, and lowered his forehead to hers. "I already know how stubborn you are."

She grinned. "Then you should know I'm not going anywhere."

THIRTEEN

The Bobcats headed into their fifth game with a 3-1 record, having beaten the Montezuma-Cortez Panthers.

There were six games left in the season, still too many to tell whether the Bobcats would realistically make the play-offs. If they could keep their current record, they'd be a shoo-in.

However, the team had been plagued with misfortunes, from Scott Porter's injured hamstring to Corey's academic probation. Practice so far had been chaotic, with news vans parked outside the field, wanting to interview the players of the winning team.

And then two of their offensive linemen had come to blows simply because they didn't like each other and decided to be immature assholes, and Cameron had to jump in and physically separate the boys. For their punishment, Blake had each of them doing extra runs. If they had the energy to hit another teammate, then they had the energy for extra sprints.

The kids had shut their mouths after that, but then Blake's cell phone started ringing, which he'd ignored twice. The third time he'd answered to one of his neighbors, bitching about Staubach escaping from the backyard and digging through her prize-winning roses. The dog was a nuisance and was bound and determined to put him on the shit list of everyone on his street.

Cameron stood next to Blake and tapped his clipboard on his thigh, watching the play unfolding on the field. His assistant coach had been in a shit mood all day after a brief conversation with Drew Spalding that morning before school. It was no secret the two men didn't like each other and the only reason Drew tolerated Cameron's presence was because Blake insisted on Cameron coaching.

What was a secret was the reason they didn't like each other. Years ago, when Cameron had still been coaching in a neighboring town, he'd had a brief but steamy fling with a woman from Blanco Valley. A woman who turned out to be Drew Spalding's wife.

As soon as Cam found out, he'd ended the affair, but the damage had already been done and Drew and his wife had eventually divorced. Needless to say, Drew blamed Cameron for the demise of his marriage and the two men had been at each other's throats ever since.

After watching one more ragged play, Blake whistled and called the team in. "Your handoffs are sloppy. You guys have gotten lazy," he told them. The kids were hot and out of breath and tired, but Blake didn't give a shit. His job was to bring home the win. "Y'all are playing like you've already won the championship game. Let me tell you something, you're not champs yet. Championships are earned, you hear me?"

"Yes, Coach!" the kids yelled on command.

Blake signaled for them to run the play again. Before they could start, Blake snagged Tanner, his backup QB, by his pads. "Listen to me. Ninety percent of the game is in between your ears. Keep your head up and your legs moving."

"Yes, Coach," the kid answered. Blake moved off the field as the kids resumed their position. He whistled one more time to signal start. As soon as they heard their cue, they moved through the play, executing each move with synchronization. Tanner completed a handoff to the offensive lineman, who rushed it for twenty yards before being tackled.

The kid went down with a crunch of pads, his helmet smacking on the grass and his cleats kicking clods of dirt in the air.

Blake sensed a presence next to him and knew it was Drew before the guy spoke. His overpowering cologne was recognizable anywhere. "The press loves Cody," Drew commented. "The kid's a natural in front of the camera."

"He's also a natural on the field, which is where he needs to be," Blake responded, without taking his eyes off the players. Cameron had them huddled, going over corrections. "We need our starting quarterback practicing with the team."

"It's important to the boosters," Drew reminded him.

Cameron ended his pep talk and resumed his stance by Blake's side. Blake felt Cam's tension as he set his clipboard down on the nearby bench and crossed his arms over his chest.

"Interesting play you have there, Cameron," Drew commented as he watched the action on the field. "Moving Riley Houghton to tight end?" Blake knew that Drew questioning Cam was more to get Cam's blood boiling than anything else. "That's not what I would have done, Let's just hope you know what you're doing."

"Oh, I know what I'm doing, Spalding," Cameron fired back. He nodded toward the athletic director, with his hands still tucked under his arms. "Just ask your ex-wife."

"You son of a bitch," Drew growled, and then lunged at Cameron and would have made bodily contact if Blake hadn't been in between the two men. Not that Cam couldn't hold his own.

Blake didn't need the distraction, especially in front of the players. He gave Drew a hard shove and pushed him away from Cameron.

Blake had never known anyone who could go from flashing a cool grin to throwing punches faster than Cameron Shaw.

Blake clutched a fistful of Drew's shirt in his hands and got in the guy's face. "You really want to be the headline of tomorrow's papers?" Blake asked through gritted teeth, knowing the media sitting on the sidelines wouldn't hesitate to put out a come-to-blows story between the assistant coach and the athletic director.

Drew jerked his head toward Cameron. "Just keep that prick away from me."

Blake glanced over his shoulder at Cameron, who offered Drew a one-sided tilt of his mouth smirk, and then flashed his middle finger in a go-eff-yourself gesture.

Drew wrenched himself away from Blake.

"Pussy," Cameron said to Drew as Drew took long-legged strides across the grass, crossing the forty-yard line and then the thirty.

Blake twisted his whistle back around, which had been thrown over his shoulder in his attempt at restraining Drew. "You never know when to shut up, do you?"

"The guy's a dick," Cameron responded.

"Look, I know Drew's a douche, but no guy wants to be

reminded that his wife was going around banging another guy." He jabbed an index finger at his friend. "Especially by the other guy."

Cameron didn't say anything, and Blake left him to his glowering. As though he didn't have enough on his plate without an athletic director and assistant coach/best friend who wanted to kill each other.

"Hold that stretch for thirty seconds," Annabelle told Scott Porter as he moved from one stretch to the next. His hamstring was in bad shape, which didn't bode well for that night's game. She'd taken the kid to the weight room while the team was on the field practicing. Blake had him sitting out anyway and she wanted to use the opportunity to try and loosen the muscle.

Despite her good intentions, she knew Scott wouldn't be able to play tonight. Not if his hamstring was going to heal properly. Annabelle hoped Blake would err on the side of caution and keep the kid out. She also knew he and the other coaches had to fill the gap Corey had left when he'd been put on academic probation.

Scott winced as he lowered his leg.

"It hurts," he told her.

She nodded and smiled. "I know. The pain is going to get worse before it gets better, but what we're doing here is trying to loosen the muscle."

Scott's brows pulled tighter over his brown eyes. "Coach is going to bench me tonight, isn't he?"

She lowered his leg. "I don't know, Scott. Your coach doesn't include me in his game plans."

Scott let out a long breath as he relaxed his leg on the mat. "But aren't you two, like...you know..."

Annabelle tilted her head to one side, waiting for Scott

to finish his question. "Aren't we what?" Although she had a pretty good idea of what he thought. Every time she and Blake were around each other, the air crackled.

A deep red filled the kid's cheeks and his gaze skittered to something over her shoulder. "Some of the guys think you guys are, like, a thing or something."

A thing or something. Whatever the hell that meant.

"Do me a favor and tell the other guys it's none of their business," she told Scott. "But if they must know, Coach and I are just friends." Friends who kissed like maniacs every time they were around each other.

Yeah, friends did stuff like that.

They fantasized about each other and tried to climb all over each other's bodies. Maybe they should just do the "sex and stuff" and get it over with. They both knew that's where they were headed and they'd continue to dance around it until then.

Annabelle patted Scott on the leg and got to her feet. "We're done here for now," she instructed him. "You know, you're welcome to come to my studio anytime you want. Just have your mom call and schedule an appointment."

Scott pushed himself off the mat and stood. He was tall, probably several inches taller than her, and good-looking. Blond hair, brown eyes, dimples. No wonder he had about three rally girls fighting over him. The kid would be any girl's dream.

"Do you think it'll get better?" he asked her. "I mean, I'm not done for the season, am I?"

Why did he have to ask her things like that? She knew he just needed to be reassured, but geez, she didn't have all the answers. She didn't want to crush his spirits, nor did she want to give him false hope. Everyone's bodies healed differently. Scott very well could be ready to play next week. Or he could continue to struggle for the rest of the season.

"I think if you keep doing these stretching exercises and taking it easy, you'll do okay," she answered.

Scott nodded. "Thanks, Ms. Turner." He walked around her, then turned back. "Oh, and I think you're good for Coach."

"How do you figure that?"

He lifted a shoulder. "He smiles more around you. He's always, like, watching you when you're not looking. The guy's hot for you."

As Scott left the weight room, heat rushed through her system. She knew Blake had some kind of physical attraction to her. Why else would they always end up plastered all over each other? But hearing someone else say it, instead of her own obsessive thoughts, was a totally different story.

Not only that, but Annabelle also realized the arcs of tension and desire between them weren't going to go away. Whether they kept things casual and moved to the next level, things were about to explode between them. The question was when?

How much longer could it keep growing before the desire imploded?

Annabelle followed Scott out of the locker room and made her way to the field.

The afternoon sun was bright and the field was a chaotic scene of cheerleaders, players, coaches, and even media. Parents and students mingled around the bleachers, watching the team practice for the game tonight. Rally girls draped themselves over the chain-link fence, their hair pulled back in orange and black ribbons, keeping their eyes glued to the players.

She let herself through the gate of the fence and wished

she hadn't left her sunglasses in the car. At first she didn't see Blake. She spotted Cameron with the other assistant coaches, gathered around each other and talking.

The players were in a circle in the middle of the field, doing that strange tackling exercise. They were bouncing on their feet, hollering, chanting, and grunting. There, in the middle of the circle, was Blake, yelling at the kids, calling them pussies and telling them to get their sorry asses off the ground when they were tackled.

Annabelle remained by the fence until the kids dispersed, gathering around the watercoolers, some drinking and some dumping the liquid over their heads. She knew practice wasn't over yet, but she used the opportunity to approach Blake.

A second before she could tap him on the shoulder, he turned and glanced at her. Which was a shame because she would really have loved the excuse to touch him. Maybe linger a moment longer than necessary just to feel that one hard ball of a muscle over his shoulder blades. The man had muscle definition in places she'd never seen definition before.

Almost as though he had muscles other men didn't have.

By now she should have been used to not being able to read his features during practices. His baseball cap pulled low over his eyes, which were covered by wraparound sunglasses, kept his secrets hidden from her. She'd gotten good at reading his eyes. They revealed him and she'd grown too dependent on that.

The stony, silent Blake she dealt with during practices was harder to get a hold on.

The wind blew across her face, catching a strand of hair in her eyelashes. Blake hooked his index finger over the lock, dragging it out of her eye and tucking it behind her ear. The gesture was excruciatingly slow, giving him time to linger over her cheek, then swirling his finger over the outer shell of her ear.

Lord, but he knew how to touch. She'd never met a man more skilled and who could snatch the breath right out of her lungs.

"Careful," she said in a voice that was more of a whisper. "Some of your players already think we've hooked up."

"Where'd you hear that?"

Her cheeks flamed. "Scott Porter."

Blake switched his attention to the players. "Nosy little shits."

"Speaking of Scott," Annabelle switched subjects. Thinking about "hooking up" with Blake was one thing. Talking about it to the man himself was out of the question. "I don't think you should play him tonight." The words came out in a rush, and the funny thing was, she didn't feel any better after she said them.

"I'm sure you don't, but he's playing," he told her.

"I really think that's a mistake," she urged him.

"Your feelings on the matter are noted, but I'm not benching him, Annabelle."

Why did the man have to be so damn stubborn?

"Blake," she said with a hand on his forearm. What an odd combination to have soft hair covering such controlled strength. "He's in a lot of pain."

His mouth was set in a hard line, contradicting how yielding it had been under hers last week at the lake. Funny how the man could go from commanding soldier on the football field to an easygoing, quick-witted temptation off the field.

Who are you kidding?

The man was a temptation no matter what he was doing.

Shouting insults at his players to get their attention. Putting her in her place in his office when she tried to tell him what to do. Or cradling her body close to his with such tender care, it made her heart melt.

"I know what I'm doing with my team, Annabelle," he told her, and then he removed her touch from his arm. Instead of keeping the contact, he dropped her hand and resumed his statue-like stillness.

Realistically, she knew he couldn't be the same attentive passionate man he was outside of football. But the rejection of her touch hurt, more than it should, considering they weren't even in a relationship. In reality, she had no right to touch him as though her hands belonged on him.

"I'm not saying you don't," she argued. "Scott needs time to heal. Surely you have backups you can use instead."

"We've already lost too many other good players for me to bench Scott. We need him."

Maybe she didn't have enough team spirit, but she cared more about the kids' health than she did a winning record. Which was odd, because Blake's future with the team depended on how the Bobcats' season ended. If they had another losing record, he'd be out of a job.

The thought of him leaving Blanco Valley and going somewhere else created a sick feeling in the pit of her stomach. She'd miss him, more than she should. More than she thought she'd be able to.

"Of course, you're the coach," she admitted with a casual lift of her shoulder. "It's clear you're willing to risk anything to win."

His mouth set into a hard line. "Scott's going to be fine."

She took a step toward him. "If you want any chance of him playing in the play-offs, or even making the play-offs, you'll keep him off the field tonight." She paused a moment to allow her warning to sink in. "I'm serious, Blake."

"And I'm seriously playing him," he shot back. "Without Scott, we may not make the play-offs."

"Coach," Cameron called from about twenty yards away. The kids were gathered and ready to continue their practice.

Without another word, he turned and strode away with that slow, lazy gait of his. Unhurried. Loose. Unbelievably sexy.

All Annabelle could think about, besides his mistake to play Scott, was how incredible his ass looked in those athletic pants he always had on.

FOURTEEN

Annabelle pulled into her driveway just as her phone rang. Her fingers were still shaking when she dug the cell out of her purse and glanced at the screen. The caller ID displayed her sister's name.

With a barely suppressed groan, Annabelle answered the call.

"You've got to come give me a hand over here," Naomi whispered. "The only thing that's keeping me from strangling Mom is my love for the woman. And the fact that I don't want to go to jail."

Annabelle pushed the car door open and exited the car. "What's wrong?" she asked her sister. "Why are you talking like that?"

"Because she's in the next room, and the woman has hearing like a freakin' bat."

Naomi rustled something in Annabelle's ear. "She's cranky today and complained about the breakfast I made.

Then she bitched at me for folding her sheets wrong. And she won't take her medication."

Ruth Turner had a way she liked things done, which was usually the exact opposite of the way Naomi did things. The two of them gave new definition to oil and water. Naomi's threshold for patience was no more than a few days before she and their mother's conversations gave way to bickering.

"Can you come over here for a little while?" Naomi asked when Annabelle didn't respond to her complaints. "I need to get out before I jab an ice pick through my eyeball."

Annabelle cradled the cell between her ear and shoulder and nudged the front door open. "I can stop by for a little while, but Stella and I are going to the game tonight. I'll get her to take her pills when I see her." If Ruth didn't take her medication, she'd be in danger of having a seizure.

"You're kidding me, right?" Naomi asked. "You can't give me a few hours because of a stupid football game?"

Annabelle let the "stupid" comment roll off her back, because she knew her sister didn't share the same passion. "Are you really going to give me a hard time, Naomi? Me, the one who spends her free time doing everything for Mom? Making her food, cleaning her house, and spending time with her? You're going to give me shit about taking a few hours to myself?"

"All right, chill," Naomi whispered. "I just thought maybe you'd want to hang here for a little while. Thanks for inviting me to the game, by the way."

Annabelle set her purse on the dining table and kicked her shoes off. "Mom isn't an invalid. She can manage on her own for one evening. I didn't think to invite you to the game because you hate football. Why would you want to go?"

"Oh, I don't know, to spend time with my sister?" Naomi said, as though she and Annabelle hadn't seen each other at all, when the truth was they'd gone to lunch a few days ago, and last night they had dinner with her mother, then watched a movie. As much as she loved her sister, and she really did despite their differences, Annabelle's patience for Naomi was wearing thin.

How did Naomi always manage to bring out the worst in her? One conversation and every resentment Annabelle held came hurtling forward.

She heaved a sigh and walked into the kitchen. "You're right," she told her sister. "I'm sorry. Of course you're welcome to come with us."

"Well, it doesn't mean anything now. I had to ask you."

True. But what the hell did Naomi want from her?

Annabelle dug around in her cupboard for a mug and set it on the kitchen counter. "Stella and I would love for you to come with us. It's not just because you asked me," she tried reassuring her younger sister. "I think you'd like it. The games are a lot of fun."

Naomi was silent for a moment before answering. "All right. I could use the break anyway. I've been flooded with calls from my assistant, because she's running the hostel for me while I'm away. You wouldn't believe how the business has boomed in the past month."

"Really," Annabelle commented automatically.

"Oh my gosh, I had this couple come through a few weeks ago who were on their honeymoon. They'd decided to travel through South America and were staying in hostels along the way." Naomi sounded out of breath. As though she were walking around. "Anyway, they were so sweet that the morning they left, they gave me this music box that plays a traditional Irish lullaby because that's where they were from."

Annabelle grabbed a tea bag from the pantry and

dropped it in her mug. "That was nice of them," she replied, growing used to her sister's endless stories about herself and not thinking to ask Annabelle how she was doing.

Water trickled through the coffee machine, and Annabelle stared at it while listening to her sister go on and on about her life, making the appropriate noncommittal noises.

"You'll have to see it all when you come down to visit," Naomi told Annabelle.

Annabelle didn't have the heart to tell her sister she'd probably never travel to South America. Not because she didn't want to, but because she couldn't afford it. Her business required constant income to keep it running, not to mention what she spent helping take care of her mother. She had a good comfortable life and made enough money to support herself. But she just couldn't seem to build her savings up enough to buy a round-trip ticket to Peru.

"Yeah, that'd be great," Annabelle said as the coffee machine stopped. She took the carafe out and poured the hot water into the mug.

Naomi was silent for a moment. "You're not really listening to me, are you?"

"What're you talking about?" Annabelle asked. She picked up the mug and blew on the hot tea. "Of course I am."

"You sound distracted."

Busted. Annabelle shook her head, trying to come up with an excuse for her lack of enthusiasm for Naomi's life in Peru. "I'm just thinking about tonight's game. The team needs the win."

"Oh," Naomi said with a twinge of disappointment lacing her voice. As though she expected Annabelle to have a more monumental worry than that. "Isn't it just a regular season game? I mean, does it matter that much?"

Annabelle took a shallow sip of her tea, testing the temperature. "To the kids it does. And the school."

"Oh," her sister said again. "I guess I've lost touch with American sports because soccer is so huge in South America. You wouldn't believe how a soccer stadium can fill with fans. Now those are exciting games," Naomi commented with a smile in her voice. "I swear my business doubles during soccer season."

The tea hit the bottom of Annabelle's stomach and churned like acid. She'd given her sister an opening to actually ask about Annabelle's life, and Naomi had successfully turned the conversation back to herself and her own life.

Because she's in her own world and doesn't care about yours.

The words hurt and were probably more extreme than they needed to be. Naomi had a way of making Annabelle think that her life in Blanco Valley, with her little physical therapy business and cooking dinner for their mother, was boring. Insignificant. Not important enough. Not exciting enough. Annabelle had never tried exotic food. She didn't speak another language. She didn't have foreigners from all over the globe giving her worldly gifts.

Deep down, Annabelle knew Naomi didn't have the superiority complex Annabelle always thought she did. Maybe it was her own insecurities coming out rather than Naomi trying to make her feel that way. They were sisters and they loved each other. Naomi would never go out of her way to make Annabelle feel bad about her life.

Despite that self-reassurance, Annabelle always ended conversations with her sister feeling exactly like that.

"Listen," Annabelle said, rubbing her fingers over her

forehead. "I need to take care of some quick chores before the game, so I've got to run."

"All right," Naomi said. "I'll just finish up with Mom before we go."

Annabelle ignored the little stab of guilt at trying to push her sister off the phone. "Stella and I will pick you up around six."

They ended the call and Annabelle leaned against the counter, suddenly feeling drained of energy. The green tea should help give her the boost she needed after a long day, but she hadn't drunk enough to kick in yet, not to mention her conversation with her sister left her moody.

She loved Naomi. Really, she did. After their mother passed on, something Annabelle didn't even want to think about, they would be all each other had. Strangely, though, she wasn't sure they'd even have each other. They lived completely different lives, with different priorities in different countries.

The thought of drifting even farther away from her only sister depressed her. It wasn't until then did Annabelle realize how lonely her life was. An aging mother, a sister she never saw. No husband. No kids. Not even a cat.

No one intended to live a solitary life, but somehow that's where she'd ended up. Once upon a time, she'd had the dream life. A handsome husband and good career in the big city. Then it had imploded and now here she was. Taking care of her mother and falling in love with a man who only wanted sex.

Her earlier excitement at going to the football game faded. How had her life become so depressing?

Two minutes after halftime, the Bobcats were holding on to their three-point lead. The lights were blindingly bright, the fans in the bleachers were chanting one school song after another, and the satisfying crunching of pads filled Blake's ears, fueling the adrenaline coursing through his system.

The Panthers had given them a tough first half, but the Bobcats had managed to hold them off. Blake was damn proud of the boys, feeling their determination not to lose another game. Cody was as focused as Blake had ever seen him, calling off the play before sending a beautiful spiral right into the hands of the receiver.

Blake adjusted his headset and followed the play down the field, tuning out the announcer. Cody was tackled, but the receiver continued to run the ball, dodging his opponents with agility and grace. Scott was out there, doing his job to keep the receiver protected.

But then Scott was tackled during the play, twenty yards from the end zone, giving the Bobcats their closest chance at scoring since the second half began. Blake signaled for a time-out, once again hearing Annabelle's words about Scott further injuring his leg. The players ran off the field and gathered around him and the other coaches.

Blake knew he needed to make fast work to get his strategy across. They couldn't blow this opportunity to put another six points on the board.

"How bad is the leg?" he asked Scott.

Scott shook his head. "It's fine, Coach. I can keep playing."

The thing was, Blake wasn't so sure of that. Scott had tried to hide his limp as they'd gathered for the time-out. Even with the lid and mouth guard, Blake could still see the lines of stress and pain on the kid's face. He'd been tackled three times already, and Blake knew that with each one, his hamstring grew tighter.

Hadn't Annabelle told him that one more tiny pull, one

tackle, and Scott would be out for the season? They'd def-initely need him for the play-offs, if in fact they made the play-offs. Which he fully intended on them doing.

So he made a snap decision to pull Scott from the game and bring in the kid's backup. Scott wasn't pleased, hurtling curse words and shaking his head. Blake didn't care if he agreed. The crowd cheered their support as Scott trotted off the field and the backup running back joined the huddle.

"These guys aren't going down without a fight," Blake told the players. "They know we need this win and they're not about to hand it over to us. We're going to do Slot Dou-ble Z XOXO," he told the players, calling the play they'd been working on all week. "Understand?" At their nod, he dismissed them. "Go do it."

The players dispersed, running back onto the field and taking their positions. Blake watched, with his heart in his throat, praying they could execute the play as well as they had in practice all week.

The clock resumed its ticking, and Cody called out the play, receiving the ball when David Cross, the center, snapped it. Cody pump faked to the wide receiver, drawing the Panthers' defense in the other direction, then pitched the ball to Tyler Hutchison, who made it to the five-yard line before he was tackled.

The crowd went in an uproar as Tyler fumbled the ball when he went down. Blake's stomach took a dive when the Panthers' safety scooped it up with effortless grace and shot down the field, toward their end zone.

The guy dodged every attempt to take him down when the Bobcats' offense was blocked by a brigade of defensive blockers. The safety crossed the fifty-yard line, then the forty, and Blake's stomach took another tumble when he closed in on the twenty and before any of his guys could even get close, completed the touchdown to give the Panthers a three-point lead.

With only twenty seconds left in the game, the Bobcats were done.

They'd officially blown it. When the clock ran out, the team trudged off the field while the Panthers celebrated their win.

This one hurt. They'd only been twenty seconds away from winning, and Scott would have been able to execute the play in his sleep.

Blake's pissed-off, irrational side, the coach side, resented the hell out of Annabelle's interference and wished she'd kept her mouth shut about Scott.

Stress hummed through his body, taking him around the locker room and drilling each player with a look that could extinguish a fire. The kids kept their gazes averted, their chests heaving up and down as their bodies came down from the hype of playing.

"Strickland!" Blake addressed one of the offensive linemen who'd been unable to break through the Panthers' defense. "You're supposed to be one of the toughest players out there!" Brian Strickland, drenched in sweat, kept his head bowed when Blake got in his face. "They handed your ass to you!" The air was heavy with disappointment, fatigue, and attitude. The kids were slumped over, sitting on benches and leaning against the walls. Sweat ran down their faces, dirt smothered their uniforms, and their hair was matted to their foreheads.

"Where's the execution?" he called out when no one said anything. He knew they wouldn't because none of them had the balls to talk back when the coach went on a tirade after a loss.

And Blake needed the tirade.

"Richardson!" Blake called out to the QB, who'd held himself hunched over through Blake's entire rampage. Cody looked up, blinking as Blake thumped him on his shoulder pad. "Good game," he told the kid. A trickle of blood ran down Cody's face from a cut on his eyebrow.

Blake turned from the players and stalked toward his office. At the door, he turned and addressed them the entire time. "But not good enough." He allowed the words to sink in, then hammered his point home. "Not nearly good enough."

FIFTEEN

Blake kicked his front door closed behind him, doing his best to ignore the teeth-gritting pain in his knee. It didn't work because the lightning pain shot down to his toes when he'd mistakenly used his bad leg to kick the door shut.

Or maybe not a mistake.

Maybe he'd done it on purpose because he was pissed off and wanted to tell the world to go eff itself.

And because Annabelle had been texting him since the game ended, asking him if he was okay. That she was sorry they lost. Like he was some Little League player who needed to be comforted by his mommy.

The last text had read something about her being proud of him for benching Scott. Telling him he'd done the right thing, or some such bullshit.

He hadn't answered her. He didn't want her sympathy or pity, especially because his decision to bench Scott had likely cost them the game.

Blake dropped his bag next to the front door, tossed his keys and cell phone on the hall table, and made for the kitchen. What he needed was something to drink. To get totally shit-faced drunk so he wouldn't have to think about how he'd allowed Annabelle to influence his game decisions.

He knew, logically anyway, that he couldn't blame her for the loss. That he was the coach and the decisions were his and his alone. But she'd gotten in his head with all her talk about keeping the kids healthy and losing Scott for the rest of the season if he played too much.

So he'd ignored his gut to keep Scott in and benched him. And they'd lost.

His phone vibrated again. Probably another text from Annabelle, wondering if he needed a shoulder to cry on. Apparently she thought he couldn't handle losing.

And, yeah, you can't handle losing, asshole.

So he was competitive. So he didn't like to lose.

Who did?

Once in the kitchen, Blake flipped on the light and snagged a beer bottle from the fridge. Staubach ambled in and stared at Blake with sleepy, deep brown eyes. Blake's Oxy was on the counter where he'd left it earlier. He stared at the bottle as he flipped the metal cap off the beer with the bottle opener. Stared at it as he chugged a slow sip. And stared at it some more when he lowered the bottle and swallowed.

It's not going to jump off the counter.

He picked the bottle up and shook out a pill in his hand. But he didn't toss it back right away. He rolled the pill over in his palm, wanting nothing more than to shove the thing down the back of his throat and do away with the pain. Instead he threw it over his shoulder, where it pinged on a surface and landed on the floor.

Blake didn't stay to see where it landed. He took his beer

and strode out of the kitchen, thinking he would just get drunk instead of numbing his pain with more pills. He'd have a bitch of a headache tomorrow, but whatever.

He went into the bedroom, the dog close on his heels, set the beer bottle on the dresser, and starting stripping his clothes off. What he needed was a shower. To wash away the sweat and dirt and loss off his skin.

What you need is to get laid.

Probably, yeah. But the only person he wanted to get laid with didn't believe in casual. Which sort of messed up his plans to get her naked. Couldn't really get a woman naked if she wasn't on board with the plans.

Once in the bathroom, he turned the shower on, then strode back into the bedroom, not giving a rip about his nudity. He'd just yanked a pair of boxers out of the dresser when someone knocked on his door. Staubach took off running, his toenails slipping on the hardwood floor. Not in the mood to converse with anyone, Blake ignored the knocking, and his dog's furious barking. Except the knocking turned into the doorbell chiming and Staubach went nuts.

Over and over again. One chime after another and it was all Blake could do to keep his head from exploding. With a few muttered curses, he made a mad grab for a bath towel and hastily wrapped it around his hips.

Only someone with a death wish would come over at this hour, especially after losing a football game. Anyone who knew him knew to give Blake a wide berth after a defeat.

"Settle your ass down," he growled at the dog, who was trying to climb up the front door. Blake pushed him aside and pointed a finger at him. "Down," he ordered with the same authoritative air Cameron had used. Staubach whined and sat, but his tail was swishing back and forth so fast, Blake was surprised the dog didn't take off like a helicopter.

With one hand holding the towel up, Blake used the other to whip open the door, fully intending to tell his visitor to eff off.

Except his visitor had long dark hair, thickly lashed eyes, and had a smile that was like a one-two punch. Annabelle blinked back at him, raking her gaze over his bare torso before dipping her eyes to the towel covering his junk.

Her attention jerked north to his face as though just her mere perusal would have him dropping the towel.

If she wasn't careful, that's exactly what he'd do.

"I..." Her tongue darted out and swiped across her lower lip. "I just wanted to see if you were okay."

Did the woman never give up? "Why wouldn't I be?" he asked. "Stay," he told Staubach when he stood and tried to nudge his wet nose past Blake's legs. Staubach whined again and thumped his wagging tail against the hall table.

She shifted on her feet. "Well, you didn't respond to any of my texts, so I thought..."

He arched a brow at her. "You thought...," he prompted.

Her throat worked when she swallowed. "That maybe you'd like some company."

He leaned against the jamb. "The only company I'm looking for is the naked kind. So unless you're up for that..." He allowed his gaze to rake down her body, enjoying the subtle flare of her hips, then stopping on her cool green eyes. God, she was beautiful. Why did he have to be such a bastard to her?

Annabelle tilted her head at him. "I know you're pissed at losing, but you can't scare me away."

"You've established that several times already." He pushed away from the front door, leaving her standing on the landing and giving his dog the opportunity to shove his nose in Annabelle's crotch. And not caring if she followed him inside.

At least that's what he told himself.

In truth, he did care. Way too much.

He wanted her to follow him in. He wanted her to tug the towel off his hips and use that magic touch of hers to make the pain in his knee go away. Or, better yet, the pain in his heart.

Because it ached every time he looked at her.

The front door closed with a soft snick and he heard Annabelle's light steps on the floor. Staubach trotted alongside her, desperately trying to get her attention. Instead of telling the dog to go away, she appeased him with a gentle rub behind his ears.

"Blake," she said to him.

"My shower's running," he told her. "If you're going to worm your way into my business, you're going to have to wait until I'm done." He stopped at his bedroom door and glanced back at her. She was at the end of the hallway, waiting. Waiting for what, he didn't know. "Unless you want to join me." When she didn't say anything, he pushed. "No?" With a shrug, he let go of the towel and it unraveled at his feet. "Your loss, then."

He turned his back on her wide-eyed expression, snagged his half-finished beer off the dresser, and tossed back a long sip.

He made quick work of the shower, soaping his body and rubbing shampoo into his hair. His rushing was not, he told himself, to catch her before she decided to ditch him. That he didn't care how her attention had skittered down to his bare ass when he'd lost the towel. That satisfaction hadn't hummed through his system when her breathing had quickened.

Funny how he was so in tune with her that he could tell her breathing patterns from down a hallway.

But really, what would he have done if she'd thrown herself at him? Just launched that coma-inducing body against his and finally showed that she wanted him just as much as he wanted her?

She's already shown you that.

More than once with each kiss they engaged in. The problem was, she was scared. Too afraid of her feelings for him to take things further.

You're scared too, he berated himself.

Hell yeah he was scared. More afraid of Annabelle Turner than he'd been of any other woman before. Because she touched a place deep inside him that no one else had. She saw past his weaknesses and demons and liked him anyway.

Annabelle Turner was a dangerous woman, plain and simple.

Dangerous and smart and too bossy for her own good.

Meddlesome. Independent. Caring.

But most of all gorgeous. Sexy enough to bring a man to his knees and shatter every defense he had.

Staubach came ambling into his bedroom, touching his wet nose to Blake's bare leg.

"What did you chew up this time?" he asked the dog.

Staubach sat and stared up at with soulful brown eyes.

Blake jabbed his index finger at the dog. "If you destroyed another pair of my shoes, you're done for. What happened to your toys?"

The dog stood and wagged his tail back and forth with such enthusiasm, his whole body moved with it.

After he dressed, Blake left the bedroom, aware of Staubach close on his heels, his toenails clicking softly on the hardwood floor. He expected, hell hoped, Annabelle had gone, knowing what was good for her.

Perhaps even taking his surly attitude as a sign he didn't want company.

But there she was. In his living room. Looking like the wet dream she was, staring at his framed football jersey hanging on the mantel of his fireplace. The number twenty-four in white, surrounded by the well-known forest green of the Packers, stared back at him. Taunting. Reminding him of what he used to be and wasn't anymore.

His fingers itched to put the jersey back on. To feel it sliding over his head and falling down over his game pads.

But those days were over. He knew he needed to move on. To focus on what he had now, which wasn't a bad gig, if he were to be totally honest with himself.

Man, he was such a mess.

Staubach's tags clinked together when he jumped on the couch, and Annabelle turned, paralyzing him with her searing gaze.

To give him a distraction, he turned toward the dog and snapped his fingers. "Down," he commanded.

Staubach just laid his head down and blinked.

Annabelle chuckled. "And you're supposed to be the alpha."

He glanced back at her, then looked at Staubach. "Down," he said again. The dog didn't move. In fact, he closed his eyes and expelled a deep sigh.

"He needs a bed," Annabelle told him.

Blake turned toward her. "The carpet is his bed."

Annabelle looked at the taupe carpet covering his living room floor. "Would you lie on the floor?"

"Why would I? I have a bed."

"Exactly," she told him with a grin.

Okay, she had him there. He'd sort of proved her point for her. "I'm also not a dog. I pay the mortgage; therefore, I get a bed."

Annabelle pointed toward his framed jersey hanging above the mantel. "Is this your actual game jersey?" she asked.

He came to stand next to her, ignoring his body's warning not to get too close. "Yeah, that's the home jersey."

"It's huge," she commented.

"It has to fit over a lot of padding," he explained. "Plus, I'm a big guy, in case you didn't notice." *You're a masochistic asshole.*

She didn't respond to that, thank goodness, because who the hell knew where the conversation would have gone.

It would go into the bedroom, so stop talking about bodies.

She stared at him for a moment. "Are you really okay?" she asked again.

"You act like that's the first game I've ever lost. It's bound to happen."

No one had ever asked him if he was okay after a loss. Most understood defeat came with the territory. Either Annabelle didn't understand that, which he doubted, or she really was that worried about him.

The last thought had his heart constricting in his chest.

"Why are you really here, Annabelle?" They both knew why she was there.

"I'm not sure," she admitted, which was bullshit. Then she held her hand up, showing a little white pill. "I found this on your floor. Your dog could have gotten a hold of it." She extended her palm, offering the OxyContin.

He stared at the pill, realizing it was the one he'd thrown, not wanting to take it because it would be too easy to toss the thing down his throat.

"Blake?" she asked when he didn't move a muscle. "Aren't you going to take this?"

A bead of sweat ran down his temple and his heart rate picked up. Hell yeah he wanted to take it. He wanted to take the whole bottle and numb the pain that lived with him all the time.

"You know what?" Annabelle said, closing her fist around the pill. "Never mind, I'm not giving you this." Then she stalked out of the living room and disappeared into the kitchen. He followed her, passing a snoring Staubach, who was completely unaware of the storm raging inside Blake.

"What the hell are you doing?" he demanded when she turned the faucet on and flipped the switch to the garbage disposal.

"What you should have done a long time ago," she told him. "You're going to kill yourself, Blake." She snagged the full bottle off the counter and shook them. "These aren't doing you any good."

Even though he knew she was right, he couldn't stand the sight of her dumping the whole bottle down the drain. He'd been better about not taking them, knowing he had a problem of breaking his need for them. But knowing they were around, giving him that comfort to fall back on, gave him relief.

So when she unscrewed the bottle and turned it upside down, emptying every single last pill down the sink, he wanted to lunge at her. She stared back at him, daring him to protest, to beg her to stop because they both knew he wanted to.

But he just stood there like the weak bastard he was, meeting her hard stare with one of his own while his security blanket was washed down the drain.

She threw the bottle on the counter, where it skittered until it hit a canister of sugar. "You'll thank me for that one day."

"I needed those," he told her through the ache in his jaw.

"What you need is help," she argued. "Why hasn't anyone else done that?" She crossed her arms over her chest so tight he was surprised she didn't tear her shirt. "It's because no one else knows, do they?" Yeah, definitely too smart for her own good. "How long have you been hiding this?" When he didn't answer, she pressed. "How long have you been fighting this by yourself?"

"You don't know what the hell you're talking about," he spat out, then left the kitchen. Left her standing there with the knowledge the she'd figured him out. Easier than anyone else had. He didn't want, or need, her figuring him out, thank you very much. He'd done just fine on his own so far, and he would continue to do so.

Being addicted to pain pills and not being able to admit it out loud is not doing fine.

Hot tears burned the backs of his eyes as he stomped down the hallway toward his bedroom. Crying? What the hell was wrong with him? The only time in his life he'd ever cried was when his grandfather died. And he'd been twelve, a perfectly acceptable age to shed some tears.

A thirty-four-year-old man getting this emotional over a woman he had growing feelings for calling him out? He had more problems than the Bobcats winning a season or overcoming his need for OxyContin.

He'd thought his early retirement from football was his official low.

This was his official low.

Annabelle was following him. Of course she wouldn't leave him alone. The woman thought she could fix everything. She was hot on his heels as he turned into his bedroom. The beer he hadn't finished was still sitting on the dresser. He snatched it off, chugged a long, deep pull, then swiped his mouth with the back of his hand.

Annabelle appeared in the doorway, all worry and care filling the depths of her bottomless green eyes. Sympathizing for him.

Feeling sorry for him.

Yeah, his official new low.

She's fighting for you, asshole. When has anyone else done that?

He turned from her, not wanting to see his own failures written all over her face. "Go away, Annabelle," he ordered her.

"No," she answered in a soft voice.

His room was a mess, his bed unmade and dirty clothes on the floor. Mostly because he'd been in a hurry that morning, oversleeping and not wanting to take the time to straighten up. He kicked a shirt out of the way and took another swig of his beer.

"Suit yourself," he told her, making her think he didn't care, wanting to make her leave. Because the ache of needing to feel her body pressed to his was at odds with his need for more pills.

"Blake, I want to help you," she told him, pushing away from the doorway and coming toward him.

"I already told you, I'm fine," he answered.

"You're not fine," she shot out, gripping his forearm with her slim fingers and turning him around. "You haven't been fine in a long time." She blinked at him, waiting for him to respond. "God, you are the most bullheaded man I have ever known. What's wrong with you? Because I know this is more than just losing tonight's game."

"You're so sure of that, aren't you?" he taunted her. "You think you can fix everything."

"I'm not trying to fix you, because you're not broken. I'm just trying to help you."

He lowered his face closer to hers. "I don't want your help. Go. Away."

Most people would have run the other direction when he drilled them with the stormy look he'd perfected over the years. The one he gave his opponents during a football game, right before the center snapped the ball into his palms.

But Annabelle, damn her to hell, didn't back away. She didn't cower or cry or tell him to go to hell. She stood tall, meeting his hard stare with one of her own. When was the last time anyone had stood up to him or offered their support so unfailingly? So completely?

No judgment.

No self-righteousness.

His mother had tried prodding into his troubles after his retirement, but that had been motherly concern and he'd been good at hiding his problems. Plus the fact that his parents lived in Arizona made it easier to pretend.

Not even Brandon, his cousin and closest friend, had any suspicions Blake was in trouble. Not until that moment did he realize how alone he was. How much he needed exactly what Annabelle had done for him. Tough love. He enacted that very thing on his players, knowing it was the best way of showing he cared about them.

What had he done when Anabelle gave him a dose of his own medicine?

He'd tried to run like the coward he was.

Annabelle slipped the beer bottle from his hands and set it on the nightstand. "I'm not leaving you alone tonight," she told him softly.

Blake knew that if he were to slip her T-shirt over her head, she'd let him. He also knew her statement had nothing to do with sex. The woman was just doing what she did best.

What she loved. Helping people who needed a shoulder to lean on.

The woman was a freakin' saint.

"I'm sorry," he rasped out. The word sounded so absurd. So asinine after the way he'd treated her. He didn't deserve her help. After the way he'd spoken to her, he wouldn't blame her for walking out.

For telling him to go to hell. Because that's where he belonged.

"You have nothing to be sorry for," she told him.

He lifted his hands and gripped her hips, pulling her toward him. Any other time he would have kissed her, and she would have welcomed him inside her mouth. But he didn't. Instead he lowered his forehead to hers and allowed his eyelids to drop closed.

Exhaustion left his limbs feeling heavy. How much longer had he expected to carry on the way he had? It had taken a one-hundred-and-twenty-pound, pint-sized firecracker to open his eyes to reality.

"You need help, Blake," she told him again.

"I know," he answered. Yeah, she was battling for him.

And, damn, he wanted to kiss her. No matter the circumstances, he always wanted to kiss her. Only this time it was different because, in a way, she'd become his savior and he wanted to show her how grateful he was.

But turning it into something sexual would ruin the precious risk she'd taken for him.

They stood in silence, foreheads leaning together, breath mingling from their mouths being so close.

His hands on her hips tightened. "I don't want you to go," he admitted, because he was just about all out of pride.

Without a word, she slipped away from him and pulled the covers back from the bed, even though they were already messed up. He stood back and watched, practically swallowing his tongue when she yanked her shirt over her head, revealing a flat tummy and full breasts supported by a lacy baby blue bra.

The woman was something else.

Then she reached out, removed his shirt, and tugged him down onto the bed with her.

As he stretched out on the cool sheets, allowing his legs to tangle with hers, Blake thought back to the last time he'd allowed himself to lie with a woman like this. No sex involved. Only comfort and acceptance and companionship.

The truth was, he couldn't think of a time. Because he'd never indulged in something as intimate as this. Yes, sex was just about as intimate as two people could get, but something about curling himself around Annabelle, pressing his chest to her back, was far more personal than any sexual encounter he'd had.

She'd stripped him bare and exposed all his secrets. Not only that, but she also knew who he was underneath and wanted to be with him anyway. She stuck by him, even though he'd tried to drive her away.

He didn't deserve her.

He closed his eyes. She laced her fingers through his, tugging his arm tighter around her and sighed. As though she were as content as him to hold each other.

In that instant, Blake knew, what was left of his heart crumbled. Annabelle Turner had taken it, as though she had every right, and held it in her soft hands.

The question was now, what would she do with it?

SIXTEEN

Annabelle had made a huge mistake. A six-foot-three, blue-eyed hunk of a mistake named Blake Carpenter.

As she'd lain with him, feeling his heart thump steadily against her back, she realized she'd crossed the point of no return.

The sun had just edged over the mountains and Blake was still fast asleep, sprawled on his back, one leg on top of the sheet, the other still tucked away. He looked relaxed and peaceful. She slipped from the bed, unable to bring herself to wake him.

With one last longing glance, Annabelle tugged her shirt back on and left the bedroom. Staubach trotted up to her, shoving his nose in her crotch and wagging his tail so hard, it had thumped against the wall.

So she let him in the backyard so he could relieve himself.

She quickly found where Blake kept his coffee and

brewed some for him. It was scary how right, how normal the morning routine felt, as though she'd been doing this for years. Then, like the concerned girlfriend she was, Annabelle left him a note on the kitchen counter.

I put Staubach in the backyard and made coffee. Take it easy today and call me if you want to talk.

A.

She's stared at her own handwriting for several moments, wanting to write more. But what would she have said?

Sorry for butting into your life.

That would have been a lie.

I loved sleeping next to you.

While truthful, Annabelle couldn't bring herself to say it. Because, after making the impulsive decision to dump his entire supply of Oxy down his disposal, she had the feeling she was on thin ice with him. So she'd left the note the way she'd written it and driven home. The whole way she told herself not to be disappointed if he didn't call. It wasn't like they were in a relationship. He wasn't obligated to check in with her.

For some reason that thought chased away the cheerful sunny morning. She woke up refreshed and more than a little turned on at the sight of the man's magnificent naked torso, and now she was gritting her teeth together.

She went home, forcing thoughts of Blake away, and took a shower. Afterward, she pulled on a pair of jeans, a racer-back tank, and sandals. Yesterday, when she'd picked Naomi up for the game, Annabelle told her sister and her mother she'd stop by so they could all have breakfast together. Naomi had grinned and said she'd be happy to make something so Annabelle and Ruth wouldn't have to worry about it.

Annabelle had accepted the offer, thinking how nice it

had been to have someone around to help out with their mom. It had been so long since she'd had someone to lean on and share the responsibilities with. It wasn't until Naomi stepped in did Annabelle realize just how much she did for her mom. How much of her time it consumed. Not that she'd ever minded. She loved her mother more than anything and was more than happy to give back what Ruth had given to both her daughters.

However, being able to take time to sit and visit with her mom, who was utilizing her cane more and more these days, and not spend all that time doing chores, had been refreshing.

As Annabelle headed out her front door, she reminded herself the help was only temporary. That it was only a matter of time before Naomi returned to her exciting and exotic life in Peru, always meeting new people and not having a care in the world. The same old resentment bubbled to the surface, but Annabelle did her best to squash it. Her only thoughts, for the moment, were to have a nice breakfast with her mother and sister.

Maybe eat while sitting on the back porch, enjoying the cool morning air and listening to the birds sing. Maybe they could spend some time talking or sharing old stories from when the girls had been kids. And not tiptoeing around the constant issue of Naomi's distance from her family.

Or a man Annabelle had spent the night sleeping next to, thinking she wanted to take care of him, if only he'd allow it. That she wanted to be the person in his life he leaned on. The only one he could confide in and dump his troubles on. As much as getting naked with him would probably be really good, she wanted something much more substantial than that. Something to build a foundation with that would last more than a few nights in bed.

Even now, after knowing each other for a few months, and everything else they'd been through, Annabelle still wasn't sure Blake was up for that. He hadn't given her any indication of wanting a solid relationship.

Which left them, where?

Of that, she had no clue and trying to pin their...whatever it was they were into a box was more exhausting than a conversation with her sister.

Annabelle pulled up to her mother's house and immediately noticed Naomi's car was missing from the driveway. Maybe she'd put it in the garage.

Since it was only about eight-thirty, Annabelle didn't expect much activity in her mother's house. Naomi was always up with the sun, but Ruth had never been an early riser. Expecting breakfast to be under way, Annabelle let herself through the front door and heard sounds from the kitchen.

Charlie trotted up to her, letting out a low growl, then barked nonstop.

She set her purse down on the hall table and glanced at the animal. "Careful or I might slip some antifreeze in your food."

Charlie didn't care, and he continued his *yap yap yap* as she made her way to the back of the house. And bit back a sigh of frustration when she saw her mother, leaning heavily on her cane with one hand and whisking something in a bowl with the other.

Annabelle rushed to her mother's side, noticing how the woman was struggling to stay upright. "Mom, what're you doing? Go sit down." Annabelle took the whisk and bowl of eggs away from her. Ruth turned and put all her weight on her cane. Deep lines of fatigue and stress were etched across her forehead, and her thinning gray hair was pulled back with a small black clip.

"I'm making breakfast. We've got to eat, Annabelle," Ruth argued.

Annabelle hooked her arm through her mother's elbow and led her out of the kitchen. "Where's Naomi?" she asked. "She's supposed to make breakfast."

They shuffled across the chocolate brown carpet, toward Ruth's favorite recliner. Charlie was already up in his seat, and Annabelle shooed him down. He immediately jumped off, giving Annabelle the stink eye. "I don't know," Ruth answered. "She was gone when I got up."

Annabelle lowered her mother to the chair and handed over her favorite blanket that had been stitched by Annabelle's grandmother. "How long have you been up?"

Ruth expelled a deep sigh and closed her eyes as Charlie hopped back into the chair and curled in a ball on her lap. "I don't know. About half an hour." She opened her faded green eyes and looked at Annabelle. "I haven't done much, Annabelle. Naomi came home last night after the game and put together a French toast casserole. It just needs to be put in the oven, but I wanted some eggs to go with it."

Annabelle put her hands on her hips, fighting back frustration for her sister. "Well, now that I'm here I can do it. But Naomi should have done it, because she's the one who said she was going to make breakfast. Anyway, she shouldn't have left you here with no breakfast already made for you."

"I'm capable of making my own food," Ruth argued.

Not really. Annabelle kept the thought to herself. "Mom, mixing an instant breakfast is not the same as making eggs or cooking a casserole. How did you expect to carry a dish from the fridge to the oven while holding a cane with one hand?"

"I was going to let Naomi do it when she came back," Ruth answered.

Annabelle glanced around the room, noticing how clean it was. One thing Annabelle had to give her sister credit for; Naomi had done a great job of keeping the house in shape. The furniture was free of dust and there were fresh flowers in a vase on the coffee table. Even the magazines in the rack had been organized.

"Did she leave a note or anything?" Annabelle asked her mother.

"No, and I was getting hungry."

Annabelle found the remote control for the television and turned it to Ruth's favorite channel. Then she leaned over and placed a soft kiss to her paper-thin cheek.

"I'll get breakfast done, Mom," Annabelle told her. "I'll bring your medication in with some juice."

"I already took my pills." Ruth smirked. "I even managed to wipe myself too."

Good grief.

She left Ruth and returned to the kitchen. In the fridge, Annabelle found the casserole covered in aluminum foil and a Post-it with the cooking directions. At least Naomi had done that much.

Where could she have gone so early in the morning? And why would she leave without telling their mother she was going, where she would be, and not taking care of breakfast?

Annabelle shook her head, biting back another sigh of annoyance, and preheated the oven. Ruth had started the eggs, cracking a couple and leaving the rest sitting on the counter. Annabelle returned the carton to the fridge and cracked the rest of the eggs in the bowl. With a brisk movement of her wrist, she whipped the eggs together, sprinkled in some salt and pepper, and whisked them some more. When the oven dinged, she stuck the dish in, set the timer, and waited for it to cook.

The casserole needed thirty minutes, so Annabelle took the next twenty to check her mother's grocery supplies, making note of what Ruth needed and what she was out of. Then she took trips through the laundry room and bathrooms and made note of other supplies she needed to pick up. After that was finished, Annabelle dropped the list in her purse and returned to the kitchen to cook the eggs.

Naomi still hadn't returned and Annabelle couldn't call because her sister didn't have a cell phone. Only a local landline in Peru, which wouldn't do her any good. If Naomi wasn't back by the time breakfast was finished, Annabelle and her mother would eat without her.

And then Annabelle would take a private moment to find out what the hell Naomi had been thinking.

She doesn't know.

The voice whispered through her head, reminding Annabelle that Naomi wasn't used to taking care of someone else or having another person depend on her.

Annabelle tried to remind herself of this, but concern for their mother trumped thoughts of giving Naomi the benefit of the doubt.

Seeing Ruth standing at the counter, putting all her weight on a flimsy cane and trying to make eggs with one hand made Annabelle's heart constrict inside her chest. Ruth wasn't a young woman anymore. Each year she grew older and older and her body continually fell apart. Right now, she was still able to do some things for herself. But for the most part, she relied heavily on her oldest daughter and would rely on her more and more as she got weaker and weaker.

The realization of her mother's mortality formed a lump in Annabelle's throat. Did Naomi think about these things? Did she think about how to take care of Ruth when the woman was no longer mobile? Did she wrestle with the decision to look into a group home?

Those thoughts weighed on Annabelle all the time, lingering in the back of her mind, a cruel reminder of how fast downhill life could go. Naomi had never given any indication that she gave a passing thought to such things. The realization burned in the pit of her stomach while also making her feel very alone. Naomi lived however many thousands of miles away, running her little business, basking in the warm South American sunshine while Annabelle used all her spare energy wondering what she was going to do with Ruth's house one day. Or how to support her mother financially if she ended up outliving her income.

Annabelle glanced at the time for the casserole, then dumped the eggs in a frying pan. Even if Naomi didn't come back in time for breakfast, that didn't mean Annabelle couldn't have a nice meal with her mother.

So she pushed her jumbled thoughts away and finished the meal.

The timer dinged just as the eggs finished. Her mother was asleep when Annabelle carried two plates of food into the living room. She set Ruth's plate on an end table and nudged her mother's shoulder.

"Mom," Annabelle whispered.

Ruth blinked open her rheumy eyes.

"Breakfast is done. Do you want some?"

"Well, of course I do," Ruth answered as she pushed herself up in the chair. King Charlie opened one black eye, stared at Annabelle as though he didn't approve, which she knew he didn't, then went back to sleep.

Annabelle handed her mom the plate, along with a fork and a napkin, then took a seat on the couch. They ate in silence for a few minutes, enjoying the delicious dish Naomi had made. It really was tasty and Annabelle had to give her credit for that much.

After a moment, her mother spoke. "I see you've been spending more time with the coach of yours."

A piece of egg and cinnamon-coated bread got stuck in Annabelle's throat. She took a swig of her orange juice to wash the food down. "First of all," she said after clearing her throat. "He's not 'my coach.' Second of all, how do you know I've been spending more time with him?"

One side of Ruth's thinning lips turned up. "I didn't until you just admitted it. Never could lie well, Annabelle."

Wasn't that the truth.

"I also haven't seen you as much lately," Ruth went on. "Figured a man was behind that."

Annabelle set her fork down on her plate. "I'm sorry," she admitted, pushing back the guilt over constantly centering her thoughts on Blake and not her mom's well-being. "You're right, I've been distracted."

Ruth discarded her plate on the end table. "Don't you dare apologize, Annabelle." She pushed herself straighter in the chair. "Do you think I like the fact that my still single daughter spends all of her free time taking care of me? You should be dating and having fun. Or, better yet, taking care of your own family."

Those thoughts had crossed Annabelle's mind a time or two. Or one hundred. Of course, she'd thought by the age of thirty she'd have a family of her own. A man who'd slip his arms around her and place a kiss on the back of her neck. Maybe one or two kids to play dress-up with or toss a football to. Even after her divorce, she'd thought by now she'd be closer to walking down the aisle again.

The sad truth was, she wasn't any closer today than when her divorce had been finalized. What did that say about her?

That her standards were too high? That maybe she didn't show enough interest in the men around her?

Except there was one who'd been getting all of her interest. Problem was, he had no plans to settle down with anyone. He didn't want to. Which left Annabelle in a strange sort of limbo, because she had no desire for anyone else.

She wanted an unattainable man. Story of her life.

"Annabelle," Ruth continued. "I've told you before I have no problems living in a retirement community."

Annabelle held her hand up. "Mom, stop. You're not going into a home because you're too young. The people in there are..."

"Are what?" Ruth demanded. "Dependent, like me? I'm not as young as you think I am, honey. My medical conditions make me different from other women my age."

"You're only in your sixties," Annabelle reminded her mother.

"Oh for Pete's sake, I'm not talking about you sticking me in some nursing home. I mean maybe a condo in a gated community with people my own age. There are some places that offer twenty-four-hour assistance and on-call nurses." Ruth huffed out a breath. "Annabelle, I know why you take care of me."

"Because you need help," she reminded her mother. Why did the woman have to be so damn stubborn?

Ruth shook her head. "You do it because you like to be needed," she told her daughter. "No, you *need* to be needed. Just like I did."

"Mom, what're you talking about? I don't need that." Except Annabelle was pretty sure her mother was right.

"Yes, you do," Ruth said. "I used to be the same way. That's why I had such a hard time when Naomi moved away. When you see your youngest child take control of their own life, reality sets in and it's hard to swallow. You go from spending every waking moment taking care of these other people, and suddenly they don't need you anymore." Ruth stared at Annabelle with understanding and also a little bit of sympathy. "Having all that free time on your hands can take a while to get used to."

Annabelle shook her head again. "Mom—"

"I'll admit at first," Ruth interrupted, "I loved having you here all the time. But now, you're just driving me crazy, Annabelle."

Wait, what?

"I didn't realize I was annoying you," Annabelle admitted, trying to squash the hurt.

Ruth leaned back in her chair. "Of course you don't annoy me. I just mean I know how much you're giving up to take care of me."

"I'm not giving anything up," she argued. "And you need me. That's why I'm here."

"What I need is for my daughter to be happy, and you're not happy. You haven't been happy since your divorce."

"I'm happy, Mom," Annabelle said in a low voice.

"But are you fulfilled? Because there's a difference between being content and being fulfilled."

To be honest, Annabelle hadn't realized there was a difference. Probably because she'd never thought about it before. Yeah, she was happy. At least she'd thought she was, until her mother, the realist she was, removed her rose-colored glasses and made Annabelle take a harder look at her own life.

Had she been deluding herself all these years? Telling herself being single wasn't that bad? That yes, she'd love to get married again and have kids but that this was okay too. Going home to an empty house, not having that special partner to share life's complications and joys with wasn't a big deal.

But you already know that's not true.

That pesky voice in her head, the one that always burst her bubble, chimed in. She had realized what she'd been missing out on. And it had hit her in the form of a six-foot-three behemoth of a man who made her laugh and feel and crave. Blake Carpenter wasn't an easy man to be around but maybe that's what she loved about him. He was complicated and deep, and a part of her connected with that.

She hadn't realized how much she really missed having another half until Blake. It also made her realize that her mother was right. True, Annabelle was happy. But not truly fulfilled.

The thing was, she didn't know how to fix it. And she was a fixer.

"Now I've gone and ruined breakfast," her mother said.

Annabelle set her empty plate on the coffee table. "You haven't ruined anything, Mom. I appreciate your honesty." She stared down at her clasped hands. "You're also right. I've grown complacent with where my life is."

Ruth nodded. "I know. It's time you start focusing on yourself. It's not normal for a woman as beautiful as you to spend all her free time at her mother's house."

The compliment warmed Annabelle from the inside out, because Ruth hadn't made a habit of tossing those out so casually. She was a tell-it-like-it-is kind of woman and rarely wasted time with pleasantries or beating around the bush. A trait both her daughters had inherited. Which was probably why she and her sister bickered so much.

At the thought of Naomi, the front door swung open and the woman in question came breezing through. A wide smile flashed across her face as Naomi pulled out her earbuds and set them, along with her iPod, on the hall table.

Charlie, the menace to society he was, launched himself off the recliner and ran toward Naomi, yapping away.

Naomi shot her foot out and shooed the dog away. "You see me every day," she said to the dog. "Why are you barking at me?" Naomi rolled her eyes. "Mom, your dog. He is so annoying."

Then she grinned at Annabelle and Ruth as though she'd just noticed their presence.

"Hey," she said, totally oblivious to the fact that Annabelle and Ruth had already eaten breakfast. The breakfast Naomi was supposed to make.

Annabelle took in her sister's running shoes, racer-back tank, and cropped leggings.

"We were wondering if you were going to come back," Ruth commented.

"What do you mean?" Naomi asked as she flopped down on the sofa, a fine sheen of sweat covering her chest and face.

"You've been gone quite a while," Annabelle told her sister. "Mom and I had to do breakfast."

"I told you I would make it. I was just going to do it when I got back."

Annabelle glanced at the clock on the mantel. "It's nine forty-five, Naomi. We weren't sure how long you'd be. You didn't even tell Mom you were leaving."

Naomi lifted a slender shoulder. "She was sleeping. I didn't want to wake her up."

Annabelle resisted an eye roll and grabbed her plate. Aware of her sister's questioning gaze, Annabelle strolled into the kitchen so she could do the dishes. Behind the closed door, she heard her mother say something to Naomi, which Naomi didn't reply to. A second later, the kitchen door swung open and her sister's sneakers treaded across the tiled floor.

"I'm sorry you guys had to make breakfast," Naomi said. "I wasn't trying to bail on you or anything. I didn't think it would be a big deal. Plus, I didn't realize we had a set time."

"Obviously," Annabelle muttered as she grabbed the pan off the stove and stuck it in the sink. Why did she have to turn into such a grump whenever her sister was in the room? They'd managed to have a good time at the game last night, without the slightest bicker. It had been nice and fun and had reminded Annabelle how much she missed having her sister around. Then Naomi slipped back into her own Naomi world, which made Annabelle want to snarl at her.

Naomi leaned against the counter, crossing her arms over her chest. Not even glancing at the French toast casserole or the other dirty dishes she could have helped with. Instead she just stood there and watched Annabelle do all the work.

"We were supposed to all have breakfast together," Annabelle blurted out.

Naomi blinked at her. "We could have if you had waited."

Annabelle squirted soap onto the sponge and swirled the thing around the dirty pan. "How long were we supposed to wait? For all we knew, you could have been gone all day."

"But I wasn't," Naomi pointed out. "I just went to the gym. Chill out."

"What was Mom supposed to do with the breakfast when she got up?"

"I already did it for her," Naomi pointed out. "All she needed to do was put the casserole in the oven."

"Which she can't do," Annabelle argued with a glance at her sister.

"Yes, she can, Tansie. Mom's capable of doing a lot more than you give her credit for. I still can't figure out why you hover over her the way you do."

Annabelle rinsed the pan and set it on the drying rack, but the thing toppled over when she dropped it with too much force. "Because she needs help." She shut the faucet off and tossed the sponge down. "One of us needs to be here to do the things for her that she can't do herself."

"You're here because you're a control freak, Tansie. Not because Mom needs you."

Annabelle spun around because the truth of her sister's words cut too deep. "And you're never here because you're too consumed with your own life. You didn't even know that Mom can't drink milk anymore."

Naomi stared back at her for a moment with a shallow pinch between her brows. "So it finally comes out," she muttered. "I knew there was something you were holding back from me."

Suddenly feeling exhausted, Annabelle leaned against the counter and lowered her head. Why did she have to act like a person she didn't recognize? Speaking without thinking had always been an issue for her, figuring honesty was always the best way to go. But some things, no matter how honest, were better left unsaid.

"Do you know why I stayed in South America?" Naomi asked. She glanced at Annabelle and continued. "Because I felt like I didn't fit in here."

The words sucked the breath from Annabelle's lungs. How could her own sister feel like a foreigner? It wasn't right, no matter how much Annabelle wished Naomi's life were different. *You want her to be more like you.* "That's crazy," Annabelle told her sister as much as telling herself.

"Maybe to you. But you had your life in order, Tansie. You had a degree and a good job and you were getting married." Naomi stared at a point across the kitchen. "You were always the more determined, responsible older sister. And

I was..." She lifted both her shoulders. "I was always the flighty one who couldn't stick with something for more than a few months."

Annabelle blinked at her sister. "I don't understand what you're trying to say."

Naomi placed her similar hazel eyes on Annabelle. "That's because you don't know what it's like to live in someone's shadow."

Naomi thought she'd been living in Annabelle's shadow? Why in the world would she think that? Had Annabelle made her own sister feel that way? The possibility was too much for her to swallow because she'd never intentionally make her own sister feel like she wasn't good enough. They might be different people with different priorities, but Naomi had her own strengths that made her good at what she did.

She was fearless and independent, something Annabelle had always struggled with.

"Naomi, I..." Annabelle shook her head. "I had no idea you felt that way." Had she been so worked up in starting her career and marrying Nathan that she'd failed to notice anything else around her? Had she lived the same selfish way she'd accused Naomi of living? That idea didn't set well with Annabelle; she'd always tried being a better person than that. Helping people who needed it, giving her time when she could.

"I know you didn't," Naomi said. "And I know it wasn't something you did intentionally. But Mom was always saying how proud she was of you, and 'Naomi, you should see the house your sister just bought,' or 'Naomi, when are you going to get a good job like your sister?' After a while it just became too much for me."

Naomi had never given any indication she'd felt that way.

"Why move to a whole other country? I mean, don't you realize how much we miss you? It sucks seeing you every two
years."

"You think I don't miss you and Mom like crazy? That
I constantly wrestle with whether or not I made a mistake
moving so far away? I know Mom is getting older and not
being here for her kills me."

"So why do you stay away?" Annabelle asked.

"Because I love what I do and I love living in South
America. I know you and Mom will never understand that,
but life down there is different than it is here. It's slower and
more laid back. In Peru I can be my own person without
pressure from anyone else."

"You can be your own person here," Annabelle argued.
"Do you know how much it kills Mom to never see you?"
Just saying the words out loud was like a knife to her heart.

When Naomi looked at Annabelle, her green eyes were
bright with moisture. "You think I don't think about that all
the time? That I don't constantly go back and forth between
loyalty to my family and following my dreams? How am I
supposed to decide between the two?"

Annabelle had never thought about it that way, because
her dreams had never taken her farther than a few hours
away. It just so happened that she loved Colorado. Loved
the majestic beauty of the mountains and the cool air. She
loved being outdoors and seeing her mother. So choosing
between her dreams and her family had never been an issue
for her.

"You did decide, Naomi," she pointed out. "You chose to
follow your dreams."

Naomi pushed away from the counter. "Don't say it in
that tone of voice, Tansie. Like you're accusing me of doing
something wrong. Like I've betrayed you or something."

Naomi spun around and pinned Annabelle with a desperate stare. "Why can't you just be supportive of me? Why do you and Mom always have to make me feel like I've done something wrong?"

When the first tear trickled over her sister's lashes, Annabelle's heart constricted. Naomi had gone from the independent, opinionated woman to the soft-spoken little girl who used to slip her smaller hand into Annabelle's and then allow Annabelle to lead her wherever she wanted to go. Because there was trust and love and understanding.

Where had all of that gone? Had Annabelle whittled it away? Had she allowed her propensity for being a know-it-all damage that part of their relationship?

If so, how in the world had she become that person? The last thing she wanted was to make her own sister feel inadequate. To damage her confidence. Annabelle knew firsthand what that was like.

Without taking a second thought, Annabelle pushed away from the counter and wrapped her sister in a tight hug. Naomi wound her arms around Annabelle's shoulders, gripping harder than she ever had. As they stood there in the silent kitchen, Annabelle thought back to the last time she'd extended this kind of affection toward her sister. The sad truth was, she couldn't remember. She was pretty sure she'd given Naomi a long hug at the airport the last time she'd visited. But that had been different. A good-bye until next time.

This was deep and emotional and long overdue.

The dreaded lump formed in Annabelle's throat, followed by hot tears pushing past her closed eyelids. Damn it, why did she have to cry? Annabelle hated crying; it always exhausted her.

But the tears came anyway and she let them fall, sliding down her cheeks and dropping to Naomi's bare shoulder.

When the first tear hit, Naomi pulled away and swiped at her own moisture. "You're not allowed to cry," she told Annabelle. "You're supposed to be the strong one."

But she wasn't strong. It was all an illusion. "I'm not as strong as you think I am." If she were, she'd give it a go with Blake. To see where they would go. But she was terrified of being hurt, so she stayed back.

"That's because you're your own worst critic," Naomi said with a small smile. "Through the eyes of a little sister, you're perfect."

Annabelle's heart turned over again and she wanted to tell her sister to stop. To stop saying things that Annabelle didn't deserve.

"I'm sorry for giving you a hard time," she told Naomi. "Of course you're free to live your life however you want to live it." She lifted one shoulder. "I just wish we saw you more. Mom and I miss you."

Naomi expelled a long breath. "I bet not as much as I miss you. Now go sit down with Mom." Naomi shooed her out of the kitchen. "I'll clean the rest of the dishes."

Annabelle turned around but stopped when she got to the door. She glanced back at her sister. "The casserole was really good."

A slow smile pulled at the corners of Naomi's mouth as she grabbed the sponge and started cleaning.

SEVENTEEN

After leaving her mother's house, Annabelle went to her studio for an appointment with Matt West.

On the way there, she'd picked up her cell phone at least three times to call Blake. Just to check on him. To see if he'd slept well or needed anything from her. She wasn't his girlfriend and if he wanted to speak with her, he'd call.

So she kept the phone in the cup holder and both hands firmly on the wheel. Two and ten and all that. But that didn't stop her from glancing at the device every thirty seconds, willing it to ring.

Which it didn't. Because he wasn't going to call. Because Blake Carpenter, the human island, didn't need anyone.

Maybe she could just text him.

No!

She'd left him a note, so the ball was in his court. And that, as they said, would just have to be that. Annabelle entered the studio and flipped on all the lights. The place was freezing, seeing as though fall had finally decided to come, dropping nighttime temps to downright cold. So she activated the heat and set her bag down. Just as she made her way to the reception desk to check messages, her phone vibrated.

The noise startled her but she tried to not be too psychotic when checking the message. It could be anyone. No reason to believe a certain man would be texting her. Maybe sending a nice good morning message. Or thanking her for the coffee. Or, even better, something like "I miss you."

An "I love you" would be great too.

Annabelle shoved that insane thought away the second it entered her mind. Because it *was* insane. Preposterous.

She pulled up the text and read a message from Stella. One simple word:

Lunch?

Annabelle glanced at the clock and tried calculating what time she'd be available after her eleven o'clock appointment with Brandon's son. *How about 12:30?*

A second later, Stella responded. *I'll meet you there and we can walk to the Cat.*

She confirmed the plans with Stella, then checked the studio's messages before Brandon and Matt arrived about ten minutes later.

Brandon was a big guy, probably about an inch or so shorter than Blake, with long legs and powerfully wide shoulders. He had the same dark hair as his cousin, though Brandon's was shaggier, and his eyes were darker, resembling a rich bourbon. Whatever Blake lacked in the carefree department, though, Brandon more than made up for. He always had a smile for everyone, especially the ladies, and then his carefree grins became quick and devilish, earning him the nickname back in high school of "Wild West."

Or so she'd heard. Brandon and Blake had graduated from Blanco Valley High School four years before her, so by the time she'd got to high school, all that had been left of them were stories.

"Good morning," she greeted Brandon and Matt.

Matt extended his hand first and offered a friendly smile. The boy had inherited his size and dark hair from his father, but his eyes were much darker, bordering on a rich chocolate. He was a sweet kid who loved football probably as much as Blake did.

"Good morning, Ms. Turner," Brandon greeted in that deep voice of his. The gravelly tone reminded her of Blake, which in turn reminded her of how he sounded murmuring in her ear. A wave of goose bumps rose on her arms, an odd sensation to be having in front of Blake's cousin.

Brandon didn't seem to notice as he let go of her hand and went on to describe the tightness Matt had been having in his neck.

"I have to go meet with one of my subcontractors," Brandon said with a glance at his watch. "I'll be back in about an hour to pick Matt up." He ruffled a hand over his son's too long hair, then strolled out the door.

Annabelle offered Matt a smile. "Your dad seems like a good guy," she told him, then led him to a treatment table. "Go ahead and lie down on your back."

Matt lifted one shoulder, then settled himself on the table. "Yeah, he's cool."

Quite the conversationalist. Annabelle positioned herself at the end of the table, near Matt's head. "I'm going to start with some cervical traction," she explained to him. "Basically it gives a gentle separation of the bones and joints in your neck, which takes pressure off the nerves." Annabelle wrapped one hand around the back of Matt's neck, then cupped her hand underneath his chin. "Try and relax for me," she explained to him. "You're going to feel a little bit of pulling in your neck." She gave Matt a moment to take and release a deep breath. Then she began the slow and gentle motion of applying the traction force to Matt's neck by leaning back and holding for ten seconds. "So how's football going for you?" she asked the kid.

"Okay, I guess," he answered in a slightly strained voice. "Wish I played more, though."

"Is this hurting?" she asked him. When he muttered a no, she gently relieved the pressure, then started the exercise over again. "I bet a lot of your teammates wish that. But it seems like Coach does a good job of keeping you all rotated." After another ten seconds, Annabelle released Matt's neck, and went through the motions one more time.

"Are you, like, Coach's girlfriend, or something?" Matt asked when Annabelle finished the last rep of tractions.

Annabelle almost answered with "or something" because she wasn't sure what she and Blake were. And because she knew a lot of the players suspected there was something going on between them. So she didn't bother to ask why Matt thought that.

"Honestly, Matt?" she asked him.

Matt pushed himself to a sitting position on the table. "Yeah. I mean, some of the other players think the two you are all hot and heavy and stuff."

She knew Blake wished they were hot and heavy, but Annabelle couldn't bring herself to take that leap.

"I'm not sure what your coach and I are. I know that we're friends, and he's a good coach," Annabelle answered as honestly as she could. "And the Bobcats mean a lot to him."

Matt huffed out a breath. "Yeah, he's a really good coach.

Probably the best coach we've ever had." He pinned his deep brown gaze on hers. "I know a lot of the parents didn't like having him here. Some of the other players had to leave the team."

Annabelle motioned for him to hop off the table. "That's because those parents are ignorant and think they know everything." The words slipped out before she had a chance to stop them, making her sound like some overprotective mother bear. She knew it was because she wanted to protect Blake. Which was ridiculous because Blake Carpenter was more than capable of taking care of himself. The man didn't need anyone's protection, least of all hers.

"That's what my dad said," Matt answered.

"Because your dad and Blake are really close, aren't they?" she asked the boy.

"Yeah, they're like best friends. They grew up together after my grandparents died."

Annabelle wanted to ask about Matt's mother, but she bit her tongue. Point for her, because Annabelle never bit her tongue about anything.

She led him through more stretches while giving some techniques on proper posture to help with the stiffness and showing him how to exercise his neck at home. They worked for another forty-five minutes before Brandon came back, strolling through the glass door with that long-legged loose-limbed walk that reminded her so much of Blake.

A navy blue polo, with *West Custom Homes* stitched in white across Brandon's left pec, was tucked into a pair of faded blue jeans.

Brandon came to a stop in front of Matt, with only a few inches in height separating the two. He placed a large hand on his son's shoulder. "Better?" he asked the teen.

Matt rotated his head from side to side. It was still a bit

stiff, but they'd definitely made progress. "Yeah, Ms. Turner knows her stuff," Matt answered, shooting Annabelle a grin. When the kid's full mouth turned up like that, he looked like an eighteen-year-old version of his dad.

"Let's go get some lunch," Brandon told his son, then guided him toward the door. "Do me a favor and grab us a table at Slices," Brandon said, indicating the pizza place two doors down from hers.

"All right," Matt answered, then glanced back at Annabelle. "Bye, Ms. Turner. Thanks for the help."

"Anytime, Matt," she told him, and watched as he went out the door and disappeared down the street. "Are you going to warn me away from your cousin?" she asked Brandon when he drilled his brown gaze into hers.

His brows pinched over his eyes. "Actually, no. I was going to ask what the hell is taking so long. When my cousin sees something he wants, he goes after it," Brandon explained. "I'm just wondering why he's taking his sweet time with you."

Annabelle tilted her head. "How do you know he hasn't gone after me?" she countered. If Annabelle were to be completely honest with Brandon, she'd correct his assumption. That *she* was the one who hadn't gone after Blake. She was the one holding back and, for all the reasons she had before, she couldn't remember a single damn one of them.

"For one thing," Brandon said, "Blake's been walking around with a stick up his ass for weeks." Brandon's eyes narrowed. "Unless you've rejected him."

"How is this any of your business, Brandon? Why are you so concerned about my relationship with Blake?"

"He's had a rough couple of years and doesn't need someone stringing him along. If you're not going to be legit with him, you need to cut him loose and move on."

Legit? "Is that what you think I'm doing with him? Stringing him along?"

Brandon studied her a moment. "If you're not, then what are you doing?"

Annabelle expelled a deep sigh. "Look, not that it's any of your business, but I like Blake—a lot. I don't want to see him hurt. And, yes, I know he's had some difficult times. But—and I've told him this from the very beginning—I don't do casual. He's made it clear he's not looking for anything more serious."

"Are you sure about that?"

"He's told me that himself more than once. I know what he's been through with his team and the surgeries on his knee—"

"He showed you his knee?"

Annabelle waited a moment before answering, trying to read Brandon's poker face, but his expression was just that. "Yeah, why?" she asked.

Brandon slowly shook his head. "No reason. But if he lets you see his jersey, the one hanging in his living room, then you'll know."

Annabelle's blood ran cold and a layer of sweat gathered on her palms. "Know what?"

Brandon slid his dark sunglasses over his eyes and opened the door. "That he's a big fat liar." Then he stepped through the door, colliding with Stella, who stumbled and dropped her cell phone.

Brandon maneuvered around her and Stella scooped her phone off the ground. "Yeah, don't worry about it," she called after him, wagging her phone in the air. "The phone's fine in case you were wondering."

But he was long gone, leaving Stella to scowl after him.

"Rude, much?" her friend muttered as she pocketed the

phone and settled her sunglasses on top of her head. "Ready for lunch?" she asked, and when Annabelle only stared, Stella took a step closer. "What's wrong? You look like you just got kicked in the stomach."

Her friend's description wasn't that far off. Brandon's words, or more accurately, a warning, had little sirens going off in her head. The same ones she usually heard right before Blake touched his lips to hers. They told her to stop, use caution, or cease and desist altogether. She hadn't listened to them before and Annabelle wasn't so sure she'd listen to them now.

Because despite how much he tried to make her think otherwise, Blake cared about her. For some reason she just instinctively *knew*. The same way she knew she'd fallen for him or that their relationship would never be casual. They had too much chemistry to maintain a simple friendship.

So where did that leave them? Damned if Annabelle could figure it out.

"Sorry," she told her friend, realizing she'd been standing there like an idiot and not speaking. "Yes, I'm ready."

"What was that?" Stella asked, pointing in the direction Brandon had disappeared to.

"I was helping Matt out with a stiff neck. Brandon just come by to pick him up, and they were headed to lunch."

Stella shook her head and slid her sunglasses over her face. "I hope it's not the same place we're going to. Something about that man doesn't sit right with me."

"I know what you mean," Annabelle agreed. "Gorgeous ass. Dreamy brown eyes. Mile-wide shoulders. That would rub any woman the wrong way."

Stella elbowed her in the ribs. "Well, it apparently rubbed you the wrong way. You should have seen the look on your face when he left. Now spill it, woman. Did he give you the whole don't-break-my-cousin's-heart-or-I'll-kill-you speech?"

Damn, sometimes Annabelle forgot just how observant her best friend could be. "More or less," she answered, grateful to have a sounding board. "Except how can I break his heart when we're not even involved?"

"Oh, honey, you're involved. You just don't know you're involved." Stella whipped her sunglasses off and pierced Annabelle with those baby blues. "You like this guy, right?" Annabelle nodded and Stella continued. "And you enjoy his company. Not to mention he's smokin' hot."

Yeah, and hell yeah.

"So then what's the problem?" Stella asked.

Annabelle opened her mouth, then shut it again. For the past few months, she'd had all kinds of reasons for not pursuing a relationship with Blake, and all of them pretty valid, thank you very much. The odd thing was, when Stella asked the question, Annabelle couldn't come up with a single one. Her logic had gone AWOL, leaving her without any kind of defense.

"You know what?" Stella waved a hand in the air. "Forget I asked that question because I already know what the problem is." She jabbed Annabelle in the chest with a skinny index finger. "You're the problem."

Annabelle narrowed her eyes at her friend. "I beg your pardon?"

"Yeah, you heard me," Stella said. "You're complicating a situation that's not complicated. That's what you do. It's your MO."

Annabelle laughed, which came out as more of a cough because her breath got stuck in her throat. "That's completely not true. I don't even have an MO." Wait. Did she?

Since her divorce, she'd tried to keep her life simple.

Pain free. Worry free. She'd thought focusing on her career and keeping men out of it had been the way to go.

Then Blake had come along with his bedroom voice and five o'clock shadow and blown all her good intentions out of the water. The scary thing was, he'd done it with such little effort. He'd kicked through her defenses with that size 13 of his and barged his way right in. Without permission. Without warning. She'd been ill prepared for his presence. Or the aftermath.

"I'm not trying to make you feel bad, Annabelle," Stella told her. "But you deserve to be happy. What's wrong with giving Blake a chance?"

See, that was the thing. There was nothing wrong with it. Being with Blake wouldn't be wrong, but so very right. Too right; she wouldn't be able to detach herself from him.

"He scares me, Stella," Annabelle whispered.

"And that's a normal thing when you have feelings for someone. Love is never simple," Stella added. "It's messy and complicated and hard, but it can also be the most rewarding thing in the world."

Annabelle shook her head and glanced at the people around them. "How do you know it'll work out?"

"You don't know," Stella answered. "Isn't the reward worth the risk?" Stella ushered Annabelle toward the diner's front doors. "It's not the fear of the unknown you have to get over, Annabelle. It's yourself."

"Or maybe it's just the one-eyed snake."

The voice, belonging to Patty Silvano, sent a cringe through Annabelle's system. And not just for intruding on hers and Stella's conversation. One-eyed snake? Seriously?

Stella pointed an index finger at the woman's button-down floral shirt. "Exactly. Tell her what she's missing out on, Patty."

Patty nodded, which didn't even nudge the beehive held together by hairspray and pins. "The ol' salami," the woman said. "The beef bayonet. Long Dong Silver—"

Annabelle pinned her hands over her ears. "Oh my Lord, I'm not listening." She pushed through the diner's doors and immediately smacked into the end of the line of people waiting to be seated.

Stella and Patty followed. "Well, there's no reason to be scared, Annabelle. It's just a muscle. Why, my Stan had a girth of five inches, but it's really not that bad. You just have to get used to it and I'm telling you, once you do, any plain old man won't do anymore."

Stella's mouth dropped open and Annabelle swore a flush of red filled her cheeks.

"That's great, Mrs. Silvano," Annabelle said to keep the woman from blurting out anything else. "But we weren't talking about a man's penis."

Patty opened her mouth, then snapped it shut, as though the thought of discussing anything else was unbelievable. To be honest, Annabelle wasn't sure why she was surprised. Patty was the most spry and spunky of the Beehive Mafia, often being teased as being a teenager trapped in an old woman's body.

She jammed her hands on her bony hips, clad in a pair of brown polyester pants. "Well, what the hell else is there to be afraid of?"

Stella nudged Patty in the ribs. "What I've been saying."

"Okay, will you both stop?" Annabelle demanded, aware of the people mingling around and not needing anything else for them to talk about. Blake had enough on his shoulders without the gossipers speculating about a relationship between them. He needed to focus on the play-offs and fending off questions about the two of them.

"Well," Patty said with a toss of her head, "if neither of you want my advice, then what am I doing here?"

Then she was gone, back out the door and letting more people in who stood in line behind them.

"Long Dong Silver?" Stella asked with a shudder. "I swear, I don't know if I should be amused or afraid."

Annabelle nodded her agreement. "Sometimes I wonder if Patty is a few cards short of a full deck."

"I actually think she's a sharp as a tack," Stella countered. "She's just eccentric."

"Excuse me," a feminine voice sounded from behind Annabelle. She turned and spotted a tall pear-shaped woman with chin-length dishwater-blond hair. She stuck out a hand with a blinking diamond on her ring finger. "I'm Misty Porter. Scott Porter's mother."

Annabelle blinked. "Oh," she replied, and took the woman's hand. "It's nice to meet you."

Misty's grin grew. "I just wanted to thank you for all the help you've given Scott this season."

Annabelle found herself grinning back. "It's my pleasure. He's a talented player, not to mention a good kid."

The compliment had Misty glowing. "Thank you. His dad and I are so proud, especially considering how rough the past two seasons were. Coach Carpenter has been so good for those kids."

The line to the counter moved, and the women moved along with it. "All they needed was some good leadership. They're talented kids."

"He's more than just a good leader for them," Misty added. "He's transformed the whole team."

Annabelle wondered if Blake knew how much the people loved him. Would he still doubt himself if he heard what Misty had to say? Annabelle would guess probably so, because Blake Carpenter was his own worst critic.

"I know a lot of people had their misgivings about him coming here," Misty went on, "but we've always stood by him, and we're so glad he's here." She leaned closer as a group of people nudged by them, toward the exit. "We're also glad he's found you. He seemed like such a lonely man, didn't he?"

Found her?

Annabelle forced a wider smile and tilted her head. "I'm sorry, I'm not sure what you mean."

"Oh, I wasn't trying to assume anything," Misty corrected. "But some of the other moms are saying that you and the coach are a thing."

"I wouldn't really say that—"

"A woman in my scrapbooking club said her daughter spotted the two of you at the lake. She went on to say how adorable you two were and how you were practically glowing."

Behind Annabelle, Stella cleared her throat and she knew it wasn't because her friend had something lodged. "We were just there having lunch."

Stella coughed this time and Annabelle wanted to smack her upside the head.

Pink flooded Misty's cheeks. "Gracie, that's my friend's daughter, said it looked like more than lunch. Scott even told me he thought you and the coach were an item."

Had someone turned up the heat? A bead of sweat slid down Annabelle's back. She didn't want to divulge any details to this woman; even though she seemed perfectly nice, Annabelle didn't know her from Adam. Even still, she wouldn't have the faintest clue how to respond. Denying always seemed like the best route.

But how much longer could she lie to herself? And other people? She knew perfectly well, just like they did, that there *was* something between her and Blake.

"Well, anyway," Misty continued, "I just wanted to say that I think it's adorable, and the kids love it."

"They do?" Annabelle queried, instead of correcting the woman.

"How could they not? Anyone could tell that man needed some softness in his life, considering what he's been through. And the players love you, so I don't think there's anyone else they'd want in their coach's life."

She peeled her tongue off the roof of her mouth and was about to force out a thank you, when Misty glanced at her watch and edged toward the door. "I've gotta run," she told Annabelle and Stella. "It was nice meeting you."

She breezed past them, allowing more people into the diner as she exited. Beside her, Stella was smirking, even though Annabelle couldn't see her face. She knew her friend well enough to recognize the tilt of her head.

"What?" Annabelle finally demanded.

Stella held her hands up. "I didn't say anything. Except ditto what she said."

EIGHTEEN

Y ou're an idiot," Blake whispered to himself after tapping the back of his knuckles on Annabelle's front door. He dipped the tips of his fingers into the front pocket of his jeans and tightened his grip on the gift bag in his other hand.

For some insane reason, he'd been looking forward to waking up next to her that morning. All his fantasies of her since they'd met had involved a bed, minimal clothing, and maybe some early morning lovemaking. The latter would have been a longshot, he knew. Especially after the way he'd acted the night before.

You mean like a Neanderthal?

Yeah, that.

After all, what woman would want to get naked with a guy who'd not only been borderline drunk, but had told her to get the hell out more than once?

He'd acted like a complete ass. He'd also all but broken

down when she'd dumped his Oxy down the drain. Like a first-class pussy.

Real manly and heroic.

Blake shifted his feet on the welcome mat and knocked on the door again. If she didn't answer with this one, he'd leave and come back later. Because he always found his way back to her. Even after showing his most vulnerable side of himself last night and allowing her to take care of him. Curling himself around her, skin to skin, feeling her deep breaths in synchronization with his had been foreign territory for him. Blake had never been big on cuddling. He didn't spoon or have breakfast in bed or share food. Even as he'd gotten in her face and told her to get out, deep inside he'd cringed at the thought of her leaving. He'd wanted her to stay. To spend the whole night lying next to him. He'd just been too much of a baby to outright ask her.

The intimacy he'd shared with Annabelle only magnified how empty his past relationships really were.

How empty he really was.

It wasn't an easy reality to swallow, but after forcing it down, Blake had been left with one conclusion.

He wanted Annabelle Turner. And not for just another meaningless screw. He wanted her in his life, in his home, and in his heart. He was in love with her, and after last night, there was no going back. She'd dug herself good and deep.

Blake was just about to turn around and go home when he heard footsteps on the other side of the door. A second later, before he had time to prepare himself, the door swung open and there she was.

Annabelle blinked at him. "Blake," she said.

"Can I come in?" he asked her.

She offered him a small smile, which turned his heart over, and stepped aside. "Of course. I was just in the backyard planting some flowers."

That was when he noticed the smear of dirt on her right thigh, hair piled on top of her head in some messy bun and freshly scrubbed, makeup-free face, which allowed the light smattering of freckles across her nose to peek out.

The woman was so beautiful he had a hard time breathing around her.

He stepped over the threshold, hoping to brush up against her, but she'd stepped too far back. On purpose? Was she trying to keep her distance from him? If he managed to scare her away after last night, he'd never forgive himself.

"I can come back if I'm interrupting," he told her.

Annabelle closed the door. "Don't be ridiculous. The flowers aren't going anywhere. And I'd hate to think things would be that awkward between us."

"Yeah, I came to apologize about that." He shoved his hand back in his pocket because if he didn't, he'd tunnel it through her hair. Then follow through with a deep, soulful kiss. "I was a dick last night and you didn't deserve the way I treated you."

She blinked those bottomless green eyes at him. "Blake, you have nothing to be sorry for. If anyone's sorry, it's me."

"What the hell do you have to be sorry for?"

Annabelle turned and led him to the living room. "For butting in. As usual," she said over her shoulder. "I have a problem with making everyone's business my own and I should have left you alone."

"I didn't want you to leave me alone." He held up a hand when she opened her mouth. "I know that's what I said to you, more than once, but I'm glad you stayed." He held his breath for a moment, then plunged forward with the ultimate confession. "I'm also glad you tossed those pills."

Annabelle's tongue darted out and swiped across her lower lip. "Are you really?"

Blake sighed and placed her gift on the coffee table. "Yeah," he admitted after a moment. "Scared the shit out of me at first. But I'm glad they're gone, and I'm glad you were the one to do it. No one else would have done that for me."

"That's because no one else knows you have a problem," she reminded him.

"That too," he agreed. "Also because I didn't want anyone else to know."

"You didn't want me to know either," she pointed out.

Damn, she was too smart for her own good. "Also true. Yet here you are," he said. "Right where I don't want you to be."

Something dark flashed across her eyes, but it was gone so fast that Blake almost thought he'd imagined it.

"Where would that be?" she asked.

He rubbed a hand over the back of his neck, where he could feel tension building. "See, that's the thing. I'm not exactly sure. I just know you're the only woman who's gotten this far." When she didn't say anything, which was probably a good thing because Blake was at a loss for words, he picked up the gift bag and held it out to her. "The other coaches and I went in together on this for you. Kind of a thank-you for your time. And for putting up with our grumpy asses," he added.

The comment coaxed a smile out of her. "You guys didn't have to do that. I told you from the beginning, I'm happy to help out." She took the bag from him. "I care about those kids."

Blake nodded. "I know. That's why you're so good at what you do. It's more than just a job for you."

Annabelle lifted a brow as she took the tissue out of the bag. "I told you to stop thinking so highly of me."

He tucked a strand of stray hair behind her ear. "You don't give me much of a choice."

A deep red colored her high cheekbones, then spread over her whole face when she pulled the gift out of the bag. The bag fell to the floor as she held the black football jersey up with her last name in bold white letters on the back and the number 1 front and center.

"Is this an actual game jersey?" she asked as her green gaze ran over the number one on the front.

"Yes, ma'am," he answered. "It's the home jersey."

She shook her head and turned the jersey around. "I don't know what to say. You really didn't need to get me anything."

"Yes, we did," he countered. Then he took the jersey from her and slipped it over her head. "You earned it for how much time you've spent with the players. Hell, you earned it for just putting up with me."

The garment fell to her hips and was too wide for her shoulders. But it was damn adorable and conjured a ridiculous image of her wearing one of his jerseys and nothing else. Except maybe a stringy little thong underneath. That he could remove with his teeth.

"Well, you were a bit of a challenge at first, I'll admit that," she told him with a coy look. She tugged the jersey down and gave herself a once-over. "It's a bit big for me."

"It's supposed to be big." He had to fist his hands at his sides to keep from sliding them under the hem and up the creamy skin of her stomach.

She lifted a brow at him. "To make room for all those pads I'll be wearing?" she teased.

"For a man, yeah. For a woman it's just meant to be cute," he told her.

Her smile slipped a fraction. "You think I look cute in this?"

Was that a loaded question or what? "I'm too much of a gentleman to say how you really look in this thing."

She took a step closer to him and touched his bottom lip with her index finger. "We both know you're not that much of a gentleman."

Her skin smelled of sunshine and sweat and lingering body wash or lotion or whatever the hell girly shit women wore. It teased his nostrils and sent a wave of awareness through his system, the same awareness he'd been tortured with last night as they'd lain side by side.

"I'm trying, anyway," he said in response to her statement. "But you're making it damn hard." In more ways than one.

"Am I?" Her cool hands gripped his fists, unfolded his fingers, and placed them on her lower back. "It's okay to touch me. I won't bite."

But it wasn't okay. Touching her was far from okay.

It's more than okay, you jackass. It's so damn good that you know you want to do more.

Hell yeah he did, but he couldn't because he was trying to respect her wishes to keep things friendly and platonic. Except there was nothing friendly about the way she moved into him, pressing her thighs to his, nudging his chest with her supple breasts.

And definitely not friendly when his palms explored the gentle curve of her lower back, then glided over the fullness of her rear end. He gave her a good tug, yanking her harder against him.

Yeah, nothing but friendly.

"Screw friendly," he muttered.

Annabelle's lips parted and her eyelids slowly blinked. "What?" she asked.

Now his brain was so muddled with desire that his filter had shut itself off.

His lips barely skimmed over hers. "You're making it hard to stay away from that casual fling you're so against."

"Maybe I changed my mind."

A growl bubbled up in his chest, which he managed to suppress. "You can't go changing your mind like that unless you mean it. Not right to mess with a man's head this way."

"What about the way you mess with mine?" she countered as she placed her palms on the flat planes of his chest.

"We should do something about that," he suggested. "Unless you want me to leave." *Please don't ask me to leave.*

She slowly nodded while sliding her hands up his pecs, over his collarbones, then curved over the muscle where his neck met his shoulders. "Yeah, you should go. We can't do this."

Liar. Her eyes, normally so bright green they reminded Blake of freshly cut grass, were dilated. Darkened with the same desire coursing through his veins like a barbiturate. They both knew she wasn't about to ask him to leave. She wanted him just as much as he wanted her. And they'd danced around each other for too long for it to dissipate now.

No, this was it. This was what they'd been leading up to since the moment she'd hit him with that hypnotic stare. Since the first time she'd swayed those hips for him. From the moment she'd argued with him and butted her nose into his business.

From the very first second their lips touched and set off a myriad of fireworks that could outshine the finale of a Fourth of July show.

His grip on her rear end tightened. "So tell me to leave," he urged.

Her fingers slid into his hair. "Leave," she whispered. The same kind of whisper made for dark corners and darker bedrooms.

"I'm not convinced."

She grinned against his lips. "I thought that sounded pretty convincing."

"Not by a long shot, Ms. Turner," he told her.

"How about, 'Get the hell out of my house.'"

He nuzzled her throat with his nose, breathing in the scent of her hair and the sensitive skin beneath her ear. "Better," he said. "But I might believe you if you could say it while you're not trying to claw your way into my clothes," he murmured in her ear.

"Oh." Her head dropped back when he placed a soft kiss on her neck. "I guess you see right through me, then."

He chuckled and satisfaction amped up his male pride when goose bumps rose on her flesh. "I don't think you're trying very hard."

"Because I'm through trying," she responded.

He lifted his head and looked at her, recognizing the need and fire in her eyes as matching his own. "I need you to be sure," he told her.

Her fingers dug harder into the back of his skull. "I am."

That was all the confirmation he needed. He'd been ready to drag her into the bedroom from the moment she'd slipped the football jersey over her head.

He bent his knees and lifted her so she could hook her legs over his hips. "Bedroom," was all he said, because getting out anything more than that was too much.

She waved a hand in some direction behind his head. "That way," she answered. "Down the hall on the left."

He figured if he kicked open enough doors, he'd eventually find her bedroom. Hell, it didn't even need to be her room. Any room with a bed would do.

Annabelle fixed her mouth on his, slipping her tongue past his lips. He opened for her, inviting her all the way in, while he carried her down the hallway. She was light and curvy and fit in the cradle of his hips so well that he never wanted to put her down.

He remembered how she'd felt straddling his legs when they'd been at the lake. How easy it had been for her to fit her thighs next to his hips and settle the curve of her rear end on his thighs. The position had always been one of his favorites in bed because it allowed the woman to have more control while he could watch the expressions on her face.

When Annabelle had thrown her leg over his, he'd been assaulted by an image of her astride him in bed. Hair trailing down her back, eyes closed, lips parted. Sweat glistening the indentation of her spine and hips rocking back and forth.

Oh yeah, it would be good.

"That one." Annabelle tore her mouth from his and pointed to a door he'd just walked past.

He was already so consumed with what they were about to do that he'd walked clear to the end of the hall.

She directed him to the correct door, which he kicked closed behind them. He didn't bother with setting her on the floor, not wanting to waste another second. Instead, he went straight for the bed, dropping her in the middle and settling himself on top of her.

Full-body contact while standing in the living room, or a kitchen, or a sandy beach was nothing compared to a soft bed. Especially a bed big enough to move around and one that smelled like her. The fresh flowery scent that always lingered on her skin was all over the sheets, sending him images of her tangled up in them.

He reluctantly tore his mouth from hers and gazed into her green eyes. "Do you know how long I've waited for this?" he asked her.

She bent her knees around his hips and threaded her fingers through his hair. "Do you know what this means to me?" she countered, instead of answering his question.

He knew exactly what it meant to her, because it meant the same to him. That this was anything but casual. The very thing he'd tried so hard to prevent, he was now smack in the middle of. A part of him wanted to blame the witchy spell she had over him. That she'd enchanted him with her slow smiles and seductive laugh and generous heart.

The truth was, it wasn't enchantment or craftiness or spells. It was just her. Annabelle Turner, a woman who made him feel alive and excited and territorial.

He framed her face with his palms and brushed his thumb across her cheekbone. "I have a pretty good idea."

And the last thing he thought about for a long time was the understanding that flashed in her eyes.

Blake hated gardening. Hated flowers, hated fertilizer and pulling weeds. They were a haven for bees and allergies and everything else he'd rather not deal with. So when Annabelle asked him if he wanted to help her in her garden, of course he'd said yes. Because he'd do anything for this woman. Which included wielding a ridiculous pink shovel thing so she could drop perky yellow flowers in the ground.

After making love like a couple of horny rabbits, they'd made some food, made love again, then got dressed. The getting dressed part had been Annabelle's idea. He'd been perfectly content with spending the rest of the afternoon in bed. Maybe mix a shower in there somewhere, because he'd been consumed with the idea of smearing soap all over her backside.

Apparently Annabelle hadn't been consumed with the same thoughts. After their second round of lovemaking, she'd slid out of bed, pulled her shorts back on, and asked him if he wanted to work in the garden with her.

He'd lain on his side, propped up on an elbow, and watched with disappointment as she fixed her bra over her breasts. "As long as you don't tell anyone the head coach of the Bobcats was planting flowers, sure," he'd told her.

That had coaxed a grin out of her and she'd leaned over the bed and dropped a kiss on his mouth. "I promise not to say a word. In fact, if someone asks, I'll tell them we were working with tools or something manly like that."

He'd quirked a brow at her. "Something manly?"

"You know"—she'd waved a hand in the air as she'd slipped her T-shirt over her head—"because we wouldn't want your ego to be compromised."

Yeah, they wouldn't want that. Which was why, half an hour later, he was digging in the dirt and sprinkling fertilizer over mums, or whatever Annabelle had called them.

Despite his dislike for gardening, it actually wasn't half bad. The sunshine was nice and the breeze was cool. Not to mention, working side by side with Annabelle, the woman who'd scored her fingernails down his back not two hours ago, was just about the best thing he'd done in months.

The conversation was easy and she'd asked him about his parents. He'd spent the next twenty minutes telling her about their retired life in Arizona and how he didn't get to see them nearly as often as he'd like. About how supportive and understanding they'd been when his football career had ended.

"Sounds like you have a great relationship with them," she commented as she pulled her wagon closer and took another tray of flowers out.

Blake dropped a bunch into a hole he'd dug with the trowel. "Yeah, I do. They're good people," he added, wishing he was able to see them more. To tell them how much the unfailing support really meant to him. They'd never once questioned him. Never asked him if he'd really done performance-enhancing drugs. Because they knew better and would never dream their only son could do something like that.

His parents and Brandon had been the only ones who'd believed him without a second thought.

Until Annabelle had come along. She hadn't judged, hadn't lectured, hadn't asked him what he'd been thinking. How he could not have known. She'd never looked at him with pity or contempt. She'd accepted and hadn't used his past mistakes against him.

"I'd say they'd have to be to raise a man like you," Annabelle responded to his statement.

He glanced at her, but her attention was on her task in the dirt. A wide-brimmed hat shaded half her face, slashing a line of shadow across her nose.

"What?" she asked when she caught him staring at her. "You think I'm blowing smoke up your ass?"

Blake shook his head. "You're just about the only woman I know who's ever said the phrase 'smoke up your ass.'" After filling the hole he'd just dropped the flower in, Blake patted the ground flat, then sprinkled fertilizer. "Tell me about your ex-husband."

Annabelle wasn't deterred from her task. She dug a hole next to a bush, then retrieved a carton of flowers from the tray. "Why would you want to know about him?"

"Because he's part of what makes you who you are."

"Nathan hasn't been a part of me for a long time."

Blake sat back on his haunches and draped his arms over his knees. "What you went through with him is a part of you."

She stared at him for a moment, her hands held frozen above the fresh dirt she'd been cultivating. With a heavy sigh, she resumed her planting. "Nathan was good-looking, charming, and successful." She shot him a grin when he glared at her. "He was also shallow, dishonest, and manipulative."

Not that she needed to add the last part. He wasn't jealous of the guy. On the contrary, Blake wanted to smack the shit out of any man who was stupid enough to take a woman like Annabelle Turner for granted. How could this Nathan asshole not see what an amazing thing he'd had with her?

On the other hand, Nathan's screw-up turned out to be Blake's good fortune. Had the prick not broken Annabelle's heart, they'd probably still be married with a couple of kids. Annabelle was the family type. She'd be the mom who'd cut the crust off the peanut butter and jelly sandwiches. Or walked their kids to the bus stop—

Wait. *Their* kids?

When had he started thinking about them in those terms? He had the sudden image of taking her out to dinner on their anniversary or rubbing her feet when her ankles would swell up from pregnancy.

Whoa. A year ago, imagining something like that would have sent terror through his system.

Blake cleared his throat and moved on to the next spot to plant another flower. "How long had you known him when you got married?"

"About six months. And before you say anything, I know it's not enough time to know someone that well—"

"I wasn't going to say anything," he told her. "My parents knew each other for two months when they got engaged. Sometimes you just know."

"Yes, but it sounds to me like your dad is nothing like Nathan."

Blake nodded and dropped another plant in a freshly dug

hole. "You're right, he's not. My point is that the length of time doesn't matter. You don't have to know someone for a long time to realize if they're the right person for you."

She looked up at him and opened her mouth as though she had something to say, but she clamped her lips tight and sighed. "Obviously with Nathan, it did matter. If I'd given the relationship more time, I might have seen him for the person he really was."

"From the way you talk about him, probably not. Or maybe you were just blinded by love," he added, having a hard time even saying the words.

"No," she answered right away. "What I had with Nathan wasn't love. At the time, yes, I thought I did love him, but now I realize I didn't."

Blake patted the dirt after placing the flower. "How can you be sure of that?"

Annabelle didn't answer right away. Her capable hands worked the roots of another carton of flowers. "Because I'm not the person I was when we were married. People grow and mature and change. It wasn't until years later, after I'd finally moved on from his betrayal, that I realized I was never in love with him. I didn't wake up needing to see him or ache for his touch. I was just"—she shrugged— "indifferent." She placed her deep green eyes on him. "You don't grow indifferent when you're truly in love with someone. That's how I knew it wasn't real."

Yeah, Blake knew that. As scary as it was, he knew exactly was she was talking about because that's how he felt about her. Love was a creepy son of a bitch who claimed victims without warning.

"Have you ever experienced that?" she asked without looking at him.

He gazed at her profile, noting how the sun glanced off

her jawline and accentuated the creaminess of her skin. "Yeah," he answered without thinking. And there he went again. Blurting shit out without taking the time to stop himself.

What an ass.

Annabelle shifted her focus to him, staring with an unreadable expression in her eyes. "Did she break your heart?"

This time he did pause before answering, because it was a question he couldn't answer. Annabelle did have the power to break his heart. Funny, but Blake had always considered himself too ironclad for that sort of thing. Men weren't supposed to have their hearts broken. They were the heartbreakers because they were pigs who wouldn't know a gem of a woman if it were to hit them in the ass.

"Blake?" she pushed when he remained silent. "Is it too painful for you to talk about?"

"No, she hasn't broken my heart yet," he answered. "But she has the power to."

Her brows pinched above her eyes, which were filled with questions. She wanted to ask, that much he could tell; Annabelle was a curious creature who wanted to know everyone's secrets and cure them.

He could tell the moment realization dawned when her mouth fell open. She shifted on her knees. "Blake—"

"You don't need to say anything," he said with a shake of his head. "I'm not even sure what it is." He gazed into her knowing eyes. "I just know I've never felt it before."

Her long lashes swept down over her eyes, and then a single tear leaked out. It crept past her lower lashes, then ran down her smooth cheek. Blake stopped the moisture before it had a chance to drop to her bare shoulder. He swiped it away with the pad of his thumb, then lingered on her cheek, taking a moment to remind himself how soft she was and how much he loved touching her.

"I'm not sure what to do," she whispered. "I know I've said I've moved on from Nathan, and I really have," she reassured him. "But I'm still scared. What I went through with him altered my entire view of relationships."

"I'm a little scared too," he admitted. "I've never felt this way about a woman before, so I'm not sure how to handle it." He dropped his hand from her face and picked up a clod of dirt. "The thing is, I need to focus on getting the Bobcats to the play-offs. Drew has made it clear if they don't get that far, I'll be out of a job."

Annabelle nodded. "And you don't need any distractions," she concluded.

He cupped her chin and lifted her face to his. "You're not a distraction, Annabelle. I just don't think I can jump into anything right now."

"Of course, you're right," she commented, resuming her digging in the dirt. Her hands gripped the trowel and slid into the soft grit to make room for another flower. "Your job has to come first, I understand that." She offered him a warm smile, but the warmth didn't reach her eyes.

The two of them continued working side by side in the warm afternoon sun, with the birds chirping around them and the breeze lifting the strands of Annabelle's hair. Blake told himself he was relieved. Relieved he'd finally gotten his feelings out for her and relieved that she wasn't going to push for more than he could give her. Even though he wanted to.

So why did he feel like he'd just blown it with her?

NINETEEN

The Bobcats were about to enter their final regular season game with a record of 5-4. Not great, but enough to get them in the play-offs, provided they won tomorrow night's game. If they lost, it would be over. Their season would end with the final tick of the game clock.

And Blake's career as a high school football coach along with it. Yeah, no pressure or anything.

He'd pushed the kids hard this week. Extra runs. Harder tackles. Screaming in their ears to get the hell off their asses. He'd felt like a dick the entire time as the kids had been pushed beyond exhaustion. But they'd never been this close to a play-off game before, and it was high time they knew what it felt like to be winners. The whole time he'd been stealing peeks at Annabelle while she stretched with the players, since it had been over a week since they'd made love, then planted flowers in her garden. Seeing her on the field and not being able to yank her in for a kiss or whip her sweatshirt over her head had been torture. Pure torture, but he was a mature, professional adult and had managed to keep his hands to himself.

Corey had come back after his academic probation and now the kid didn't have anything lower than a B minus. Probably because he was too scared shitless to have anything worse than that. Scott had sat out the last two games, but Blake fully intended on playing him tomorrow night because, damn it, they needed him.

And Cody Richardson...well, that one was a different matter. Blake didn't know what to make of their quarter-back. He was as likely to show up to practice pumping his team up as he was not wanting to participate. In last week's game, which they'd lost, Cody's attitude had been shit. Not listening, changing plays, and talking back to the coaches. His defiance had caused tension between him and other players, which had resulted in a fist-on-fist brawl in the locker room at halftime. Blake had been in the middle of reaming their asses when Brian Strickland had taken a shot at the QB. Just planted his fist into Cody's too-pretty square jaw and knocked him off the bench. Cameron had jumped in, which had earned him a black eye, and broken the two kids up.

Since then, tension on the team had been high. The locker room crackled with it, and it was the last thing Blake needed as they entered their most important game of the season.

The team had practiced that morning and after school, and Blake left to run a quick errand. He pulled up to Cody's house and parked along the curb. The Richardson parents were the only parents Blake had never met. They'd never come to watch a practice and had never been to a game.

The home was a modest one-story ranch with black shutters

bracketing newly updated windows and a neatly trimmed yard. He made his way up the walk, not sure how these people would respond to a visit by their son's football coach. Blake didn't know a whole lot of coaches who did this kind of thing, but... what the hell?

He tapped the back of his knuckles on the stained-glass window of the door. A second later came the sound of rapid high heels on hardwood floors, followed by the door opening. On the other side stood an attractive woman with blond hair cropped to her shoulders and long legs covered in a pair of elegant slacks.

Blake nudged the brim of his hat up his forehead so she could see his eyes. "Mrs. Richardson?" he asked.

"No, I'm Mrs. Warren," she answered in a cool voice.

Blake glanced behind him, then turned back to her. "I'm looking for the parents of Cody Richardson."

The woman pressed a hand to her chest. "Why, did something happen to him?"

Blake shook his head. "No, ma'am." He stuck out his hand in greeting. "I'm Blake Carpenter, Cody's football coach."

She blinked at him, then shook her head. "I'm Gabby Warren." She offered her hand to his. "I'm sorry for the confusion," she told him. "Cody's dad and I divorced several years before he passed away, so the last names are different."

Blake nodded. "I apologize. I wasn't aware of that. May I come in for a minute?"

Gabby considered him, probably wondering whether or not to comply or shut the door in his face. Eventually she relented and stood back for him to enter.

The interior of the home was cool and quiet. Nicely decorated with curtains covering the windows, family photos on the walls, and plump pillows decorating the furniture.

"Can I get you some coffee or tea or anything?" Gabby asked.

"No, thank you. I need to make this quick and get back to work."

Gabby clasped her hands in front of her and waited for Blake to continue.

"Mrs. Warren, I was wondering if something was going on with Cody at home. Anything that could be affecting his attitude on the field."

Gabby tilted her head to one side. "Has my son been uncooperative with you?"

To say the least. "He's an excellent football player. Probably one of the best on the team. But he's not the easiest player to work with. Especially the last few weeks."

Gabby nodded. "I'm sorry for that, Mr. Carpenter. His stepdad and I will definitely talk to him about it. Is there anything else?"

For a moment, Blake thought about just thanking her for her time and getting back to business, but the little voice in his head told him to hold off. He had a hunch about the root of Cody's issue and wanted to see if he was on track.

"Mrs. Warren, is there a reason you and your husband don't attend the games?"

She lifted both shoulders, which were covered in an expensive-looking blouse. "My husband and I aren't really into football. Cody understands that."

Blake wasn't so sure. Cody had left an environment where he'd been loved and adored, practically held on a pedestal for throwing a pigskin ball around. He'd played in a stadium that held thousands of people and was the center of every high school sports story. He'd dominated every championship game he'd played in an arena that the entire state of Texas attended.

Now he was in a small-potatoes league where even his own parents had no interest in the sport.

"I bet it would mean a lot to him if you and your husband came tomorrow night. Maybe show a little support."

Gabby's eyes narrowed. "My husband and I support him plenty. Cody knows how proud we are of him."

"I'm sure he does, Mrs. Warren. I don't mean to overstep my bounds here, but I can't help but think that your son's poor sportsmanship is because he thinks no one cares."

Cody's mother lowered her gaze to the floor, then she paced to the other side of the room. "I know it's not the same here as it was in Texas. Football is everything down there and his father was his number one fan." Gabby lowered herself to a pristine white couch. "Cody stayed with him after the divorce, but when Cody's dad died last spring, it totally devastated him. Not only did he not have his father, but Cody was also forced to leave the only home he'd ever known and move here with me and his stepdad." Gabby waved a hand in the air. "I encouraged him to play football, thinking it would make the transition easier, but I know it hasn't. He's not the same."

Blake lowered himself to the adjacent love seat. "Mrs. Warren, I'm sure you're doing the best you can with him. I really think what Cody needs right now is your encouragement and support. Expressing some interest in what he loves the most will probably go a long way with him. To be honest with you, I think the kid needs the attention. If you can, try to come to the game. If we win, the team will make the play-offs, so it's an important game."

The woman's chin quivered, showing Blake just how much her son really meant to her. "I honestly had no idea my interest meant that much to him. He's always told me he doesn't care."

"Because that's what teenagers do. I can promise you he cares more than he lets on."

She nodded again. "I appreciate your honesty. I'm sorry he's been giving you trouble."

"Mrs. Warren, your son is a good kid. And a damn fine ball player. He just needs some guidance right now. And extra love."

Blake left the Warrens' home, not entirely sure he'd done the right thing.

Out on the field, the team went through the plays, tackling, smacking each other's pads, grunting, hollering, and kicking up clods of dirt with their cleats.

"Where the hell's Richardson?" Cameron muttered as he and Blake watched the players execute a Slot Double Z XOXO.

As soon as his assistant coach asked the question, the QB came strolling onto the field, red jersey hanging over his pads and helmet dangling from his fingertips. Blake approached the kid and intercepted him before he made it halfway across the field.

"Practice starts at four. I expect you here at four," he told Cody.

Cody stared back at him, then continued on his way, walking around Blake and cutting across the field.

Blake turned around and hooked his hands on his hips. "Did you hear what I said?" he asked the kid.

Cody, probably knowing the push-ups and extra runs he'd have to do, turned around and nodded. "Yes, Coach."

Thankfully he didn't say anything else, because Blake wasn't in the mood to throw any more shit on the already huge pile he was dealing with.

Practice continued with Cody repeatedly fumbling the ball

and allowing himself to be sacked again and again. When he was taken down, and his lid ripped off in the process, Blake blew his whistle and stomped across the field.

"Listen to me, son. Do you realize the game we're playing tomorrow night?"

Cody nodded.

"Mental errors like that aren't acceptable. Now play smart."

Damn, why did everyone have to be such a pain in the ass? More importantly, why was he so irritable?

Actually, he knew why. He hadn't had any sort of time with Annabelle since they'd tumbled into bed together. He missed her. He missed her laugh. He missed the way she busted his balls. Missed the way she pushed him to be a better version of himself. And his lack of Annabelle time made him a surly son of a bitch. Maybe he ought to go for an extra-long run tonight to expel the tension from his body.

Blake went through the rest of his day without hearing from Annabelle. He thought about calling her, or even texting, but stopped himself each time.

He'd hurt her. That much he knew when he'd all but told her she was nothing but a distraction to him. And yeah, she did distract him. But what he'd failed to tell her was that it was the best kind of distraction. The kind that made him forget himself and football and his sketchy future. Of course, being the oaf he was, it had come out all wrong and now he didn't know how to fix it.

So he left it alone and decided to give the woman some space.

"Your days are numbered," Blake told Staubach that evening after he'd found the dog chewing on one of his belts. "Where the hell are your toys?"

Staubach turned his head to the side as though he understood what Blake had said. The dog's nails clicked on the hardwood floor as he followed Blake down the hall, nudging Blake's calf with his wet nose.

Damn it, he didn't want to be attached to this dog. But he was cute, with this golden fur, deep brown eyes, and swooshing tail. Blake tickled the dog's head with his fingers as the two of them entered the living room.

Blake was just about to settle on the couch with a beer when his phone rang.

Staubach launched himself on the couch, completely ignoring Blake's threats to stay the hell off.

"Yeah," he answered on the third ring.

"I was wondering if you'd like to come over and prune my roses for me," his cousin Brandon greeted. "Seeing as you're so good with flowers and all."

Blake leaned his head back on the couch and closed his eyes. "How did you know about that?"

"I know all, see all, my friend," Brandon replied. "Plus the fact that Annabelle lives next door to one of the nosiest women in all of Colorado. Whose daughter-in-law is the sister of a mother of one of your players. You know how it goes. She told her daughter-in-law, who told her sister, who told her son, who told Matt, who told me."

Blake blew out a long breath. "Please kill me," he muttered.

"I had no idea my best friend had turned into Bob Vila. Not to mention you finally got yourself laid. About damn time too."

Blake pulled the phone away from his ear. "You're breaking up real bad because I'm about to go through a tunnel." He ended the call and set the device down on the end table.

A second later, it rang, which he ignored.

When Blake didn't answer, the phone vibrated twice, indicating a new text.

With a weary sigh, Blake picked the thing up and read the message.

There are no tunnels in Blanco Valley, asshole.

Blake answered, *That's because I'm not in Blanco Valley. I moved to Montana.*

God knows when you're lying.

Whatever. Blake left his phone alone and flipped the television on. With one hand stroking Staubach's head, he surfed the channels, briefly pausing on ESPN, then almost changing it. The current story, however, stopped his finger from pressing the button. The anchors, with their pinstripe suits and bright ties, were listing off the top ten quarterbacks to ever play football. Blake listened with half interest as they rattled on about Joe Namath, then switched to him.

They played old game footage of some of his greatest plays, rattling off his stats and briefly mentioning his college career. Blake watched himself, with the old familiar nostalgia bubbling to the surface. Strangely, though, gazing upon his own image, watching his former teammates on his former home turf, wasn't as debilitating as it used to be. The usual regret and shame and wishful thinking didn't blindside him and make him want to ram his fist into a wall.

He felt…calm. As though that chapter on his life could finally be closed. And why not close it? Why couldn't he turn the page and start a new chapter?

Hadn't he already, though?

Wasn't his life here, in Blanco Valley, coaching the Bobcats, supposed to be the new chapter? How was it he'd failed to realize he'd moved on to a new phase in life?

Was it because he was so stuck on his past mistakes, worried about what people saw when they looked at him?

A sharp pain crept up the back of his skull as the game footage on the television faded and returned to the anchors in the newsroom.

Blake flipped the channel, but not before catching the guy say, "Blake Carpenter will forever have an asterisk next to his name because of his steroid scandal."

At the end of the day, he'd been responsible for his own actions. If the world forever saw him as tainted, it was his own fault. But the thing was, he no longer cared. Maybe that meant he'd matured. Maybe it also meant he was just too damn old to care.

Either way, it was way past time to stop acting like such a pussy. And that would include making sure Annabelle knew just how much she meant to him.

Watching the Bobcats play the final game of their season, basically a do-or-die situation against the Grand Junction Central Warriors, was like watching game seven of the World Series. In the bottom of the ninth and one out left. Annabelle stood in the bleachers next to Stella, because everyone else was standing and waving their signs and black and orange pom-poms in the air. The kids in front of her and Stella kept whacking them in the face, and the only reason she forgave the girls was because they were so damn cute with the face paint.

The team came back from halftime with a three-point lead, but the Warriors had controlled the ball for most of the second half so far. Finally the Bobcats exploited a bad pass and intercepted.

Annabelle kept one eye on Blake as he stood on the sidelines, looking tall and stoic with his headset, and the other on Cody Richardson, who was sacked before he could get rid of the ball. He went down hard, prompting raucous cheers from the visiting spectators along with collective groans from the Bobcats fans.

The kid in front of her hollered out a screeching, "Come on!" before tossing her pom on the bench in front of her. When she threw it down, the thing whacked Virginia McAllister in the back of her stiff beehive, which had been painted orange. The Beehive Mafia had arranged themselves on the bench so their colored hives were alternating black and orange. As nosy as they were, Annabelle had to hand it to them for their creativity.

Stella threw her hands up in the air. "These guys are killing me," she commented as Cody got back to his feet.

"At least they retained possession of the ball," Annabelle said, sparing a glance at Blake, who'd removed his headset to converse with Cameron. The two men had their heads bent over a clipboard, before Blake replaced his headphones and drew his attention back to the game.

This time, when Cody received the snap, he took two steps to the right and fake pumped to the wide receiver.

"Come on, Bobcats," Stella muttered when Cody took off running, weaving his way through defensive blockers, dodging one player after another and narrowly missing attempts at taking him down.

The kid made it for thirty yards before he was tackled. Feet stomped on the metal bleachers and Annabelle and Stella were jumping up and down with the rest of the fans. The two of them slapped each other a high five when the Bobcats scored a touchdown two plays later.

The clock ran out on the third quarter, and the Bobcats moved to the final twelve minutes of the game, leading their opponent by ten points. Everyone remained on their feet, energy pulsing through them like a live wire. It was damn stressful, watching them come closer to the play-offs than they had in years.

She could only imagine how those kids felt, after a long season of trying to obtain what had previously been out of their reach.

"Give it to 'em good, Bobcats!" Lois shouted from below them, with as much bravado as her elderly voice would allow. "Stick those kids where they belong!" Next to Lois, Beverly sniggered and waved her orange foam finger in the air. She was waving the darn thing so hard, she whacked her own beehive.

Virginia yanked the thing off Beverly's hand. "What do you think you're doing?" Beverly demanded.

"You've smacked me in the head about five times," Virginia scolded. "You're only allowed to have this if you know how to use it."

Stella gripped Annabelle's forearm, her fingers digging into the soft flesh. "I don't know how much more of this I can take."

"Do you mean the game or the Beehive Mafia?"

Stella snorted. "Both."

"Tell me about it," Annabelle muttered.

In the first play of the quarter, the Warriors forced a fumble, scooped the ball up, and took off running until the opposing player was finally tackled at the Bobcats' twenty-yard line. The two teams repositioned their lines for the next play. Their QB received the snap from the center, then sent the ball flying to their wide receiver. But the ball was picked off by Evan Christiansen, the Bobcats' safety, who spun around and ran, dancing left then right, executing a beautiful play of footwork. Annabelle glanced at Blake to see him yank off his headset and holler something as the safety sprinted into the end zone.

The Bobcats' fans, including the two girls in front of Annabelle and Stella and the Beehive Mafia, foam fingers included, went crazy as their kicker effortlessly added the extra point.

And with four minutes and forty-three seconds left on the clock, the Bobcats were *this* close to closing out a winning season and making their first play-off game in eighteen years. "Oh my Lord, I think I'm going to pee my pants," Stella panted as the kids resumed their positions and moved into the next play. Cody called out the play, received the snap, and handed the ball off to their running back.

Annabelle sneaked a peek at Blake, who had his hands jammed on his lean hips, moving up and down the sidelines as he followed the actions of his players.

Forty-five seconds left and the Bobcats scored another touchdown. The stands were in an uproar, screaming and stomping and cheering, and the band played a school song, which the kids sang along to and made the appropriate hand gestures in the air.

Annabelle and Stella joined in because the energy was infectious and thrummed in the air like a synchronized heartbeat. The Bobcats put another point on the board when they made the field goal.

The clock ran out without the Warriors able to make another score.

The Bobcats rushed the field as soon as the buzzer sounded, jumping all over each other and mixing with students and parents and cheerleaders. The band played a traditional fight song, but the crowd was more interested in celebrating than singing along. Annabelle and Stella tried to stay out of the way, or risk death by trampling on the metal bleachers. But there really was no place to go, so they made their way down the aisle, holding on to each other's hands so they didn't get separated in the throng of people.

Annabelle had lost sight of Blake, not long after someone had dumped the Gatorade dispenser over his head, sending liquid and ice all over the place. She knew there'd be no hope of finding him, since the field had turned into a mass of people, jerseys mixing with plainclothes and cheerleader outfits. Annabelle and Stella made it to the bottom of the bleachers and pushed their way through the people.

It wasn't easy going against the flow and continually bumping into girls who were crying over the victory and little kids with painted faces or Bobcats T-shirts.

Stella glanced over her shoulder as she pulled Annabelle along. "If you want to stay, you'll have to ditch me," she called out. "Because I can't stand all these people. It's making my anxiety go haywire."

Annabelle shook her head, warring with needing to get away from the madness and congratulate Blake. "It's all right. We can go grab a bite to eat."

"Are you crazy?" Stella shouted. "We'll never get a table anywhere in town."

That was true. The Cat would be a madhouse tonight.

"Besides," Stella continued. Then she stopped and leaned closer to Annabelle, whispering in her ear. "You need to call Blake so you can have some congratulatory sex."

Call Blake? Would he want to hear from her tonight? After all the hype from the game and preparing for the playoffs, a goal that he'd been working for all season, he'd likely not want the distraction. Because she knew where they'd end up. He had a job to focus on and he didn't need her nosing around where she wasn't needed.

TWENTY

November in Colorado was crisp and cool with brightly colored trees, snowy peaks, and Thanksgiving turkeys on people's minds. But this year the meal planning had taken second place to the play-off game happening in just a few days.

When Annabelle had arrived that morning for weight training with the players, she'd seen Blake right away, hands perched on his hips as he'd answered questions for all the reporters clamoring for attention. His baseball cap had been pulled low over his eyes, and his black Bobcats hooded sweatshirt was stretched over his wide chest. He'd looked good. Because the man always looked good and she'd been thinking about him nonstop over the past week and a half since they'd won their last regular season game.

That night she'd texted him congratulations. Thirty minutes had gone by before he'd responded and she'd thought maybe he was trying to avoid her. The dynamic between them had been a bit awkward since their conversation in her garden. When he'd basically called her a distraction. She'd be lying to herself if she said his words hadn't hurt, that it didn't matter whether he wanted to give a relationship between them a chance. He obviously didn't and what happened in her bedroom, when he'd been so gentle yet passionate, had been a one-time thing.

She'd succumbed to the very thing she'd been trying to avoid with him. Becoming nothing more than a fling. The harsh reality afterward had been impossible to ignore. He'd been trying to get into her pants since the first day they met, and she'd given him the invitation, opening her door, as well as her heart, to him.

He'd taken it and moved on without looking back.

Although, Annabelle thought as she stood over Matt for some more neck stretches, Blake had been hinting at something more. There had been something in his eyes when he'd looked at her, an emotion she hadn't seen before. But after days, then weeks had gone by without him mentioning it anymore, she'd been forced to admit she'd misread him. That maybe it had been her own wishful thinking more than anything else.

Because she'd wanted something substantial with Blake. Something beyond flirtations and fiery kisses and incredible lovemaking. While she knew the connection between them wasn't in her head, for some reason they'd hit the pause button.

Annabelle suppressed a sigh as she let go of Matt's head and motioned for him to get off the table.

"How's that feel?" she asked him.

Matt moved his head from side to side. "It's good," he told her. "I think the stretches have been helping."

"I'm glad to hear that," she told him with a smile. "Are

you ready for Friday's game?" she asked, trying to distract herself because she could hear Blake talking in the other room. Why did his voice always have to give her chills? Maybe because it reminded her of how he'd whispered in her ear when he'd been inside her. She held back another shudder.

"More ready than I've ever been for anything else," he answered.

She was just about to tell him good luck when Blake appeared in the doorway.

"West," he said to the kid.

Matt turned around.

"How's the neck?" Blake asked.

"It's good, Coach," Matt answered.

Blake eyed him for a moment, then nodded once. "Good, because you're starting on Friday."

"Really?" Matt asked, a grin lighting up his face. He glanced at Annabelle, then back to his coach. "You're going to start me?"

"Don't look so surprised, son. You've earned it."

Matt took a few steps forward. "I promise I won't let you down."

"Now, don't start crying on me, Matt. It's just a football game."

Annabelle knew it was more than that, but she kept her mouth shut.

Matt nodded. "Yes, sir." Then he left the room and Annabelle and Blake were alone.

She stayed in her spot, hands folded in front of her when all she wanted to do was thread them through his hair. And kiss him. Because he looked so good that her body practically hummed with the tension of wanting to feel him against her. It had been too long since they'd touched; being away from him was like going through withdrawal from an addictive drug.

"I think you just made his entire year," she commented, trying to keep the conversation on neutral ground.

"Matt's a good kid," Blake said. "He has the potential to be a great player. He just needs to find himself."

Annabelle took a few steps toward him, slowly, because the urge to launch herself in his arms was overwhelming. "So, you think you're ready for Friday's game?" she asked. Damn, who knew trying to make idle conversation would be so hard? And awkward?

Was she the only one who noticed it?

The casual set of his shoulders, hands slid in his pants, mouth relaxed, indicated Blake didn't have a care in the world. That he was just as at ease with himself, and being around her, as he was before they'd been intimate. Had he put the whole thing behind him? Had she become just another conquest to him?

"The team looked really together yesterday at practice," she added when he didn't answer her question. "I noticed—"

"I don't want to talk about football, Annabelle."

His gruff words stopped her short and a shiver of awareness slithered down her spine. "Oh?" The word came out as more of a sigh. "Then what would you like to talk about?"

He stepped all the way into the room and closed the door behind him. "I don't want to talk at all," he told her.

Before she could do anything, or prepare herself in any way, Blake grabbed her, winding one strong arm around her waist and splaying his palm over the small of her back. The contact sent a rush of heat up her spine and had her breath catching in her throat. Her eyes drifted shut when his other palm, so warm and big and rough, cradled her face, cupping her jaw and dipping his fingers into the hollow spot just behind her ear.

Out of pure instinct, her hands came up and braced on his chest. His heart beat strong and sure beneath her fingertips, which matched the thumping of her own heart against her rib cage. He was nothing but solid muscle beneath the soft sweatshirt, contrasting her feminine curves, plush breasts, and flare of her hips.

He dipped his head and nuzzled her nose with his. "I've missed you," he whispered.

She brought her mouth closer to his, urging him to kiss her already. "Could've fooled me," she joked, only she wasn't really joking.

He stilled, holding his lips a whisper away from hers. "I know I upset you before when I said I didn't need any distractions."

Annabelle shook her head, not needing the knife to be dug any deeper than it already was. "Blake, you don't have to explain—"

"I meant what I said about you not being a distraction. At least not in the way you're thinking."

She pulled back, keeping her hands on his chest but allowing herself to run her gaze over his features. "Maybe you'd better explain it again."

He blew out a soft breath and skimmed his thumb over her jawline. "Okay, yeah, you distract me. But the thing you have to understand about me, Annabelle, is when I see something I want, I go no holds barred. I jump in headfirst and you would be no different. There's no way I would be able to split my attention between you and everything else. I can't give everything I have to a relationship right now. Not with these play-offs coming up."

She nodded as warmth curled in her belly. "I understand that."

He dipped his head and looked her in the eye. "See, I wasn't sure you did."

"Okay, I didn't," she admitted. "I didn't completely understand how you could decide between one and the other, especially since I wasn't the one you chose."

Blake shook his head. "It's not about deciding between one and the other. It's about focusing on what needs to get done right now. If we jumped into something, I'd want to drown myself in everything *you*. I wouldn't be able to do that without taking away from the team."

In other words, he was committed heart and soul to those kids and he planned on seeing it through. Yeah, she'd been hurt and upset when she thought he'd chosen football over giving them a chance. But holding himself back so he could give all of his energy and attention to a bunch of high school kids was beyond heroic. The guy was selfless and strong and just about the sweetest thing ever.

"What?" Blake asked her when she hadn't been able to hold back her grin.

She traced the tip of her index finger over the *Bobcats* stitched across his pec. "I'm kind of crushing on you, Blake Carpenter."

One side of his mouth kicked up in a devilish grin. The same one that had captured her attention the first time he'd flashed it. "Tell me something I don't know," he teased.

Was it possible for a man to be just as sexy when he teased as when he was surly? Blake practically turned it into an art.

"I'm pretty sure you didn't know that. You're just amazingly sure of yourself." Never mind the fact that he had every right to be.

ERIN KERN

"Really?" he wanted to know, moving his hand to cradle the back of her head. "So you're telling me I've misread all the looks you've given me?" His mouth hovered just above hers. "Every time you bite your lip. When the pulse right here"—he accentuated his point by brushing the pad of his thumb near her collarbone—"flutters into high gear. Or maybe"—he pressed a featherlight kiss on the corner of her mouth—"I've misread those sharp breaths you take when I touch you just the right way."

Okay, so the guy was good at reading body language. "Maybe I'm just a really good actress." Her eyes dropped closed when his lips explored hers, feeling the texture without prodding for them to open.

His chuckle was deep and sexy. "Sweetheart, no one acts that good. No one can make their eyes dilate when they come."

The words were whispered along her lips and that was when she opened for him. Because she couldn't take any more of his teasing. He'd touched and teased and tested and now she wanted.

Her lips opened just barely, hinting for him to take the plunge because she was done with all the teasing. Playful seduction was nice and all. Heck, better than nice when a man like Blake Carpenter was the one giving it. But sometimes a woman just needed to be taken. Ravished. And every other corny cliché she'd read in those old romance novels. The burning in her system wouldn't subside until he took it all the way.

So when he stepped away from her, removing his mouth without so much as a hint of tongue, the burning increased and she wanted to scream.

Did the man know what he was doing to her? Did he know that she wouldn't be able to concentrate on anything else until he gave her the same pleasure he'd given her before?

"You're a tease, Blake Carpenter," she accused while taking a deep breath to slow her heartbeat.

"Just returning the favor," he said, and with a gentle squeeze of her chin, was out the door. Leaving her alone, aching and burning and ready to explode.

Annabelle gripped the steering wheel as she drove toward her mother's house. It was still early, only about eight a.m., and she had some time before her first appointment. So she decided to go see her mom and her sister, since she'd been so busy and hadn't had much time to spend with either one of them.

The neighborhood was alive with lawn mowers, dogs on leashes, and joggers. Annabelle just barely dodged a man with a beagle as she got out of her car and walked toward the front door of her mom's house.

The morning was cool with a breeze that sent the remaining leaves in the trees rustling, signaling that winter wasn't far away. Annabelle rubbed her hands up and down her arms, wishing that she'd put on a thicker coat.

She let herself in the front door when she found it unlocked and walked into a quiet home. No television and no smells from the kitchen.

"Hello?" she called out. No answer. "Mom?"

Even King Charlie was absent. What a nice thing to be able to walk through the door without the overgrown rat trying to tear through her jeans with his pathetic claws.

The place was spotless, with bright flowers on the coffee table and her mom's favorite blanket folded neatly on the back of the couch. It also smelled good, like fresh laundry and cool morning air.

Annabelle dropped her keys and purse on the floor next to the television and was about to head toward the bedrooms when she heard voices from outside. The sliding glass door was open and the slight breeze billowed the sheer curtains that were pulled back. There, on the wooden deck, beneath the overhang, were her sister and mother, seated at the patio table. Steam unfurled from the mugs cupped in their hands and they were engaged in quiet conversation. Annabelle stood back and observed them, noting the easy smile that curved the corners of Ruth's mouth and the relaxed set of her shoulders.

When was the last time her mom had enjoyed a quiet, cool morning like this one? More importantly, when was the last time Annabelle had sat down and encouraged her to do so? She thought back over the past few months and couldn't remember ever sitting on the patio together and sipping a cup of coffee. Did that mean she was too consumed with structure? Too worried about doing things a certain way and making sure everything was in order to think about something as simple as having a cup of coffee with her own mom?

Naomi thought about things like that. She was good at the carefree stuff, always had been. Annabelle was the organized, responsible sister. Naomi was the fun, happy go-lucky one. The roles had always suited them, and Annabelle had been content at filling hers. And good at it. She'd plugged along, making her lists and handling her responsibilities, going from one task to the next seamlessly. And that had been enough for her. Or had it?

Nowadays she wasn't so sure. Her feelings for Blake and seeing the dynamic between Naomi and Ruth had made her reevaluate the person she always thought she'd wanted to be. Maybe having that serious relationship wasn't all that it was cracked up to be. Maybe constantly worrying about how her mom was going to cook a meal or wash her own sheets didn't need to be the priority she'd always made it.

Had Annabelle become that person? The one who didn't know how to unwind or have fun or let loose?

You certainly let loose with Blake in the bedroom.

Yeah, and it had been the best time she'd had in forever. Maybe that ought to tell her something. That she needed to let loose more often. That she was better as that person than the one who liked everything just so.

Annabelle pushed aside the curtain and slid the screen door open with one hand, holding her smoothie with the other.

"Annabelle?" her mother called out. "Is that you?"

She plastered a smile for her mom and sister. "Yeah, it's me. I had some time before my first appointment and thought I'd stop by for a minute."

"Want some coffee?" Naomi asked.

Annabelle held up her Styrofoam cup and took a seat at the table. "Thanks, but I've got this. Where's the pit bull?" she asked her mom.

Ruth lowered a hand to her lap. "Right here, being a good boy."

As though sensing the conversation was about him, Charlie lifted his head and pinned his black eyes on Annabelle. She supposed he thought his throaty growl was meant to be intimidating. Despite how annoying the dog could be, he was kind of cute. In a demonic sort of way.

"Your sister and I were just talking about the possibility of her moving back to the States," Ruth commented with a warm grin directed at her youngest daughter.

Annabelle tossed a surprised look at Naomi. "Are you serious?"

Naomi lifted a shoulder. "Just something I've been thinking about."

"But you said you love Peru," Annabelle reminded her sister. "What about your business?"

"I can always sell it," Naomi answered. "Hostels do really well down there, so I'd have no problem finding a buyer."

"But..." Annabelle shifted in her seat. "Why would you leave a place you love and move back here?"

Naomi sipped her coffee, slowly, then set the mug back down. She turned the cup around in circles, as though she herself didn't understand her own reasoning. "Because you and Mom are the only family I have. And that's more important."

"Stop discouraging her, Annabelle," Ruth chimed in with a swat to Annabelle's arm. "If she wants to move back home, then we should be encouraging her."

"I'm not discouraging her, Mom," Annabelle responded. "I'm just trying to understand where this is coming from." She placed her attention on her sister. "Every time we talk, you go on and on about how much you love South America and how well your business is doing. And now you want to walk away from it?"

"I figured this would make you happy," Naomi countered, instead of responding to Annabelle's questions. "Don't the two of you want me closer?"

"Of course we do," Ruth said before Annabelle had a chance to respond.

"We both would love having you back home," she told her sister. "I guess I just want to make sure you're doing this for the right reasons and not because you think that's what we want. Don't live your life for us."

"But that's the problem, Tansie," Naomi argued. "I've

spent too much time living for myself. Only thinking about what makes me happy and focusing too much on my life in Peru. And not enough time thinking about you and Mom back home." She placed a comforting hand on Annabelle's arm. "About how much you've sacrificed and picked up the slack that I haven't been able to carry. Or wanted to carry, I guess you could say."

Annabelle shook her head. "That's not entirely true."

"No, it is. I liked not having responsibilities. I liked not having to think about anyone but myself. I took off and did my own thing and didn't stop to think about what I was leaving you with."

"Can you please not talk about me like I'm a child?" Ruth demanded. "I'm right here, and I am still your mother. Don't think the both of you are too old for a good whooping."

"I'm not talking about next week, or anything," Naomi went on, brushing aside their mother's non-threatening promise. "Just sometime in the near future. Maybe within the next year. In the meantime, tell me more about this hot coach you've been seeing."

The change of subject was so abrupt that Annabelle had to take a minute before answering. Plus, she didn't know how to answer. "Why does everyone keep assuming we're seeing each other?"

Naomi exchanged a glance with their mother. "Uh, because you keep spending time with the guy? And when you're not, you're either thinking about him or ogling him."

"What your sister is trying to say," Ruth butted in, "is that we want to know more about the man who's captured your attention."

"You've never been this secretive about a guy before," Naomi added.

Annabelle shook her head. "That's not true."

"Name one," her sister challenged.

They wanted an actual name? As in a real guy? Annabelle opened her mouth, then snapped it shut because her brain had decided to shut down on her. Also, her sister was right. She couldn't come up with one man who'd turned her so upside down.

"See?" Naomi prodded. "I'm right," she whispered.

"Okay, whatever," Annabelle responded with a flip of her hand. "So I'm a little tight-lipped about him."

Naomi waved her hand in a "continue" gesture. "Which means?"

"Which means...I think I might be in love with him." As soon as the words were out, because speaking them and having them float around in her brain were not the same thing, a weight lifted off her shoulders. The cobwebs in her mind cleared. Sort of like gray clouds breaking up after a gloomy day and allowing the sunshine to sneak through and warm the ground. Because that's how she felt. Warm and complete and whole. Peaceful.

Naomi slapped a hand on the table, rattling the coffee mugs. "I knew it. I saw it all over your face when you brought him here that one day." She jabbed a finger toward Annabelle. "That's why you haven't brought him back around, isn't it?"

"Are you ashamed of us, Annabelle?" her mother asked.

"What?" She tossed a look at her mom. "No. Why would you think that?"

Naomi waved a hand in the air. "We don't think that. We think you're so head over heels for this guy that you're terrified for him to be around us."

"That doesn't make any sense." She picked up her forgotten smoothie and winced when it had grown too warm.

"It's because we know you," Naomi went on. "We know you well enough to see right through that indifferent attitude you try having around him."

Apparently so did Blake.

Apparently, also, her jig was up.

Naomi sipped her coffee, then swallowed. "You should know better than to try and pretend around us."

"I do know better," Annabelle commented. "I guess I thought if I denied the feelings long enough, they'd go away."

Naomi's brows pinched together. "Why would you deny it? If I fell for a man like that, I'd embrace it."

Because Naomi was uninhibited. She didn't have the fears or trust issues that Annabelle had. She threw herself into everything she did with total abandon. So, yeah, Naomi would be the one to welcome love with open arms. She'd put out an ad in the paper and have shirts made.

"Sounds like love to me," Naomi stated. "Maybe instead of trying to identify what it is, you should decide what you're going to do about it."

What could she do about it? Blake had all but said he couldn't give her anything, at least not until the Bobcats' season was over. How much longer would it go? What if they made the championship? Then what after that?

Should she wait for him to make the next move? Or would it be better if she took the reins and exhibited some control over her own life? After all, wasn't it high time she did something for herself for a change?

TWENTY-ONE

Blake eyed the kid sitting across the desk from him, slouched back in the chair, chin lifted in defiance and a screw-you attitude hardening whiskey-colored eyes that should have gleamed with teenage mischief.

Cody Richardson should have been the bane of Blake's existence. A quarterback with a mind of his own who constantly changed plays and challenged coaches left and right was a recipe for a headache. Not to mention conflict and tension between the players, which had already been prevalent throughout the season.

But the thing was, Blake couldn't bring himself to write the kid off. He couldn't be sure, but he didn't remember seeing the kid's mom and stepdad at the game two weeks ago. The one where their boy had played his ass off and had been a major contributor to bringing his team to the play-offs.

"Tell me what's on your mind, Cody," Blake urged, even though he'd been the one to call him to the office.

Cody bounced his leg up and down and tightened his arms over his chest. "I know you came to my house," he stated.

"Yeah, I did," Blake admitted. "Is that something you'd like to talk about?"

"No," Cody answered immediately. His knee continued its rapid bouncing. "I mean, do you, like, always go to players' houses and talk to their moms?"

Blake paused before answering, because he knew he needed to consider his words carefully. Cody didn't strike him as the type of boy who'd want people prying beyond what he wanted them to see. Another thing he identified with. With everything that had happened to him, Blake had never wanted anyone investigating or forcing him to reveal all the ugliness that churned inside his gut. For years his weaknesses had held him captive, taking over until they had ruled him, telling him how to act, where to go, and who to spend time with.

Only tough love, the act of someone who saw underneath the I-don't-have-any-problems defiance, could break the armor holding in the demons. Someone had done it for him, a woman who'd captured his heart and soul, and Blake wanted to find a way to do it for Cody.

Pay it forward and all that.

"Sometimes, yeah," Blake answered, not seeing the need to deny it. "When I feel the need to."

"Why did you feel the need to, Coach?" Cody asked without looking at him.

Blake leaned back in his chair and shoved his baseball cap up his forehead. "I wanted to invite your mom and step-dad to the game. I noticed they don't go that much."

Cody jerked one shoulder in a half shrug. "Yeah, well, they don't really like football, so..."

Blake sat silent and waited for the kid to finish. "So...what?" he urged. "Don't you want them to come and support you?" Cody didn't say anything. Just stared at the ground and continued bouncing that knee. Blake barely suppressed a sigh. "Son, if there's something on your mind, you can tell me. I promise you it'll stay in this room."

With those last words, Cody's hard-as-nails exterior cracked and he shifted his stormy gaze to Blake's. The contact was minimal, just a touch, and then his attention was back on the ground. A tremor of hope lit through Blake's system, knowing he'd crossed the most major hurdle.

"I just want to play football, sir," Cody answered, instead of taking the bait.

Blake nodded, trying to communicate to Cody that the two of them were on the same side. "I understand that. In fact"—Blake leaned forward and rested his forearms on the desk—"no one will understand that better than me." Blake studied the kid, taking in his too-long brown hair and not-quite-there teenager fuzz coating his jaw. "Cody..." With a long sigh, Blake debated just how much to share with Cody. "Do you know why I left the NFL?"

Cody tilted his head and lifted his chin once more. "I know you retired because of drugs."

Okay, but not quite. That was pretty much the watered-down, condensed version of what had really happened.

Blake decided not to go into all the details of that part, because it was simply too complex. Instead he focused on the story most people didn't know. The darker side that had sent him spiraling down the rocky path of addiction and dependence. And might have eventually killed him.

"Yeah, but did you know I was probably already on my way out?"

Cody gazed back at him. "I remember you blowing out your knee and missing an entire season."

Blake nodded. "That's right," he admitted. "But I bet you didn't know that because of my injury, I became addicted to OxyContin."

Cody's brows lifted a fraction, surprise flashing across his face. And then the look was gone, but tension in his jaw had lessened a fraction. Not by much, but enough to know Blake was cracking through.

"Bet you didn't know that, did you?" Blake went on. "That your coach was addicted to painkillers." He kept using past tense, as though he were over his addiction. But he wasn't, he still craved the stuff every day. Each morning he woke up with trembling fingers and sweat coating his skin. He wanted his pills when he showered or went jogging with Brandon. He craved them when he drank his morning coffee and when he called plays to his team. All the time. Day and night, it never stopped.

A line of tension appeared between Cody's brows. "No, sir, I didn't."

"My point is I had a problem that I tried to hide from everyone. I thought I had it handled on my own, but I didn't."

"So how'd you get over it?" Cody asked.

I'm not over it.

The confession was right there, aching to get out, to tell everyone that it hadn't gone away. That it wouldn't go away for a long time. At least on its own. But Cody wasn't the one to share that burden with, and it was beside Blake's point anyway.

"Someone saw through me," Blake told him.

"Was it Ms. Turner?" Cody asked, staring back at Blake with no apology in his eyes for stating something so bold. When Blake cracked a smile, Cody shifted his shoulders. "I mean, she just seems like that type of person. She's always, like, trying to help people and stuff."

Yeah, she was that. And so much more.

Blake waited before answering, debating on how deep he should go, how much was appropriate to tell a kid, not to mention a kid who was one of his players. "Yeah, it was Ms. Turner." Why should he hold that back? Why not be honest with Cody and give him an incentive to display the same honesty?

"So you two are, like, a thing, then? Because some of the other guys think you've hooked up."

Blake knew what the guys thought. He wasn't about to reveal that part of his relationship with Annabelle. "My relationship with Ms. Turner isn't anyone's business but mine and Ms. Turner's," Blake told him. "It's beside the point anyway. What I'm trying to tell is you that I know what it feels like to push everyone away. I know what it feels like to keep secrets bottled up and pretend there's no problem or that no one cares." Blake paused and watched Cody. "Do you understand what I'm saying, son?"

Cody didn't move for a moment, then slowly nodded. "Yeah, I think so."

"Good," Blake said. "Good. So then you'll also understand that you, too, have people who care. That if there's something going on that's troubling you, this would be a safe place to unload."

The muscles in Cody's jaw tightened, relaxed, then tightened again. His hands ran up and down his thighs, then curved over his knees, fingers relaxed. "I don't like it here," he stated matter-of-factly.

Blake should have been surprised by the admission, but he wasn't. Cody probably hadn't been happy from the moment he'd crossed the Colorado state line. In fact, the kid most likely hadn't known happiness since his father had breathed his last breath.

"I know you've had a hard time, Cody," Blake told him. "I've never lost a parent, so I can't say I know what that's like. And no one would blame you for struggling to adjust here."

"I don't want to adjust here, Coach," Cody told him. "I want to go back to Texas."

"Well, I'd like to have my knee back," Blake argued. "I'd like to go back to the NFL and erase all the scandals. But we can't always have what we want. That's part of life and growing up—"

"And maturing and all that," Cody finished. "My mom's told me this already."

Cody didn't want to hear it again. Message received loud and clear. But Blake wasn't about to give up so easily.

"You know," he urged, "no one's forcing you to play on this team. You're free to walk anytime you want."

Cody snorted. "I can't do that."

"Why not?"

"Because we both know this team needs me," Cody answered.

Yeah, that was true, but Blake guessed there was more. "I don't think that's why. I don't think you're really playing for yourself." Blake gazed back at the kid. "Are you?"

Cody's shoulders jerked. "I don't know what you mean."

Blake ran a hand along his jaw, knowing he needed to tread delicately. "Your father loved football, didn't he?"

"Yeah, so?"

"So, that's why you're here," Blake guessed. "You're not doing this just to pass the time or because your mom makes you. You're playing because your dad loved the sport and it makes you feel closer to him." Blake paused to give his words time to soak in. "Do you think I'm right?"

"I think you don't know shit," Cody answered.

Well, then.

"Maybe I don't," Blake said with a lift of his shoulders. "Maybe I don't know shit about shit. What I do know is that you need to take whatever anger you have toward whomever you have it for and leave it on the field. Use it as motivation, because this game is the most important one this team has played in, and we need your focus. Do we understand each other?"

Cody's knee resumed its bouncing. "Friday's just another day I get to play football, Coach."

"Maybe to you, but not to some of the other players," Blake told him. "Try to remember that it's not all about you." When Cody only sat there and didn't say anything, Blake jerked his head toward the door. "You're dismissed."

Without another word, Cody stood from the chair and left the office, with his you-don't-know-shit attitude trailing behind him like a rank stench. Along with frustration for everything left unsaid and unfinished.

Damn, but he thought he'd at least crack that wall of Cody's. Something to say Blake had made some headway, that maybe they'd come to some kind of truce or understanding.

Two steps forward, one step back.

Blake leaned back in his chair and dug the heels of his hands into his eye sockets. His fingers were still trembling and there wasn't a damn thing he could do about it.

It was way past time he started living with higher standards. To be the better man that Annabelle thought he was. And that was what it really boiled down to.

Annabelle.

She looked at him with hero worship, like she thought he could walk on water or make all her fantasies come true. While he wasn't sure where she got those impressions from, there was no reason why he couldn't at least attempt to fulfill the role.

Cameron appeared in the doorway of his office and tapped his fingers on the frame.

"Doesn't look like it went too well," his friend commented.

Blake stared up at the ceiling and blew out a breath. "As long as he ditches the attitude when he's on the field, I don't really care."

Cameron coughed and said "bullshit" at the same time.

Blake lifted his head and pinned his attention on Cameron.

"You care too much," Cameron explained. "That's your problem."

"I didn't realize caring could be a problem," Blake countered.

Cameron plopped into the chair Cody had vacated. "For you it is." Cam leaned forward, grabbed a handful of M&M's out of a glass dish, and dropped a few in his mouth. "I was going over some game film last night," Cam told him as he crunched candy between his teeth. "I think we ought to move Matt to right guard."

Blake thought for a moment, mentally calculating pros and cons.

"Aren't you sure glad one of us is the brains of the operation?" Cam asked with a cocky grin that created little smile lines at the corners of his eyes.

Blake couldn't help but grin back. "Keep on and I'll stick you with laundry duty."

Cameron downed the last of his candy and pushed out of the chair. "But I'll still have the brains." He offered a mock salute, then turned to leave and bumped into Annabelle.

Blake just about shot out of his chair when his friend

braced his hands on Annabelle's shoulders to steady her. *Hands off, asshole.*

The warning flashed through his mind and came *this* close to tumbling out of his mouth. But he shoved it back because it was Cameron, for crying out loud.

"Do us a favor and make some noise when you enter a room," Cam said with a warm smile.

"Maybe I should put a bell around my neck," Annabelle offered.

Cameron tugged on Annabelle's hair. "On the other hand, it's kind of nice to see that guy"—Cameron jerked his head toward Blake—"caught off guard." He leaned over and whispered something in Annabelle's ear, which she answered with a slow smile.

She patted him on the chest. "You're a good friend."

Then they were alone when Cameron shut the door.

Annabelle sat in the chair and tucked a strand of her rich brown hair behind one ear. She'd left it down today, which, Blake decided, he liked best. Gave him ample opportunity to dive his hands into it and feel the cool strands sifting around his fingers.

"What'd he say to you?" Blake blurted out, just because he was a nosy asshole when it came to this woman.

"He just asked me to give him a call if things between you and me go south," she answered.

The playful gleam in her eye told him she wasn't serious. And Blake knew Cameron well enough to know he'd never say anything like that to Annabelle. At least not seriously. Because he knew how bad Blake had it and was enjoying the show too much to end it.

Sick bastard.

"See, I don't know that Cam's the right guy for you," Blake commented.

Annabelle glanced back at the door, where Cameron had just made his exit. "I don't know. He's pretty hot. I bet the guy's got women scrambling for his attention."

Blake only lifted a brow, because that ugly green monster had him tongue-tied. He wanted her talking about *him* like that.

She jerked a shoulder. "Maybe I will give him a call before some other woman snatches him up."

Blake gripped his hands tighter on the desk, because the tension was no longer from his need for more pills. Over his dead body she'd call Cameron Shaw.

She narrowed her eyes at him. "You wouldn't have a problem with that, would you?"

What did she expect him to do? Piss a circle around her? Brand his name on her ass? Because if that's what it would take, that's what he'd do.

Take for what?

Take for the world to know she was his and no man had better put a hand on her.

The wave of possessiveness was sudden but fierce. The only thing he'd ever felt possessive for was a game ball.

"He'd have to get through me first," Blake told her. "Cameron might be bigger, but I'm meaner."

One corner of her mouth turned up. "In other words, you'll kill him if he lays a hand on me."

"You got that right," Blake confirmed.

"You know, some women would be offended by that. Every feminist bone in my body should be bristling."

He stood from the chair and came around the desk, perching himself on the corner and crowding her. His legs brushed hers and he could see the flecks of gold in her hazel eyes. But she didn't back up. She just tilted her chin, matching his stubbornness with her own. Normally anyone who challenged him in such a way was put in their place. Blake was an alpha male who liked to call the shots and hated having his authority questioned.

Annabelle Turner had challenged him from day one. She's strolled into his office, with her stubborn chin, you-can't-tell-me-what-to-do boldness and straight up put him in his place from the very beginning.

Which was wrapped around her finger.

He gripped her chin with his thumb and index finger, tilting her head so the lights from his office highlighted the straight line of her pert nose.

"Let's get something straight, Annabelle," he stated with a gruff voice. "I may not be able to put a label on whatever we have, or even exactly what I feel for you. But this is it for me."

"It?" she repeated.

"Yeah, *it*. The real thing, if you catch my drift."

Her eyes widened and she blew out a shuddering breath, teasing his knuckles and making the hairs on the back of his hand stand up.

"Maybe you'd better spell it out for me," she said.

She was going to drag it out of him, wasn't she? He should have known she wouldn't make it easy for him. But then again, he supposed love was never an easy thing.

"What I mean is," he started, rubbing the pad of his thumb back and forth along her jawline, "I don't want any other man having a go at you. Including Cameron, or anyone else associated with me."

One of her delicate brows arched. "Having a go?" she repeated.

He couldn't help but smile. Yeah, not the best choice of words. "You know what I mean."

"I guess I do," she replied. "I just like seeing you squirm."

Which was something he'd been doing a lot around her.

"I just stopped by to wish you good luck at the game," she added. "And to give you this." Blake dropped his hand from her chin when she dug something out of her back pocket. Her trim fingers worked to unfold a glossy packet, which she then handed to him.

"It's information on a substance abuse support group," she told him. "They meet in the evenings a few days a week. If you're interested, that is."

Blake eyed the brochure with mixed feelings. He'd never considered going to a support group before, mostly because he'd always thought they were for pussies who couldn't handle their problems. Sitting among a bunch of strangers, introducing themselves like they were back in kindergarten, then crying about their problems hadn't exactly been his cup of tea. So he'd pushed that option aside because he was a big tough man who didn't need anyone's help.

Only he did need help; if left to his own devices, he'd probably end up back at his doctor's office, begging for more pills like a heroin addict.

"Thank you," he told her.

Her body stiffened for a moment. "You mean, you're not upset?"

"Why would I be upset?"

"Some people might think that's a presumptuous thing to do."

"What, try to help?"

She stood from the chair and smoothed her hands down her thighs. "I sometimes have a habit of trying to help too much."

Blake set the brochure down and reached for her, gripping her pinched waist with his hands. He gave her a solid tug, drawing her into the open V of his legs. "Some people might think that. But it's actually what I love most about you." The second the words were out of his mouth, Blake realized what he'd admitted to. It was the closest admission of love he'd ever made to a woman. Except for maybe his mother.

Annabelle must have realized it, too, because her eyes widened and turned impossibly green. Blake had never realized it was possible for eyes to actually change color. But Annabelle's did. Sometimes they were brownish green and other times they were more green than anything else.

She huffed out a breath and toyed with the collar on his shirt. "Blake..."

Then his office door opened, and Cameron stuck his head in, completely unconcerned for the moment Blake and Annabelle were having. "Did you forget you have a team out here ready to practice? Or would you like me to run it for you so you can make out with your girlfriend?"

If Blake didn't love Cam like a freakin' brother, he would have lunged across the office and smashed a fist into the man's shadowed jaw. Like the asshole he was, Cam lifted a brow in a silent dare.

"You want to give us a minute here?" Blake said, and sent his friend a look that said, *Keep on, asswipe.*

But Annabelle dowsed a bucket of water over the flame when she tugged out of his grasp and stepped away. "It's all right," she said with a shake of her head. "You're busy and I have to go anyway."

A part of him, the one that was wrapped so tightly around her finger, didn't know which way was up, wanted to demand she stay. Demand she have some kind of response for his admission. Because he knew she felt the same way. He could see her love for him in her eyes. Could feel it when she melted into his embrace and her heart thudded against his chest, thumping a rhythm that was like repeating his name over and over again.

So he just sat there, perched on the edge of his desk, and watched her leave. Just ran out of his office without so much as a backward glance. And Blake let her go, like the coward he was, not sure if he should feel relieved or rejected.

TWENTY-TWO

An hour before the Bobcats' first play-off game in eighteen years, and Blake had lost his damn mind. He was supposed to be with his team as the stadium filled to the gills with fans, press, and students. He should have been with his other coaches, going through the game plan, reviewing plays and praying the kids could remember everything they'd learned throughout the season.

Instead he was in his truck, gripping the steering wheel until his knuckles cracked, going after a woman. Replaying Cameron's *"Where the hell are you going?"* over in his mind when he'd abruptly strolled out of the locker room, leaving the kids gaping after him. He'd pushed through the parking lot, ignoring the quizzical gazes from fans and the *"Does he know something we don't?"* from Virginia McAllister.

Yeah, he was insane. Freaking out after receiving a text from Annabelle that she'd be unable to attend tonight's game because her mother was sick with the flu.

Or was she? His paranoid mind kept telling him there was more to her excuse. Like maybe she was pissed at him and decided not to come to the game. He couldn't stand the thought she might think he'd blown her off. Had he completely ruined things between them? Damn it, he shouldn't have called her a distraction. She deserved better than that. She deserved someone who put her first, made her the center of a man's universe. He'd done a piss-poor job so far, even though he hadn't been able to assign a label to whatever it was they had. What he did know was that he needed her there. The thing was, Blake didn't even realize how much her presence meant to him. He needed her support. He needed to be able to glance in the stands and see her beautiful face smiling back at him. Cheering the kids on.

Cheering him on.

Okay, yeah, she said she'd understood about the distraction thing. She'd told him that very thing. Only something in her eyes had contradicted the reassuring smile. It hadn't been until later that night, as he lay in bed, that he'd gone over the conversation in his mind. Seeing the light of uncertainty flash across her face as she told him she understood.

So here he was, flying across town toward her mother's house, when he should have been preparing for the biggest game of the season.

A distraction?

Heck yeah she was.

But the best kind, and he needed to tell her that. He needed her to know how he felt, point-blank. No holds barred. There was no way he could get through the game thinking she was unsure about their future.

His phone vibrated for the third time since he'd run out of the stadium. He knew it was Cameron without even checking the message. Blake turned onto Ruth Turner's street and checked his phone.

If you're not kidnapped by aliens or being held for ransom, I'm gonna murder you. What the hell, Blake???

Having ignored Cam's first two messages, Blake knew he couldn't keep ignoring his assistant coach. Cam at least deserved to know Blake wasn't flaking on them.

Chill. I'll be back by kickoff.

Blake set the phone down, then picked it up again.

Promise.

Like that last word would keep the vein in Cameron's forehead from popping out.

A minute later, he arrived at Ruth's house and pulled alongside the curb. Annabelle's car was in the driveway. Parked neatly and precisely. Just like her.

As he was about to exit the truck, and most likely make an ass of himself, his phone vibrated again. He grabbed it, fully intending to tell Cam to take a damn Midol already, when he saw it was Brandon.

Please tell me that wasn't your truck I saw leaving the stadium. Matt said you just up and ran out of the locker room. Everything all right?

With a heavy sigh, Blake shot a quick reply.

Just need to take care of something, which I could do much faster if everyone would stop fussing over me like a damn woman.

His phone vibrated with Brandon's response.

Geez, sorry. And tell Annabelle hello for me.

Blake lifted his eyes skyward as he exited the truck. Was he that predictable?

His heart thumped wildly in his chest as he made his way to the front door. What if she didn't feel the same way? What if she slammed the door in his face? What if she was too hurt to give him a chance to prove she wasn't a distraction?

What if you stop acting like a damn pussy and man up?

Pretty hard to do when his palms were sweaty.

Without giving himself time to rethink his stupidity, Blake knocked on the door and waited. Waited to see what kind of fate Annabelle had in store for them. A second later, the door swung open, and there she was. Wide-eyed and soft and so damn beautiful that Blake wanted to kick his own ass for pushing her away. He opened his mouth to speak, but the punch in his gut had knocked the breath out of him.

"Blake," Annabelle greeted with a surprised, wide-eyed look. "What're you doing here? Did something happen with the team?"

"Is your mom really sick?" he blurted out, like a complete ass.

Her brow furrowed. "What?"

"Is she really sick, or were you just saying that to avoid seeing me tonight?"

She blinked at him once, then stepped out onto the porch, closing the door behind her. "What're you talking about? You think I would lie about my mom being sick just to avoid seeing you?"

When she put it like that, he really did sound like an ass. A terrified jerk who didn't have a clue how to tell her how he really felt. He only knew he couldn't go forward with tonight's game without her knowing.

"Blake, you need to be with your team," she told him. "This is an important game and they need you there."

He shook his head. "It doesn't matter. I would miss the whole thing if it meant..." He blew out a breath and shook his head again. Damn, he'd given dozens of press conferences. Given television and radio interviews, speeches, and tons of public appearances. So why couldn't he tell this one woman how he felt? How did she manage to tie his tongue in knots?

She took a step toward him and touched his arm, which only made him crazier. "Blake, what's wrong?"

"None of it means anything without you," he finally told her. "I would miss the whole thing if you asked me to."

Her green eyes darkened with confusion. "I would never ask you to do that."

"I know. I'm just saying, if you asked me to, I'd walk away from it."

She blinked, a slow sweeping of her dark lashes over her stunning eyes. Then she pulled a shuddering breath. "You would walk away from a play-off game for me? Even if it meant your coaching job?"

"In a heartbeat," he answered.

"But those kids mean everything to you," she reminded him.

"You mean more."

The pulse at the base of her neck fluttered, which matched the trembling of her full lips. "Blake," she whispered, then swiped her tongue along her lower lips. "I know this is the part where I say something in return, but I'm not sure what."

"You don't have to say anything." He glanced at his watch, knowing he needed to get his ass in gear if he was going to make it back by kickoff. "I needed you to know that you're not a distraction. I mean you are, but..." He paused. Shit, it was coming out all wrong. "You're a distraction I need. I mean, want. But yeah, I need you too—"

"Blake—"

He shook his head. "No, I told you you didn't need to say

anything. Just let me get this out before I screw it up. I said you were a distraction because I was scared. I was scared that if you got too close, that would be it for me. I would lose my focus for everything I'd been working for since the beginning of the year, and I thought that was more important to me."

She opened her mouth to speak, but he held up a hand. "But it's not. I don't care if we go to state or not."

"Yes, you do, Blake. The team has worked too hard, not to mention your job is on the line."

"I don't care about the job," he argued.

"Don't tell me that," she said. "You care about those kids more than you realize."

"Of course I do," he agreed. "But you mean more to me than the football season. I meant what I said before that I'd walk away from it if you asked me to."

"I—" She blew out a shuddering breath, then swiped at her eyes. "No one's made that kind of sacrifice for me before."

"I know." He took her hand and rubbed his fingers over her softer ones. "You're always the one making sacrifices for other people. Someone should do the same for you for a change."

One side of her mouth kicked up, contradicting the emotion swimming in her eyes. "And that someone is you?"

"Why not?" He shrugged. "I love you." So yeah, there it was. His soul pretty much bared for her to see. Flaws and all.

"You...what?" she whispered.

He came closer, crowding her so he could breathe her in and fill his senses with everything that was Annabelle. Just in case she told him to take a hike, he could leave remembering how she smelled.

"I said I love you. If you asked me to walk away from this team, I would."

"You keep saying that, and I keep telling you I would never ask you to do that," she reminded him.

"That's because you're the least selfish person I know." He grabbed her other hand. "And how about you go ahead and tell me you love me back. I already know you do."

She offered him a small smile. "Always so sure of yourself."

"About this? Hell yeah."

"Okay," she countered, taking a step closer to him. "How about this? I love you too much to allow you to miss tonight's game. So get your ass back there and win this one."

Her admission sent a ribbon of warmth through his system, prompting the corners of his mouth to curl up.

She nudged his arm. "Yeah, you heard me right." She pressed her lips to his, finally giving him what he'd been craving all day, hell, his entire damn life. Her sweet scent wrapped around him, causing everything else weighing on his mind to fade away. The game, his job, her rejection. It all diminished when her cool lips touched his. How could he question anything in his life when he had her? She was his strength, his foundation.

"Now go," she whispered against his lips. "Those kids need you."

"*I* need you," he clarified.

She rubbed her hands over his shoulders. "I know. And I'll be here to congratulate you when you win. Despite your doubt, my mother really is sick."

How could he have doubted her? Of course she would never pull anything like that. She was the most genuine, honest person he'd ever known.

He kissed her again, allowing his mouth to linger on hers, not ready to break the contact so he could absorb all of her strength and sweetness. "I'll be back," he told her.

"And I'll be here."

With one last lingering look, Blake turned and left, striding down the sidewalk with more confidence he'd felt in a long time. Because he couldn't let her down. Annabelle was the first thing in his life worth keeping around, worth fighting for. And he wasn't about to let her down or let her go.

EPILOGUE

Five months later...

Stop pacing," Annabelle told him. "You're making me nervous."

Blake stopped in the middle of the worn linoleum flooring and glanced at her. "*You're* nervous? You're not the one who has to talk to five hundred high school seniors."

The corner of her full mouth twitched, and if Blake didn't know any better, he'd have sworn she was trying to hide a grin. At his expense.

"So glad I amuse you," he muttered, and continued his back and forth pacing along the hallway outside the Pagosa Springs High School multipurpose room. On the other side of the closed heavy-duty double doors was the entire senior class sitting through a fifteen-minute educational video about performance-enhancing drugs and the devastating effects they could have on one's body. Blake knew better than anyone else the downward spiral that type of abuse could cause. Which was why the school board had asked him to speak today at a special assembly for the students.

At first Blake had turned them down. He'd been mourning the end of the Bobcats' season five months ago, after they'd lost the first game of the play-offs. It had been a devastating loss, going into overtime. In the aftermath, he'd been damn proud of his players, encouraging every one of them to be just as proud of themselves and how far the team had come, when no one had expected them to do anything.

More than that, he'd worked too long and hard to peel the negative image away from his life, only to dive right back into the dirty details.

"Look at how hard you've worked," Annabelle had told him one night after they'd shared a dinner on the patio. "Don't look at it as opening old wounds. Look at it as being an inspiration to others. As giving those kids a chance to make an informed decision. Giving them the information that you never had."

Of course she was right. Annabelle Turner was rarely wrong. And she'd been looking out for him, the way she'd done since the day they'd met. Only then he hadn't seen her persistence in such a positive light. He'd been too stubborn and dead inside to see anything other than his own monsters.

So he'd called the school board back and told them he'd only do it if he could pass a drug rehab program. Those kids deserved someone better than a man who was still battling monsters and couldn't even put his own life back together. He'd needed a detox, literally, so he could present himself with a clear mind and clean slate.

Sixty days later, he'd achieved his goal and had been declared clean and sober from the drug that had been running his life.

With a fresh start and Annabelle by his side, Blake had entered a new phase in his life. One where he'd been able to finally shut that part of the book and start a new chapter.

Except now, as he waited outside the multipurpose room, with Annabelle gazing at him like he'd lost his mind, probably because he was fidgeting like a kid before the prom, Blake had to push back a strange feeling of doubt. Nerves. Second-guessing.

All feelings that were foreign to him. He'd been a huge star once. Confident in front of the camera. Thrived in front of a screaming crowd. That had been his life and he'd craved the rush of admiring fans and thrill of victory.

So why did a room full of seventeen-year-olds make him sweat?

He blew out a breath and shoved a hand through his hair.

Annabelle approached him and grabbed his hand. "Will you stop?" she pleaded. "You're messing up the hair that you just got cut."

"Those kids aren't going to notice my hair," he told her.

Her sweet lips tugged in a wider grin. "But I notice it, and I love it." She pressed a soft and lingering kiss to his mouth. "So quit making a mess of it."

He grunted and pulled her closer when she ended the kiss too soon. "Let's just blow this joint and find a janitor's closet somewhere."

Her chuckle tickled his jaw. "How romantic."

His palms gripped her lush hips. "You didn't seem to mind when we were in the field house last week."

A soft pink flush bloomed across her high cheekbones. "That's because you didn't have a room full of kids waiting for you," she reminded him.

Blake pressed his forehead against hers and drank in her

strength. "So? I don't belong in there anyway. I don't know any of those kids."

"Hey." She leaned back slightly and gazed at him out of crystal-clear hazel eyes. "How many times do I have to tell you? You've earned this. You have more right to be here than anyone else." Her cool fingers curved along his smooth jaw. "Yes, you've been through a lot. Yes, you went through a dark time. But that's what makes you special enough to guide those kids. Only someone who's lived it can teach it."

Damn, she was right. Again. "That sounds like something from a fortune cookie," he said with a curve of his lips.

She rolled one delicate shoulder. "Maybe it is. Doesn't mean it's not true."

From inside the auditorium, Blake heard the video shut off, followed by the voice of the principal speaking through a microphone. The words were inaudible, but the magnified voice matched the thumping of his heart.

"Quit that," Annabelle urged.

Amazing how the woman could figure him out with a simple look.

She's had you figured out from day one.

Yeah, that was true. Only he hadn't wanted to see it, then he'd spent too much time denying it. Amazing how a little pride could force a person to waste months of what would have been bliss with a beautiful woman.

A little pride?

Okay, yeah, he'd been more stubborn than a mule. But only a woman like Annabelle, a determined, gorgeous, and persistent pistol in a petite package, could have shattered all that bull-headedness.

Not that he'd gone down easily. No, he'd fought it.

Then it had only been when she'd fought back that he had realized he'd been fighting a losing battle.

Blake heard his name spoken over the microphone, followed by an uproar from the students.

Annabelle glanced back at the door, then offered him a full smile. "Almost time." She took his face in her soft hands. "You're going to kill it."

He gripped her face in return and touched his lips to hers. The kiss, which was only supposed to be quick, turned deeper. They always did with her, because he couldn't help himself. He simply couldn't get enough of the woman.

"Mmmm," Annabelle groaned when the kiss ended. She swiped her tongue across her bottom lip.

"I'm still going to drag you off to a closet after this. The house is too far away."

"I'm going to hold you to that," she said with a smack of her palm to his ass.

With one last kiss and a lingering look, he left her and pushed through the doors to the auditorium and the raging ruckus of five hundred kids who rushed to their feet when they saw him.

Yeah, this was going to be a total touchdown.

Love Always Wins in Champion Valley!

Brandon West wants his teenage son to snag the eye of a recruiter for a football scholarship. But when he enlists an ex–professional ballet dancer to train his son, Brandon is the one caught by her clear blues eyes . . .

Please see the next page for a preview of

Back in the Game,
coming in Spring 2017.

ONE

You know, if you didn't want to come this afternoon, you could have just said so."

Stella Davenport feigned an I-don't-know-what-you're-talking-about look at her friend Annabelle Turner, who practically glowed under the hot Colorado sun while Stella had her hair plastered to her neck and streams of sweat running down her back. If Stella didn't adore the woman to pieces, she'd resent the hell out of Annabelle for her ability to look like a sun goddess while Stella felt like a roasted pig, even with her best efforts.

Ten rows below them, the Blanco Valley Bobcats, who were coming out of their first winning season in...well, Stella had no clue how long, were in the middle of the third game of the season. The kids were playing their hearts out, the taste of victory still fresh on their minds after making the play-offs the previous season. The accomplishment had been well earned, not to mention a long time coming, and had brought the whole town together, Stella included. Even though she'd never been a huge football fan, the Bobcats had become her adopted team and she'd ended up going to every home game last season.

Stella nudged her sunglasses higher after they'd glided down the bridge of her nose for the umpteenth time. Why did it have to be so freakin' hot? "It's not that I didn't want to come. It's just…"

You didn't want to come.

Yeah, that.

Okay, so she'd been a bit off her game lately. Distracted. Restless.

In other words, she'd been in one place too long and that itchy feeling had begun to crawl through her system. Moving from one place to the next as a kid, thank you very much, Gloria Davenport, had become the norm by age ten. The two-plus years she'd been in Blanco Valley, otherwise known as God's painting canvas, far exceeded any time she'd spent anywhere else. Except for her years with the Chicago Ballet Company. The urge to pick up and move wherever the wind blew her was more muscle memory than anything else, but the itch was there.

The feeling contradicted her memories as a kid, because she'd hated moving around. Hated staying in one place long enough to make a few good friends, only to leave. The lack of stability had cemented her urge to put down roots as an adult. But now…after two years in the southwestern corner of Colorado, Stella felt like she needed to pick up and go. As though there were somewhere else she needed to be. Somewhere more beautiful or diverse, as her mother always said. Gloria Davenport was a drifter at heart and had dragged her daughter from one part of the country to the next, always following that one guy who'd made meaningless promises to take care of them.

Whatever.

Stella had learned a long time ago that promises were easy, but contentment was hard to come by. Gloria Davenport had never been content, thus creating the same itchy, wandering tendencies in her daughter.

"Okay, whatever." Annabelle nudged Stella's shoulder with her own, just as the Bobcats' defense sacked the opponent's quarterback with a shuddering crunch. "Sit there and be silent," Annabelle went on. "We both know that this is way better than what you were doing at home."

That was true.

Why did Annabelle always have to be right?

Trying to mend the holes in her deceased grandmother's favorite blanket, when everyone who knew her knew she couldn't sew for shit, was downright masochistic. Her mother's mother was what had brought her to Blanco Valley two years ago when she'd been diagnosed with stage 4 cancer. At the time Gloria had been off gallivanting in who-knows-where and Stella had been the only one to take care of Grammy Rose. Stella's subsequent retirement from professional ballet after multiple knee injuries had been perfect timing. Although, at the time, *perfect* hadn't been the word Stella had used to describe the all but forced retirement from something that had been her life. Her reason for living. The only solid and constant thing she'd had growing up.

And now she didn't have her grandmother. Her sweet, frail Grammy who'd been strong and resilient through her cancer treatment and into the last days of her life. Stella had watched her slip away, slowly succumb to the tumors that had ravaged her body and then breathe her last breath two months ago. A piece of Stella had died along with Grammy and she hadn't felt the same since then.

Which was probably why she hadn't felt like watching her home team play football.

Yeah, Annabelle knew that. Annabelle knew everything about her.

The grieving part of Stella thanked her friend for dragging her out of the house, when all Stella had been doing was sloppily mending an old blanket while tears streamed down her face.

The stubborn part, the one that bullied all of her other parts into submission, wouldn't admit in a million years that this was better.

The Bobcats intercepted the ball, turning the play around in their favor, and gained twenty yards. The fans surged to their feet, Annabelle and Stella included. Only Annabelle blew a kiss to Blake Carpenter, the team's head coach, former professional football player and all-around hottie. The man towered over his players in both height and intimidation, but the hard set of that square jaw of his, which was hardly ever without a shadow of a scruff, softened when he locked gazes with his fiancée.

The corner of his mouth tilted just slightly enough to minimize the bad-assery the man always had going on.

Annabelle's love-struck sigh was enough to have Stella's stomach turn over. Sometimes people in love were annoying with all their love and happiness and . . . love.

"Isn't he the dreamiest?" Annabelle said.

The two of them sat back down on the bleachers. "I think you've mistaken me for a character in *Grease*."

"Just because you don't believe in love doesn't mean it doesn't exist," Annabelle commented.

Stella pushed her sunglasses up when they slid down again. "I never said it doesn't exist. It just doesn't exist for me."

"That's what everyone says until they fall in love," Annabelle reminded her.

Which probably won't ever happen for me.

Everything happens at least once. That's what Grammy used to always say and Stella had believed her. Until she'd grown up and one too many failed relationships, including the one she'd given up her dreams for, had smacked the rose-colored glasses off her face so fast she'd had whiplash.

Not everybody fell in love and Stella had come to the realization that it wasn't in the cards for her. Which was totally a-okay with her because the less strings she had tied to her heart, the less likely she was to trip over them.

Did that make her a cynic?

Her mother would say it made her a realist.

The whole is-the-glass-half-empty-or-half-full question. Some people said half full. Some said half empty. Gloria Davenport would say that someone beat her to the punch and drank half her water.

Grammy Rose would say the glass is whatever you want it to be.

Just the thought of her soft-spoken grandmother, with her rheumy blue eyes, thinning gray hair, and never-failing optimism brought the lump back and pulled her thoughts away from the game in front of her.

"Hey," Annabelle said with a comforting touch to Stella's shoulder. "Don't do that. Rose wouldn't want you to sit here and be all glum," Annabelle urged, knowing what a driving force Grammy Rose had been in Stella's life and how hard she'd taken the woman's death. Annabelle had been there the day Rose had slipped away, had held Stella's hand and cried with her when her grandmother had left the world. She'd taken Stella's grief as her own, and then her sympathy had turned into tough love when she'd urged Stella time and again to get the hell out of the house and do something with herself.

With the exception of her dance studio, which she owned and taught classes, Stella hadn't done a whole lot of anything.

Annabelle had recognized the wallowing after her divorce from her cheating husband years ago.

"You're right, she wouldn't," Stella agreed.

"She'd tell you to get your shit together and live your life," Annabelle went on. Then she fingered the top of Stella's head, running her index finger over the part. "She'd also tell you to get your roots done."

Stella swatted Annabelle's hand away. "Thank you."

Annabelle held her hand up in surrender. "All right, fine. Then she'd tell you to check out Cameron Shaw's spectacular ass. And remind you that he's single."

Cam was a sight to look at. Tall. Broad shouldered. Easy, graceful walk and cocky enough to heat up a woman's cheeks. But the guy just didn't float her boat. Okay, yeah, she could look at him just about all day. What woman wouldn't enjoy mentally undressing that prime piece of male meat?

Annabelle leaned closer and whispered, "Then she'd say you need to get laid."

Stella jerked away from her friend. "Excuse me? I'm perfectly fine the way I am."

Her friend chuckled. "That's what I said before I met Blake, and I'm pretty sure I remember you telling me to just do him already."

"I didn't say that," she hedged. "I never would have said that."

"Okay, forget Cameron. I don't think you're his type either."

Stella whistled with her two fingers when the Bobcats sacked the opponent's QB again. "If I would have known you were going to turn this into a matchmaking session, I would have stayed at home. Besides," Stella went on, "it wouldn't make sense for me to have a relationship right now anyway."

Annabelle scanned the field. "I told you before not to talk about that. Anyway, I'm not talking about a relationship. I'm talking about time between the sheets."

"Why can't we talk about it?" Stella wanted to know. "I'm not leaving for good. And time between the sheets always leads to the R word. Just look at you and Blake."

"It'll only lead to a relationship if you want it to." Annabelle was silent for a moment. "How do I know you'll come back? You'll get to Chicago, realize how much you miss it there, and you'll want to stay."

Stella studied her friend's profile, noting the firm set of her mouth and eyes hidden behind dark aviators. The two of them had hit it off two years ago when Stella had moved to Colorado from Chicago and let herself through the doors of Annabelle's physical therapy practice. Her knee had been in bad shape and she'd needed time to heal before she could open her studio and teach. Annabelle had pushed her until she'd wanted to strangle the woman, but the toughness had been necessary. Stella's knee had eventually regained its strength and mobility and she'd been able to move forward with her dance studio.

Now the two of them were closer than any friendship she'd ever had.

Stella laid a hand on Annabelle's bare shoulder. "I promise I'll be back," she told her friend. "Because if I don't, no one will be here to nag you about your nauseating relationship with the hottie coach."

The corner of Annabelle's mouth turned up. Good. Humor she could do. The sappy stuff was totally lost on her. "Methinks you're jealous. And I know you have to go. Just promise me you won't ditch me."

"You know I won't. I'm not leaving for another four months anyway."

Annabelle sighed. "I still can't believe you're going to miss State for some stupid choreography job." Annabelle placed her attention on Stella. "*Rapunzel* over State, Stella?"

"Aren't you jumping the gun a little bit?" Stella reminded her friend. "They've only played two games."

Annabelle placed a hand over Stella's mouth. "Hush, you'll jinx them. They may have only made it to playoffs last year, but they're making State this year. Mark my words, Ms. Davenport."

"Joking," she said behind Annabelle's hand, then removed the thing from her face. "Plus, I heard there are financial problems."

Annabelle tossed her friend a startled look. "What're you talking about?"

Stella lifted a shoulder and followed the play on the field. "About the boosters. That they're not donating as much as the team needs. Going to State is expensive and they need the money."

"Rumors and lies," Annabelle argued.

Stella watched Annabelle for a moment. "Honestly?"

"Honestly?" Annabelle answered with a weary sigh. "I don't know. Blake doesn't talk about that part of it and I only know what I catch in passing. When I ask him, he just tells me not to worry about it. I think as long as West Custom Homes keeps backing them, they'll be okay."

Just the name West sent a shiver down her spine. And as the tingling feeling snaked down her back, the man himself appeared, as though her body's reaction to his name summoned him from wherever he'd been lurking. Because where she was, he appeared. Just like that. Simple, yet complicated because Stella couldn't figure the guy out.

More like you can't figure out how you feel about him.

Okay, that too.

Because he'd become *that* guy.

That guy she didn't want to think about. That guy who made her teeth grind together.

That guy her mind constantly drummed up fantasies about, most of them without clothing.

The one who'd taken her out on one glorious, romantic, unforgettable date. Sweet-talked her. Bought her dinner. Melted her bones with that subtle curl of his full lips. And then never called her again.

Probably because you threw up all over him.

Yeah, there was that.

What guy would want to go on another date with a woman who'd ruined his shoes with regurgitated prime rib?

Obviously not Brandon West.

He probably hadn't given her another thought after that, other than his dry-cleaning bill. Which she should have offered to pay for, but the humiliating memory of doubling over in front of him had been too fresh in her mind. Especially since he'd been about to lean in for a kiss. Because a girl instinctively knew when she was about to be kissed and Brandon had had that look about him.

As though he'd been waiting for the appropriate moment all evening.

And Stella would be lying if she'd denied the same feeling.

But after never hearing from him, she'd realized said feelings had been one-sided. Almost as humiliating as throwing up all over the guy.

Brandon stood at the bottom of the bleachers, cradling something wrapped in foil in one large hand and stopping to shake hands with another man.

Brandon had large hands. Long-fingered. Thickly veined. Tanned.

Man's hands.

They were probably covered in calluses, given what he did for a living. Yes, now that she remembered from their date, he did have calluses. When he'd her helped down out of his truck, he'd offered his hand and she'd taken it. Which had been a mistake because she'd spent the rest of the evening wondering what his hands would feel like on the rest of her body.

Brandon chuckled at something the other man said. Funny how she could hear his deep-throated laugh over the sounds of the game and cheering from the fans. He glanced up at the stands, but Stella couldn't tell if he was looking at her or not.

But she stared back, wondering what was going on behind those dark sunglasses of his. He lifted the hot dog to his mouth, took a big bite, and slowly chewed while staring in her general direction.

Annabelle stood from the bleachers. "I'm hungry," she stated. "Want something from the snack shack?"

Stella made a desperate grab for her friend's arm. "Wait," she blurted out. "I'll go with you." She sneaked a peek at Brandon, and the man he'd been talking to walked away.

"If we both get up, we'll lose our seats," Annabelle pointed out.

Brandon turned toward the bleachers and started climbing. In their direction. Those long legs moving from one metal bench to the other, dodging the various people sitting around. "Then let me go instead." Brandon was now five rows down from them.

Annabelle tugged her arm free. "But I have to go to the bathroom."

Three rows down. Shit.

"Can you hold it for a few minutes? I'll go first, and then you can go after me."

Two rows.

"What?" Annabelle queried. "No, I can't hold it. What's wrong with you?"

What's wrong with me is coming up the bleachers.

Stella waved a hand at Annabelle and admitted defeat when Brandon's shadow fell over the both of them. "Just go."

Annabelle stared at her a moment longer, then accepted Brandon's outstretched hand to help her down the bleaches. "Ms. Turner," he greeted Annabelle.

"Thank you." She beamed at him. "Do me a favor and keep Stella company. I'll be back in a few minutes."

She's under his spell; she doesn't know what she's doing.

That could be the only explanation for Annabelle abandoning her to the man she knew good and well Stella didn't want to be around.

Brandon placed his attention on Stella, looming over her from one row down like the overpowering...man he was.

She couldn't even think of a good word to describe him, because he scrambled her brain and made her feel like she had the IQ of a walnut.

He took another bite of the hot dog, chewed slowly and carefully before saying, "My pleasure."

Someone please kill her.

"Brandon West, if you drip mustard on me, I'll have

to swat that cute little behind of yours." Beverly Rowley, born during World War II, stood at about five foot four but had the authoritative presence of a general. She and her three equally opinionated longest-standing-Blanco-Valley-residents had been dubbed the Beehive Mafia to pay homage to the pewter gray, top-heavy hairdos they'd been trying to bring back in style for the past thirty years.

Beverly blinked up at Brandon, way up because she was hunched over on the metal bleacher next to Brandon's legs. She tapped one of her orthopedic shoes. "Have a seat, boy."

One side of Brandon's mouth kicked up. Stella wasn't sure if he was more amused at being called "boy" or having one of his greatest assets described as "cute" and "little."

"How are you today, Mrs. Rowley?" he asked her, not moving from his spot.

She swatted his leg with one sun-spotted hand that was adorned with a petite gold watch. "I'll be better once you're not hovering over me like some guard dog. You're making my hearing aid buzz."

Stella hid a grin, because Beverly didn't take kindly to people laughing at her. Not that Stella would have the nerve to poke fun at a woman who'd written an open letter to the mayor of Blanco Valley because he had the "poor taste" to order the demolition of one of the city's historical buildings. Beverly hadn't cared that the building had been condemned because of asbestos and an abundance of rats and other sewer creatures. But anyone who had the gumption to openly lecture the mayor was a woman not to be messed with.

Even if she was seventy-two and weighed as much as a seventh grader.

Brandon obeyed her order, wisely keeping any argument to himself.

"Will I see you at the Meet the Bobcats next week, Mrs. Rowley?" Brandon asked the old woman.

Beverly kept her focus on the game, tapping her hands on her polyester-covered legs. "That depends if the Shouting Bean decides to stop serving that god-awful soy crap they insist on inundating us with." She turned and glanced at Stella and Brandon, her painted-pink lips pinched in a look of distaste. "Some of us like good old-fashioned vitamin D."

The place was called the Screamin' Beans, but Stella didn't correct her. "I believe you can still have regular milk, Beverly. The soy is only an option."

Beverly gazed at Stella over the top of her ginormous sunglasses, pinning her with a disapproving stare she probably reserved for unruly three-year-olds. "Well, in any event I don't like that stuff. And the reason I do my cardio at the park is so I can get away with drinking the real stuff."

Brandon opened his mouth to say something, probably argue with her because Brandon West wasn't intimidated by any of the Beehive Mafia like half the town was, but Stella leaned forward and placed a hand on Beverly's frail shoulder. Which was also covered in polyester. "I agree, Mrs. Rowley. You drink whatever you damn well want."

Beverly lifted her pointy chin, then nodded once. "I knew there was a reason I liked you, Stella Davenport." Then she turned her attention back to the game, ending their conversation.

One of Brandon's brows arched above the rim of his sunglasses. "Impressive."

"One just has to know how to sweet-talk her. It's a talent only a few of us possess."

"And what about you?" he asked her as he dipped his head toward her ear, sending shivers down her spine. "Will you be at the meet and greet?"

She kept her gaze averted, because if she turned her face, their noses would be inches apart. "That depends."

"On what?"

On if you'll be there.

"If you keep fidgeting like that, I'm going to start to think you don't want to sit next to me," Brandon said after Stella's traitorous friend had abandoned her for nachos and a soda.

That's because I don't want to sit next to you.

As if she needed another reminder of what a big guy Brandon West was. How overpowering he was. All-consuming.

And she wasn't going to even mention the way he smelled.

The people who'd been sitting in front of her and Annabelle returned to their seats, which had forced Brandon to spread his thighs from the lack of space. At five foot seven, Stella wasn't exactly little. Her own legs were cramped and had been forced to rub against his. Who knew the friction of denim against a bare leg could be so...nerve-wracking? All her girly parts, which had been so neglected they were practically covered in cobwebs, awoke with a startling jolt.

"Why do they have to put the bleachers so damn close together?" she griped, trying not to cram her knees into the girl in front of her, but when she moved them aside, that only shoved her up against Brandon even more.

"Sit still," he told her. "You're driving me nuts."

"You know, you didn't have to sit here," she reminded him. "I could have kept myself company."

His only reply was a deep-throated grunt as he lifted the foot-long hot dog to his mouth and took another bite. The scent of the food, along with the swirls of ketchup and mustard smeared on the dog, made Stella realize she hadn't had anything to eat since breakfast. Her stomach protested at the lack of protein and made its discomfort known when Brandon bit off more hot dog.

"Want some?" he offered.

Yes, please. "I'm fine, thanks," she told him.

He held up the hot dog. "Sure? Because your stomach is saying otherwise."

Stella took her attention off the play-making on the field and placed it on the virile man next to her. "I'd think you wouldn't want me eating in close proximity to you again."

His mouth twitched. "I didn't say I was going to give you any. I just asked if you wanted some." And then to really drive the knife in deep, he sank his teeth into the hot dog, bit off a huge chunk, then chewed. Slowly, working the muscles in his square jaw, which was covered by a layer of dark stubble, and swallowed. His Adam's apple moved up and down, and holy Lord the sight shouldn't have turned her on. It was a throat for crying out loud. What kind of a woman got turned on by a throat?

The kind who's seen as much action as a retirement community.

"It's good," he told her, swiping a napkin across his mouth.

Stella turned away and watched the game in front of her. "You're a tease, Brandon West."

"Worse things have been said about me," he commented. "Want the last bite?" He held the stubby end of the dog in front of her, temping her to just take it. Take the thing and quiet the stomach. And what was the harm in sharing a little food with the man, anyway?

But for some reason, the thought of biting where he'd just bitten rattled the ironclad shield she'd erected between the two of them after their date.

"Last chance," he urged. "I know you want it, so open up."

Yeah, she wanted it. And she wasn't talking about the hot dog. At least not the one in his hand.

Her stomach let out another audible growl. "All right, give me the thing." She made a grab for it, but Brandon held it just out of reach. "You offer it to me, and now you won't let me have it?"

His mouth, the wicked thing, turned up in another grin. "I said open up."

Say what?

"On second thought, I'm not that hungry," she told him.

He chuckled. "Liar. Your stomach's been talking ever since I sat down. When was the last time you ate anything?"

She turned away from him again. "That's hardly the point."

"Maybe not, but you still want this." He waved the dog in her face again.

Why did the man have to be so insufferable? Worse, why did he have to look so damn good doing it? She knew for a fact his eyes underneath those black-as-pitch shades were the same color as creamy milk chocolate and had the ability to see down into her soul. Hence the reason for the wall she'd erected between them. She didn't want Brandon West seeing into her soul because then he'd melt it. The man was dangerous and the realization had hit Stella about halfway through their date.

They'd been sitting at dinner talking about this and that and Stella had asked about Matt. Brandon had fished a picture out of his wallet and shown it to her. She'd taken the photograph and gazed down at a much younger Brandon—she'd guessed him to be about twenty-two or twenty-three—with Matt. The kid had probably been about five or six and the two of them had been sound asleep on a hammock, hats covering their faces, no shirts and wearing cutoff shorts and bare feet. And she'd thought, *Oh yeah.*

This is a man she could lose her heart to. When he'd taken the picture back and said something to the effect of "I'd do anything for that kid," she'd just about lost it. And the thing was, it hadn't even been what he'd said that had stuck with her. It had been the way he'd said it and the look on his face. Here was a man who'd dedicated his life to a child he most likely hadn't planned for but would do anything for. The concept was foreign to Stella, however strange that sounded, because her mother, Gloria Davenport, hadn't lived by the same motto.

Gloria lived in Gloria's world, and most of the time, Stella had just been along for the ride. Not that she didn't love her mother. Gloria had her good qualities and Stella knew she'd been loved. But Gloria was self-centered and thought everyone around her should cater to her whims.

Instinctively, Stella knew Brandon wasn't like that. There was something about him that told Stella he'd move heaven and earth for his son, and Stella admired him for that. In fact, a part of her sort of loved him for it.

Which was why she needed to stay away from him. Even after being here two years, Stella wasn't entirely sure Blanco Valley was her permanent home.

"You want this or not?" Brandon asked again after she'd spaced out.

"All right, fine. But you're not"—she made a mad grab for the hot dog, managing to yank the thing out of his big hand—"feeding this to me." She tossed it into her mouth before he could take it back.

"Spoilsport," he told her.

She lifted one shoulder, which was a mistake because it was the one that kept rubbing up against him. "One of us has to be the mature one." Or keep whatever weird dynamic they had going on in check.

Brandon either didn't notice it or didn't care.

The Bobcats, whom Stella had been ignoring since Annabelle had invited Brandon to completely invade her personal space, intercepted the ball and gained twenty yards. The two of them surged to their feet along with the rest of the crowd as the team ended the third quarter four points ahead and with possession of the ball.

"By the way, I never thanked you for attending Grammy Rose's funeral," she told him as they sat back down. "It meant a lot to me that you were there."

Brandon gazed at her from behind his dark sunglasses. "Rose was a good woman," he replied. "She'll be missed. I'm sorry you had to go through all that alone."

"I wasn't alone. I had Annabelle."

"That's not what I mean."

Their faces were inches apart, thanks to the close quarters, and Stella had to resist the urge to lay her head on his shoulder, just to see how solid he was. "Then what do you mean?"

He shifted on the bench, bringing his hip in contact with hers. Yeah, definitely solid. "I mean, someone you share things with."

"You mean, like a man?"

"If that's what floats your boat," he answered with a smirk.

You and I both know that's exactly what floats my boat.

The man practically drove her boat.

"I got through it just fine," she hedged, not mentioning that she couldn't even think about Grammy without her throat closing up.

"Is that a fact?"

She narrowed her eyes at him. "You don't believe me?"

"Not entirely. Your eyes give you away."

See? This was why she needed to keep distance from him. He saw way too much. Things he had no business seeing. Like how she carried around Grammy's death but plastered a smile on her face so people wouldn't notice.

"You can't even see my eyes," she argued.

He brought his hand up next to her face, the heat from his palm melting into her skin and scorching her cheeks. She would have jerked back, but there was nowhere to go. Anyway, Stella wasn't entirely sure she wanted to move away. Her inner desire, which contradicted the sensible side of her brain, wanted to lean into him. To feel his large palm, with its work-roughened surface, cup her cheek and tell her she'd be okay. That she could go on without her sweet but sensible grandmother to light up her life.

But he didn't touch her. Instead he lifted her sunglasses, just enough to get a peek of her eyes. She squinted against the bright afternoon sun and forced herself not to look away.

"See?" He settled the glasses on top of her head and skimmed the tip of his index finger just underneath one eye. "It's right here."

His finger went back and forth, beneath her left eye, just barely brushing her lower lashes and sending a zing to the pit of her stomach. Before she did something really stupid, like turn her face and press a kiss to the palm of his hand, she pulled back and replaced her sunglasses.

Brandon didn't protest. In fact, he didn't react at all other than dropping his hand. Was she the only one fazed by their attraction to each other?

Then it hit her. Like someone dropping an ice cube down the back of her shirt. Maybe Brandon wasn't attracted to her at all. Maybe all the stuff going on in her body was one sided and that's why he'd never asked her out again. Maybe she was the only one confused and hot at the same time.

Maybe she had no effect on him at all.

Heat burned her cheeks at the reality she didn't want to swallow.

"You could see that through my sunglasses?"

"What can I say?" he asked as he lifted one hip off the bench and withdrew his cell phone. "I have a gift."

Out of the corner of her eye, Stella saw Brandon's long fingers flying over the keypad of his phone as he texted someone. She forced her attention to the game, because the guy had already distracted her enough.

The players broke from their huddle, and Matt jogged onto the field.

Stella nudged Brandon in the ribs. "Your kid's out there."

"I see him," he replied, never taking his gaze off his phone.

"How can you see him when you're doing that?"

He lifted his head and pinned her with his gaze. "I can do more than one thing at a time."

Clearly.

They sat in silence for a moment when Brandon finally put his phone away. Was he texting a woman?

As the thought flitted through her mind, Stella realized that may have been the reason he'd never asked her out again. He had another woman in his life.

Oh, Lord, why hadn't she realized it before? Of course Brandon would have a woman, or girlfriend or whatever. A man like him wouldn't be single for long. Not that she cared. Hadn't she just told Annabelle she didn't want a relationship anyway? Because she was leaving in four months after accepting a job with her former ballet company choreographing their end-of-the-year production of *Rapunzel*. It had been an opportunity she'd been awaiting for years, and after already turning it down once, she wasn't about to let it slip away again.

Unfortunately, it meant being gone for several months, which wasn't exactly conducive to a new relationship.

"You should bring Matt to my studio," she blurted out. What the hell?

"Why would I bring my football-playing son to a ballet studio?" Brandon asked without taking his attention off the field.

"Lots of football players take ballet lessons. It can help with balance and coordination."

Brandon snorted. "No son of mine is taking ballet."

"Why, because ballet is for girls?"

He slid her a look. "Ballet *is* for girls."

"Says who?"

"Men."

"Oh, I get it," she concluded. "You think it'll like impede his masculinity or something. That I'll make him put on a pair of tights and dance on his toes."

"Isn't that what ballet dancers do?"

"Well yeah, but—"

"Then forget it," he finished. "He doesn't need ballet lessons."

"Fine, be stubborn," Stella fumed, wondering how she could go from wanting to jump a man's bones to wanting to strangle the guy.

Fall in Love with Forever Romance

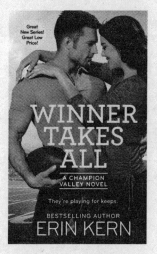

WINNER TAKES ALL
By Erin Kern

The first book in Erin Kern's brand-new Champion Valley series, perfect for fans of *Friday Night Lights*! Former football player Blake Carpenter is determined to rebuild his life as the new coach of his Colorado hometown's high school team. Annabelle Turner, the team's physical therapist, will be damned if the scandal that cost Blake his NFL career hurts *her* team. But what she doesn't count on is their intense attraction that turns every heated run-in into wildly erotic competition…

LAST KISS OF SUMMER
By Marina Adair

Kennedy Sinclair, pie shop and orchard owner extraordinaire, is all that stands between Luke Callahan and the success of his hard cider business. But when the negotiations start heating up, will they lose their hearts? Or seal the deal? Fans of Rachel Gibson, Kristan Higgins, and Jill Shalvis will gobble up the latest sexy contemporary from Marina Adair.

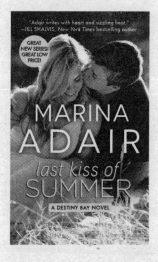

Fall in Love with Forever Romance

MEANT TO BE MINE
By Lisa Marie Perry

In the tradition of Jessica Lemmon and Marie Force, comes a contemporary romance about a former bad boy seeking redemption. After years apart, Sofia Mercer and Burke Wolf reunite in Cape Cod. Their wounds may be deep, but their sizzling attraction is as hot as ever.

RUN TO YOU
By Rachel Lacey

The first book in Rachel Lacey's new contemporary romance series will appeal to fans of Kristan Higgins, Rachel Gibson, and Jill Shalvis! Ethan Hunter's grandmother, Haven, North Carolina's resident match-maker, is convinced Gabby Winter and her grandson are meant to be to-gether. Rather than break her heart, Ethan and Gabby fake a relationship, but if they continue, they won't just fool the town—they might fool themselves, too...

Fall in Love with Forever Romance

AN INDECENT PROPOSAL
By Katee Robert

New York Times and *USA Today* bestselling author Katee Robert continues her smoking-hot series about the O'Malleys—wealthy, powerful, and full of scandalous family secrets. Olivia Rashidi left behind her Russian mob family for the sake of her daughter. When she meets Cillian O'Malley, she recognizes his family name, but can't help falling for the smoldering, tortured man. Cillian knows that there is no escape from the life, but Olivia is worth trying—and dying—for…